THE LONG RIDE HOME

THE FIGHT AGAINST THE GREEN GHOST

DALE PEROUTKA

Primix Publishing
11620 Wilshire Blvd
Suite 900, West Wilshire Center, Los Angeles, CA, 90025
www.primixpublishing.com
Phone: 1-800-538-5788

Published by Primix Publishing: 05/07/2024

ISBN: 979-8-89194-127-4(sc)
ISBN: 979-8-89194-128-1(e)

CONTENTS

PROLOGUE

And the universe began!

Suddenly, there was light, but no light we could see.

Suddenly, there was matter, but no matter we could feel.

Suddenly, there was energy, but no energy we could perceive.

There was an enormous nuclear and subnuclear reaction, an explosion that encompassed and comprised the known universe. A person, if such a person existed at that instant, would have no frame of reference for the enormity of the explosion. As the minuscule brain of an ant cannot comprehend the solar system, the galaxy, or the distances between such galaxies, such a person could not comprehend what has frequently been called "The Big Bang!"

Many forms of life were created and immediately extinguished in that initial millisecond in time. The great thinker Einstein proved that time itself and the levels of space were warped by the stress of the forces of the explosion. Some very primitive forms of life lived through this event and were later modified or extinguished. Strange elements were modified by the violent passage of mesons, quirks (both two up and one down), pions, W and Z bosons, and other subnuclear particles yet to be discovered. Only the strong survived, although sometimes, the strong was an imprecise definition because some life developed a memory that allowed it to modify itself to survive that caustic, hostile environment.

Among this later form of what loosely might be called life, was a virulent form of absorption that existed on energy, electrical energy given off by nuclear reactions, explosions, lightening and the rubbing of one positively charged piece of matter against a negatively charged piece of matter.

In the first micro millisecond of "The Big Bang," this form of life or absorption was instantly created;

within the next micro millisecond it was destroyed, unfortunately, within the third micro millisecond, it was immediately recreated, but not destroyed.

This form of absorption or life permeated certain parts of primeval matter. Much formed around itself. Most of this life was ultimately attracted to, absorbed by, and decimated by larger energy sources such as suns, novas, and later the universe's abundant black holes.

A small amount remained dormant in undisturbed primal rock, floating in uncharted space between galaxies. This rock, irregularly and roughly shaped with little refraction, was about the size of half of a small compact car and, if on earth, would weigh about two and a half tons.

Eons passed.

Gravitational waves ebbed and flowed.

Galaxies continued their unrelenting rotation around the center of the universe, some traveling through space faster than the average of approximately .02 percent of the speed of light, some traveling slower.

Some galaxies slowly collided with cataclysmic violence! A small part of the original dust and rock coalesced into planets; most such planets remained cold, grey, and lifeless while other planets condensed liquids out of the original dust and rock to start the long, painful journey to support life.

The forefathers, or more accurately, the forethings of thinking, reasoning beings poked their heads (or upper part of their bodies) out of ancient slimy mud and slowly evolved.

Years, multiples of millions of years passed.

Civilizations were born, rose to heights of glory and died. Some civilizations never progressed beyond the nuclear age, choosing instead to decimate themselves through an inability to compromise and peacefully resolve their differences. For life to survive, it must compete and win at any cost!

Slowly, ever so slowly, the rock was nudged out of its solitary position between galaxies by infinitesimal gravity waves. It was passively drawn to a flat spiral galaxy thought to be in the middle of the universe of millions of such galaxies.

Gradually, it drifted into the edge of this galaxy. Gravitational waves caused by the violent collisions between stars influenced its movement more and more. Its speed increased due to the faint pull of gravity. Gravitational waves, as infinitesimal as a grain of sand on a planet, still had an influence upon its movement.

No intelligent, reasoning eyes or senses saw its movement. It passed through the edge of this galaxy and plunged through first one solar system and then another, narrowly missing a star here and a planet there, all the while having its course altered and modified.

It reached a solar system with nine planets, one of which is a huge gas giant. It skimmed this gaseous planet and due to the planet's huge gravitational pull, it received a change in its direction and a radical lessening of its speed. It missed a red planet. It approached a beautiful greenish blue and brown, practically all water covered planet and at an altitude of just under a hundred miles, slightly penetrated its atmosphere.

This planet, with its attendant atmosphere, was rotating about eleven hundred miles an hour at its equator. Again, gravity exerted its pull and pulled the object closer to the planet, bouncing the object several times at the outer edge of the atmosphere like a thrown pebble skimming the surface of a smooth pond. Its speed was slowed even more; the blue and green planet's gravity exerted a greater and greater influence upon the object.

The friction of the atmosphere heated the rock and rubbed off tiny particles like sandpaper rubbing against a brick causing the object to become electrically charged. It eventually burned and submerged itself through the planet's heavy atmosphere.

As things sometimes occur, the rock unfortunately passed through a thunderstorm. Since it was part ancient metal, and electrically charged, it attracted lightning and was struck, not once, not twice but with many violent strikes before it crashed into the ground with a shattering impact. The ancient rock, and the life inside, received jolts, charges of millions of volts of lightning like a comatose human body receiving an electrical jolt from a defibrillation machine. The place of impact was in the south-central part of Central America near a lightning scarred, metal filled mountain.

It slowly awakened. It started ravenously feeding on the electricity, its food, because of its starvation all those eons of years. It was frenzied in its search for food, food! It terrified the local natives whose primitive direct current electrical generators attracted life.

It reproduced itself. The original self, the original "life" was eaten, although, eaten is a poor description of being devoured by your starving offspring, who are multiplying and being devoured by their offspring.

Ah . . ., rain, thunderstorms, lightning, electricity, the essence of life! More, more, it multiplied and broadened its mindless search for more electricity.

A long night began. . ..

CHAPTER ONE

Gunshots!

    Sharp, echoing gunshots from over a block away echoed through the metal and concrete stairwell.

What the hell is going on? He recognized the weapon as an AK-47 with its signature "boom." The responding weapon was an M-16 with its sharp crack and hissing exhaust.

Daniel Peterson, trudging up the echoing metal and concrete steps to the third floor of the brick city building, puffed as he reached the second level. Resting for a moment by leaning against a dusty iron railing, he felt the grainy dust fluttering around his fingers. He promised himself that he had to lose some weight and get himself into condition again. The ache in his side throbbed as his lungs labored for more air. Memories of running up three or four flights of stairs without breathing heavy were long gone.

Suddenly, more gunshots, yells and screams from almost next door scared him out of his lethargy.

Running up the remaining flight of stairs to the third floor, he mumbled, "Dam, I'm glad my office isn't on the tenth floor."

He had sold his car in April for financial and physical reasons, a year or so ago after his ex-wife had taken all their savings. After moving home within walking or at least bus-taking distance of his office, he had thought that the daily walk to work would help both economically and physically, but he still was at least twenty pounds overweight and terribly out of condition.

"Daniel Dwight Peterson, just because you're a Service Assistant to the City Board doesn't mean you can be late for work," Joyce Travier, his secretary, mumbled as she crouched behind her desk.

"Well, Joyce, some of us can be late, like you, and some of us can't, like me," Dan Peterson said as he gasped for air clutching a file cabinet to recover his breath. "Whatever it was, they are no longer shooting at each other. That sounded all over. You know very well that in my twelve years of service in this fair city, I'm almost always on time for work."

He took off his worn, navy-blue sports coat and hung it in the corner on a clothes tree; both had seen better days. His tie, which matched no known color in the universe, hung over his well filled wrinkled shirt. Even though the tie was a subject of much unwanted attention, Dan was going to wear it no matter what because it was a gift from his son.

He turned to his secretary, "Did you hear those gunshots and screams a minute ago?"

"What gunshots? I always hide beneath my desk! Of course, I heard them. They sounded close. I would have called the police, but our phones were out too. Not even 911 works now. I tried my cell phone, but all I got was a vicious kind of static."

Joyce Travier, Secretary to the Service Assistant to the City Board, looked fondly at her boss of nearly eight years; this nearly six- foot brown haired overweight man with deep gray eyes was the gentlest and kindest person she knew. She knew of the enormous difficulties he had with his ex-wife, Kathy, and was saddened to see the terrible effect her problems had on him. He had tried to find a second job so he could afford to keep his family together, but the demands of his ex-wife were too much.

"There's not much I can do here, Dan," Joyce reluctantly complained, crawling out from underneath her desk. "Since the electricity went out, I can't use my typewriter or computer, and the only light in here is from down the hall."

"Well, since about ninety per cent of our job involves handling paperwork for our precious city board upstairs, this lack of electricity is a blessing in disguise. And that's about the only blessing I can think of," Dan continued. "I hate looking like this," he gestured at his waist and his wrinkled shirt, "but, without any electrical power, I couldn't even iron my shirt."

Joyce nodded, her frizzy blonde hair flying, "Same here, I haven't had a bath for a couple of days, too."

Dan looked at her, a small smile of approval creasing his face; her habit of wearing tight clothes served her well: besides flaunting her substantial upper body prominences, her snug clothes didn't show many wrinkles. When she had been hired by Dan, she emitted sexual energy like a lioness in heat, however, that energy was directed to only one man: her husband. Dan often wondered how her husband was able to walk in the morning, but no other man ever got to first base, much less in the ballpark with her. Regardless, she was still the best secretary he ever had.

"Any idea what's going on?" she asked.

Dan shook his head, "No. There's wrecked or burnt cars all over the city. And I've contacted just about everyone I can think of, but when the electricity stopped a few days ago, and never came back on, everything else seemed to just stop."

"Say, Dan, did you try to contact Sam Albright, your lieutenant friend of the L.A. Sheriff's Department? He might know something."

"I did yesterday, but the telephone lines were terribly scratchy, as if we were talking to the moon or underwater or something. Sam kept yelling something about 'The Green Ghost,' whatever that was, and said to not use any electricity because things were going to get worse. Most of the rest of his conversation was nearly unintelligible. He said to protect ourselves because Los Angeles and Orange County were going to starve and riot in about a week."

"What! You're kidding?"

Dan shook his head, "I believe him. He has never lied to me and as a lieutenant in the Sheriff's Department, he has seen just about everything, but he sounded scared. And it takes a lot to scare someone like him! But I just don't know what he was talking about."

"I know one thing for sure, I miss our morning coffee," he mused.

Joyce smiled; she would grind fresh Columbian coffee beans for him in the morning and the pungent aroma of freshly percolated coffee would permeate through the office. They kept their coffee beans frozen in a small, battered, but still serviceable refrigerator that Dan had scrounged from somewhere. When Joyce had first started grinding fresh coffee for Dan in the mornings, the rest of the city staff would just happen to wonder in for a staff conference or to flirt with Joyce and casually ask, "Oh by the way, do you have any coffee?"

It took Joyce a week to realize that frequently the reason for the staff conferences was Dan's coffee, not her or Dan. She knew that since Dan was too kind and generous to charge his fellow workers, she therefore placed, and rigidly enforced, a charge of a quarter a cup on each cup of fresh coffee.

But now, no coffee because there is no electricity.

"Joyce, do you have that disaster plan we prepared a couple of years ago?"

"Sure, I'll get it for you. You realize that no one even looked at that plan after we put so much work into it."

"I know, but there might be something in there that will give me some idea of what to do."

Joyce rummaged around in a dusty storage closet looking for the report. All Dan could see of her on her knees was her tightly-clad nicely rounded buttocks sticking out of the closet. (This job had some benefits!) After throwing out old paperwork behind her like a gopher throwing dirt out of a hole, she finally located the report.

"Here," she said as she tossed the three-inch report to him after dusting it off. "I need to get on our janitorial staff to clean out that closet. There's stuff in there that haven't seen for years. I had the feeling that something was looking out at me."

Dan recalled doing a considerable amount of research on the plan including contacting every local agency he could think of and receiving stacks of documents from both the state and federal disaster agencies. It seemed to him that too much of the planning consisted of generating useless paperwork. Joyce's frequent comment was "Well, here's another tree lost."

During the initial part of their research, they received a two hundred and ninety-three-page manuscript from someone in Washington D.C. Holding the manuscript in his hand, Dan groused, "Look; this nitwit obtained a government grant of about $37,500 to catalog all of the other disaster plans. He's used his manuscript as a basis for a thesis statement to some college around Washington D.C. Useless!"

Thereafter, whenever anything came in that was a worthless document or an unnecessary piece of government paperwork, Joyce and Dan would refer to it as "Another document from Washington 'U'."

"There's sure a lot of documents from Washington 'U,'" Dan said quietly one afternoon, shaking his head.

Dan's review of their disaster plan revealed that nothing seemed to apply to their entire lack of electricity. A comprehensive discussion of ten-year, twenty-year, fifty and hundred-year floods didn't seem to help. Earthquake preparation, while relevant, assumed that there would be some sort of electrical power available. Tornados in Southern California were usually very weak. Nuclear war or terrorist attacks were the providence of the federal or state authorities and/or the police forces.

Originally, deep into their research, Dan had said confidentially to Joyce, "You know, I've come to the conclusion that there wasn't much the supervisors or mayor of our fair city could do in the event of a major disaster."

Robert Sandoval, one of the few city employees who bothered to show up for work, strolled in while Dan was reviewing the disaster plan.

"Anything in there that might help us, Mr. Peterson?"

"Oh, hello Robert. No, I don't think so."

He paused for a second, paging through the disaster plan and occasionally reading from it, "Let's see, the Sanitation Department has the responsibility for the sewer and sanitation problems, Southern California Gas Company has to handle their approximately sixty two thousand miles of gas lines, the water company has to repair their approximately fifty nine thousand miles of pipes and get water flowing again, and Caltrans, the authority for repairing streets, roads and bridges has to repair or dig them out."

"What about Southern California Edison?" Joyce asked.

"Well, they're in charge of the electrical power and repairs to get their facilities back online." Dan shook his head, "But here, the power is off all over. We get our power mostly from the electrical grid with Washington, Oregon, and the Colorado River. There are a few California power plants, but they generate only a small amount of electricity."

"Well, I saw an accident involving four cars about three blocks from here and it seemed to be caused by a light green something that attacked the car's motors," Sandoval said. "And there's wrecked cars all over."

"I've seen that too, Robert. See if you can borrow a bicycle or something to ride down to the Edison electrical plant in Huntington Beach on Pacific Highway to find out what's going on. Our phones are all out. We've been given orders not to use any vehicles. Try to find out if they have some answers. Here, read this."

Robert Sandoval glanced at the handwritten memo, scribbled on the city's stationary that had been signed by the mayor,

Until further notice, no one, absolutely no one will drive any of the city's vehicles!

"That was shoved under our door about three nights ago, but I can't find out any further information. The lords upstairs haven't shown up for work the last couple of days, either. See if you find out something," Dan said. "I'll be in my office if I can find something to do."

"Sure, I'll be back as soon as I can."

Robert and Joyce watched Dan meander down the darkened hall to his office.

"How is he doing?" Robert asked, quietly. "I was here when his ex-wife stormed into here and threw a tantrum and embarrassed the hell out of him because he couldn't afford something. What a bitch! I think he must have married her on the rebound after his first wife died. And he is such a decent guy."

"He's doing much better since she left," Joyce said. "Did you hear that she took their cute little red-headed girl and went to live in a commune?"

"No, but it doesn't surprise me, she always acted as if her panty hose was too tight," Robert said, a gleam in his eye. "She had a great body, but her brains were in her boobs."

"Hay!"

"Well, present company excepted, of course," Robert apologized, smiling.

Several hours later, he reported back, his face tight with worry.

"Dan, all of the entrances to that electrical plant were closed and locked. It seemed totally locked down! The few very nervous guards patrolled the plant. They wouldn't tell me anything and they refused to even let me talk to a supervisor. And I saw more wrecked cars than I ever thought possible! Pacific Coast Highway is totally blocked."

"Did it look like the plant was operating?" Joyce asked.

"No, absolutely not! You know that place always looked like a beehive of activity withlights, steam and smoke everywhere, but now, it looks like it's totally shut down."

Robert Sandoval then blurted, "What's going on, Dan? Something's wrong. Something's very wrong."

Dan shook his head, "I don't have any idea what's going on, but why don't you both take the rest of the day off. We can't accomplish much here anyway."

"I'm worried too, Dan, what are we going to do?" Joyce asked, worry radiating from her bright blue and now slightly bloodshot eyes.

❦❦❦❦❦

Joyce wasn't the only one who was worried. About twenty some miles north-west, at a Los Angeles County Sheriff's station in one of the small cities to the west of the Long Beach Freeway, Samuel R. (for Roosevelt) Albright, Lieutenant, Los Angeles County Sheriff's Department, was also worried.

After twenty-eight years on the Sheriff's Department, he had worked just about everything interesting the Sheriff's Department had to offer, including a patrol deputy at a substation, detective bureau (robbery and homicide), Central Jail, and the Training Academy. Now, he was the Watch Commander and for all practical purposes, the Station Commander at this Sheriff's Station and he thought he had seen just about everything society had to offer.

During the last three days, his mechanics kept coming to him complaining, "We can't keep our patrol cars running. Something keeps going wrong with the electrical systems and the radios refuse to keep their frequencies. All our batteries seem to go dead without any explanation."

Lieutenant Roosevelt had noticed that frequently a patrol vehicle with all the lights and radios simply stopped running, leaving a disgruntled deputy sheriff on foot.

"If I had wanted to go on some crummy foot patrol, I would have joined L.A.P.D.," more than one deputy sheriff complained.

Lieutenant Albright's dark brown eyes reflected his wary attitude of viewing anything he heard or read with a great deal of cynicism. While his skepticism kept him alive on more than one occasion, his attitude carried over into his relations with supervisors, particularly those supervisors who had not earned his respect.

The direct order he had just received, however, taxed his faculty for judgment and reason; a judgment and reason honed in a world frequently devoted to ascertaining unique ways to kill, maim or rob its fellow citizens.

Patrick Dollar, Captain, Los Angeles County Sheriff's Department, and David Rodenski, Sergeant, Los Angeles County Sheriff's Department, both of whom Samuel Albright had spent many nights within a patrol or radio car as patrol deputies, had just called him with some astonishing information. Both were old time cops now assigned to what Sam considered plush jobs at the Sheriff's Technical Services Division.

Sam was told, "We want you to shut down all of your electricity and electrical generators in your station."

"Sam, this is a Direct Order," said Captain Patrick Dollar, one of the few people Sam Albright truly respected in the department.

Sergeant Rodenski interrupted, "Sam, you remember what effect a Direct Order has, don't you?"

"What the hell are you guys talking about, Pat, David?" Sam Albright growled; his voice hoarse from the perpetual cigar stuck in his mouth. Of course, Sam Albright knew what a "Direct Order" was, he often referred to them as "myopic decrees from the ivory tower."

"Sam, this order comes from the Sheriff himself. He received the directive from the governor's office in Sacramento."

"So? What's going on? I just can't shut down my station simply because some four-eyed desk-bound nitwit in the Governor's office says so."

"Sam, listen," Pat Dollar said patiently, an edge creeping into his voice (while a great patrol leader, diplomacy was not one of Sam's strong suits), "There's a form of life around that eats electricity; they call it 'The Green Ghost.' It attacks anything that uses or produces electricity: cars, radio transmitters, anything that uses electricity. I know it sounds crazy, but it's true."

Pat Dollar waited a moment for Sam to absorb the information.

"I must repeat The Direct Order, Sam: shut off all generators, all emergency 911 power systems, all radio broadcast facilities, and, most importantly, do not drive any patrol cars or any motor vehicles."

"What?" Sam Albright yelled with disbelief, "What have you been drinking, Pat?" even though he knew that Pat hadn't touched a drop of alcohol since he joined A.A. nine and a half years ago.

"We're not kidding, Sam," Sergeant Rodenski stated flatly. "No one else here believed it either, but your power went off a few days ago. We got through to you only because this phone line is underground, but we don't expect this line to last very long, either."

As if to punctuate Sergeant Rodenski's statement, a harsh wave of static flowed through the telephone wires.

"Sam, I bet the emergency gasoline generators for your station are running very rough, and probably on occasion, just stop running," Pat Dollar said. "And how about your radio cars? I bet half of them stopped running, too."

"Well, sure, but, but" Sam uncharistically sputtered, "what, what am I supposed to do for patrolling my cities, get horses?"

"You'll have to stop all patrolling except your immediate area foot patrol, Sam. All the other stations, including all the other police departments, are having the same problem. Pull in all your deputies. Make sure all your patrol vehicles are in the station. The Sheriff said to try to protect our people, the station, and then the citizens, specifically in that order! I don't have any other information to give you."

Captain Pat Dollar hesitated for a second and then said with a husky voice, "My Friend!"

The words "My Friend" abruptly stopped whatever expletive based complaints that Sam Albright was mumbling.

The phrase "My Friend" referred to a time when neither had broken under terrible questioning by the Sheriff's Department's feared Internal Investigations Bureau (I.I.B.) with the assistance of a Chief Deputy District Attorney. Both Sam and Pat came from the old school where whatever happened in a patrol radio car stayed in the car. As a matter of fact, their lives all too frequently depended on such trust.

A citizen, whose name shall remain hidden in the mists of history, had been stopped by Sam and Pat for drunk driving. The citizen could not walk, he was so drunk. Never-the-less, he thought that since he couldn't walk, he could drive.

After watching the citizen's new Mercedes Benz convertible weave from lane to lane nearly striking a parked car, Pat, driving the patrol car had asked Sam, "Do you want another drunk driver?"

Since Sam was the "bookman" and was required to write any arrest reports, he had the final authority to approve any arrests. His first comment was, "Oh hell no, I've got enough paperwork to keep me busy all night. Let's see if we can kick him loose."

After following the Mercedes Benz with their red lights flashing and an occasional tap on the siren, the new convertible finally stopped by running into a curb.

When approached by Sam, the citizen made it very clear to Sam and Pat that since he had contributed large sums of money to the political campaigns of the District Attorney and the Sheriff, he wasn't subject to the laws of the great State of California. His slurred comments told Sam to do a sexually impossible act with himself. After absolutely refusing to get out of his new Mercedes Benz convertible, the citizen was "gently" removed from his automobile without the benefit of opening the doors.

The citizen, still not seeing the light, belligerently doubted the legitimacy of both Pat and Sam's parents' marriages at the time of their conception.

Clutching onto the heated black hood of their highly polished black and white patrol car, the citizen refused to quiet down and slurred, "Are you clowns what they call a salt and pepper team? I bet you still have the same mother. Who were your fathers anyway?"

Neither Pat nor Sam gave a dam what color the other was; their interest was in what that officer carried in his heart. Pat, however, who had lost his father about three weeks prior to this, started to see red and drew back his fist.

Sam grabbed Pat's arm, "Easy, guy, easy, he's not worth it."

The citizen, drool dripping on his hand made custom pinstriped silk suit, let his mouth overload the lower back end of his rotund anatomy and spouted through his sour alcoholic breath, "You two morons think that you can pick on me just because I can buy and sell a dozen of you. Look at my new car. The closest either of you two will get to a car like that is as my valet."

Sam quietly looked at the citizen, and then with a big grin said, "How true. But the wonderful thing is that you are under arrest."

The citizen's reply was an unoriginal, "Well, piss on you."

At that, he zipped down his fly, pulled out his penis and tried to urinate on the two uniformed officers.

It was later alleged that in his rookie days, Sam had allegedly purchased a pair of what were called "Thumb Cuffs." These were tiny locking cuffs, usually attached to the thumb or a finger of a suspect and were used for children or people with very small wrists who could slip out of a set of adult Peerless or Smith & Wesson handcuffs. Each cuff was attached to the other cuff by a two-inch stainless-steel chain and served the same purpose as a regular set of handcuffs, except that they were much smaller.

If the citizen's version was to be believed, one of the tiny cuffs somehow found its way onto his penis!

The other cuff was quickly attached to the base of the heavy-duty whip radio antenna of the patrol car. Since, at that time, the whip radio antenna was fastened on top of the left rear fender of the patrol car, according to the citizen, he was forced to stand on his toes to prevent any stretching. . .

If the citizen's version was to be further believed, the two officers threatened to start broadcasting over their radio, thereby electrically charging the antenna. At least that was the citizen's version. The obvious intent of the two renegade officers (the citizen's description) was to harass him. Then, according to the citizen, the two officers reportedly gave the microphone to him and told him to call for the Sheriff.

A direct quote was alleged, "We personally guarantee that if you press this button and call for the Sheriff, somebody will come."

The two officers, laughing hysterically, climbed into their patrol car and started to drive slowly away with the poor citizen running alongside.

They eventually took mercy on him, unhooked him from the antenna, attached regular handcuffs to him, transported him to the station and booked him. To add insult to injury, they towed away and stored his new convertible. Usually unmentioned in the investigation of Pat and Sam was the fact that this innocent citizen had a blood alcohol level of .26, more than twice the legal limit at that time.

An exhaustive early morning search of Sam and Pat's lockers, cars, and homes without search warrants or prior notice by officers of Internal Investigations Bureau and the D.A.'s office, failed to turn up any evidence of said "Thumb Cuffs." Of course, both Sam and Pat denied any knowledge whatsoever of any of the ridiculous allegations of the drunken citizen. It seems that the citizen also waited about a week before he reported the incident to the District Attorney's office.

The citizen's tale was at least partially true. He had in fact contributed substantial amounts of money to the campaigns of both the Sheriff and the District Attorney. The interrogations of Sam and Pat by I.I.B. and the D.A.'s office were physically brutal, lengthy and without the presence of any independent witnesses.

A common thread running through the questioning by the lead investigator was that both Sam and Pat were often referred to as "My Friend."

Thereafter, whenever absolute sincerity was necessary between the two former patrol car partners, the phase was utilized.

After hearing Pat say, "My Friend," Sam felt his heart sink.

"We're signing off now, Sam," Sergeant Rodenski yelled over waves of crackling static. "We are going to try to reach some of the other stations and warn them. Take care of yourself."

Sam heard a static "Via Con Dias, My Friend," as the connection was severed.

Samuel R. Albright, Lieutenant, reflected on what he had been told as he absent-mindedly pulled on his gray speckled mustache and brushed a few strands of his half-eaten cigar off his military pressed tan shirt holding his six pointed highly polished star. The lieutenant's gold bars on his shoulders suddenly seemed heavy. After a few moments of depressed thought, he shook himself, got to his feet and walked to the door of his office.

"Dispatcher!"

His voice echoed down the heavily waxed (by inmate trusties) government-green hallway that ran the length of the station,

"Yes Sir!"

"Have all units 10-19 the station, code two. Check if we have any undercover units' code 5 on some house, if so, have them 10-22 the code 5 and 10-19. All Sergeants report to my office, now!"

"Now, Sir?"

"Now!"

About three minutes later, Sam's four sergeants were standing in his office. The foul odor of a half smoked half chewed cigar permeated the air.

"What's going on, Sam? Why are we having all our field units coming into the station, and why code two?" Sergeant Judy Livingston asked.

"And why are we canceling all units that are code 5," Sergeant Joseph Armento interrupted, "You know we have two continuing stakeouts on those crack houses in the north end?"

"Listen up people, forget about the stakeouts," Sam growled, "We have a bigger problem on our hands."

Samuel (R. for Roosevelt) Albright then briefed his sergeants on what he had been told by Captain Dollar finishing with "A couple of you know Pat Dollar and Dave Rodenski and know that what they say, you can make bank on. Judy, you know Pat Dollar, don't you?"

Sergeant Judy Livingston caught herself smiling at memories of a weekend on a Mexican cruise ship where she and Pat Dollar never left their stateroom, her body tingling, before she jerked herself back to the present. "Sure, I know him, if he says something, that's the way it is," she said huskily.

Sam gave his sergeants a few minutes to absorb what he told them. He watched them closely: these men and woman who had indeed made life and death decisions, these men and woman who were required to carry a firearm with them every day of their life since joining the Sheriff's Department (and if rumor was correct, more than one of them carried their firearms with them into bed, especially with a member of the opposite sex! Sam had assumed that the weapons were unloaded.).

Sam stated flatly, "Our last direct orders were to protect our deputies, our station and then the populace. We are in charge and I intend to do everything I can to protect our people. I just don't know what else to do."

Silence.

"If any of you have any other ideas, let me know, now. Our society is going to go to hell and we, as officers, must stay together."

Another silence.

Sergeant Bob Douglas, the senior sergeant at the station cleared his throat, started, hesitated for a moment, and then said, "This station is like a second home for most of us, or when our spouses kicked us out, our first home. Sam, this isn't really a voting situation, but I, for one, intend to follow you. You have always had us and your deputies' interests in mind and I intend to support you. Anyone disagree?"

Another silence, then almost simultaneously, the three other sergeants shook their heads

"No."

Sam waited for a moment, not daring to speak. Something seemed to be in his eyes.

"All right, I've ordered all of our units to 10-19, code two. Judy, once they return to the station, get the keys to the cars, and lock those keys up. Understand?"

"Yes Sir."

"Joe, about six months ago, you did an inventory on our disaster supplies. Would you grab about three deputies, a couple of shotguns and a couple of trustees and head on over to that Ralph's grocery store. Forget about taking a car, they don't run anyway. Take some carts or wagons and grab all the food and supplies you can think of that we'll need for long term. Don't forget water. The station fund money is in the safe, take it with you and try to pay for whatever you take. Oh yes, get as many candles as you can find."

"Well, what if the store is closed?"

"Well, what do you think?" Sam asked.

A heavy silence filled the room.

And continued to fill the room.

Eyes refused to meet eyes.

The magnitude of their problem seeped into their souls: they were no longer the enforcers of the law, they had to become the law.

"As I said, try to pay for the supplies that you take, however, you get them. Understand, Joe?"

"Yes Sir!"

"Bob, you're our Watch Sergeant today," Sam looked at Sergeant Bob Douglas. "Would you get me a list of all personnel we have here at the station right now, including secretaries, everyone. Determine who is married and who isn't."

"Judy, once Bob's list is finished, work with him and set up a rotating guard duty of the station perimeter. I think this city is going to go bonkers when word gets out and I want to protect our station. Be sure to put someone on the roof. Get the AR-15s out of the armory and issue one to each of the deputies on the roof. Make sure each is currently qualified with that weapon. Oh hell, forget about the qualification, just find out if they can shoot the dam weapon!"

"Pete, you're in charge of our jail, how many inmates do we have here, excluding trustees?" Sam asked.

"We have fourteen, Lieutenant, mostly misdemeanors."

"Any Charley Manson, Hillside Stalker, Richard Ramirez, Geoffrey Dahmer types?"

"Naw, just the usual array of drunks, dopers and a few Grand Theft Auto suspects. How about if we kick all of them loose? If what you say is true, I don't want to have to feed them."

"Good thinking. Why not?" Sam said. "Give them a citation and a promise to appear and kick them out the door. About three quarters of them wouldn't show up for trial and as screwed up as our warrant system is, we wouldn't find them anyway. As soon as you're done with the trusties, send them home too. I don't want to have to feed them."

"Oh yes, Bob, Judy, before you run off, shut down the entire station. Shut down the gasoline generators we have in the garage since they haven't been running well anyway, take away and lock up all patrol car keys, shut off all 911 emergency generators, all radio broadcasting equipment and anything else that uses electricity. In fact, pull all the electrical plugs on the NCIC computers, the California Auto Status computers, CLETS, AFIS, and our booking computer systems; most of those computers have batteries in them and I don't want the station being attacked by that Green whatever the hell it is."

"What about water and toilet facilities?" Sergeant Bob Douglas asked.

"Christ! I haven't even thought that far yet. Why don't you investigate that? We'll need a shed and a latrine out back somewhere. There's that vacant lot next door, use that, but remember we'll need to change the hole every so often. Get some of your trusties to dig one or two for us before you kick them loose. I think we have three of those portable toilets out back."

"Any questions, anyone?" Sam asked, unconsciously pulling on his mustache, his eyes radiating deep concern.

An awkward silence followed.

They realized the magnitude of the problem when they first saw Sam without a cigar stuck in his mouth. (Sam _always_ had a cigar in his mouth. Rumor had it that he even slept with his cigar, there were several other more interesting rumors that more than one attempt was made by an enterprising member of the opposite sex to find out if that was always true.)

"Brief all of our deputies, but go easy on them. This thing is a helliva shock."

Sam paused heavily for a second, "Something else needs to be said, perhaps to _all_ of us. For many years, this gold star that we wear on our left chest was the only law around. We've been handed a situation no one ever dreamed of, but fortunately, I've got you Sergeants, I'm proud of each of you, and we've got good people here. We've been trained to do a job as leaders and supervisors." He paused again for a second and then with steel in his voice said, "Let's do it right!"

Three days passed.

Three long strenuous days.

Shortly after a static filled telephone call from his close friend, Dan Peterson, Sam sent as many of the married deputies' home as he could. A few came back, dragging their families and a few possessions with them. One, Deputy Ralph Gomez, told Sam, "Sir, this station has been my second home for over five years. My family needs the protection of the station and I can help out around here."

Sam nodded, "Sure, check with Sergeant Douglas; he's the Watch Sergeant and is in charge of housing; we'll probably put you and your family up in the old trusty quarters."

He looked at Deputy Gomez's family, a dark haired, slightly plump woman with two pre-teenaged children hanging onto her skirt, "You understand that your family will have to work and help out here?"

"Yes Sir! My wife is a good cook, and the kids can help keep the station clean. Thank you, thank you very much, Sir."

Two days ago, Sergeant Judy Livingston ran frantically into his office, "Sam, Deputy Almanto grabbed one of the patrol cars and left the station!"

"Aw crap, "Sam exclaimed as they ran out of the station. "Where was he headed?"

I don't know," Sergeant Livingston panted as they ran to the back gate of the station.

Suddenly, an explosion about two hundred yards down the street shook the area. They could see what was left of a new Chevrolet black and white patrol car with its interior heavily engulfed in flames. Hovering over and around the car were sheets of a green transparent substance, flowing in and out of the remains of the wreck.

"What happened, Thomas?" Sam asked a stunned deputy sheriff crouching nearby.

"I don't know exactly, Sir. He had a spare key to a sergeant's car and was using that to start it; a little later he drove off."

"Did he say anything?"

"Yes Sir. He's been really depressed the last two days. He said he was going for help. He was broadcasting on all of the radio frequencies when he left."

Apparently, the deputy might have lived, but he had turned on his radios and was attempting to contact someone, anyone. The energy attacked not only the engine compartment of the vehicle, but also struck the trunk which contained the broadcasting equipment. The trunk, full of ammunition, flares and a full gas tank resulted in an explosion that blew the car apart and killed the deputy.

Fortunately, the station had plenty of food. Their station was a local disaster area center and contained a basement nearly full of emergency supplies. Sam and his deputies settled in for a long wait, hoping that someone, anyone, would help them.

✦━◆━◆━◆━◆━✦

After talking with Robert Sandoval and reviewing his disaster plan, Dan Peterson frustratingly tossed it on top of a dusty file cabinet, "There's nothing in there that covers a total lack of electricity. I simply don't know what to do."

"Oh, Dan. A Mr. Robinson of some security outfit stopped early today and asked for you."

"Robinson? Robinson, Joe Robinson?"

"Yes, I think that was his first name, he wanted to see you today. He seemed to think that it was important."

Joyce scratched the dark roots of her bleached frizzy blonde hair as she rummaged through the top of her unusually messy desk and retrieved a scribbled upon piece of scratch paper. "I hate not being able to take a shower," she complained.

With considerable effort, Dan refrained from pursuing the thought of Joyce standing in a shower, the soapy water running down full tight, well rounded. . ..

"Here, he left his address and asked for you to come over to see him as soon as possible today," Joyce said.

Dan looked at the address and noted that it was only a block or two away. He thought for a moment, but couldn't place the building at the address.

"Dan, is that your friend Joe Robinson who we got those letters of recommendation for a couple of years ago?"

"Sure. The last time I heard from him, he was working for the Department of Defense or the Army or something like that in one of those hush-hush jobs where nobody knows what you're doing."

"I remember typing those recommendations from the councilmen upstairs, but I don't remember why."

"Well, he was my roommate in college and we became close friends. He later met and married some bimbo and dropped out of college. I thought he was relatively happy until he caught his wife in bed with another man."

"Oh no," Joyce exclaimed.

"Oh yes! Joe went a little crazy and nearly killed both. He was arrested for assault with intent to commit murder and jailed. He called me from a jail cell and asked for help. I obtained a good criminal attorney who managed to convince the judge to lower Joe's bail which I posted."

"What happened to him?"

"Well, when it was time for trial on the assault charges, neither Joe's wife nor the man, who also turned out to be married, were very interested in pressing charges and having their entire sordid affair aired publicly. Joe's criminal attorney convinced the prosecuting District Attorney to drop the charges to 415."

"What's a '415?'"

"A 415 is Section 415 of the California Penal Code, Disturbing the Peace," Dan smiled. "I never quite figured out exactly whose "peace" was being disturbed. It seemed to me that someone's 'peace' had been considerably disrupted when Joe walked into their bedroom, but, in any event, he was free."

Giggling, Joyce looked at him, "415, huh? I've heard quickies or nooners called a lot of things, but never that. I'll have to remember a 415."

After rummaging through his desk in the darkened office with nothing to do, Dan told Joyce, "I'm going to walk over to see Joe Robinson. Why don't you go home? There isn't much we can do until we get some electricity on."

"All right, thanks, but will you promise to let me know if you find out something?"

"Of course."

The clear, windless Southern California day with, strangely, no smog felt heavy on Dan's face. No buses or cars were running on the deserted streets with only a few people walking around. The few people Dan saw avoided his eyes and were hurrying, almost as if they were looking over their shoulders at an unseen object. Pigeons and doves, usually noisy, frequenting the roofs of the city buildings cooed forlornly, their calls seeming to stop in mid-cry.

Dan's footsteps echoed from the concrete buildings as he jaywalked through an electricity-less intersection. There were no signal lights at intersections and no streetlights at night. He also recalled that there hadn't been any radio or television the past few days or so! Even the emergency bands on his son's battery-operated short-wave radio had nothing on them but heavy waves of static.

The address he received for Joe Robinson was an all-enclosed mirrored office building with no open windows. Later, he would remember that the building had no name on it, but several nasty looking toughs were loitering around the front entrance. Even though it felt like a clear warm day, each of the men idling around the front entrance had long jackets or always coats on with at least one hand in a pocket.

"I'm here to see Joe Robinson, please," Dan said to a hard-looking, unshaved, crew-cut character at the guard station at the front entrance. A rank odor hovering over the man like flies assailed Dan's nose and indicated that he too hadn't had a bath for at least several days.

"So, who are you?" the guard growled, his bloodshot eyes constantly scanning the street behind Dan.

"I'm Daniel Peterson. Joe Robinson left a message that I'm supposed to see him today."

Igor, as Dan silently nicknamed the guard, had several suspicious looking bulges in his obviously slept in clothes. Igor carefully looked over a hand-written list, "Got any identification?"

After a very close examination of Dan and his expired driver's license, Igor pointed to a set of carpeted stairs, "Go directly to the waiting room on the second floor; do not stop. Do not go anyplace else. Understand?"

Dan met Igor's eyes, nodded, and climbed the stairs to the second floor. Igor was obviously accustomed to command, but there was tension, even fear, in his eyes.

The building felt damp and musty, as if the air conditioning system had been off for some time. Even the walls were soggy with occasional tiny puddles of moisture adhering to them. A stale odor like his son's gym bag permeated the place. There were no lights, the building dark and dingy, but pieces of candles could be seen scattered in the hallways and in the waiting room. Strange sounding thumps echoed from down the long hallways, but Dan saw no one.

Dan's curiosity was aroused, but he did as he was told. The waiting room was divided in two by a chest high battered light green wood counter. There were two doors, one, the door that Dan entered and the second, a sheet metal covered door with a single Yale lock with no door handles.

Trying not to pant from his walk up the stairs, he walked up to the expressionless man wearing Army camouflage fatigues behind the counter. Dark brown eyes watched him warily.

"I'm here to see Joe Robinson."

The man adjusted a handgun appearing bulge under his fatigue shirt and pointed at a decrepit old sofa, "Sit down and wait."

"Well, do you know if he's here?"

"Sit!"

Dan sat.

"What kind of place is this?" Dan asked. A cold stare like a scientist examining a not very interesting bug was his only reply.

After a few minutes, Dan became bored and looked at some of the magazines scattered in the waiting room. The magazines dealt with such esoteric and diverse subjects as statistical analysis, physics radioastronomy and steam engines. In a relatively recent magazine on high-tech chemistry, even the table of contents proved to be unreadable. There was an old and much used "Mother Earth" magazine.

"What is going on here?" Dan speculated to himself. He heard a key turn in the lock in the sheet metal covered door.

"Dan! It's good to see you!" Joe Robinson smiled as he flung open the door and strode into the waiting room. "Come in."

They warmly shook hands, nearly hugging each other. While they had frequently talked on the telephone, they hadn't physically spent much time with each other since Dan married his second wife.

"You put on some weight, guy," Joe Robinson remarked, his hazel eyes smiling.

Joe's six-foot, one-inch body, on the other hand, seemed to be as slim as ever. He looked disgustingly healthy with a nice tan, Dan noted ruefully. He still had a physical presence that more than a few women had found attractive, but his crew cut was new. Joe's army camouflage fatigues had no insignia of rank, but his black webbed belt held a high-rise holster containing what looked like a large, well-used 9 .mm caliber dark steel automatic. He wore the traditional Army combat boots; however, these boots hadn't been in the neighborhood of shoe polish for months.

"Are you about ready, Ron?" Joe Robinson said to the man behind the counter,

He glanced at Dan.

"It's ok, he's good people."

"They said about a half an hour, Sir."

Joe nodded, "I'll only be a few minutes. As soon as you are ready, let me know."

"Yes Sir."

"Follow me, please," Joe said to Dan. "I'm glad you got here when you did."

He escorted Dan down a dark, gloomy, government olive colored hallway past a few closed metal doors and reached a metal office door. It had no door handles, but only a single circular lock on the right side of the door. Dan raised his eyebrows as Joe unlocked the heavy metal door, let them in, and relocked it after them.

Dan's eyes swept over a gray metal desk with a surprisingly bright orange cloth covered high backed chair behind the desk illuminated by light flowing in from the single window. There were two armless metal chairs in front of the desk, one of which was chained to the floor with handcuffs welded to it. On one wall what appeared to be a map of the world was partially covered with black cloth.

Joe sat behind the desk and whispered, "Grab that chair and bring it over here."

Joe had four metal ball swinging gadgets that if an end ball was struck, the other end would bounce outward. He set all four in motion, the net result was that the air was filled with the sound of metal balls hitting each other. Dan realized that anyone eavesdropping would have difficulty in hearing any voices clearly.

"Dan, there is a reason for all this, but I must have your promise that what I tell you here today will not leave this room," Joe whispered.

He continued, "I have only a few minutes to give you. I'm going out on a limb for you and my job, such as it is, would be in jeopardy if the general public finds out what I'm about to tell you and that I told you."

"I owe much to you and, no, don't make any comments, I simply owe you," interrupted Joe as Dan started to protest. "You are probably the most decent person I know. Your life, our life, is in considerable danger.

"Just listen!" Joe ordered in a voice that was accustomed to command. The new lines of worry around his eyes tightened as his eyes turned steely.

Dan sat; nodded his head and listened; this was a side of Joe Robinson that he didn't know existed.

"Dan, I'm in charge of group funded under the National Security Agency via the U.S. Army that works with the Central Intelligence Agency. I have military people working for me because they are the most qualified to do the things we were assigned. We accomplish things that because of legal reasons either the FBI, the CIA, or the military can't or wouldn't even touch! As you may know, there was a large meteor strike in the southern part of Central America a few weeks ago. We believe that this meteor carried with it a substance, a form of life."

Dan interrupted, "Why, that's incredible news, but . . . but what has that got to do with all this?" He gestured at the locked door.

"Let me finish, remember, this is top secret. That life form was brought to our attention by the local jungle natives who called it El Fantasia Verde, or in English: The Green Ghost! That stuff terrified the hell out of the natives. In fact, the natives down there were so afraid of that stuff that they chose the lesser of two evils: the local authorities instead of El Fantasia Verde. That life form, for lack of a better definition, eats electricity."

"What?" Dan stammered. "You're kidding, aren't you?"

Then he nodded, "Well, now, that does make some sense." His office and home had been without any electrical power for the last couple of days or so and the telephone conversation with Lt. Sam Albright fell into place.

"Wait a second, what does this stuff, this life force look like?"

"When you can see it, it has a greenish faint phosphoric light. That's the reason the jungle natives called it El Fantasia Verde. Why?" Joe asked.

"Well, two or three nights ago, I saw a greenish light occasionally glowing close to the ground not too far from my house, but I didn't know what it was. Is that it?"

"That's it! We know it's here," said Joe, heavily, his tanned face radiating an apprehension, an unaccustomed fear. "We think it reproduces by feeding on any object generating any electrical current. After a short period of time, it blankets an area and destroys everything using electricity."

He gestured at the wall map, "We've asked that all reports of that stuff be forwarded to us here. Two days ago, we received part of a hysterical radio report of a gigantic tsunami near the west coast of Japan. In the middle of the report, behind the voice of our agent, we could hear the sound of a deep rumbling, a scream and then nothing. We think one of our nuclear submarines in the Sea of Japan had one or more of its nuclear warheads explode off the coast of Japan."

He paused for a very depressed moment, "It will get worse!"

Joe's eyes developed the glazed "thousand-yard stare" that Dan had seen in men who just returned from violent combat. They had seen and done things in a hell that men should never have been subjected to!

"After investigating that force, we were flying back from Central America with two older cargo C-130's. You might remember that the C-130s have four of those big Allison turboprops that use Jet Assisted Take Off units to take off from short or non-concrete runways. We had only a very short dirty runway deep in the jungle and we had to use those JATO units to get out of there. Well, we had a third EC-130 flying electronic support above us at its ceiling of about 34,000 feet. It had the usual array of full electronic gear including communication lasers, radar jamming and so on. It was broadcasting a message to us and to Langley, Virginia, our CIA -headquarters, when streamers of El Fantasia Verde attacked both of its port engines."

Joe paused a moment, reliving the horror of that moment, "We think that most of the crew bailed out over northern Mexico before the plane blew up in midair. The captain, a friend of mine, didn't make it because he was fighting to save his aircraft to the last possible minute. We have a tape of his last words. . . ."

Joe shook himself slightly, his haunted eyes focusing on Dan, "We landed as soon as possible over here in Orange County. We nearly crashed landing our plane!"

"I'm so sorry, my friend," Dan said quietly, shaking his head.

A long moment of silence followed, broken only by the constant clicking of the steel balls.

"Well, what about power plants or cars or buses or planes?" Dan thought out loud. "You know, public transportation has stopped and all of the streetlights and traffic signals are off. And I saw a lot of wrecked or burnt cars. Does this stuff, this life force affect cars and regular electrical power?"

"Our latest information is that this life eats anything that makes any appreciable amount of electricity. Batteries themselves haven't been attacked, but when a battery is utilized in any kind of electrical system, that system has been attacked."

Joe continued, "We haven't had any reports of humans being attacked, and my people think that the electricity in a human or animal body is too little to attract this life form."

Joe leaned forward and whispered in Dan's ear, "This is absolutely Top Secret, but we notified most state governments to cease the use of electricity or cars and buses because this stuff attacks them. Right after we advised the lower government units, or hope we got to them, to shut down all their electrical and generation systems, we lost all contact with pretty much the rest of the world! I don't know if the big dams or the nuclear power plants ever got the message."

Joe then leaned back in his chair, "There are about one hundred and nine nuclear power plants in the North American area and I pray that they had the time to shut themselves down."

"We never got that message to shut off our facilities, we were only told that we couldn't drive any city vehicles."

Dan paused for a moment, then Joe's comments started to take effect, tiny shivers of fear fluttering down his spine, "My God, Joe, that, that means worldwide starvation, disaster . . . You know that the average family has only enough food and supplies for about a week. What is the government doing about it?"

Joe just sat and looked at Dan.

The clicking of the steel balls continued through the darkened room.

Dan opened his mouth as if to ask something, but then shut it unspoken.

The silence grew, punctuated only by the clicking of the steel balls.

And grew!

And grew!

Dan finally, with a terrible, cold sinking feeling in his stomach, realized that he wasn't going to hear an answer to his question. Even more horrible was the sudden realization that there may not have been an answer to his question.

"Is, is that why you asked to see me today?" asked Dan with a trembling voice from a dry mouth after several stuttered attempts.

"I owe you more than I can ever repay," Joe said. "I would be in serious trouble, very serious trouble if this information ever leaked out and I was found to be the source."

He paused for a moment and then continued, "I strongly suggest that you start to really take care of yourself from now on. I just can't tell you much more. Hell, I don't know much more, but the worldwide conditions are grave, catastrophic! I was part of the decision-making process to recommend to the President of the United States that he activate the National Guard to preserve law and order. We hoped the President decided to follow our recommendations and he did activate the National Guard about two days ago, however, by the time he made the decision, we were unable to even broadcast the decree because that stuff ate our transmitters."

After a sad pause, Joe's tension filled voice continued, "Locally, we've lost contact with the whole Los Angeles area to the west of us from essentially the Harbor Freeway westward to the Pacific Ocean. We have reports of terrible looting and gunfights between some of the gangs, the Crips and the Bloods, over there. I understand that the police departments and the sheriff's stations are simply entrenched in their station buildings; in a few places, the police can't even get out of their substations or police stations."

Dan just stared at his friend, attempting to absorb what he had been told. So, some of the terrible rumors he had heard were true.

After a while, Dan shook himself, "Do you have any suggestions? What in God's name can we do?"

"You have relatives somewhere in the Midwest, don't you?" asked Joe.

"Sure," a stunned Dan replied. "I, I have a whole bunch of family in Wisconsin." He slowly continued, "And as a matter of fact, my parents, the last time we talked on the telephone, asked me to come home to their farm."

"Try to make it there. This area, and most big cities will be a war zone in a few days. After about a week with no food or water, people will get desperate. There will be no controlling these cities, or probably much of the world when this information gets out," Joe warned as he rose from his chair.

"Now, Dan, I've got too much to do and you have to leave. I'll escort you out of this building. My people are scared. Hell, I'm scared. They will shoot first and maybe ask questions later if they don't know who you are."

Before Joe unlocked the office door, he said, "We are shutting down this operation within the next couple of days. Our scientists tell us that, at least at the present time, we can't stop this force."

Joe paused for a moment and then said painfully, "We lost a number of very good men attempting to capture a part of that stuff. Our scientists think that The Green Ghost was around probably since the beginning of the universe. It ate through everything we put around it; we can't even run tests on the stuff because our testing equipment uses electricity. Water, lead, graphite, nothing seems to stop the stuff. They tried to use those giant magnets up near Livermore, California, and down in Texas to hold the stuff, but it ate the magnets to get to the electricity."

"A few of us have a place picked out, and I have a couple of scientists working on the Green Ghost, but at this time, there seems to be no future for any electrical society. We'll attempt to preserve some semblance of civilization, but I can't take any strangers," Joe apologized.

"I suggest that you take your family and leave. Don't stay here in Southern California, or near any large city, because there's no way this area can obtain enough food to fight off starvation. Also, don't try to drive a car, that stuff will eat your engine and possibly kill you," Joe urged.

"You leave as soon as possible. Don't wait! You understand?"

Dan numbly nodded.

Joe continued quietly and thoughtfully, "We've attempted to set up a conference at the University of

Chicago in about a year for all of our scientists to discuss this force; hopefully, there will be some alive to attend . . ..”

They slowly walked together down the hall to the front of the building, the only sound was their hollow footsteps on the scruffy carpets; Dan was still in shock and nearly speechless.

Dan looked, really looked at his friend, aware that this was probably the last time they would see each other.

Dan said heartfeltly, “Thank you, my friend.”

They looked at each other, clasped their hands in a rock like vice and then instinctively hugged each other. They broke apart and again clasped hands and hugged. Both turned and walked away, neither wanting the other to see the tears streaming down their faces.

CHAPTER TWO

Shocked, Dan Peterson stumbled almost mindless through the deserted city streets. The day was bright, nearly too bright as if the sun was pounding down on a defenseless city. There was little air movement, and what breezes there were brought with them a putrid odor like a sunbaked dumpster behind a Chinese restaurant. A small pack of dogs trotted around a corner, but they didn't seem to be as afraid of humans.

Dan Peterson took off his jacket and loosened his tie on his sweat-stained shirt. His tie, the tie given to him by his son, was dropped somewhere while he attempted to absorb, attempted to understand what had happened to his life and his society. His mind was blank while he struggled within himself to realize that he had to go on. His friend Joe Robinson had told him the truth about the force; Dan had realized something was wrong when he couldn't obtain any answers or information about what had happened to the electrical power.

A crash of breaking glass from around the next block caught his attention.

He cautiously peered around the corner of a building and locked eyes with two men crouching in the middle of the street waiving metal baseball bats. One of the men growled, "You want to help us or you want to be gone?"

Behind the men, about a half dozen men and women crawled out of broken front windows of a large red bricked electronics store carrying computers, television sets and electrical appliances.

No police were in sight nor was there the sound of an alarm or any sirens. Dan shook his head and turned away.

"So it starts."

He plodded his way onto the street where he lived. The thought, *"Things aren't the same,"* penetrated his stunned mind.

There was no laughter by the neighborhood kids, lawns were uncut, and the streets hadn't been cleaned for some time. It was amazing how seedy the neighborhood looked after about a week of lack of care and water. In fact, garbage hadn't been picked up and the tin cans and garbage bags were starting to stink. Large black slinking rats with long hairless tails were frequently seen in broad daylight. And they too didn't seem afraid of humans.

Concern, worry for himself and his kids was starting to flood his mind. A tightness of fear grew in his chest. Sweat was staining his shirt from his armpits and down his back, not only from the warmth of the day, but from his feelings of tension.

More fear, laced with terror, was attempting to clamor its way into the outer fringes of his mind.

"What was he going to do?"

"What could he do?"

"What about his family, his kids?"

Dan thought of his conversation with his friend, Joe Robinson, and Joe's warning was etched in his brain: "Get out of these cities, out of Southern California, this area will be a war zone because the police can't protect you."

The key question kept occurring to him whether he should or even could give up this life in California and try for a different life somewhere-anywhere, even Wisconsin.

A second dreaded thought of *"Could we even make it to Wisconsin?"* kept repeating itself in his sense of reason.

"I sure hate to give up everything I've worked for here, my home, my books, my life here, my friends, everything," he mumbled to himself as he stumbled to the front of his typical southern California rented tract home.

His home with the traditional Southern California red tiled roof was as unseen to Dan as the cracks in the brown stucco sided walls that indicated the effects of the frequent Southern California earthquakes. Beside the house, next to the concrete walkway, Dan's prized six-foot tall red, white and orange roses were blooming, and wilting. The small front lawn was turning brown; it badly needed watering, however, there wasn't any water pressure or water.

He had tried so hard, so very hard, to make a decent and warm home for his kids and family, could he give this up?

But they couldn't stay here!

Once inside his home, Dan saw his sixteen year old son, Tom, sitting and looking out the front windows. Tom's long brown hair was uncombed on top of his five-foot, eight inch, one-hundred-and-forty-pound body. Dan smiled with pride at his boy, a quiet, physically strong young man, who had been getting just average grades at school, but who excelled at sports and played a mean second base-shortstop for his high school baseball team. He had Dan's physical stature (minus about eighty pounds), but his deceased mother's deep sensitivity to others.

Neither Tom nor his nine-year old sister, Sue, had been to school for a week. The buses never arrived and the phones stopped working a few days later. The first few days were exciting since both kids typically weren't all that enthused about attending school; lately, however, both had started to worry.

"Dad, we're running out of food and all of the grocery stores were closed this morning," Tom said with concern in his blue-green eyes. "We are almost out of charcoal and lighter fluid for the barbecue, too."

"I went down to old man Mott's store and traded him some books for some cans of food. I hope that was ok?" he asked. "You know how he likes to read."

"Sure, sure," Dan absently replied as he walked slowly up the stairs, dragging his coat on the floor, his shoulders hunched over.

Sue walked over to Tom, "What's wrong with Dad? Is it something to do with us not going to school?"

Tom shrugged his shoulders, "I don't know, Sis. He seems changed for some reason."

Dan wandered almost in a daze from room to room, memories flooding back: here was Tom's first tiny rocker, there was Sue's shoe, on the wall, a photograph of many happier days when they were all together and Judy, his first wife, Tom and Sue's mother, was still alive. Next to it was the last photograph they had of Ginger, his youngest daughter. Her flaming red hair surrounded an impish smile on a five-year old face.

His favorite room in the house, his study, was dark, and now, almost dingy because of no lights. His computer was lifeless, a useless piece of furniture. He had spent considerable time in this room, planning and working on how to provide a better home and living for his family. He still came here to think. Here were a few valued items such as his autographed baseball by his beloved California (or now Los Angeles or whatever) world champion Angels and his lucky Angel baseball cap he wore to every one of Tom's baseball games. The hat, so faded and worn as to be almost colorless had been a good luck charm for Tom's games, first in little league and then in high school. Books on almost any subject were haphazardly stacked on the four walnut-colored bookshelves.

Dan wasn't sure when he realized he and his family had little choice. He was hearing gunshots every night and he had heard rumors of violent race and food riots over in the western part of Los Angeles County which Joe Robinson and Lt. Sam Albright had essentially confirmed.

Dan now realized that he hadn't seen a police car or fire truck for over a week.

And Southern California's most frequently heard noise, sirens, had been conspicuously absent. It was probable there were no more police patrols since they needed patrol cars and radio communications to perform their duties. There also were no fire engines or ambulances since they all needed electricity and they had no way of responding to the widespread traffic accidents. After his conversation with Joe Robinson, Dan now understood the terrible reason why.

He realized the normally very noisy southern California scene was now silent and had been so for some time. He hadn't realized it until after his meeting with Joe Robinson, but he also hadn't heard the constant drone of planes either.

Dan slowly shuffled down the worn carpeted stairs and sat down heavily, the smell of charcoal barbecue permeating the house through the open back patio doors.

"Tom, Sue, come here please," he said with a deep sigh.

Some families meet at the kitchen table or at the fireplace during times of great family crisis. Dan's family, for some reason, met at the steps.

Tom and Sue's eyes met and flashed with worry.

They remembered the times they met on the steps: when their Dad had sadly told them of their mother's death; when he later introduced them to Kathy and asked her to be their new mother; and later, when he had to tell them that Kathy simply ran away with their sister, Ginger.

"I've got some bad news, kids," Dan said.

"What, Dad?" Tom asked, his blue green eyes blinking rapidly.

Dan, as well as he could, told Tom and Sue what had been disclosed by Joe Robinson and Lt. Sam Albright, and what he had seen within the last few days.

"Joe also told me that they believed that this entire Southern California area was going to become a war zone. Since we don't have any transportation to haul food and once the food runs out, people will get desperate. He said that we should try to escape from here because the police and fire departments are now useless."

"What, what about the rest of the United States?" Tom asked, his voice trembling.

"If I understood Joe correctly, that too!"

Long moments of silence followed.

Twice, Tom opened his mouth to say something, then stopped, his eyes deep in his taut face.

"You kids remember the last time we talked to Grandpa and Grandma in Wisconsin?"

"Sure," Tom nodded. "They said we should try to come there to live or at least for a vacation. They hadn't seen us since you married Kathy."

"Yes," Sue agreed, "Grandma really wanted to see us, too."

After a moment of silence, Dan went on, "It feels like we're being forced to do something that we don't want to do. But you know that we don't have much food left. The refrigerator doesn't work and we had to eat the frozen food before it spoiled, and there is no water or gas either because there is no electricity."

He added after a moment, "And we're almost out of charcoal and lighter fluid, too. The toilets aren't running either because we don't have any water pressure." After the first couple of days, they kept the bathroom doors closed to prevent the odor from permeating throughout the house.

"Tom, you remember my friend on the L.A. Sheriff's Department, Lieutenant Sam Albright?"

"Sure. How could I forget him? He came to our party as a guest with a black and white patrol car and scared three-quarters of my friends away. And he wasn't even in uniform!"

"I called him and he warned me of The Green Ghost. He said that we should be very, very careful."

Dan concluded, "Joe Robinson also said and felt strongly that we should get out of Southern California. He said, and I agree, that most families have only enough food for about seven days or less. After that, people, us, will be in dire straits."

Both Tom and Sue were silent, almost deathly still for moments. A few far-off gunshots sharply punctured the brooding silence.

"Another problem that we have is that we can't drive or fly or take buses because of The Green Ghost. I haven't even given any thought on how we'll get to Grandpa and Grandma's if we decide to go there."

Sue's little face, framed by her long light brown hair, was white and drawn, tears leaking down from her brown eyes.

"I don't want to leave," she whimpered, pushing a wisp of hair out of her face.

"I don't either, Honey," Dan whispered.

Tom broke the silence by looking at his father and somberly shaking his head, "Well, it looks like we can't stay here, it's just too dangerous. I forgot to tell you that one of your upstairs' bedroom windows was shot out this morning. And a couple of hours ago, I heard a lot of automatic gunfire about three or four blocks west of us. I think it came from that Von's shopping center over there."

He continued, shaking his head quietly, "And we have very little food left."

Sue and Tom looked at each other, a silent communication flowed between them, and both almost nodded together with tears streaming down Sue's face.

Tom said with a lopsided grin too close to a grimace, "Well, Dad, let's go visit Grandpa and Grandma!"

All three were cognizant then that their life, as they knew it, was changed forever. Dan, with tears of pride in his eyes, reached out and grabbed his kids in a fervent hug. He had never been prouder of them than that minute.

Sue sniffled through her sobs, "But, what about Ginger, Daddy? I love her and miss her so much."

Dan nodded, "I love her too, Sweetie."

He recalled fondly the close bond that had developed between Sue and Ginger almost from the moment that Ginger had been born. For some reason, their relationship seemed to be more than just an average sister-sister friendship. Dan thought that Kathy, Dan's ex-wife and Ginger's mother, with her separatist attitude about protecting "her" precious baby from Dan's children, had exactly the opposite effect: her stance forced the children closer together. When Sue started school, she sat down with her homework and taught her three-year old sister how to print her name and address.

"Well, Dad," Tom muttered, gently touching Sue's shoulder, "If this force thing lasts for a while, we may never be able to see her again, no matter where we are."

"Joe Robinson said that we can't fight the Green Ghost now. He felt that our scientists had no tools or knowledge sufficient to combat that stuff."

"Dad," Tom said, "You remember, Sue and I received two post cards from her a couple of months ago. The postcards were postmarked in a small town near Durango, Colorado."

Dan nodded, "Sure, I recall that. We couldn't find the town on the map, but the postmarked zip code was in that area."

"Well," Sue said, matter-of-factly, "If we're going to see Grandpa and Grandma, we'll simply have to go get her." There was no discussion; Dan and his son looked at each other and nodded, they knew that they had to find their Ginger.

Once the decision was made to leave, however, what then?

What can be taken?

What must be left?

What <u>must</u> be taken?

Finally, after some argument and longer silences, Dan said gently, "You guys make a list of those things that you absolutely, only absolutely need and want to take with us; we'll sort that stuff out later."

Afterward, Dan looked into Tom's room and saw the heartbreaking decisions that had to be made. Tom didn't want to take his favorite baseball glove that helped win the school championship or his trophies, but he was placing in a small pile articles such as knives, boots, a survival book he found somewhere, and rough clothes.

Sue's room was a different story, however. Sue's room had always been a different story. At the best of times, it looked like a hurricane had blown through and improved the room's organization. She refused to throw out anything. And she had a psychological aversion to picking up anything on the floor. Dan had tried everything he could think of to get her to keep her room neat: from "grounding" her with no television or telephone, to out-and-out bribery. Nothing seemed to work and Dan finally gave up. Once every other week or so, he would pick up and wash her clothes. Sue would help him hang her clothes and put the clean clothes in her dresser, but she seemed incapable of doing anything further. During the "clothes-pick-up" time, Dan would take a few large trash bags to clean her room. It continually amazed him how such a pretty-little girl could accumulate so much junk and trash.

Dan saw her sitting in the middle of her room surrounded by dolls, photographs and knickknacks, tears flooding down her cheeks, heartfelt sobs racking her small body. Dan's heart went out to her and he held her tightly in his arms.

"I know how hard it is, Honey. Take what you think you can carry, but be sure to take photographs of Mom, too, OK?"

"I, I know, Daddy," Sue sobbed. "I'm s-s-sorry, it just so hard!"

"We'll do this together, Honey, it'll work out, you'll see," Dan mumbled as he hugged his daughter. He averted his face so she would not see the tears running down his cheeks.

"I've got to leave for a while. You and Tom watch this place, OK? I'll be back soon. It'll be all right, Honey," Dan murmured, stroking his daughter's fine light brown hair as he held her.

It was dark when Dan left his home. He had changed from his normal white shirt and worn dark dress pants to jeans, tennis shoes and a dark short sleeved shirt. He put a small pry bar in his pocket, more for protection than for anything else. There was residual heating coming from the pavement and sour odors in the air as if he was smelling Tom's high school gym bag full of unwashed sneakers or socks.

A shortcut through an alley led him to the back of a small sports store. It was about three thousand square feet and was part of and approximately in the middle of a small, east facing, shopping center. The neighborhood was warm, quiet and dark. The moon hadn't come up yet, although he remembered that last night had a full moon.

The alley was dark and deserted; overhanging tree branches gave the alley an appearance of a dim and forbidding cave. Garbage cans lay on the pavement as if thrown there by a giant's hand. Garbage and litter crunched softly under his feet as he crept to the back of the store. No lights were on anywhere, not even a candle or fire burning.

The back door he looked for was barricaded with wrought iron, but the molding around the locks was free. Obviously, the owner needed to somehow get into the store. Dan moved around to the side of the shopping center and peered out at the street.

Nothing moved, not even a breath of fresh air.

The little store's location was almost hidden from the street. The entire shopping center consisted of only a few stores with a dozen parking places. There were a few large leafy eucalyptus trees still oozing sap from being burnt by the energy force; it smelled like cough drops. A still smoldering burnt new bright red Cadillac was tilted on flat tires to one side with both front doors open, abandoned in the driveway to the shopping center. Huge, jagged holes in the hood of the car and from the interior oozed wisps of corrosive smoke. Dark reddish scrape spots on the ground looked suspiciously like dried blood.

He looked for an alarm system on the back door of the store and found the wires; he then mumbled to himself, "Come on dummy, there's no electricity to operate the alarm system."

His heart was beating rapidly, so loud that he was certain that someone else could hear it. His hands shaking, he fitted the pry bar to the backdoor lock and pried gently.

Nothing.

He tried harder.

Still nothing.

He pounded on the top of the pry bar with his bare hand to drive it further into the space between the door and the wall and felt the wood give a little.

He stopped, looked around and wiped the sweat off his brow. He wondered why burglars never suffered heart attacks, his was beating so hard.

He tried again, harder this time and felt the door frame move a little more. Encouraged, he forced the pry bar into the space between the door and door frame and gave a sharp, quick jerk. The door popped open with a soft squeak, pieces of the lock fell to the ground, tinkling loudly in the dark alley.

Startled, clutching the pry bar in his sweaty hands, Dan ran a few cautious steps to the corner of the building to flee if someone came out or yelled.

Nothing.

Absolute quiet!

Dan's breathing slowed; his heart stopped pounding in his ears. He returned to the rear door and this time, slowly and quietly pulled it open and peered into the back of the store.

There were no interior lights, but a soft moon-light flowed in from the front windows. No one appeared to be there. He tiptoed in and pulled the door shut behind him, clutching the pry bar in a trembling, sweating hand. He examined the interior of the store and clearly, there was no one there.

There: on the wall, a Colt AR-15 rifle and below it, boxes of new .223 ammunition for it. Since the owner couldn't legally sell such a weapon in California, he must have kept it for display. Dan crept behind the counter, grabbed the AR-15 and examined it.

"I hope this thing still fires," he mumbled to himself.

It was identical to the Colt M-16 he had used in the Army except this weapon was semi-automatic rather than a military full-automatic rifle. His hands fondled the new rifle even to the black plastic covering over the muzzle's dark green flash suppressor, the metal cool under his hands. He broke open the weapon and peered down the barrel, it appeared clean and clear.

He quickly filled two fifteen round clips and loaded the weapon, the sharp metallic click of the clip sliding firmly into the bottom of the AR-15 echoed loudly throughout the store. He pulled back and held the T-handle, pressed down on the release level on the left side, and quietly and slowly allowed the T-handle to slide forward; a .223 cartridge slid smoothly into the chamber with a whisper of copper jacketed metal sliding home.

He ejected the clip from the weapon, ejected the .223 cartridge from the receiver, and flipping the safety lever to fire, pulled the trigger. The click of the firing pin echoed throughout the store.

"*Wonderful, it works!*"

On the opposite wall were a few power bows of the multiple pulley variety. He needed to get Tom to tell him about the bows.

It was amazing how much better he felt having a familiar weapon on his back. His heartbeat slowed. He started to think more calmly and rationally.

"*Priorities? Come on, guy, priorities.*"

A bed roll still in its original plastic container was found and placed beside the back door. He found a gold mine of supplies: two wire racks full of freeze-dried food.

"*I wonder what happened to the old guy who owned this store,*" he idly speculated while he crammed the freeze-dried food into a large green canvas duffle bag.

After filling the duffle bag full of food, it felt like it weighed about fifty pounds. He quietly staggered to the back door, carrying the stuffed duffle bag on one shoulder and the seven-pound bed roll and his rifle on the other.

He quietly peered out the back door, his eyes searching for any movement.

Nothing.

Nothing appeared to have changed.

He crept into the alley with his hoard and quietly closed the door, bracing it with a dusty plank he found along the wall. Keeping to the shadows, he crept home and slid in the back door.

"Tom?"

"What, Dad?"

"Come here, I need your help, we must bring as much of this stuff home as we can to help us on our trip."

"Sure, Dad! Say, where did you get that gun? Is that a real M—16?"

"Close enough, come on, gang, I need your help."

"Put on some dark clothes and tennis shoes. Hurry up, we have little time," Dan urged.

A few minutes later, Dan silently led a darkly dressed Tom and Sue through the still deserted shadowy alley to the back of the store, the Colt AR-15 strapped snugly on Dan's shoulder.

"Quiet, absolutely quiet," he whispered.

Tom and Sue looked at each other with wide questioning eyes, "Where was their father taking them?"

As they entered the store, Tom whispered admiringly, "Well, I'll be. I didn't think you had it in you to do this, Dad."

"I simply don't have a choice," was the sad reply.

"What a find!" Tom whispered, his eyes glinting as he surveyed the interior of the store. It never occurred to Dan that his son didn't seem to be at all disturbed by their burglary of the store.

"Sue, you look for good walking shoes while we try to plan what we need. Tom, you look for food that we can carry. Forget cans because they weigh too much," Dan whispered. "I'll look for weapons and things. And be quiet."

By this time, the yellow full moon was creeping over the eastern horizon and shining directly into the front windows of the store. There was enough light for them to nearly read a book, in any event, there was ample light for them to examine the total contents of the store.

Dan found a 9 mm. chrome plated H & K semi-automatic handgun with black rubberized hand grips. Nearby were three nine-round clips for the gun. He took the clips, three boxes each containing 50 copper jacketed hollow point bullets with a brown Bianci shoulder holster for the weapon. In a drawer in the rear of the store, he found an old Smith and Wesson five shot Chief .38 caliber revolver with the serial number ground off it. The Smith and Wesson Chief had brown checkered wood grips that were chipped and worn as if someone had used the weapon to pound nails. The action seemed smooth and tight, however, as he dry-fired it, the "click" of the hammer falling echoing loudly throughout the store.

After more searching, Dan found two small .22 caliber pearl handled, Smith & Wesson automatic handguns that were concealable in a pocket. In separate drawers, he found four small boxes containing fifty shells each of .22 caliber long rifle ammunition for the .22 automatics and a single box of 50 high velocity "Super-Vel" metal jacketed hollow nosed bullets for the .38 revolver.

"Dad, we should take this light-weight crossbow for Sue, she can easily carry it," Tom whispered as he waved a small, hand-cockable crossbow toward Sue.

"Sure, as long as it's not too heavy."

"We should take these two power bows for you and me, too. I'll show you how to handle them," Tom said as he picked up a power bow, pulled back on the nylon enforced wired string and released it. The sharp sound of the released bowstring strumming throughout the store startled Sue.

"Quiet, Tom!" she exclaimed in a hushed voice.

"Ok, Ok, kids. Calm down. Tom, I'll grab arrows and arrowheads, and there are two quivers at the end of this aisle," Dan said.

Two more bedrolls, canteens, more ammo, all the freeze-dried food and beef jerky, and two nasty hunting knives were taken. Dan found a vial of water purification tablets that might be worth its weight in gold.

"Dad, can I take this?" Tom asked.

He was waving a giant hunting knife with about a sixteen- inch blade that weighed nearly seven pounds. It seemed to contain everything but the kitchen sink in its handle.

"Try to find something smaller, Tom," Dan suggested. "Some guy by the name of Rambo is the only one who can handle a knife like that."

Both Tom and Sue strapped smaller hunting knives on their waists with Velcro webbed belts while Dan strapped a dark green, razor sharp, Army K-Bar knife to his waist.

Dan found two adult lightweight metal framed backpacks for him and Tom, and a child's backpack little more than a school backpack that fit Sue.

They made at least a half-dozen trips back and forth to their home before the night was half over. Each time, the pile in their living room grew alarmingly.

"We'll never be able to carry all of this stuff," Tom worried as he surveyed the pile before one of their last trips to the store.

"I know," Dan replied, "But I want to get everything we can before someone else discovers the store."

On their last trip, Tom and Sue tried on several pairs of heavy-duty shoes.

"I suggest that we each take two pair of shoes because I don't know when we'll be able to get replacements."

Dan had his picked out. He settled on a pair of soft leather walking shoes and a pair of heavy leather work shoes. Sue, of course, simply had to have the pink colored hiking shoes. Tom made a more sensible choice of half-leather, half canvas hunting boots and thought they would not be difficult to break in.

Included within the final things they took were small aluminum individual eating containers that were sturdy, yet light weight with each containing a small knife, fork and spoon. Sue took four, one for each of them and, "This extra one is for Ginger."

"Tom, how much do you think that stuff we took is worth?" Dan asked.

"Well, I'd say at least a thousand dollars; those bows and that AR-15 is worth at least that, why?"

"I don't know if the owner will ever get back, but I'm going to leave about four hundred dollars, that's all I have on me. I hated to do this," he gestured, "But I feel I have to take care of us."

Tom said nothing, but he looked at his father for a long moment . . ..

After they returned to their home, they examined the mound of loot with critical eyes.

"Dad, we simply can't carry all of this stuff," Tom said.

"I know, and I've been thinking about that, maybe we can pull a small cart or wagon or something."

"Daddy, Daddy, can I take my bike I got for Christmas?" Sue asked, excitedly.

"Bikes!" exclaimed Dan and Tom simultaneously.

"Sweetheart, you have just answered our problem. If we fix up your bike and Tom's bike in the garage, maybe we can ride to Wisconsin."

"Do either of you know where I can get an adult's bike, preferably a heavy-duty kind?"

"Well . . .." Tom said, thinking, "The Swackies down the street ride all the time and they have all kinds of bikes."

"But they're on vacation in Europe or Spain," Sue objected.

"Well," Dan said, "If they are over there, and if Joe Robinson is correct, they are going to stay there because there's no transportation back to the United States."

"Tom, get that pry bar, grab a candle and come with me."

A few minutes later, after prying open the back door of the Swackies' home, even knowing that the Swackies could never return, Dan refused to examine the drawers of the house like they had searched the store's contents.

"Son, I don't want to go through their house. I hate to do this, but we must take care of ourselves."

It was near dawn and they didn't want to waste time nor did they want to pry into the Swackies' personal affairs. They only looked in the garage and with the flickering candlelight, found as Tom had said, several kinds of bikes, some in excellent condition and others in pieces.

"I think Mr. Swackie does, did, his own repairs to his bikes," Tom murmured.

After examining the contents of the garage by the light of his small candle, Dan decided that they would use the Swackies' bikes rather than the cheap bikes he could only afford for his family.

"Tom, run back home and get Sue. These bikes are in much better condition than ours and she'll need to choose her own," Dan said.

Tom left to get Sue. The Swackie bikes had derailleurs with gears and levers for them to climb hills and appeared to be the much sturdier wide-tired mountain bikes rather than the cheap Peterson bikes.

Dan found a small trailer as Tom and Sue returned.

"Look Tom, Mr. Swackie modified the original trailer by attaching dual wheels on each side and widening it. It looks like he used the same size wheels as the bike that's towing this trailer."

Small repair kits, extra tires and tubes for each bike and a small hand air pump found their way into the trailer.

Tom suggested, "Dad, we should take along extra chains, too."

"You know, Dad," Tom said as he stacked spare tires and parts in the trailer, "We just might have a chance with these bikes."

After returning home with three bikes and the trailer, and after having been awake all night, Sue immediately fell asleep on the sofa. Dan carried her up to her bed and gently laid her on it.

"Tom, you sleep up here and I'll sleep downstairs. I don't want anybody trying to break in and rob us," Dan said. "We should pack all of this stuff this afternoon or evening and try to leave as soon as possible. I suggest that we plan on leaving tonight, late."

"OK," Tom yawned as Dan hugged him, "I'll wake you or you wake me, whoever gets up first."

Their sleep that morning and afternoon was punctured with an occasional gunshot, a few seemed only a block or two away. . ..

CHAPTER THREE

"D ad?"
"Dad? Dad, wake up," a small voice pleaded.

Dan drudged himself out of a deep sleep and looked at the source of the voice: Sue. She had washed her face with some of their limited amount of water and had brushed her hair until it floated like a halo around her head.

"Good morning, Rabbit," Dan said fondly. "Come here and give me a hug."

Dan looked over her shoulder; it was late afternoon. They had slept nearly the whole day.

"Daddy, I'm hungry. Will we be all right?"

"I hope so, Honey, it will not be easy and we may have some hard times ahead of us, but I think we'll be all right," Dan said to her head he hugged against his chest.

"Well, let's use the food we can't take with us. And then, we'll pack; I want to leave tonight if possible. Is Tom up?"

Tom strolled into the living room, yawning, "Hi Dad."

"Good morning little skunk," he said to his sister. Little skunk was his name for her since she had a violent attack of gas when she was four. After many heated arguments later, Tom learned to use the nickname only when they were alone and as a term of fondness.

Cans of cold beans and creamed corn washed down with their final bottle of cola constituted dinner. After dinner, in the diminishing daylight, they returned to the living room and stared with dismay at the large, jumbled pile of sleeping bags, bows and arrows, food, extra shoes, extra knives, three backpacks and other plunder in the middle of the floor.

"Tom, get the trailer in here while it's still light outside. Sue, you bring down what you want to take with us," Dan told the kids.

The sorting began; difficult decisions of what to take and what to leave had to be made on a strictly practical basis since their space was very limited. Dan couldn't even consider his computer since the batteries would attract the Green Ghost. Most of the family photo albums had to be left with only a few irreplaceable photographs allowed along.

"How about suitcases?" Tom asked.

After a moment's thought Dan shook his head, "I don't think so, that trailer has a plastic bottom which will protect our things, and suitcases are additional weight that I don't want to lug across the country. What I do think though is that we should use one of the small overnight suitcases for our vitamins, toothpaste and brushes, and so on."

The pile of what to take was still too large even after they had heartbreakingly sorted out the nonessentials. Weight was a major problem. Sheets, pillowcases and most blankets were discarded for sleeping bags (each weighing six to eight pounds) with a plastic sheet for each. Extra boots or shoes, toilet paper(!), food which might weigh as much as ninety pounds, a few small cooking pots, weapons and ammunition, extra clothes including only a single towel for each, jackets, light weight rain coats, bars of soap, a box of Tide and a small bottle of bleach for washing dishes, a very few treasured books, Sue's doll, Ginger's doll she had left behind, matches, bows and arrows, and extra hunting knives all had to be included. Shouldn't forget the first aid kits and a small toolbox with tubes, tires and extra chains for the bikes. A two-pound box of candles might be worth its weight in gold.

"Dad, I think we should place our extra clothes and shoes, and things we don't need right away on the bottom of the trailer," Tom suggested.

"Sure, that makes sense; we'll keep the raincoats and jackets on top, next will be our sleeping bags, then our food. I would like to keep our food in those two green duffle bags over there, they will help protect the food if we get caught in a rainstorm. On the bottom with the extra clothes will go that tiny toolbox with the extra tires and tubes."

"Tom, Sue, each of you should carry one of these throw-away cigarette lighters; we found a whole box of them which will go on the bottom of the trailer."

Fortunately, Dan thought, both of his kids were healthy and didn't need special medication. Vitamins should be taken, though; they were going into some hard times and they needed all the help they could get. Dan had belonged to one of the warehouse stores in Southern California and he had purchased a three-pound bottle of vitamins. Tom placed the bottle on the pile commenting, "Well, now we have enough vitamins to supply the whole state of Wisconsin." Dan glared through Sue's giggle.

Eventually, the pile was whittled down. Much was compressed into the lightweight backpacks that Dan and Tom would carry. Sue could carry only a small amount but she was carrying her toothpaste and brushes, extra ammunition, extra clothes, and of course, most importantly, her doll!

"I want each of you to carry one of these little .22 automatics. They'll fit in a jacket pocket and if something happens to me, no one will think of searching either of you," Dan said.

"Let me show you how to work and shoot this weapon," Dan said to his daughter.

"Here, you take a bullet and you insert it into this clip. The clip will hold from six to about a dozen bullets. Take the clip and you do it."

After Sue had practiced filling the clip with the three-quarter inch bronze-colored cartridges and sliding the clip into the little weapon, Dan said, "Pull back on the top slide and let it go; it will load one of the bullets directly into the chamber. Never point the gun at anything you don't want to shoot, understand."

Sue nodded; her big eyes wide.

"Ok, now, when you pull the trigger, just pull it gently; don't yank it."

"Daddy, I don't want to!"

"Sue, you must, if something happens to either Dad or me, you're the only one who could help us," Tom argued.

With a shaking hand, Sue fired an experimental shot. The sharp bark of the gunshot almost caused her to drop the weapon.

With ears plugged with cotton, they shot off half of a box of .22 Long Rifle cartridges in a closet so both Sue and Tom could become familiar with their guns.

After looking at a destroyed telephone directory full of .22 holes, Tom said, "I bet that's a use for the yellow pages that you'll never find in the yellow pages."

Sue also carried the smaller, lighter crossbow with its lightweight shafts. She practiced loading, cocking, and firing it until the living room wall was full of holes.

Tom looked at his sister happily puncturing the wall, "Dad, we've created an Annie Oakley."

Looking at the wall, Dan said, "Do you think the landlord will be able to find you to repair your holes in that wall?"

After a second's thought, her response was a flash of teeth from a grin.

"Tom, you took archery in high school. Show me how these bows work."

"Sure Dad. See, these pulleys on the ends of each bow allow you to take about a thirty-pound pull on the bowstring and turn it into a seventy pound thrust. Plus, the nice thing is that these bows weigh only about five pounds each."

Dan pulled the bowstring back; it surprised him when it flowed easily and seemed to sit comfortably against his cheek.

"See, Dad, both of these bows have magnesium handles with laminated graphite/fiberglass limbs. This one is a recurve bow with the tips or ends of the bow curving toward the front while the other bow had straight tips. These are nice and quite expensive bows!"

"I need a small screwdriver," Tom said. "I want to attach these aiming devices on the bows." To Dan, the aiming devices looked simply like a small flat bar with needles sticking out of it.

"Look here, Dad. Each point on these aiming mechanisms is for approximately ten yards. Each pin up is for a further distance and we need to experiment with each pin to figure out exact distance," Tom explained, pointing. "See, these overdraw rests are used if you draw the string and arrow too far back; when you do that, you can still shoot because the arrow will sit on the rests."

From the side, both bows looked just plain nasty. Both were mottled in brown and green camouflage markings. Tom loved them! He also approved of the few black graphite shafts his father had found. Most of the arrow shafts were of dark colored aluminum, however.

"Dad, when we practice shooting these bows, we should use the graphite shafts," Tom suggested. "That way when an arrow glances off an object or if it doesn't hit it straight on, the graphite arrows will bend and then resume their shape."

He continued his demonstration by gently bending first a graphite arrow and then gently twisting an aluminum shaft. "See how the graphite bends and comes back to its original shape; the aluminum might stay bent and then it is useless."

A little time was spent screwing and gluing razor sharp two-edged broadhead arrowheads to the shafts. Dan thought that the two-edged broadhead arrows would bring down anything they would hunt, and silently, Dan thought that if they had to use the bows for defense, the approximately 350-gram arrows would knock a person down!

"Tom, do we need to unstring these bows? I remember the old-style wooden bows that had to be unstrung except when we used them."

"No. These new power bows are different in that they always remain strung without hurting them."

They attached brown leather quivers to each bow. Tom's quiver had five arrows; Dan's had nine. The arrow points faced up and were contained within the quiver, while the shaft and feathers hung down.

"I'm impressed, Son, you know what you're talking about," Dan complimented, his hand squeezing his son's shoulder.

Dan fitted the brown Bianca leather holster containing the 9 .mm automatic to his left lower armpit; he snugly snapped the lower part of the holster to his belt and the upper straps wrapped around his left shoulder and extended to his right shoulder. The .38 Smith and Wesson Chief was hooked to his right rear belt.

After watching his father practice drawing the weapon a few times, Tom drawled, "Sue, you remember who Wyatt Earp was?"

"Aw, no, I don't think so."

"He was an old-time sheriff on television. And he was supposed to have one of the fastest draws in the West."

"Oh, sure, we used to watch him on T.V."

"Well, don't look at Dad if you want to see a Wyatt Earp."

After suffering through a giggle from his daughter, Dan replied, "Well, I think we should leave as soon as we finish packing." As if to emphasize the need to escape, a distant burst of automatic weapon gunfire punctured the silence.

They felt physically rested, but emotionally drained after making the aching decisions of what to take and what to leave.

"I think it will be safer traveling at night here in the city," Dan said. "There is a full moon with no clouds in the sky and we should have sufficient light to see where we're going."

The smell of smoke and old barbecue fumes combined with the acidic odor of rotting garbage caressed their faces. A far-off scream was punctured by several gunshots.

While Dan was searching through his upstairs bedroom, he glanced out the west facing window. Off in the distance somewhere near the Huntington Beach library, he saw a flash of light and a moment later, felt a rumble like a sonic boom.

Tom came running into the bedroom, "What was that?"

Dan pointed out the window, "I think one of the oil tanks in Huntington Beach blew up. Look, you can see the flames from here!"

The far flames illuminated the dismay in Tom's eyes; it echoed the apprehension in Dan's heart.

"Tom, Sue, we have to get out of here! There is no one to protect us," Dan urged his kids. "There are no fire departments anymore."

Both Tom and Sue somberly nodded; they knew that their home and the neighborhood weren't safe any longer.

Dan and Tom examined an old auto club map for the route they would take. Ginger's postcards showed pictures of a resort near Durango, Colorado. Both Sue and Tom believed this area was where she was staying; in addition, the faded postmarks all indicated a tiny town in Southwestern Colorado. From what was readable, the scrawled childish hand-printing of their Ginger on the postcards said that she was at a camp. Ginger could not have traveled far to mail the postcards.

First, however, they had to get out of the city.

"After looking at this map, it seems that the only possible way for us to travel northeast is to follow the freeways, either on the freeways themselves or on the adjoining surface streets," Dan said.

"I agree," Tom nodded somberly. "We should probably get up to and follow the Riverside or 91 Freeway northeast and then pick up Interstate 15 northward. Do you think that the freeways will be open?"

"Well, I guess we'll find out."

Dan thought they could travel maybe five or ten miles an hour, depending on the street conditions. It had been some time since he had done any serious bike riding; while the kids had ridden their bikes frequently and were in sound physical condition, Dan knew that the first week or two would be physically stressful for him.

❖ ❖ ❖ ❖ ❖ ❖ ❖

Fourteen miles below the surface of the Pacific Coast, the Pacific North American Plate continued its slow, almost infinitesimal movement. The major dividing line, commonly called a fault line or more precisely, the San Andreas Fault line, between the two plates was expected to fracture soon. The pressure, sometimes sufficient to heat or melt rock, continued and spread under the Southern California area. However, the San Andreas did not "let go" as the locals defined it; instead, a lessor fault known as the Newport-Inglewood Fault line that ran through a more populated area moved slightly and released a little of its pressure.

The Newport-Inglewood fault ran from the mostly white and all upper-class Newport Beach, where the popular conception of a sailboat in every garage was nearly true, through Long Beach and extended to mostly black and lower-class Inglewood, where several residents were just lucky enough to even have water in their homes! The release of the fault, commonly called an earthquake, would have registered about a 4.0 on the Richter scale if the instruments had been functioning. As earthquakes go, Southern Californians take such things in stride as did the Petersons.

A few buildings were cracked, several plate glass windows in probably Southern California's largest indoor shopping center, South Coast Plaza, were shattered. Goods fell off a few shelves, the head of a mannikin broke off and noisily bounced down a flight of stairs, scaring half to death a lowly hungry mouse creeping around for food. Some freeway overpasses were slightly damaged, and all in all, a relatively normal Southern California earthquake!

Unfortunately, in Torrance, just south of the Newport-Inglewood fault line, a massive oil refinery had been built by men whose primary emphasis was on money, not safety or location. When the trembler shook the Southern California area, a three-inch pipeline, still containing pressurized octane gasoline, fractured. A fine spray blew out of the puncture wound on the pipe. As the trembler continued shaking the pipe and the braces holding it, one metal piece broke and struck another pipe, causing a tiny spark.

The explosion was violent, but localized. Under normal circumstances, the automatic sprinklers and fire-retardant sprayers would have been immediately triggered and extinguished the fire. However, with no electricity and therefore no water or fire-retardant pressure, the fire spread, unstoppable!

❖ ❖ ❖ ❖

Miles away to the east, Dan suggested, "Kids, let's go through the house one more time before we leave; make sure we've taken everything we want."

"Sure, Dad, but first, I want to run over to see my best friend, Ronnie, and tell him what happened and," Tom continued sadly, "to say goodbye. He only lives the next block over."

"Ok, Son. But take your gun and knife with you; don't waste any time because we need to leave as soon as possible."

Dan wandered through his home one last time. He had originally hoped to purchase a house, but he could never earn enough money to raise his children and save for a down payment. In addition, after Ginger was born, Kathy refused to even attempt to work. She insisted on staying home to raise "her" child her way excluding everyone else in the family.

Dan had thought of getting a second job to save for a down payment on a house, but it seemed he spent most of his time refereeing fights between Kathy with her unreasonable demands and tantrums, and Tom and/or Sue. She demanded that Tom and Sue act as mature adults while forgetting that they were still children.

Memories! A few photographs on the walls with smiling faces and arms clasped around each other had to be left behind. In this room, they had prepared a bed for Ginger if she somehow ever made it back to them. Her things that had been left behind when Kathy took the little girl and ran away had been carefully and lovingly stored here.

Memories, some not so sweet, like the bed in Dan's bedroom, never much love spilled between Dan and Kathy after Ginger was born; Dan recalled the terrible loneliness he suffered when he could not even touch or hug Kathy. The bleakly lonesome, constant physical and emotional rejection he had received from her still hurt.

Dan sadly remembered seeing Kathy walk around nude in the bathroom or bedroom but refusing to let him touch her or fondle her or even just hold her. He had thought about possibly having an affair simply to receive some physical or emotional tenderness, but that went nowhere.

There, hanging on the wall, was one of the last photographs of their smiling red-haired Ginger; it must be taken.

Clutching the photograph of his Ginger, Dan slowly walked down the darkened hallway to Sue's room. She was sitting on her bed holding a candle for light.

"I'm saying goodbye, Dad. Maybe we'll be able to come back some time, huh?" she said with a soft quiver in her voice.

She got up, walked to the door, said, "Goodbye Room!" and firmly closed the door. She put her soft, small hand in Dan's large hand, and one last time, they walked down the hallway to Tom's room.

He had returned and they found him standing in the middle of his room, holding one of his high school trophies. A candle was perched on his dresser emitting a flickering little light. Obviously lost in his memories, he startled at their entrance and looked at them with glistening eyes. A weak smile creased his face, "Let's go!"

"Son, take along your glove and a baseball; that's too important to leave here. We'll just have to carry the extra weight!"

Dan wasn't a particularly religious person, but before they left, he gathered his family in a circle of arms and each said a small prayer for them, for their house, for help in finding their beloved Ginger and getting "home."

Dan applied one final coat of lightweight oil on the chains of their bikes and greased the ball bearings in the wheels of the trailer.

"We ought to bless Mr. Swackie, he sure made this trailer sturdy."

"This ten-foot square plastic covering should help protect the trailer and we can use it for protection of our sleeping bags on the ground," Tom said as he folded a heavy plastic sheet over the trailer.

Back packs were hoisted on bent backs and strapped on. Each person had carried a lighted candle down the stairs; now, each almost ceremoniously blew out his or her candle, first Sue, then Tom, and then with both children looking at him with wide, fearful eyes, Dan!

In the silence, too silent darkness, Sue with her bike led them out of the back-patio door and around the house to the driveway. Dan firmly pulled the patio door shut; maybe someday they might return!

He gently touched a beautiful stark white rose just starting to bloom as he pushed his bike past it, his face lined with sorrow.

No dogs barked.

No horns honked.

Nothing.

An overwhelming tension filled silence continued to fill the city.

They formed up on the driveway with Dan leading, Sue in the middle and Tom bringing up the rear.

"Everyone ready?" Dan whispered.

Their tears were finished, a fear with much excitement went through them. They were starting something brand new.

"Listen, I want to stop and tell Joyce, my secretary, where we're going and why," Dan said. "She's been with me for a long time, and I want to give her a chance and to say goodbye. She lives only about three blocks from here, OK?"

"Sure Dad. Lead off."

Dan led them out onto the street and turned east. He wobbled badly from side to side on his bike, his balance was being thrown off by the heavy backpack on his back.

"Dad, stop!" Tom called softly.

"Here, let me carry the AR-15; you have two handguns with you and I can balance my load better then you."

"OK, Son, I'll teach you how to use that weapon tomorrow."

Dan thought it might be around midnight, but he wasn't sure. He had thrown away all their watches because they had batteries in them. The city was deathly quiet with no one on the streets, not even a stray dog or cat. It was as if people were hiding in their homes, knowing that something was about to happen, but afraid to venture out to investigate. They could see wrecked cars everywhere. There were no streetlights. The smell of smoke drifted more pungently throughout the still night air.

They turned onto a tree shrouded street with the few requisite Southern Californian molty looking palm trees and stopped at a single-story house about halfway down the street.

"Let's park up here in the driveway, out of sight of the rest of the neighbors," Tom suggested quietly.

"Good boy," Dan whispered. "You're starting to think of our safety."

Dan cautiously approached the side door and quietly knocked. He waited a moment and knocked again.

"Who's there?" an alarmed voice called out. The unmistakable sounds of a pump action shotgun being cocked could be heard.

"Dan. Dan Peterson!"

"Joyce, it's me: Dan Peterson."

The side door opened a crack and then opened all the way.

"What's wrong, Dan? Why are you here?" Joyce said as she and her husband framed the doorway. Her eyes opened wide as she saw the bikes and Tom and Sue.

"Joyce, I found out what happened to our electricity. The electricity, for lack of a better definition, has been shut off permanently."

"Oh my God! Why?"

Dan told them briefly what he had heard of the future conditions in Los Angeles and Orange Counties, and the rest of the world. He summarized his conversation with Joe Robinson and his recommendations.

"I knew something was dreadfully wrong when you didn't come back yesterday," Joyce whispered huskily. "I even walked over to your friend Joe Robinson's place, but they were in the process of leaving and they told me to come back tomorrow."

Dan continued, "We don't have much time. The kids and I are leaving and we're going to try to make it to Wisconsin. We want to try to find Ginger, my daughter, in Durango, Colorado, before we get to Wisconsin. I wanted to tell you because, well, we've been close for a long time, and I wanted you to have at least a chance. This entire Southern California will be a war zone very soon."

After giving them a moment to absorb what he said, Dan suggested to Joyce and her husband, "You might consider trying to leave if you have family or friends someplace else. Do not try to drive. You will be killed, or worse," he warned.

"We have got to go now," Dan whispered. "You take care of yourselves, OK?"

Joyce, with tears flowing from her eyes, nodded and hugged Dan. As her heavy breasts pressed warmly into Dan' chest, it occurred to him that in the years they knew each other, this was the first time they ever physically touched. Joyce then ran over to the kids and gave them both hugs.

"Thanks, from both of us!" her husband whispered. "At least now, we know what happened; we'll have to do something." They shook hands and Dan mounted his bike. They waved and Dan led the kids back onto the street.

The streets were relatively level here, Dan noted with relief. He wanted them to get into a routine before they hit the major hills. The trailer towed easily, although it took more effort to stop because it lacked brakes and Dan could feel the heavy tug of it bouncing over cracks in the pavement.

"I suggest that we stop in an hour or so, just to rest," Dan called back to Tom and Sue.

Both protested that they wanted to go on. Dan, however, was adamant about a brief rest; his kids were in good physical condition, he was not!

They slowly worked their way east and north.

"It feels funny not having to stop at the stoplights and not having to travel on the right side of the street," Tom said to Sue. "In my driver's training class, they taught us all of those rules of the road."

"Well, I'm sorry I couldn't buy a car for you to drive," his dad said softly. "You know how hard it was to keep anything when Kathy was here."

"That's ok, Dad, don't worry about it," Tom replied, meeting Sue's eyes. They both knew that their father did not know that Tom and his friend Ronnie had put more miles on Ronnie's dad's car than Ronnie's dad. They also both knew that neither boy had licenses to drive. And Sue got much mileage out of not telling her father what the boys did in Ronnie's father's car, particularly that certain afternoon Tom came home smelling heavily of beer, and a little later, listening to him throw up in the bathroom. (Sue never knew of the two girls they picked up and what happened in the back seat.) The next morning, Tom's hangover masqueraded as the flu.

"Tom, I think if we follow the major streets until we get to that pass to Corona and Riverside, it'll be easier riding."

"Sure, I've been watching the freeway and it looks pretty clear."

"Do you think we should chance it?"

"Well, if it's clear, we should make good time, and if it isn't, we can always get off of it. You know we have to get on it anyway, later on."

After their short rest, they mounted their bikes and tried to get up a ramp. While it was a steep ramp to the freeway, Tom and Sue climbed it easily. They made it about halfway up when Dan stumbled off his bike. He was gasping, the right side of his chest throbbing.

"Dam!" he mumbled. "What in the hell am I doing, dragging my kids two thousand miles across the country, and I can't even get up this stupid on ramp."

"Come on Dad. You can make it," Sue called as she and Tom waited for him at the top of the ramp.

"Sure, sure," Dan wheezed, his heart pounding, "You're thirty some years' younger than me, and you're in condition, I'm not."

Nevertheless, a little embarrassed, he pushed the bike and trailer and reached the top of the on ramp without making too much of a fool of himself. He rested a moment to catch his breath, and looked back toward a major part of the city.

Darkness, absolute darkness met their view with a reddish glow far to the west that looked like an out-of-control fire just north of the Los Angeles harbor area, near Torrance. Closer to them, they could see towering flames.

"Tom, that closer fire looks like the Huntington Beach oil tanks near their library; I didn't know they still stored flammable materials there."

Southeast of them, they could see an ugly green pulsating phosphorous light filling part of the southern nighttime sky.

"Tom, look! That must be coming from that closed nuclear power plant down at San Onofre; that energy or whatever it is must be huge. It's strange because that plant has been closed for some time."

"I think you're right, Dad. We are over forty miles from that plant and we can still see it over the hills."

It was a city without lights, not even automobile or truck lights or even a flashlight blinking here or there. The lights from the oil refineries that normally illuminated the night sky like large, smelly Christmas trees or a small Las Vegas were now dark. The only illumination was an ironically benevolent yellow light from the smiling moon.

Even stranger was the absence of sound: no airplane noise, no traffic noise, no children playing, no adults visiting and talking, and sadly, no radio or television blaring somewhere. The city was collectively holding its breath for what was going to happen.

"I sure don't like the looks of that glow south of us, nor do I like the looks of that fire over by Wilmington, West Long Beach area," Dan said.

"Dad, that fire is huge. And it's further west than Long Beach. We are twenty or thirty miles from there and look how large it is," Tom exclaimed. "It's a couple of miles in diameter."

Suddenly, they saw a large yellow-white explosion that doubled the fire area.

"There goes one of the fuel tanks at the refinery," Dan muttered.

A tiny "I'm scared!" came from Sue.

"I agree, Sis, let's move."

Later, huge concrete overpasses crept out of the moonlit darkness like a silent giant praying mathis seeking to envelop them in a dark tunnel; fortunately, the moonlight gave a light at the end of this tunnel.

The freeway was remarkably clear. There were a few nasty wrecks with overturned and burnt cars, but most people got off the freeway before their cars were attacked. They kept their speed down because while the full moon was bright, shadows from trees or buildings concealed holes or ruts in the freeway. In addition, Dan wanted to get them in condition before doing any long distance or speed riding. Truthfully,

Dan needed to get himself into condition. His legs burned with long unused muscles protesting their treatment.

Privately, Tom was worrying about his father. Tom tried to make sure that about every half hour, they stopped for a brief rest. Tom knew that his father was out of condition and fairly old. From Tom's perspective, anyone over thirty was "fairly old!"

They finally stopped at what was once a golf course and camped out rather than seek shelter since the weather was nice. In addition, Dan wasn't sure of their reception at any buildings or homes.

That first night, or more precisely, that first early morning, after they made a tiny, fireless camp, Sue, with wide fearful eyes, looked around her at the silent all-encompassing darkness.

"Dad, it's spooky out here," she complained.

"Well, we'll have to get used to it. We have some pretty good weapons here to defend ourselves," Tom said as he patted the power bows and the AR-15.

"You're right," Dan said. "I think after tonight we should try to travel during the day and pick out better camping places. We really need to get out of this area as soon as possible. Let's try to sleep a little and when the sun comes up, we'll move on."

"Dad, do you think one of us should stay awake to guard us?" Tom asked.

"I don't think so, Son. We're fairly hidden down here off the freeway. If someone or something is coming around, it or they will have to see too; and it's very dark down here."

"Sue, come over here and snuggle up to me. Tom, we'll just have to learn to become light sleepers."

After their first "spooky" night, they tried traveling during daylight, avoiding areas that looked wrong or dangerous. That first morning, Dan's legs were so sore he couldn't get out of his sleeping bag. Tom had to help him crawl out of the bag and pull him into a standing position. After about twenty minutes' effort, with sweat pouring off his face, Dan was at least able to hobble around the camp.

"Thanks Tom! Let's see how far we can get today before my legs give out."

"Don't worry Daddy; don't hurt yourself," Sue said. "We'll make it!"

Once they paddled, Dan's legs seemed to loosen and they rode for more than a few miles. However, Tom was pulling the trailer rather than his father.

The second night, they had stopped near a housing track north of the Riverside Freeway. They were sleeping lightly when they heard yelling and screaming coming from the dark houses with a barrage of automatic weapon gunfire. They hastily quenched their small campfire and huddled together; their weapons drawn. An ominous silence settled over the track. They slept little that night and left at first light.

The next day, they had traveled only a few miles and had camped by one of the freeway roadside emergency call boxes. This call box had been solar powered during the day and apparently, was battery powered during the night.

They had just eaten, the sun was going down and they were just relaxing before going to sleep when Sue exclaimed, "Dad, look!"

They could see a faint greenish substance in the air flowing around the emergency call box. The call box sparkled almost like a firework's Roman Candle.

"Get away from there," Dan yelled.

He grabbed Sue by the arm and dragged her away from the call box!

Tom bent to pick up his backpack.

"Leave your stuff," Dan yelled at Tom. "We'll come back for it."

They ran about fifty yards away and stopped to look.

The call box burst into flames with vicious tentacles of green darting into the base of the call box like translucent green sharks attacking a defenseless small fish. While the fire quickly burnt itself out, a faint odor of ozone drifted toward the Petersons. The green flowing substance just disappeared into the air.

"What was that?" a shaking Sue asked.

Tom exclaimed, "I think that's the Green Ghost that Dad's friend told him about!"

"I believe so too, Honey," Dan said. "It is attracted only to electricity and it shouldn't harm us if we stay out of its way."

They cautiously approached their camp, grabbed their belongings, and moved about a hundred yards away.

"I think we'll be safe here," Dan said. "But we've learned something: we'll have to stay away from any solar powered signs."

Far off to their rear in the daylight, they could see two very large fires under towering black smoke clouds with an occasional flare as if something exploded. The fires appeared to devour everything in their path. Dan knew, with a heavy heart, there was no human way the fire could be stopped because the energy force prohibited the use of fire trucks and air tankers. Los Angeles and Orange County could only pray for rain, and heavy rain, at that.

The fourth day on the road, they passed large herds of cattle meandering around the freeway and the surrounding countryside.

"Where did all those cows come from, Dad?" Sue asked.

"They have large cattle farms near the Riverside area where we and the rest of Orange County get some of our milk and meat."

"How come they're walking around loose?"

"Well, I think somebody released them," Tom replied. "If you don't have electricity, it's kind of hard to feed them."

The Petersons rested near one such farm. They found two bales of straw to use as a target for practicing with the power bows. When Tom lifted a bale of straw, a small brown cottontail rabbit bolted out from under it and nearly ran into Sue. It was difficult to tell who was more startled, the rabbit or Sue.

Dan had noticed that at the start of the trip, his legs and lungs hurt. He had to have Tom assist him in even standing; now, however, his legs were strengthening and his lungs and chest did not ache quite as much.

They passed other groups of people walking, riding bicycles and even a horse or two. Sometimes, they quickly rode past people stripping wrecked vehicles.

Tom asked, "I don't think we should ask them if they own those cars, do you?"

"Well, I agree, plus, what are they going to do with those parts of the vehicles."

"Good point!"

Shortly after passing Interstate 10, they approached a line of people trudging toward them. The leader was a large, stout, highly coiffured white-haired woman with a fur coat draped over her shoulders. Her considerable breasts protruded through the front of her fur coat like ponderous pontoons penetrating a fury sea. Carried gingerly in her arms was a small white poodle whose sole purpose in life appeared to be yapping.

Plodding behind woman were apparent members of her family, each carrying or dragging suitcases, clothes or pulling small red wagons piled high with goods.

After examining the Petersons like they were illegal aliens or bugs from another planet, the white-haired woman demanded with a sniff, her nose slightly upturned, "Where are you people going?"

With a glance at Tom, Dan responded, "Well, we're headed up the road; how far are you folks going?"

Sniff!

"We are proceeding to," and here she named a town closer to Los Angeles, "We will stay with my brother, he's the mayor of that city; you, of course, have heard of him."

"Well, I know of him, but we're going in a different direction."

Sniff!

"I see you are riding bicycles rather than driving; neither of our Lincoln Town Cars nor the Cadillac will run. Do you have any credible information why they wouldn't even start?"

"Yes. Something happened to the electricity," Dan said.

Sniff!

"Well, I know that!"

Sniff!

The nose went a little higher. "George, come along, we don't have all day to waste here. We'll get no useful information from them!"

And with that, cradling her yapping poodle, she marched off followed by a little old man and their entourage.

Tom watched the group trudge off, shaking his head. "Kathy at sixty-five."

Sue giggled, nodding her head.

They slowly made their way to the base of the mountains. Sue looked at the road up over the mountain pass, "We've got to go over that?"

Tom answered, "Sure do. I think we'll be walking up most of it."

"I agree," Dan said. "If we take it easy, I think it'll take at least a couple of days to climb."

They started slowly up the hill. Tom took the bike with the trailer and led the way. Sue was in the middle and Dan brought up the rear. They spent most of their time walking and pushing their bikes. As loaded as they were, with the heavy backpacks and the trailer, they made poor time.

Tom insisted on resting when he saw his father gasping for air and refusing to stop until the kids felt like stopping.

Tom angrily stated, "Darn it, Dad, don't push so hard! We'll get there; you must take care of yourself, you're a whole lot older than Sue and me."

"Nonsense," Dan wheezed with perspiration beading his forehead, "I'm not that old, just keep walking."

Tom and Sue looked at each other, shook their heads, walked to the side of the road, and sat down.

"OK, OK," their father gasped. "You win."

They rested one afternoon in a tiny park immediately off the freeway with a small spring running through it.

"Let's spend the night here, OK, Dad?" Sue asked with a glance at Tom.

"I agree. Dad?"

"OK, OK."

Tom froze. He waived them motionless. He slowly lifted his bow off his bike's handlebars, notched an arrow, and slowly drew the string back. He took careful aim and let fly. The arrow flew close to thirty-five yards and struck a large rabbit sitting beside a bush.

Dinner!

Sue at first refused to eat. "I don't want to eat that little rabbit," she complained.

After Tom and Dan had skinned and cleaned the rabbit, Dan lit a small fire in one of the park's barbecue pits. Sue obtained a pot of water from a nearby stream, and using a water purification tablet, they boiled the water, added a freeze-dried package of soup, and had a delicious rabbit stew. After smelling the odor of cooking throughout the small park, and since she had several days of eating cold food, Sue finally broke down and ate some stew. Dan smiled when she came back for seconds.

They watched the sun go down over the horizon. The horizon appeared dusty or cloudy. Later that night, the reason became obvious. Fire, fire raged out of control in the city and county

below them. The fire was sweeping through an area at least a dozen miles wide. They looked with horror at the fire; they could see flames leaping what seemed like hundreds of feet into

the air. Fortunately, they were many miles away from the fire, but there was nothing to stop it from burning through the entire city! They didn't sleep well that night.

CHAPTER FOUR

"I hurt!" Dan Peterson mumbled to himself.

Tender nerve endings shot ribbons of pain through his legs from the five days of arduous paddling needed to climb the Cahon Pass from nearly sea level to a 4100-foot altitude. The fifth day started cloudy and windy, and by the time the Petersons had a meager breakfast of cooked oatmeal and freeze-dried orange juice, a cold driving rain battered their faces.

Sue huddled in her sleeping bag complaining, "Daddy, I don't want to ride in the rain, I'll get wet and cold. I'm cold now."

"Sure, Honey, we'll wait, I think we escaped from Orange County just in time."

"I think so too," Tom agreed, lines of unaccustomed worry etching his sixteen-year-old face. "There is no way those big fires we saw are going to be stopped. I sure hope some of my friends from school will be all right."

"Well, if they're lucky, this rain will continue down and either stop or put a damper on some of those fires."

The remainder of the morning was spent huddled under a freeway overpass. The area was sheltered from the wind and driving cold rain. Tom had built a small fire the evening before and now, they just simply replenished the fire. While they had brought along light raincoats and hats, Dan needed to rest his legs, his calves and thighs burned with a dull ache. Both Tom and he worked a little on the bikes and the trailer, tightening the bolts and screws, adjusting the seats and repacking their trailer.

As they traveled, Dan and Tom experimented with who was carrying what supplies, guns and bows. Usually, Tom carried the AR-15 on his back with his backpack, Dan carried the chrome H & K 9 mm.

semi-automatic in its brown leather Bianci shoulder holster on his left side and the .38 Chief in its brown hard leather snap holster attached to his belt on his right back hip just under his backpack. Sue carried her little pearl handled .22 automatic in her jacket pocket while Tom just stuck his .22 in his shirt pocket. The power bows were finally attached to the trailer for traveling.

Tom smiled, "We look like a couple of hit men, every time we camp at night, I take off the power bows and the AR-15, you take off your 9 mm. and the Smith & Wesson Chief, and Sue takes out her little .22 automatic."

"Well, I don't want to have to use any of these weapons, but I want us to be prepared just in case," his father said, a little defensively.

Around midmorning after the rain stopped, they kicked out the fire, strapped on their heavy backpacks and resumed their journey. To the side, a glorious rainbow simmered under the breaking dark cumulus clouds. A pungent odor of wet earth with a subtle high desert tang drifted past their faces.

At the top of the pass, they rested at the sign on the side of the freeway stating Cahon Pass, Elevation 4190 Feet. Ahead and to the side in the brownish tawny colored high desert were abandoned buildings, their open doors swinging listlessly in the desert breeze.

"Dad, where is everyone?" Tom asked.

"I don't know, son, but with no electricity, water or gas, it's pretty hard living out here."

They followed the concrete freeway except in two places: the first was a large burnt-out area of wrecked cars and trucks just to the south of a California high desert town called Victorville. The sharp odor of ozone lingered in the air and an acidic oozing substance still bubbled on the freeway like pudding in a cooking pot.

"Looks like the 'Green Ghost' caught those vehicles and devoured the electricity in the engines and batteries," Dan pointed.

"That must have been an inferno when that gas truck exploded," Tom replied, his nose wrinkling from the remnants of acerbic and sour smoke drifting by. "Look, it's burnt all over that freeway."

The second place they had to detour was in a construction zone. An overpass had been under construction and some of the wood pilings or supports had caught fire or had been set on fire. The burning had weakened the supports and the entire overpass collapsed onto the freeway making it impassable.

They backtracked about a mile to an off-ramp and found a street that appeared to skirt the construction zone. As they slowly rode through a group of small business buildings, Dan had been holding the handlebars with his left hand and was just simply relaxing, riding along.

Suddenly, two filthy, black haired, unshaven men clad in ragged blue jeans darted out from one of the buildings.

Jail tattoos proclaiming membership in a local Mexican gang adorned dark completed arms. One brown skinned arm was still oozing blood from a partially collapsed vein caused by numerous illegal narcotic injections. A teardrop tattooed just below one eye decorated the shorter of the two.

The barefooted taller and more skeletal of the two waived an ancient, long, double barreled 12-gauge shotgun.

"Stop! Get 'em up!" he yelled.

The shorter man, clutching a dark blue metal baseball bat in his hand, jerked around with saliva drooling down his unshaven chin, the pupils in his bloodshot eyes widely dilated. With a pulse rate of 120 beats a minute, he had the classic signs of a methamphetamine freak. (Dan didn't know of the three small off-white rocks in a small plastic bag in the man's right front pants pocket.)

"Shoot em, Shoot em!"

The man with the shotgun fumbled with his right thumb and pulled back the hammers of the shotgun.

Tom and Sue skidded to a halt, their hearts in their throats.

As the man with the shotgun pulled back on the hammers to cock his shotgun, Dan's range of focus narrowed to only the creature pulling back on the hammers of the shotgun, everything else was blocked out.

His right hand flashed behind his right hip, yanked the small .38 Chief Smith & Wesson five shot revolver from its snap holster, pointed the gun in the general direction of the shotgun and fired.

To this day, Dan could not remember hearing the shots he fired.

One of the shots, a .38 caliber copper-jacketed hollow point lead slug blasted out of Dan's Smith & Wesson Chief at thirteen hundred feet per second. The slug struck the man with the shotgun in the right leg just below the knee.

He dropped the shotgun. It struck the concrete roadway and discharged, the explosion echoing throughout the buildings. Lead pellets whistled as they screamed past Dan's head and shattered the windows of a building across the street.

As Dan's hollow point bullet penetrated the man's leg, the leg whipped backward, a red mist of blood spurting out the back of the leg.

He screamed, tumbled to the ground, and crawled away clutching his leg. His filthy long-haired buddy sobered up enough to grab his friend and drag him back toward the buildings they had been hiding.

"Let's get out of here," Dan yelled, his heart pounding.

Tom leaped off his bike and grabbed the shotgun as they made their panic-stricken escape. Pumping the paddles of their bikes as hard as they could, Dan gasped, "Are you kids all right?"

Both nodded, breathing heavily.

They quickly escaped onto the freeway and rode about a mile before they stopped. Dan was still shaking.

His right wrist and thumb throbbed from the sharp recoil of the small .38 revolver firing high velocity bullets. He had never actually shot at a man. Strangely, he felt no guilt; later, he realized that two weeks ago, he would not have even thought of doing such a thing.

Both Tom and Sue crowded around their father and held him, each trying to calm the other.

Tom, still panting, grinned, "Good shot! Were you aiming at his leg?"

"No! I really didn't want to hit him, but he was pointing that shotgun at us and I didn't have much of a choice."

"Are you kids sure you're both OK?"

"We're all right, Dad!"

"Do you realize that you fired three shots?"

"Oh no. I fired only once."

"Wrong, Dad! You fired three shots: the first ricocheted off the pavement in front of that man, the second hit him and I don't know where the third went. Here, let me see your gun."

"See, three empty cartridges," Tom said as he pushed the cylinder release on the left side of the blue steel weapon and flipped the still warm cylinder open. He pushed the ejection rod and ejected the shells from the revolver.

"Still, it was great shooting. Where did you put the box of .38 shells? I'll reload it for you."

After loading the Smith and Wesson Chief, Tom handed the empty cartridges to his father, "Here, you can keep them as a souvenir."

They later examined the shotgun, it was an old, worn blue steel, double barreled, 12-gauge with a live shell in the left chamber. It had dual hammers and dual triggers which seemed to be serviceable, but the brown wooden stock appeared to have a thin crack running the length of it. He recalled seeing dark spots and drag marks on the street where the attempted robbery had taken place.

Tom watched his dad's deep eyes become a steely grey when he said, "You know, Son, the more I think about it, the more I wish that I had been a better shot."

Tom was quiet. From deep within him came a trembling thought, *I've never seen Dad with that look before. . . He always seemed so weak, so laid back.*

After riding for a few miles, they found that strong winds had created a sand drift over both north and south bound lanes of the freeway. Apparently, some of the sand and dirt had come from abandoned Little League fields off to the East side of the freeway. They had no choice but to push and pull their bikes through a three-foot high, twenty-foot-wide drift of sand. The trailer was the hardest to pull through and it took all three of them, Tom and Sue pushing and Dan pulling to get it across, as Sue put it, "The Sahara desert in the middle of a Southern California freeway."

Later that day, they stopped at a small campground near an off ramp of the freeway. They found it difficult traveling through the town as there had been no maintenance of the roads. Street signs over the freeway were down, either burnt by the Green Ghost and blown over by the wind or sometimes, crashed down by vehicles running into them.

"Tom, I'm concerned. Did you see the eyes in that last group of people we passed? They're getting desperate because of no food or any help from the government."

"I think so too, Dad. We need to be more careful."

They found a small group of people already camped at the campground; both groups approached each other with caution.

"Where are you folks from?" Dan asked.

"We're from Barstow and we're riding down to stay with our family on the outskirts of Riverside. I'm George Dickerson, that's my wife Peg and the kids over there are the rest of our family."

George Dickerson, a big, burly, slightly balding man and Peg, a small, mousey woman with long brown hair with bright vivacious eyes turned out to be the parents of the kids.

"How are conditions from your direction?" George asked.

"Well, there was quite a bit of fire down in Los Angeles and Orange counties when we left that area. I don't know if that rain did any good down there," Dan said. He explained that they were going to find their daughter in Colorado. "By the way, how is the road from here to Barstow?"

"The road from Barstow to here is open but take plenty of water. We heard rumors of some gang activity on the overpasses; they have a gunman sit on the overpass and draw down on anybody coming along. The rest of the bunch would come from behind and strip them. I've heard that they wouldn't bother any large group. . . ."

Sue found another little girl and they were soon the best of friends. Tom made eye contact with a younger teenage boy and they wandered off together. Peg Dickerson's bright eyes occasionally secretly glanced slowly up and down Dan's body, her twitching hips quietly displaying more than an academic interest in him.

When Peg in her tight jeans strolled from one side of the camp to the other, the sway of her hips was a little more pronounced.

"Not now!" drifted through Dan's mind even though there was a reaction in parts of his body that had been dormant for a protracted time. *"Dam! It's been a long time,"* came an unwanted thought.

George Dickerson looked admiringly at Dan's arsenal. "Say, I've got a couple of boxes of 12-gauge shells. I sure do like that old shotgun."

Dan explained how they had acquired the shotgun and described the general location of the incident. George's comment was a laconic, "Hit 'em seven inches below the belly button: that way they don't reproduce."

"Well," George drawled, closely examining the old shotgun, "We've got a couple of extra five-gallon water bottles, I'll trade you for this old shotgun."

He added, "You'll need them to cross the desert if you're going to make it to Colorado."

"A deal," Dan said. He had been thinking of water and was worrying about how they could store or carry it. The five-gallon container they had taken from the store didn't last long.

After a rest of two days, and a sad parting since they had made friends with the Dickerson's, they continued north on the freeway. They had discussed road conditions with Dickerson's and finally planned to take whatever was left of Interstate 40 eastbound from the Interstate 15 highway.

Dan told the kids what he had learned about the gang robberies on the freeway.

"Well, we should have a contingency plan in case we get stopped," Tom said.

"What did you have in mind?"

"I've been reading my survival book at night and it shows hand signals, like if I hold my hand up, it means stop, if I make a fist, it means enemy sighted, and so on."

Sue shook her head, "Why can't you just tell me? I'm right here."

"Well, that's if I can't say anything."

"Why not? I wouldn't go anyplace, and no one has ever shut you up before."

Tom gave up, sputtering, "Aw, forget it."

After a night's rest in the clear high desert air, they started early in the morning. In the unpaved center of the freeway between the northbound and southbound lanes grew small dusty-pale green bushy trees. These same small trees or bushes grew naturally in the desert, stretching off as far as the eye could see. The center of the freeway, like most freeways in Southern California, was dotted with parts of truck tires, trash, paper, and once, Dan saw an old diaper.

An occasional tiny grey-green lizard was glimpsed running from shadow to shadow. The monotonous desert with its pale browns and greens extending off to the gently rolling hills was broken only by the occasional brightly garnished billboard. The Petersons' eyes feasted on the rounded and weather-beaten ancient volcanic cones colored with red, bright yellow and greenish earth dotting the landscape.

The only sound was the soft murmuring of the bike tires on the highway. When they stopped to rest, the silence was a quiet nature softness that was comfortably all encompassing. It felt to Dan that nature was giving them time to delve inside of themselves with its benevolent solitude.

Even Tom noticed it, "It just doesn't feel like Los Angeles or Orange County up here. Down there, you always heard noise and felt tension or stress, but up here, it's much quieter, much slower somehow."

"It's strange," Sue exclaimed.

"What's strange?"

"I can hear myself breathe, it's so quiet."

Their daytime temperature was comfortable, but very dry mid-70's. During one of their rest stops, they looked behind them to the southwest and could see snow-covered mountains far in the distance.

Tom said, "It's a good thing we're not going through those mountains."

"Well, I too hope we don't have to go through those mountains in Colorado," his father thoughtfully replied. "Our map, however, shows that the Durango area is fairly high. By the time we get there, it should be early summer or summer. Hopefully the snow will be gone by then."

"Think we'll find Ginger?" Sue asked.

"I don't know, Sweetie," her father replied, his eyes deep, "But we've got to try."

That night, after Tom and Sue were asleep, Dan retrieved the precious color photograph of their Ginger. He sat with it in both of his hands near the campfire, the all-encompassing silent darkness surrounding them. With his shoulders hunched over the photograph, the flickering flames reflected the impish smile of his little red-headed daughter. He murmured to the photograph, "We're going to find you, Sweetheart."

He carefully wiped a little dust off the photograph with his handkerchief and gently placed it back on their trailer.

They continued their monotonous ride, the faded yellow lines on the freeway slipped slowly under their whispering bike tires. Tom and Sue would occasionally weave back and forth between the raised lane indicator bumps placed on the road. They rode under severely burnt electrical power lines crossing the road. The energy had attacked these power lines and sometimes, had started small fires that spread to dry brush in the desert. Fortunately, there wasn't much to burn and the fires soon extinguished themselves.

About thirty miles onward, they had just passed a bullet riddled road sign stating, "SIDEWINDER RD- 1 MILE."

"Dad, what's a sidewinder?" Sue asked.

"A sidewinder is a form of rattlesnake or something devious or dirty."

Dan was slightly in the lead when they came over a small rise in the freeway. About a hundred yards ahead of them, they saw an overpass with two figures on it.

Suddenly, a rifle bullet ricocheted sharply off the pavement next to Dan! A second rifle bullet creased Dan's left arm, leaving a bloody furrow.

"Off the bikes!" Dan screamed.

All three hurdled off their bikes and rolled frantically into the chest-high tall grass, bushes and debris in the ditch on the side of the road.

"Stay down," he exclaimed while he struggled to unsnap the straps holding his backpack.

"Tom, give me the gun!"

Tom slipped the AR-15 off his back and his hands shaking, gave it to his father. Dan had loaded it with a fifteen-round magazine taped upside down to another fifteen-round magazine. He lay on his stomach in the chest-high grass and bushes in the ditch. Sue was behind him, breathing rapidly, her hands quivering. She had drawn her little .22 caliber pearl handle automatic and was waving it around.

"Put that away, Honey, you're too far away," Dan whispered.

"Watch behind us, Tom, there may be more of them, and stay down!"

"Stay right here and keep your heads down," Dan ordered.

He crept about twenty feet away and to the side from his kids. He took his faded California Angel baseball cap, put it on the end of his rifle, and slowly lifted it above the grass around a small bush.

A shot echoed sharply off the overpass and a bullet grazed the top of the hat. More gunshots echoed off the overpass and surrounding hills as other bullets whizzed through the grass and bushes around him.

"Dam, my favorite hat," Dan muttered.

His left arm throbbing from the crease by the bullet, the blood oozing slowly, he crawled back close to his kids near the edge of the tall grass and carefully parted it. He could see the top of the overpass and now, there were three figures looking down at the road. The figure in the center was yelling and waving his arms at the other two men.

His heart pounding, Dan's right thumb flicked the dark green metal lever safety on the left side of the AR-15 downward toward the trigger, the weapon was now ready to fire. The AR-15 had been loaded with a .223 cartridge in its chamber.

He wrapped the canvas sling around his left wrist, braced the front hard black plastic covering of the rifle barrel over his left hand and wrist and pulled the stock into his right shoulder.

He centered the front sight of the barrel between the two prongs of the rear sight. Focused on the sight pattern of the rifle was the middle figure on the overpass, obviously the leader.

Dan inhaled a deep breath and slowly let it out, an instruction from a Master Sergeant firearms instructor long ago ingrained in his mind: "Squeeze the trigger as if you are caressing a woman's breast."

Dan caressed this trigger.

A .223 caliber bullet with a weight of .52(or about the size of a 22 long rifle bullet) ounces exploded from the muzzle of Dan's rifle at a speed of 3100 feet a second!

The bullet, with a flat and slightly rising trajectory, struck the center figure before he even heard the gunshot. The bullet struck the figure about two inches below dead center of his chest. The bullet continued through the rib cage, angled slightly upward and mushroomed through the heart until a shattered vertebrate stopped the deformed spent bullet. The figure's arms flew up and he flew backwards off the overpass. He was dead before he hit the road.

Immediately upon firing his first shot, Dan jerked the trigger as fast as he could and fired the entire fifteen round magazine in a little over four seconds. He sprayed the entire top of the overpass with bullets. He fought to keep the muzzle of his weapon from rising from the rapid recoil. An almost continuous six-inch blaze of white-yellow fire blasted from the flash suppressor on the front of Dan's AR-15 rifle as each bullet cleaved the air searching for a target!

Bronze colored cartridges ejected high out of the right side of his rifle in an unrelenting stream. He felt, rather than heard, the recoil spring twanging in the hard, dark plastic stock of the rifle next to his cheek.

God, he loved this weapon.

Dust, dirt and concrete chips flew where his bullets were impacting. He saw another figure flop up and down and roll over a few times. Through the dust kicked up by the bullets, the third figure could faintly be seen crawling off the overpass and then running at top speed down the side road. Dan fired a final shot at the third figure but couldn't see if he hit it or not.

The gas-powered hard metal chamber of the Colt AR-15 locked open.

Silence.

Sudden silence!

Sudden painful silence after the ear-piercing blasts from the AR-15 next to their heads.

They waited with noiseless breaths, the hot barrel of Dan's rifle oozing a thin stream of blue smoke. The acidic smell of cordite combined with a tangy aroma of large wild sweet clover and the odor of their perspiration caressed their faces.

"Where do these people come from, so far out in the sticks?" Dan wondered to himself as he ejected the spent clip and slammed home a new fifteen-round clip.

After a minute or two, Tom noticed a flock of crows hovering over the overpass. A few landed on the road. He said, "Dad, if there was anyone alive there, those crows wouldn't have landed."

"I think you are right. But let's play it safe."

"Here, Tom, you keep the AR-15 and the Chief revolver, I'm going to check out that overpass. The rifle is cocked and loaded, so be careful. Don't touch the trigger! I will take my 9 mm. with me. Sue, you watch very carefully behind us. I don't want anyone sneaking up behind us."

He crouched, and then half-crawled, half-ran to the overpass.

As he approached the overpass, the crows flew up, cawing loudly. He pulled back the slide of the chrome automatic, softly and quietly chambering a copper jacketed cartridge into its chamber.

He peered out of the tall grass just before the overpass.

Nothing moved.

Cautiously, trying to look everywhere and hear everything, he darted under the overpass panting, his heart pounding.

He found a rough camp with a small tent and the smoldering smelly remains of a small mesquite fire. Dan glanced into the interior of the tent, but except for a pile of clothing, it was empty. He found piles of what looked like stolen things, one of just papers and books and the second looked like discarded backpacks. No one alive was there, however. He could see the body of the man he shot just on the outside of the camp. The body had landed on its head and neck, and if he didn't have physical problems before he fell, the impact on the concrete roadway resolved whatever chiropractic symptoms he had.

Dan climbed up the concrete side of the overpass. He paused about halfway up, rolled over on his back and examined where his kids were hiding. He could see both peering wide eyed out of the grass. There was a soft breeze in his face with a mild not unpleasant tang of dry desert air. The only sounds were the crows cawing loudly above him.

Tom pointed upward and shrugged his shoulders and hands indicating that he could see nothing above Dan.

Dan climbed up to the top and quickly sneaked a peek over the concrete curb separating the road from the highway below.

"Squawk!"

A terrified crow flashed up from the pavement nearly striking Dan! It was unknown who was more frightened, the crow or Dan.

Dan waited a moment longer, his heart pounding, and then again sneaked a quick peek over the curb.
No movement.
He looked again, longer this time.
There was a body lying motionless facing Dan. The eyes were open.
All three of them!

One of Dan's shots had hit the suspect's head right above the bushy dirty eyebrows. A large puddle of blood lay pooled on and under the body. He obviously would not harm Dan or his kids. No one else was on the overpass.

Dan climbed over the concrete divider and crouching, looked around. A sharp look down the dirt side road where the third person had run revealed no one in sight.

Dan motioned that his kids should stay where they were. He didn't want Sue to see the bodies or the blood. There was an old M-14 lying partially under the body, soaked with blood. Dan left it but found several boxes of .223 ammunition. The top of the overpass was strewn with rusty cans, shell casings, discarded filthy clothing and a few pornographic books and magazines. Whoever the men were, they had been here for some time.

Dan climbed down the side of the overpass and examined the camp below. It was also filthy. He found a few books on explosives and guns.

"What on earth kind of people are these?" Dan muttered to himself.

He found several green and brown colored military ammunition cans full of ammunition. In addition, he found what looked like a carefully wrapped package of plastic explosives including, strangely, instructions on using it. The instructions were issued by the U.S. Army and were apparently from a course on utilizing these explosives.

Food, personal mementos like photographs and wallets, clothing, and a small pile of miscellaneous guns were carelessly strewn about.

After carefully examining the piles and camp, Dan took only what they needed and could easily carry.

"Tom," he called. "Come up here and bring the trailer, Sue, you stay back there guarding our rear, OK?"

As Tom paddled Dan's bike and trailer to the overpass, he looked for a moment at the body lying on the road, shook his head, but said nothing. He helped search through the piles of goods that looked like they had been stolen from other unfortunates passing through the area. Both examined the weapons and Dan showed Tom the package of explosives. Most guns were in very poor condition. All were dirty and dusty, a few were dismantled and most were unserviceable.

Interestingly, they found an Ithaca 12-gauge pump shotgun with the words "Los Angeles County Sheriff-130-S" stenciled on the dark brown wooden stock.

"How did they get this?" Tom asked waving the shotgun around.

"I don't know. That shotgun came from one of the L.A. County Sheriff's stations, Lakewood, I think. That 'S' on the stock means that it was a Sergeant's weapon. These, whatever they are called, probably held up a patrol car and took the weapon. I don't want to know what happened to the officer."

"Dad, there's something strange here: there's no food! What did these guys eat? I bet there's another camp down that road." Tom pointed with the shotgun down the side road in the direction the third person had escaped.

"I think you're right; we should get out of here. Now!"

"Dad, we should take the explosives, ammunition and books, they don't weigh much and they very well might come in handy."

"Ok, but let's hurry. I don't know if there are any more of this bunch out there."

The body on the road was dragged to the side and covered with some rags.

"Tom, climb up on top and get those weapons and any ammunition and pile it in this tent."

Dan trotted back to Sue to retrieve Tom's bike.

"Is everything all right?" she asked.

"Sure, we are all right, but come on. You did a good job guarding our rear."

As Dan and Sue rode up to the overpass, Dan said, "You guys start riding and wait for me about a half a mile down the freeway. Tom, take the trailer, I'll catch up with you in a minute."

Dan trotted back to the overpass. He had found a small red painted can of kerosene that the gang had been using to light fires. He spread it over the piles of stuff, heavily doused the remaining guns, unusable ammunition, clothes and tent. After pouring a trail of kerosene away from the camp, he bent down, flicked his small cigarette lighter and lit the trail. The kerosene caught fire and flared back to the camp. Dan ran back to his bike, jumped on it and hurriedly left to join his kids.

"I want to make sure no one else gets held up by them," he told the kids.

They rode about three-quarters of a mile away from the overpass and stopped, watching the fire burn. The fire was burning heavily with a cloud of black smoke flowing over the top of the overpass.

Suddenly, a violent white and yellow explosion rocked the overpass, strewing debris and flames over a two-hundred-yard area. What appeared to be flares, small rockets or fireworks rose lazily in the still desert air; in descending, one flare or rockets landed on an unfortunate large leafless tree and blew it to bits. The Petersons ducked, but the explosion did not reach them.

"I think we missed something, huh, Dad?" Tom grinned.

"Oh wow, just like the Fourth of July!" Sue exclaimed.

A sound like muffled firecrackers echoed over the desert.

"Firecrackers, Dad?"

"No, that's the ammunition 'cooking' in those metal ammunition cans because of the fire. Remember, we couldn't use that ammo and I doused it with kerosene. I wanted to make sure they couldn't use it either."

"Well, come on gang, we've got a lot of miles to go. And if they don't know that we were here before, they sure do now!"

The days passed.

They were averaging nearly forty to fifty miles a day on the freeway. While detours were an occasional problem because there hadn't been any maintenance on the roads for some time, the further they traveled into the desert or high country, the less they saw of burnt vehicles or blocked roads.

The hot summer months had not yet arrived in the desert. If they had waited another month or two, Dan thought, they would not be able to stand the heat and burning sun. The days were steadily warming. They had fallen into the routine of stopping every hour to rest, and a longer rest at noon. They had filled their water bottles at a campground just outside of Barstow before turning eastward.

They passed a restaurant with golden arches in an old railroad car. "I'd give my left arm for a decent hamburger and some French fries," complained Tom.

"Me too," said Sue.

Dan remarked to Tom, "I would have thought that there would be more people traveling, but we haven't seen all that many."

"I think you're right; I wonder where everyone is, maybe they are just staying home, hoping to wait this thing out."

An informal system of barter and information exchange developed among the travelers and between the travelers and the townspeople. Everyone was hungry for news and information; most didn't know precisely what had happened to their society. Most survivors, however, learned quickly to have nothing to do with electricity.

They could see a faint appalling greenish glow on the far nighttime southern horizon from the general direction of Phoenix. Dan had heard rumors that the nuclear power plant at Palo Verdi, just outside Phoenix, had been savagely attacked by the life force. A grizzled old desert man told him he had seen with his own eyes mutated live plants and animals. Dan listened to the tale with some skepticism, but others fleeing from the southwestern Arizona area agreed with the desert man. They swore that the earth was constantly shaking around the Western Phoenix area as if there was a continual earthquake. They told stories that their animals refused to even travel toward Phoenix.

Dan and his family made it through the flat, gently rolling, but monotonous desert in relatively good shape. At night, the sky was clear and cloudless; they could almost touch each star!

"How many stars are there, Daddy?" Sue asked.

"Well, we can see about four thousand or so stars on a very clear night, but there are about a hundred billion stars in our galaxy alone."

"Oh," came a small voice.

"But there's more, astronomers think that there might be millions more galaxies besides ours. You see, Honey, space above us is so huge that we are looking at light that left that star years, decades or centuries ago."

"Where's the North Star, Dad?" Tom asked.

"The easiest way is to find the Big Dipper. There, see, that group of stars that looks like a dipper?"

Upon receiving nods, Dan continued, "Now look for the two stars making up the side of the bowl opposite the handle. Imagine a line with those two stars directly overhead. That line will run into a bright star: The North Star or Polaris. Now, if you look a little further, the North Star is the end star of the handle of the Little Dipper. See, it looks like a small dipper."

"I remember reading about it, but I don't remember why it's important."

"It's important because the ancient sailors used it to navigate at sea; to them, it never seemed to change its position in the sky."

After a pause, Dan continued, "Modernly, we used electronic compasses, radar and satellites to tell us where on earth we were, but now, maybe The North Star will again be important.'"

The monotony of the dusty brown land was broken only by the flashy, and frequently tasteless billboards advertising either some Las Vegas showroom, suntan oil, or in one instance, women's underwear. Off to the side were black areas.

"What are they, Daddy?"

"I think that they are lava flows from an old volcano. I'd like to take time to find out, but maybe sometime later."

As they approached and passed through Needles on the west side of the Colorado River, they stopped at a bluff overlooking the river valley.

"Oh my!" Tom exclaimed.

They looked in amazement at what was below them.

It was as if God had taken a large fire hose and washed a smooth channel through the original Colorado Riverbed. Far off in the distance to the south, they could see a huge, smoldering, jumbled, pile of debris, tree trunks, parts of houses, bridges and anything that was near the flood.

"What happened?" Dan asked one of the local people, an older man in dust covered overalls.

"Well, from what we understand, a couple of those dams upriver all burst at the same time. I heard Parker Dam and Hoover or Boulder Dam had been destroyed by a green force of some kind," was the shaken reply.

"That night, without warning, a wall of water about forty or fifty feet high and a half a mile wide washed through here. It tore out all the bridges and any homes near the river and just wiped that channel clean! All those casinos that were near the river are just gone. I had heard that most of them were closed anyway because right before the flood, all the electricity was out in this whole area."

His wife continued, "We had a thunderstorm here, and lightning was around. As well as we could figure that green stuff was attracted by the lightning, and what the flood didn't ruin, the green stuff burnt."

They found an old couple named Thunerman by the riverbank. Mrs. Thunerman's life history was written in the seams of her face capped by bright silver hair; when she smiled, the immediate area seemed brighter. Mr. Thunerman was stooped, a crippling arthritic condition caused him to shuffle when he walked.

The Thunerman's had a small boat they somehow had attached a rope to and had jury-rigged this rope across the now languid muddy river. They used their small boat to ferry people and goods across the river for a price, depending on what the travelers had and what the Thunermans needed.

Later, Dan realized that when he was talking to Mr. Thunerman, Mrs. Thunerman stayed away from them and close to their trailer with both hands under her apron. The apron did not quite conceal the bulge of a chrome plated .357 Colt Magnum.

"This is the only passage across that river for miles," Mr. Thunerman said. "You're welcome to try some other place, but I guarantee you there ain't nothing around here to help you ford that river."

Dan felt he had no choice. The roads up and down the riverbank seemed impassable even if the roads still existed.

"Well, what do you want?" Dan asked frustrated. "We don't have anything worth trading. We're just on the road to Colorado to try to find our little daughter."

"Well, we don't need anything that you might have. But I tell you what: I can't chop wood anymore and Grandma needs wood for the stove. How about if you chop some wood for us and we'll call it even?"

"Sure, if you have a saw and an ax."

Both Dan and Tom sawed and chopped wood for about a day while Sue helped stack the wood, piece by piece, by the Thunerman's house. Mrs. Thunerman showed Dan a photograph of her granddaughter, a girl about the same age as Sue.

"They live near that big baseball stadium in Anaheim in Southern California. Do you know where that is?"

"Sure," replied Dan, "My son and I used to take the bus to watch the Angels play baseball there. They changed the name to the Los Angeles Angels. I don't know too much about the conditions in that area, though." He thought it unnecessary to tell her of the huge fires and terrible devastation, even if the fires were quite a distance away from her daughter's home.

Several times during the day, Mrs. Thunerman brought home-baked cookies and bread out to Dan and his family. The smell of baking bread spread through the area making Tom's stomach growl.

During one of their breaks, Mrs. Thunerman invited Sue to sit on her lap. Sue, shy at first, finally agreed. Mrs. Thunerman, tentatively at first, put her arms around Sue. Sue looked up at her with big eyes, decided that "Grandma Thunerman" was all right and hugged her back. Dan looked away when he saw tears running down "Grandma's" face. They both knew that it was probably the last time "Grandma" would hold a small "Grandchild!"

It was nice to see at least some kind of happiness for these folks.

Dan and his family spent the night with the Thunermans. Tom fell asleep quickly, physically sore from the woodcutting. Sue fell asleep in "Grandma's" arms, to "Grandma's" great joy. Dan never did find out what "Grandma's" first name was, but Mr. Thunerman said, "Just call me Sam."

They talked long into the night, a soft desert wind whispering gently though their hair, the stars so bright, one could almost read by them.

"We've been here for over ten years after I retired from L.A.P.D. Grandma likes to play bingo and we could walk to the various casinos."

Sam pointed to where the wildly violent water carrying debris of all kinds from upriver came nearly to their home. Dan could see the scars of the flood less than fifty feet from the front door. Sam husky voice told of the terrible earthshaking noise coming out of the night as the flood thrust its inexorable way southward.

"As long as I live," Sam said, "I'll never forget that night! I've been in some tough places and dark alleys, but I've never been as scared as I was that night. That sound was like a hundred locomotives coming down the river. And there was not a thing we could do about it."

Mrs. Thunerman silently nodded, agreeing with her husband.

Like most people the Petersons had met, the Thunermans were hungry for information and news.

Dan briefly told them of the information he received from Joe Robinson, thinking to himself that the label "Secret" was academic. Dan detailed their experiences traveling and of their ultimate search for their Ginger.

Finally, Dan was getting sleepy. He offered to pick up Sue from "Grandma," but she refused. "Grandma" slowly got out of her rocking chair and gently, gently, laid Sue in her own bed. Dan started to protest that it was unnecessary, but Sam clasped his shoulder and shook his head.

Sam took Dan outside and said softly with misty eyes in his weather-beaten leathery face, "Son, your daughter is in good hands in there, you and I both know that we'll probably never see my kids or grandkids again. Your daughter, so sweet, will help make my wife's memories a little more bearable."

Dan and Sam half-carried, half-walked a sleeping Tom to one of the spare bedrooms and just put him on the bed. Dan took off Tom's shoes, loosened his belt, and pulled a blanket over his son. Tom softly snored as Dan gently brushed a wayward lock of hair off his face. Dan stretched out on his sleeping bag in the Thunerman's living room and fell into an exhausted sleep.

About mid-morning, Dan woke and stretched to the smell of baking bread and a happy conversation between Sue and "Grandma."

"Well, about time you get up, sleepyhead," a rosy checked, radiant "Grandma" with a flour coated apron smiled.

His Sue also had an apron on, but she had flour in her hair, on her face, and up to her elbows. She planted a flour tasting kiss on her father's check, "Daddy, she's baking bread to take with us."

Tom walked in followed by Sam. "Good morning, Dad. Sam and I were checking out the bikes and trailer. We tightened everything and greased the wheels and chains. He's a pretty good mechanic. He adjusted the rear sprocket and derailleur on Sue's bike. She had problems getting into high gear, remember? She'll find it easier to keep up with us now."

"Thank you, Sam," Dan yawned, a full body stretch racked his body. He hadn't slept so soundly for weeks.

"It was nice to sleep with a roof over our heads," he smiled. "Thanks again."

"No, Son, Thank you! Nice boy you have there," Sam said.

Sam motioned to his wife, "Grandma, where did we put those supplies that we found in that abandoned trailer?"

"Good thinking, we don't need them, we've got plenty. They are in the back of the shed outside."

"Come on, Son, and you too, Tom," Sam said. Somehow, Dan had earned the nickname "Son" from Sam.

Mystified, both Dan and Tom followed Sam to the shed. He entered it with Tom, and Tom came back out staggering with two large boxes. Sam said, "Here you are let's figure out what you can carry."

Tom and Dan looked at each other with questions in their eyes. Dan squatted down and opened the top box.

"Well, I'll be!" Dan exclaimed.

"What, what?"

The boxes were full of condensed and freeze-dried food, enough to last for weeks. What a Godsend! They were getting low on supplies and Dan was worrying about food for them. This food was worth its weight in gold.

"I, I can't pay for all this stuff, Sam."

"Son, you already have, more than you will ever know," Sam replied, his bony arthritic hand clutching Dan's shoulder. "Tom, bring your trailer over here and I'll help you pack."

After packing and repacking the trailer, Dan thought it would weigh about sixty or seventy pounds more, but he could live with that.

"Son, I know you are anxious to go, but let's break bread together one last time," Sam asked almost formally.

"Sure, of course."

Their last meal was subdued, each knowing they would not see each other again.

Finally, Dan clasped Sam's gnarled hand and said simply and deeply, "Thank you!"

Grandma, smelling of flour and baking, hugged Dan. The wonderful odor of freshly baked bread triggered Dan's memories of his mother and grandmother in an old home in central Wisconsin. Grandma held on to Tom for a longer moment. She then ran back to the house, and in a minute was back carrying two large, still warm loaves of bread. She wrapped the bread in battered tin foil and fastened the loaves on the trailer saying, "You can eat this on the way."

She gave Sue a tiny freshly baked apple pie, still steaming, saying, "This is a little surprise for you, Honey. I'm sorry we didn't have any more apples."

Sue smiled her thanks, her big eyes wide.

They walked the bikes down to the riverbank and one by one, Sam took them across the river in his rickety, old, but still serviceable boat. On the last trip, Sue and "Grandma" came across by themselves with Sue's bike, holding hands.

Sam gave Dan directions on the safest way he knew to Kingman, Arizona. That said, Sam's gnarled hands grasped Dan's hands in a final handshake. Sue flung herself at "Grandma" and they held each other for long minutes. Sobs shook a tiny body being held against a grandmother's loving final embrace. Tears seamed roads down floury checks. Finally, they broke apart, embraced again, and for the last time, broke apart.

"Come on kids, we have to go," Dan said softly, his voice husky, something seemed to be in his eyes.

They mounted their bikes and rode off. They looked back, waving. They could see Sam and "Grandma" with their arms around each other, waving goodbye. An occasional sob racked Sue's body. Dan rode alongside her and just rubbed her back and hair.

"You know," Tom said philosophically, "Those two people make up for all those we ran into with the shotgun and on that overpass."

"Well," Dan said. "They have water, food and quite a bit of firewood, now. I think they'll be all right."

"I sure hope so," Sue exclaimed. "She was so nice.

Dan just nodded at his daughter, knowing that there wasn't much he could say. Because of what they had been through, he was grateful that his kids could see there were decent people still around.

They passed a burnt Arizona inspection station shortly after crossing the river. They stopped briefly and looked at the charred shell of the buildings. Each building was riddled with bullet holes.

"You think there is any government left, Dad?" Tom asked.

"Well, according to Joe Robinson, if there is a government left, it is essentially useless now. The only communication anywhere would be like the olden days: letters, writing and personal appearances; no more phones, no more televisions. . . . But I sure hope someone is trying to fight that force!"

Tom commented slowly, "You know, Dad, what you did to get all of the guns and things from that store was the bravest thing I ever saw you do."

"Well, thank you Son. We didn't have much choice. I hope that somewhere, somehow, somebody is working on something to fight the life force. If we have to put up with that every time there is electricity, our society, heck, our world will regress to the dark ages."

The road to Kingman was an uphill climb almost all the way.

About a day later, they passed what was once Kingman. They were told that most of the city was burnt and that it wasn't safe to enter it. Fortunately, the main road they were traveling on didn't enter the city.

They passed a wide burnt area where a forest fire had recently consumed an approximately two-mile wide area of devastation up the side of a mountain. With no forest fighting equipment or personnel, the local people were powerless to stop or control the blaze until a severe rainstorm over the area quenched the fire. Dan and his family could see the effect the heat of the fire had on the road, the tar between the concrete slabs was burnt and, in a few places, still smoldering. The blacktop roads had simply melted from the heat.

It took over seven days for them to reach Flagstaff, nearly one hundred and fifty miles. They rode from an elevation of about three hundred feet at the Colorado River to an elevation of six thousand, nine hundred feet at Flagstaff.

"This area is so beautiful," Dan said, looking around the Flagstaff area. The evergreen pine trees surrounding the city scented the air. Deer, fox and once, a rangy looking black bear lumbered across the road in front of them. Rabbits, gophers and families of pheasants and quail densely populated the freeway. Dan and his family ate wild game each night. Sue, with her small crossbow shot a big male pheasant one evening. Delicious. She later took one of the tail feathers and stuck it in her hat.

They rested for a few days on the outskirts of Flagstaff. Dan and Tom were told that the center of Flagstaff wasn't safe at night. Apparently, a few of the Los Angeles gangs had made their way to Flagstaff before the life force and had established a rough form of territory.

One of the residents, a skinny, leathery looking cowboy named Parker, "Just call me, 'Park'" told Dan, "We should travel though the center of town in the early morning just after sunrise. It seems that most of the gang wars and fights are at night and they sleep during the day. Our advice when traveling through there is to shoot first and maybe ask questions later."

He offered, "If you're going to go through the town, I'll go with you. My business is finished here and I need to get home."

He was riding a beautiful golden palomino mare. "Ain't she pretty? I raised her from a baby," he said proudly, patting the snorting horse.

Early the next morning, before they left, Park asked for Dan and Tom's help in putting rubber shoes on his horse. The rubber shoes were made from parts of a thick tire and they were velcro'ed on the horse's feet. The horse wasn't happy with the "rubbers", but Park explained that the "rubbers" deadened the sound of the hooves on the concrete freeway.

"Can hardly hear her coming with these things on," he said.

"Well, let's go," he directed. "Keep your guns handy!"

He was carrying a black, wicked looking Ozi 9 mm. in a homemade side-draw holster.

They rode east bound on Interstate 40. Sue was riding between Dan and Tom. Tom was carrying the AR-15 across his handlebars; it was loaded and cocked with the safety in the on position. Dan was holding the 38-cal. pistol with his 9 mm. in his shoulder holster. They were approaching an off ramp called Butler Ave. when a bullet twanged off the pavement in front of them. Another bullet went through the outer part of Park's right sleeve.

"Over there, by that building," Park shouted as he yanked his 9 mm. Ozi from its snap holster.

They could see a figure with a rifle pointing at them. Three weapons spoke as one, the figure flew backward into a dark alley.

"Come on," Dan shouted. "Let's get out of here!" The four rode as fast as they could.

"Dam bikes aren't made for speed," Dan gasped.

Tom turned, and riding without holding onto the handlebars, flicked the safety on the AR-15 downward. Pulling the trigger as fast as he could, he swept the front of the building with the AR-15, shooting at windows, doors and anything that was in the neighborhood. Glass was breaking, windows were shattering, bullets ricocheting all over, chunks of concrete and dust were flying! The sound of the AR-15 echoed off the buildings and concrete dividers of the freeway. It sounded like fifty AR-15's in a war zone. He went through a fifteen-round magazine in less than five seconds.

"That ought to keep them down," he grinned.

Secretly, he had wanted to do that ever since he got to carry the AR-15. He just never had the opportunity and he knew that they couldn't waste ammunition. By this time, they had passed through a slight hollow and bend in the freeway and were sheltered from any return fire.

"Everybody OK?" Dan asked.

He then told Park to stow the bad language, his shirt could be mended, but there was a child present.

While they rested, Dan showed Park his map and pointing up in the general direction of Durango, Colorado, asked, "Do you know what the roads are like up in this area?"

Park replied, "Well, you have two choices, one is to go straight up from here to Durango, but I wouldn't recommend that. That whole area is quite rough. I think that your best bet is to go over to Gallop, New Mexico, and then turn northward. The roads are in better condition."

He paused for a moment of thought, "You'll be traveling through that Indian reservation going north, but I don't think that they will bother you; they'll probably be better than some of the people around here."

They amicably parted with Park on the outskirts of Flagstaff after helping him remove the "rubbers" from his horse.

"Carry plenty of water through that area," he said. "And good luck on finding your little one up in Durango. I'd like to help, but I have family here, you understand. Be careful!"

❖❖❖❖❖❖

CHAPTER FIVE

The days, miles and towns passed. Intriguingly named Winona or Two Guns were ridden through without stopping.

"I don't want to stop at these towns," Dan grumbled. "Every time we stop, people ask us questions and we wind up wasting more time. I just want to get to the Durango area and look for Ginger."

"Dad, do you think we'll ever find her?" Sue asked her big eyes wide in her face.

"And if we find her, do you really think Kathy will give her to us willingly?" Tom asked.

"Well, to be honest with you kids, I don't plan on asking her."

Unseen by Dan was the exchange of smiles between Tom and Sue.

They stopped and spent an entire day at the Meteor Crater to the west of Winslow, Arizona. Dan had been pushing his family hard eastward, always eastward to find their beloved Ginger, and he felt they could use the rest. The Meteor Crater itself was about six miles south of the main highway over a winding two lane asphalt road. A large jack rabbit squirted out of the tall, dusty brown grass and bounded across the road in front of them as they rode over a culvert in a small ditch. It was unknown who was more startled, Sue or the rabbit.

"We may never be back this way again, and I think this Meteor Crater is something worth seeing," Dan said. Little did he know what effect this place held for the far future.

While the main building or buildings were ransacked, Dan and Tom found most exhibits intact.

"Dad, this is interesting," Tom said, absorbed, "This area must have been like an atomic bomb when that meteor hit."

They leaned over the railing looking down into the crater itself. At the bottom, they could see a small shed in about the center of the huge hole left by the meteor.

"What's that little building for, Dad?"

"Well, according to this plaque, scientists went down into the hole and dug out parts of the original meteor."

"Fascinating!"

Sue quickly became bored with the whole thing; she was more interested in watching a couple of bunnies play in the tall, green grass surrounding the buildings.

About two days later, they stopped at the Petrified Forest National Park. Now, Sue was interested. She quickly loaded her pockets with two pounds of vividly colored petrified trees.

"I had a friend who went through this Petrified Forest Park a couple of years ago and he got a ticket for taking rocks out of the park," Dan said.

"Why?"

"Well, apparently the Rangers feel that if everyone who came through here took a piece of the forest, there wouldn't be any left."

"Oh, all right, I understand," Sue said as she threw away most of her carefully selected rocks.

As they turned northward toward Durango at Gallup, New Mexico, fireplace, and barbecue smoke hovered over the scrawling housing tracts surrounding the city. About ten miles north of Gallop, they crossed into the Navajo Indian Reservation.

After paddling a few miles, Sue asked, "Dad, where are all the Indians?"

Tom laughed, "Sue, just because we are on their land doesn't mean that they live right here. Most live in small towns or regular cities in regular houses."

Sue was disappointed, "Aw, I thought I would see real live Indians, tepees, and things."

Tom waved his hands, "Look around us here, there's nothing out here but small bushes and trees. There's not even any decent grass to feed a cow or steer. Plus, this area doesn't look like it gets much rain."

They could see that Tom was correct: the bare, rolling, reddish colored land was occasionally covered with dusty green small bushes and dry trees with a solitary lowly cactus adding its sharp-edged color. Off in the distance, thousands of feet tall reddish buttes stood as sentries over the barren land. The road frequently crossed areas where flash floods had violently gouged gullies and arroyos through the dry land.

Meanwhile, a solitary figure on a horse overlooked the highway. Wearing what remained of a charcoal gray/black New Mexico State Police uniform with a faded silver stripe down the pants legs, the figure had long coal black hair nearly down to his shoulders. His dark eyes peered out of a sunburned face with high cheekbones protected by a non-regulation black and now floppy "Smoky the Bear" hat. A black Sam Browne webbed belt held a 6-inch .357 Colt Python revolver. A container on the back held a set of Peerless stainless-steel handcuffs while two small circular containers in the front of the belt held rubberized speedy loaders for the revolver. While most of his department had gone to 9 .mm or 10 caliber semi-automatics, this person preferred his revolver. He knew *this* weapon didn't jam!

Over the left breast pocket of the dusty charcoal gray/black uniform shirt hung a slightly tarnished New Mexico State Police badge. On the right side of the uniform shirt was a name tag, "Patrolman James Blue Cloud."

Patrolman James Blue Cloud's regular steed, a new Plymouth state police vehicle with a high-performance engine, heavy duty shocks, overhead flashing red and blue lights, prisoner cage surrounding the back seat, and three sets of radios (one for the State Police, one for the County area he was assigned to, and the last for a state-wide emergency broadcast net) was resting on its side in a deep ditch below him.

Nearly a month before, in the early evening, he had been on routine patrol near the border of the Reservation when he spotted a just reported hijacked stolen car being driven by two local gang members. After making a violent U-turn, the rear wheels on his high-powered Plymouth screeching, he went into pursuit.

Adrenaline flooding, he had picked up his police radio microphone and was broadcasting, "101, Gallop dispatcher, I'm in pursuit of a stolen light blue, four door 99 Chevrolet northbound out of Gallop," when his hand-held microphone suddenly blossomed with a green heat that burned his hand.

Patrolman Blue Cloud stared at the microphone in amazement as he flung it away from him. Waves of violent static punctured the always busy police airways. The engine of his police vehicle, running smoothly at about 4500 R.P.M. or nearly 120 M.P.H., shuddered as if a giant hand was shaking the engine. Jagged holes appeared in the hood of his highly polished vehicle like fire through tissue paper.

His heart pounding, instinctively, he slammed on his brakes.

The engine beneath the hood radiated a greenish, pulsating light. His four-wheel locked skid from 120 M.P.H. was doing fine until he hit a three-inch deep hole in the concrete highway.

The right front tire shredded, blew out and collapsed. His violently decelerating police vehicle was thrown into an uncontrollable sideways slide.

At this second, the high-powered Plymouth engine, unable to defend itself against the attack of the "Green Ghost," screeched through a clamor of tortured pistons and stopped running. The effect was that Patrolman Blue Cloud lost the power steering and brakes on his vehicle. His vehicle, in a cloud of dust and acidic smoke from his severely abused tires, spun, slid sideways off the road into a deep, dry ditch and rolled on its left side.

The sight of the ground crashing into Patrolman Blue Cloud's open left front driver's window caused nightmares for days to come.

Unbuckling his belts in the middle of his vehicle shoulder harness, Patrolman Blue Cloud grabbed the departmental issued Ithica 12-gauge pump shotgun, his personal 30-30 lever-action Winchester carbine and his utility briefcase containing extra ammunition, papers, and handcuffs. He stood up on the counsel, pushed open the right front door and crawled out onto the side of his patrol car. He slid off the side and quickly scrambled away from the smoldering vehicle.

He sat for a few minutes in the dirt on the side of the ditch, the dust settling on him like flour over a loaf of bread. After taking deep breaths to calm himself, and wishing he hadn't quit smoking a few years ago, he looked around for the stolen car.

The stolen car had also been attacked, but its driver refused to stop. The last time Patrolman Blue Cloud saw the stolen car, he vaguely remembered that it was airborne into a deep arroyo with swarms of green transparent substances attacking it in midair. Since the arroyo was at least several hundred feet deep, Blue Cloud didn't even bother to climb down to the bottom to see if there was anyone alive.

Now, nearly a month later, as he watched the figures on the highway below him, Patrolman James Blue Cloud recalled a conversation he had with a tribal elder several months ago.

Could this man on the bicycle be the person he was searching for?

The elder, a wizened old man, had skin baked to a leathery texture by the harsh desert sun. Long black hair sprayed wildly from underneath a Stetson hat, a sweat stained Stetson hat whose color many moons ago had been an off-white, but what was now a floppy streaky brown that somehow seemed to blend with the desert its owner lived with. Knarled, weather-beaten hands stuck out like branches from a buckskin jacket so faded and weathered, it was almost white. The revered elder seemed to be a part of the land, a part that seemed to have existed long before the white man ever trod on the Navajo's, on the People's sacred lands. While his body was ancient and frail, his voice a whisper in the dry desert air, the elder's unquenchable spirit radiated from his dark eyes.

The elder had taken Blue Cloud away from the others during a frequent, but typically useless tribal meeting to talk to him.

"My son, we are proud of you. You have adapted to the white man's ways, to the white man's justice, yet you honor us with your presence and you honor our people."

The elder's voice was as soft as the night wind, "You see much, but you say little. And what you do say is wise. Is good! Two moons ago, I fasted for five suns with the forefathers for guidance, for answers."

Blue Cloud blinked: he was surprised, not only at the old man's fast, but that the mention of the purpose of the fast was unusual. This elder was respected, even revered by the more stable minds of his community. This elder, while being uneducated himself, had led his people through the very difficult process of obtaining better education for their children, better jobs for the men and better homes for the families while maintaining their heritage with their land. He had also led the fight against the scourge of alcoholism that swept through the tribe like a plague.

Blue Cloud, however, reverently said nothing; while visions by the elders were rare, they were given great weight. No amount of education, logical thinking and militaristic police academy training could erase such a fundamental part of his beliefs. He respectfully nodded his head for the elder to continue.

"I was given a vision, a vision of a terrible fire from the sky, but it wasn't fire. The fire destroyed the white man's cities, all the white man's works. Much sadness was over the land, but joy, too. I don't know why; the fathers would not tell me! The vision showed me that our people would also suffer."

Blue Cloud, deeply puzzled, asked, "What is this 'fire?'"

An outsider hearing the conversation would have been surprised that Blue Cloud did not dispute what the elder had seen. Blue Cloud, while educated in the Indian schools and later in the "white man's" colleges knew that all the meaning of life, all the answers were not written on the blackboards of schools or in books, or as one song put it, "... on the subway walls!"

"It was not of the sun, it was not of the land," the elder replied, his dark eyes looking inward at the vivid memory of the vision.

"*What is this?*" Blue Cloud asked himself. "*Is this the start of an atomic war? Is he telling me that he foresaw war?*"

"Was this fire an explosion of some kind?" he mumbled to the elder.

After a moment during which chills of terror fluttered up and down Patrolman James Blue Cloud's back, the elder shook his head.

"No, the fire was old, old as the Great Spirit. It was not like the sun, not like our campfires, but like the color of the young pine trees in the mountains. It is evil!"

The elder's body shook with suppressed fear, "The fathers said that you, my son, must follow the white man's obligation," as he pointed to Blue Cloud's badge on his left chest.

"A man will ride from the great salty water in the southwest to a (Here, he used an untranslatable Navajo word with the essential meaning of fresh, clear water.) sea in the east. He will cross our land in search of a little child with hair like the setting sun. While he is on our land, especially the northern lands, he must, he must be protected. Danger comes from there," he pointed toward the northern mountains.

The elder's voice strengthened as he clasped Blue Cloud's uniformed right arm with his talon-like hands, "He must be protected! Do you understand? He will ride tall over our land, but he must be protected while he is here. You must . . ..! "

"How will I know him?"

The elder shook his head. His dark eyes radiated with the fierceness of his command to the young patrolman, his dark black eyes a deep passageway to the fear in his heart.

"If he is protected, the fork in The People's journey is toward brightness, peace, not only for our people, but also for all people. If this man is not protected, the fork is toward where animals, both four and two legged, will again rule."

At that, the elder's body seemed to deflate almost like a balloon. He wearily sat on a nearby stump and seemed to withdraw inside of himself, he rocked back and forth, mumbling to people or things only he could see. He had delivered his message!

Patrolman James Blue Cloud had left the elder sitting on the stump. He had walked slowly back to his patrol car and, almost in a daze, driven back to his station. From then until about a month ago, when he lost his patrol car, he had worried about the elder's vision. He never doubted the elder's vision, he simply didn't know what it meant.

Therefore, when his patrol car was attacked early one evening while chasing suspects in a stolen car northbound from Gallop, he was not altogether surprised when the engine in his vehicle was attacked by a green transparent, ghost-like substance.

"So that was the fire that didn't come from the sun," he mumbled to himself.

After unsuccessfully trying to find a working vehicle, he walked back to the nearest settlement and borrowed a horse. He had tried to report back to his duty station in Gallup, but chaos in the city with no electricity prevented him from getting anywhere near the station. Eventually, he gave up trying to report to his headquarters and returned to the reservation to keep his promise, his promise not only to the people of the State of New Mexico to serve and to protect, but his promise to the tribal elder.

Now, as he saw the figures on bicycles below him, he wondered if this was the man he was to protect.

The day was overcast; a huge black cloud had formed over the southern Chuska Mountain range; lightning, thunder, and heavy rain interspersed with inch thick balls of hail pelted the southern range. Several miles in diameter, the heavy rainstorm buffeted the higher slopes of the mountains, mountains at least five to ten miles from the two-lane highway.

Frequent gusts of cold, dusty, dirty wind from the northwest blew dust and sand into the Petersons' eyes as they paddled northward. It was difficult paddling their bikes against the chilly wind, the swirling sand and dust searching for crevices in their clothing.

"Dad, we should stop," Sue complained. "This wind is blowing dirt and sand and it's getting into my mouth and eyes."

"Sure, sweetheart. Tom, how about right up ahead by the culvert? We can camp in the gulch and we'll be sheltered from the wind."

"It seems ok to me, Dad, it looks only about ten feet deep."

They stopped by the culvert that bridged a gulch about ten feet deep and about sixty feet wide. The bikes were moved to the other side of the road, but camp was made in the bottom of the gulch. It was early in the afternoon and the sleeping bags were left on the trailer for later. A small fire was started from the meager supply of dry small trees and bushes. Sand and dust blown by the wind whipped over their heads. No one seemed interested in making a meal right now.

Patrolman James Blue Cloud carefully watched the heavy thunderstorm. He got off his horse, tied the reins to a scrubby bush, and walked about twenty yards away. The chilly wind whipping at his charcoal-black shirt was ignored. He knelt, scooped out a small hollow in the desert sand and dirt and lay flat on the ground.

He placed his ear in the small hollow; his eyes closed, he allowed his breathing to slow, his heartbeat to become one with the earth.

There!

Far off, he could hear a very faint rumbling, like a train locomotive moving down its tracks. This, however, wasn't a train. He listened a moment more, now certain what it was.

The patrolman leaped to his feet, and ran to his horse.

"Hi Ya!" He yelled as he mounted his horse and galloped down the side of the hill. He hoped that he would be on time.

Precious moments passed as Patrolman Blue Cloud carefully made his way through the boulder strewn, crevice riddled bottom of the hill to the highway. He galloped his horse up on the highway and turned toward the gulch that sheltered the Petersons.

He whipped his horse faster and faster. The coming terrible danger could not be stopped and they needed to escape from it.

Meanwhile, Dan Peterson was just relaxing by the fire, trying to keep it lit by adding small pieces of wood and dried brush to the flickering flame.

Suddenly, they could hear the frantic galloping of a horse on the highway above them. Dan grabbed his Colt AR-15 while Tom retrieved his power bow.

"Sue, get behind us! Whoever that is is in one heck of a hurry. Tom, let's climb up the side of this gulch."

As they climbed back up the side of the gulch, they could suddenly feel a faint rumbling in the ground coming from the northwest.

"What the heck is going on, Tom?" Dan asked.

Tom shook his head silently; he didn't know either.

The horse's frenzied galloping came closer and closer. Suddenly it skidded to a stop above them on the culvert.

Patrolman James Blue Cloud stared down on the Petersons huddling by the side of the gulch, Dan's Colt AR-15 pointed at him, Tom's power bow was notched with a hunting arrow ready to fire.

They looked up and saw a rider on a horse, a single eagle feather attached to a "Smokey Bear" hat covering a bronzed face wearing what remained of a New Mexico State Police uniform.

"Get out of there!" Blue Cloud yelled, his horse dancing with lather dripping from its sweaty, heaving sides.

"Hurry!" Blue Cloud shouted again as he swiftly jumped off his horse and ran to the side of the gulch. The Petersons now could feel and hear a terrible rumbling coming from the northwest.

He reached for the Petersons, "Here, give me your hands."

Dan saw the badge on the Indian's chest and grabbed Sue. He heaved her up to the Indian to pull up onto the road, he then pushed Tom to the top of the gulch, sand and dirt tumbling into his face as Tom scrambled to the top. Both Tom and the Indian grasped Dan's hand and they pulled him to the roadway.

"Get out of here, get to high ground!"

He pointed up the gulch, "Can you hear it?"

"What is it?" Tom asked as they ran to their bikes.

"It's a huge flash flood coming down these arroyos," Blue Cloud shouted. "Hurry, get up to the top of that hill, we might be safe there."

Suddenly, the thundering water was upon them!

They could feel the spray from the flood rushing down the gulch beneath them.

Both Dan and Tom, however, had left their backpacks up on the highway. Precious seconds were wasted lifting the backpacks onto their shoulders.

The onrushing-muddy water, filled with dry brush and debris, flooded over the road. It clutched for the humans with a deep roaring like angry, hungry locomotives.

As the Petersons jumped onto their bikes, the turbulent water reached their bicycle wheels, the spray from the tumbling water soaked their faces. Both Tom and Sue easily fled ahead out of danger. Dan's bike, however, was pulling the trailer and it took a critical second longer to get started.

The violently tumbling water reached nearly to the hub of the trailer before Dan got it started. As Dan stood on his paddles to pull the trailer out of the water, the debris laden water viciously pulled the trailer and Dan toward the gulch.

Desperately, Dan jumped off the bike and started dragging his bike and trailer out of the rushing water by hand.

Blue Cloud suddenly appeared alongside Dan and together, they pulled the trailer out of the rampaging waters.

"Let's get higher, sometimes these floods will double in size as other streams join them," Blue Cloud shouted over the thundering flood.

Meanwhile, Tom and Sue had reached the top of the hill. Tom dropped his backpack and bike saying, "You stay here, Sue. I'm going to help them." He ran back to Blue Cloud and Dan, and all three pulling the bike and loaded trailer, reached the top of the hill.

Below them, they could hear and see the flash flood, its force tumbling large boulders down the gulch in a fierce turmoil of violent destruction, the thunder shaking the ground and pounding their ears.

After a few minutes, the thunder subsided, the water dissipated, and the only thing left was a small muddy stream. The water had washed out the road like a jagged saw through a loaf of bread. All that remained was a fifty-foot crevice where once was small gulch.

Sue started to shake, to cry. Dan ran to her and held her to his chest, murmuring, "It's all right, Honey, we're safe now."

He held her for a few moments, rubbing her back, her voice trembling, "Daddy, I was so scared."

"I know, Honey, but this man saved us," Dan said as he turned to Blue Cloud.

Dan reached out to shake Blue Cloud's hand, "I don't know how you knew that we were in danger there, but our deepest thanks."

"I agree," Tom said, looking at Blue Cloud's uniform. "Are you or were you a State Police Officer?"

"Well, I guess I still am an officer, Officer James Blue Cloud, maybe still of the New Mexico State Police," he smiled as he shook Dan's hand.

"We're the Petersons, Tom, Sue and I'm Dan."

"Would you like to spend the night with us," Tom offered after glancing at his father, "It doesn't look like we're going any place today. We've got a little extra food we can share if you like."

"Thanks, I'll be glad to. Let me take care of my horse first. I had to ride her hard to reach you in time."

Later, they sat around a campfire and talked.

Sue, gazing at Blue Cloud, asked shyly, "Are you a real Indian?"

"Sure am," James Blue Cloud smiled gently at her. "One hundred percent Navajo. I was born on the reservation, but I went to school in Gallup and in Albuquerque. I joined the State Police about two years ago and was assigned to this area. By the way, where are you folks from, where are you headed?"

Cold chills of awe ran up and down his back as Dan told him they were from Los Angeles, California (No one ever heard of Orange County.) and the search for their Ginger in the Durango area.

When Dan told him of El Fantasia Verde, he exclaimed to himself, "So the elder's vision was true!" A sense of pride, almost of reverence, caused his chest to swell, he was so pleased.

They spent the night together, Dan telling the patrolman of the conditions from Orange County, California to this point in their journey. He briefly mentioned their search for their little girl; however, the patrolman knew little about Durango, Colorado.

The morning dawned clear. Patrolman James Blue Cloud, late of the New Mexico State Police, after riding with them for a few miles, bid them goodbye.

"I think the roads ahead of you to Durango are clear. I haven't heard much because there has been hardly any traffic since the 'Green Ghost' arrived."

Dan said with deep feeling, "Officer, I wish there was some way we could repay you for what you did for us."

"You continue your journey; you find your little red-headed daughter and you finish your journey to near the great lake. That's how you can thank me," Blue Cloud said cryptically. "So long." He had not told them of the elder's vision.

A few miles after they parted, Tom asked his father, "I wonder what Officer Blue Cloud meant when he said that the way we can thank him is to finish our journey."

"I don't know either, Son. I've been thinking of his final comments, but it doesn't make sense to me. We're doing what we have to do; I hope we can find our Ginger, and I'd like to get to Wisconsin."

"Wait a second, Dad!"

Tom's eyes were wide in his sunburned face as his bike skidded to a halt.

"What?"

"Dad, we never told him we were going to Wisconsin!"

"No, we didn't, and how did he know Ginger's hair was red?" Sue exclaimed. "How would he know that? We never told him that either."

"Oh my," Dan said. He thought for a moment and then said with chills running up and down <u>his</u> back, "You're right, we never told him our ultimate destination, the subject never came up. How did he know?"

The days passed. After some detours because the roads were out, the Colorado-New Mexico border came and went.

One morning, it had been raining. They had spent the night at a turnout on the main road about halfway down a long winding mountain pass, and decided that they would wait until the rain stopped. Around noon, the rain stopped and the clouds were dissolved by a gentle breeze.

The air was crystal-clear, a racy smell of wet earth and evergreen cedar and pine trees caressed their faces. Mountain tops to the sides and extending off in the distance were still covered with snow while clouds gathered around a solitary snow- covered peak like a halo. The view was breathtaking, the all-encompassing silence broken only with the lonely moan of a slight wind and the cry of a flying hawk.

After finishing their meal of quail, they had shot and roasted the night before, they packed their bags, loaded up the trailer and were on their way.

Dan and Sue gradually pulled ahead of Tom. He was just riding along, riding Dan's bike, pulling the trailer, and enjoying the scenery. A few times, they were nearly a mile ahead of Tom, and he was out of sight when they went around a curve in the road. It was coming to evening and Dan was thinking about finding a place to spend the night.

As Dan and Sue rode around a sharp curve, their way was suddenly blocked by three unshaven men wearing unwashed plaid shirts with dirty jeans. The dirt in their long stringy hair matched their jeans. All three were armed and they motioned with their guns for Dan and Sue to stop.

"Get off the bikes!"

"Keep your hands up where I can see them!"

Two more men joined the party on the road from behind them; they had been hiding on the side of the road.

"Well, well, what do we have here?" the apparent leader sneered.

He was taller than the other four men at about six feet three inches and weighed at least two hundred and twenty pounds. An old baseball cap partially covered his long brown hair. His unkempt beard covered a small cruel mouth. None of the men had shaved recently and it probably had been weeks since they had washed or taken a bath. Their clothes were filthy and stinky. Dan was downwind of three of the men and the odor was almost overpowering; he had smelled pigs who were cleaner.

Sue started to sob. Dan looked around at her and out of the corner of his eye, saw Tom just coming around the beginning of the curve.

Dan raised his hands higher and shouted at Sue, "Shut up, just shut up."

Sue stared at him in dumbfounded surprise, then she howled!

"Shut up, I said," Dan shouted again.

Sue and Dan had the immediate attention of the five men. When Dan sneaked a glance out of the corner of his eye, Tom was not in sight.

"Good boy, Tom," Dan thought to himself.

"What are you doing out here?" the leader demanded.

We're just passing through to get to Durango," Dan replied. "We don't mean anyone any harm."

"P-P-Please, let us go," Sue stuttered.

This plea met with rude laughter from the men. "Take them over to the camp and tie them up," the leader ordered. "We'll figure out what to do with them later."

"Gar, get his guns and then see what they have in their backpacks, maybe it'll be something we can use."

"Gar" sidled up to Dan and with his gun in his right hand away from Dan, yanked Dan's 9 mm. from his shoulder holster and snatched Dan's .38 Chief from his belt, leering at him with blackened cavity ridden teeth. The only time "Gar" ever saw a dentist, the dentist was on television. His breath would have caused a hog to fall in love with him. Narrow dark eyes under stringy black hair radiated meanness, an unnecessary cruelty as he shoved Sue and Dan toward the camp.

"Get over there, next to that tree," Gar ordered, viciously poking a gun in Dan's back. "Kid, you make one funny move and I'll kill your old man, understand?"

Sue nodded, her small body trembling, her face drawn and pale.

"Sit down by that tree," Gar ordered, pointing at a four-inch-thick sapling. "Hands behind your back around that tree trunk." A thin rope tied tightly around Dan's wrists effectively negated any thought of escape.

A woman had been tied to another tree, her long hair hanging over her face. Sue was dragged over to and tied to the same tree as the woman except that Sue was tied facing away from the camp.

One of the men had been conscripted as cook. The others loudly and profanely complained about his cooking, but all five ate whatever he had made. By the time the so-called cook had prepared the meal, it was dark. The men didn't bother to offer any food or drink to the captives.

Empty whiskey and wine bottles were strewn around showing that the men had been at the camp for some time. Worn, dirty clothes were thrown about with a few hung from nearby pine tree branches. Two yellow nylon tents were partially hidden under a few pine trees on the south side of the camp. It seemed that they used this spot as an ambush to lay in wait for any unlucky people traveling on the road. Other backpacks were stacked against trees; Dan didn't think their owners were anywhere in sight.

After eating, the leader stood up, belched loudly, walked to the edge of the camp, zipped down his fly and urinated into the bushes. He threw a few extra logs on the already substantial fire and then swaggered over to where Sue and the woman were tied together. He untied the woman from the tree and dragged her to the center of the camp near the fire.

A trickle of dried blood on her dirt covered face showed that the woman had been beaten, but she was conscious. When Dan saw her face in the bright firelight, something moved deeply within him. She had long blondish brown hair that framed a face of beauty. She had full lips and wide, deep dark eyes. He didn't know how old she was, but even soiled with her white blouse and calico skirt covered with dirt, in the campfire light she looked younger than he was.

Despite having been beaten and in obvious physical pain, her eyes spat fire at the man dragging her. Her hands were tied tightly behind her back and her feet were bound with a thin rope. The leader dropped her to the ground close to the campfire and yanked a large knife out of his belt.

He waved the knife around in front of the woman bragging, "Get ready, we're going to have some fun." He bent down and cut the rope binding her feet.

He grabbed her calico skirt in one hand and with the other hand clutching his knife, he slit her calico skirt from the hem between her legs up though her waist. The woman tried to roll over and kick him, but wearing his heavy leather shoes, he simply kicked her in the ribs, ordering huskily, "Knock it off."

He grabbed her white blouse and ripped it open, the buttons flying. With a sharp jerk, he yanked both the blouse and the calico skirt off her. Her white bra and panties gleamed stark white in the campfire.

A smirk gleaming through his greasy beard, he waved the knife around and said, "Watch, boys, you're going to see something nice."

He then playfully pushed his knife under her bra between her breasts and swiftly pulled the knife upward, severing her bra in half. He grabbed a piece of the bra with his left hand and yanked. Her full firm breasts flopped free.

He leered, "Boys, look at those, ain't they beauties?"

He bent over, hooked a filthy claw-like hand into the top of her white panties, and ripped them off her slim hips.

She tried to cross her legs to hide the dark triangle at the top of her long legs, but the man kicked her legs open. One of the other men, Dan thought it was Gar, took a drink from his whiskey bottle, staggered over to the woman, and grabbed a leg. She attempted to kick him, but she was clearly overpowered. She said absolutely nothing, but her face and eyes steamed fear and hate.

Suddenly, Dan felt a tug at his ropes binding him to the tree.

"Shhh," a voice breathed in his ear.

"Thank you, Lord, oh thank you!"

Dan whispered a heartfelt prayer: it was Tom.

He felt another tug and suddenly, his hands and arms were free. Dan didn't move, trying to get the circulation back into his hands and wrists.

"Good boy," Dan whispered.

By this time, the men's attention was concentrated on the victim of the planned rape. They didn't notice Dan moving slowly to his knees in the deep shadows next to the tree.

"Here, Dad," Tom handed Dan his power bow.

"I can't hold it yet, rub my hands and wrists until I get some circulation back in them," Dan whispered.

"There may be some more of them down the road. I don't want to use the guns and alert the rest of them," Tom whispered softly, his hands quickly massaging his father's cold hands and arms.

Meanwhile, the leader was straddling the woman on the ground while he unbuckled his pants. He dropped them and his erect penis sprung up out of a thatch of filthy dark hair like an evil engorged snake. He kicked his pants away and said hoarsely, "Well, girly, I've got something for you! Let's see how good you are."

Off to the side in the dark forest, Dan and Tom suddenly heard the snarls and growls of two different animals like the howls of tortured creatures!

One howl sounded like a powerfully voiced high-pitched baby screaming, the other howl seemed to come from deep within a powerful dog's chest. Dan and Tom looked at each other in amazement, neither had ever heard such yowling before, but the sounds were a little distance back in the trees and didn't seem to threaten them.

As the leader stroked his penis and started to bend over the woman, Dan whispered to Tom, "Take the man on the right holding her leg, I'll shoot at the leader."

Tom nodded, his face a grim mask as he slipped a graphite arrow from his quiver.

Dan quietly snapped a dark arrow from the brown leather quiver of his recurve bow, fitted the arrow to the drawstring, drew it back to his cheek and fired almost all in one motion.

His 32-inch, black, three hundred and fifty-two-gram graphite arrow with its two-razor sharp broadhead edges left his bow at nearly 430 feet per second. It sprang from Dan's bow with a soft twang, flew and arched slightly downward.

The arrow impacted the leader's body above the left hip about two inches from the backbone, slicing slightly downward though the lower part of the left kidney, penetrating the lower intestine and exiting about four inches below his navel. The razor-sharp arrowhead struck the leader's erect penis and stopped after half severing it.

The leader's last conscious scream was a satisfying, "AHHHHH!"

The leader fell to his knees, staring in horror at the arrow sticking out of his abdomen and penetrating his erection.

The woman drew back her free leg and kicked the leader full in the face. He fell back onto the campfire, his hair and greasy beard flashing into flames. He lurched back to his feet, one dirty hand pawing at his flaming beard while the other hand attempted to grip the fatal arrow.

Dan quickly snapped another arrow out of his quiver, drew back and fired again at the leader. This arrow, designed to bring down a deer or other wild animal, struck him in the neck.

It was enough!

He reeled and staggered out of the camp not realizing that his sordid and evil life was over. Shortly after, they heard a crash in the dark forest, then silence.

At the same time, Tom's 32-inch, black graphite arrow, weighing approximately three hundred and sixty-two grams, traveling at about 415 feet per second, struck "Gar" in the front of his throat, penetrated through the larynx, the neck muscles and shattered on the vertebrate between C-3 and C-4. "Gar's" hands, grasping upward toward the arrow, never reached his throat before he hit the ground. He rolled over several times, snapping the arrow in half before rolling into a tiny tree, his legs twitched violently, and then were still.

Both Dan and Tom notched their next arrows and fired at the three remaining men. Due to the poor light, Dan's arrow narrowly missed a gaping face, but Tom's arrow struck a man's upper right arm, glanced off the bone and stopped halfway through the arm.

All three remaining men, excited by the impending rape, then horrified by the sudden and mysterious slaying of their leaders, seeing the silent arrows magically appearing out of the deep darkness, and hearing the terrible howls of the animals echoing in the dark forest, panicked and ran screaming from the camp. They could be heard crashing through the bushes in the distance. A long-drawn-out cry of a falling body was heard as one of the men fell over a cliff.

"Come on," Dan muttered. "Let's get our Sue."

Tom and Dan ran to Sue and untied her. Dan clasped her to his chest and held her trembling body, gently stroking her hair murmuring, "Its ok, now, Honey, its ok now." Dan could see that physically, Sue was all right, only shaken by the experience.

"Tom, take Sue to the edge of the campground and stay with her," Dan said. "Let me borrow your knife, they took mine."

Dan ran to the woman and dropped his power bow next to her.

She was lying on her side in the dirt and dust of the campground, her eyes darting frantically like a terrified doe deer caught in headlights of a speeding automobile.

She saw, materializing out of the darkness, a man carrying a power bow, and wearing a dark plaid shirt and jeans topped by a faded California Angel baseball cap. His grey eyes under light brown hair glinted in the flickering firelight. Her legs curled into a partial fetal position in defense of her nudity.

"It's ok now, you'll be all right, you're safe now," his composed soft voice was like cool water flowing over her terrified beating heart.

"It's over! You're safe now," his voice murmured softly.

"Just try to relax. I'm going to cut these ropes on your wrists."

A sharp tug and her arms were free. He retrieved her blouse and skirt and said, "Here, I'm going to slide your blouse back on, try and sit up."

"Easy now, easy. I'm going to wrap your skirt around you," he said quietly as he tied her skirt around her naked waist. "You will be all right now. Understand?"

She shuddered and nodded yes, her eyes wide, like pools of dark warm water. Her hands and wrists were cold, numb, and useless, just pieces of wood hanging from her shoulders. He rubbed her hands and arms briefly, and then said, "I've got to take care of my daughter."

He repeated, "You'll be all right, you're safe now!"

Dan then ran to Sue and Tom and held them in a tearful embrace.

"Easy Honey, its ok now, easy, easy, Baby." Dan soothed Sue, now relatively calm. Dan never asked specifically, but he thought she might not have seen the attempted rape and the shooting. She had been tied facing away from the campfire.

"Tom, I'm so proud of you, you saved our lives."

Tom's only reply was a tighter hug from his family and a sheepish grin of pride. After long moments of holding each other, a soft drum roll-like sound flowed around them. They separated, turned, and looked toward the woman by the campfire.

"What the. . . " Tom exclaimed.

Their mouths fell open.

They were astonished to see the woman they had saved petting and rubbing a huge cat-like animal and a brown German Shepard dog. The animals were lying on their backs and having their bellies rubbed. The cat-like animal was friendly growling so loud, they could hear it throughout the camp site. Both animals would roll over and lick the woman's arms or face and then lay back down to have their stomachs rubbed again.

"What on earth?" Dan whispered, amazed. "Tom, I bet those are the animals we heard howling before."

"I think so too, Dad."

The woman looked at the trio and her hoarse whisper flowed across the now calm clearing, "Thank you. Thank you so much!"

"Come over here and meet my babies," she called. "They wouldn't hurt you."

With some reluctance, all three approached the animals, Sue clutching onto Dan. The cat, a cougar, was large, with a broad face and wide head with soft brown fur, a dark spot and mouth gave it a slightly smiling expression. The tips of its ears and the end of its long tail were dark brown or almost black, but the soft fur on its belly was white. When it stood up, its shoulders reached to Sue's chest. The dog was a German Shepard. Both animals examined Dan and his family with soft intelligent eyes. The cat's eyes were yellowish-green orbs glowing in the campfire light.

The woman put limp hands on each of their heads and whispered gently to the animals, "It's ok, they're my friends."

"Come here, kids." She reached out and rubbed their hands with her still cold and lifeless hands, then took each of their hands and let the animals smell them.

The cougar licked Sue's hands. She giggled because it felt like wet, warm sandpaper.

"Can I pet him?" she asked.

"Sure, just scratch behind his ears and under his jaw, he loves that."

Sue slowly reached behind the cougar's head and softly, then more firmly, scratched behind his ears. The big cat's eyes squinted in pleasure, a soft rumbling emitting from his broad chest.

"His fur is so soft," Sue exclaimed.

"Sure, I brush his fur with a large wire brush, it helps keep him soft and clean," the woman said.

The cougar reached up and licked Sue's face with a moist swipe of his tongue. She hugged the cougar, unafraid!

"He likes me, he likes me," she exclaimed. His response could be heard throughout the camp.

Tom knelt to one knee and placed his power bow on the ground. He called gently to the dog to come to him.

The dog strolled over to Tom, smelled, and licked Tom's hands, and allowed Tom to scratch him behind the ears of his proud head. Its long drooping tail was wagging briskly.

Tom softly murmured to the dog, "Hi big boy, how are you doing?" and other boy-dog small talk. The dog snuggled up to his leg and lay down.

The woman struggled to her knees and with Dan's assistance, managed to stand up.

Dan asked, "Sue, would you tie or button her dress and blouse a little better, I don't think she can help herself yet."

While she lacked any feeling in her hands or an ability to grasp anything because her hands had been tied for so long, she fumbled to hold Dan's hands in hers. Her icy touch was like velvet, a spark flew between them. Her cold, limp hands reached up and touched his face as if memorizing his features.

"Come here, please," her voice caressed him. "I want you to meet my babies too."

She held Dan's hands and looked at the cougar. It looked up at her, left Sue's side and strolled to the woman. She took Dan's hands and let the cougar smell and lick him. Dan scratched the back of the cat's broad head between its ears. He had never seen such an animal up close; it had a presence about it that was intimidating, but its fur was soft. Its purr emitting from a powerful chest was a soft drum roll rumbling through the camp. The big cat's yellowish-green eyes examined Dan with an almost inherent superior intelligence and seemed to accept him as a slightly inferior equal. The dog smelled Dan's legs and hands, and submitted to a back rub.

"What's his name?" Sue asked referring to the cougar.

"Well, I really don't have a name for him, I raised him from a baby when he was two or three days old and he just comes when I call."

"Then, I'll name him," Sue declared.

"What about the rest of the gang members?" Dan asked, looking around, concerned. Getting captured once was enough.

The woman voice changed, "I'll take care of them."

She called the animals to her and held each head in her hands. She looked deep into their eyes: the cougar snarled with his lips pulled back showing his long, sharp, yellowish fangs, its high squeaky voice raised the hair on the back of Dan's head; the dog rumbled deep in its chest. Both animals left the campsite with silent bounds.

Dan and Tom dragged the body of the slain gang member away from the fire and heaved it into the bushes. They retrieved the backpacks, but their weapons were missing.

A minute later, they heard first one then a second blood curdling scream from a man's terrified voice in the darkened forest. They then heard an almost unearthly howl from the dog.

Then silence!

Dan glanced at the woman, her face a pale, grim mask.

"Tom, is there somewhere we can camp around here other than this place?" Dan asked.

"Sure, I left the bike and trailer in a small clearing behind us up the road. It looked like it had a stream there, too."

"Let's spend the night there, not here," Sue whimpered.

"I agree, p-p-please," the woman said, softly. She swayed, tears staining the dirt on her face. Both Tom and Dan grabbed her and gently sat her down.

"Easy now, it's ok now, you're safe with us," Dan murmured as he gently rubbed her back.

"It's all right now," Tom said as he massaged her hands.

"I-I-I'm sorry, I was just so scared," she said, shaking her head, her body quivering, her tears flying. "G-G-Give me a minute, I-I'll be all right."

She continued with a shudder racking her body, "This place is too horrible to spend any more time." Her voice caressed Dan like the soft fur on a kitten's back.

"What about the animals?" Sue asked.

After a shuddering deep breath, the woman said through her tears, "Oh they'll find us, no matter where we are."

"In fact, I can assure you that we will not be bothered by anyone else," she stated flatly. A cold shiver ran down Dan's back when he heard that pronouncement.

"You see," she mumbled, her body still quivering. "The men had guns and I was afraid they would kill my babies if I called them. The wind was blowing away from us and my babies didn't smell them until too late. Those, those men surprised me before I could call them."

She explained softly, "I can call my babies and they would return to me, but I have to hold them to communicate what needs to be done. It takes time; they are both highly intelligent, but they are both very independent. By the time I did that, those . . . those vermin would have killed my babies!"

Dan was impressed, not only by what the woman was saying, but how she was saying it. She seemed to have a soft face covering a hard exterior protecting a delicate and sensitive interior.

They found the bikes that Dan and Sue had been riding and the woman's backpack.

The woman looked at them and said, "I, I can't walk. I can hardly feel my legs and hands."

"That's ok. We'll put you on our bike and hold you. Just try to relax," said Tom.

Her body appeared to be firm, but her callused hands were soft on Dan's shoulders and neck as he carried her.

"Sue, Honey, go and kick some dirt over that fire, please," Dan said. "Make sure it's out."

They waited for Sue to put out the fire and rejoin them. The stars were so bright that they could easily see the road.

They balanced and supported the woman on Dan's bike while they trudged slowly back up the road. Sue was walking her bike alongside them, the woman's backpack draped over Sue's handlebars.

Dan asked, "Tom, how did you know exactly where we were?

"Well, once I saw you, with your hands up, I knew that something was wrong. I left the guns there because I didn't want to alert anybody else. Do you remember that overpass with that other probable camp?"

Dan nodded, "Good thinking."

Tom continued, "I took the bows and crept down the side of the road; there are small trees all over. It was dark when I got to the camp, but I came onto it on the other side. I could see where Sue was, but it took me quite a while to crawl around to your side of the camp to find you, Dad. I didn't know how many of them there were or if they had a sentry guarding the camp."

"Besides, they were drunk," Tom added nonchalantly. "And it wasn't much."

"Tom, you saved our lives!" Sue exclaimed. She stopped and hugged him again, her big eyes brimming with admiration.

Dan reached out and grabbed his son's shoulder, "Son, your 'wasn't much' saved our lives and this woman from a fate worse than death."

Dan looked his son straight in the eye and said, "Tom, I've never been prouder of you than this moment."

The woman stopped the bike, reached and wrapped her arms around Tom and just hugged him. She couldn't grasp him since her hands were still mostly useless, but her arms held him, her tears dampening his shirt. An embarrassed, but pleased Tom led them back to where he had left the bike and trailer. They lowered the woman and helped her sit on one of their sleeping bags. The illumination from the Milky Way gave them enough light to see what they were doing.

"Tom, please get some firewood. I'll get a pot so we can boil some water," said Dan. While Tom dragged larger pieces of wood to the fire, Dan and Sue used some of their precious freeze-dried supplies since it was too dark for Tom to hunt.

By this time, the dog had returned and lay down by the woman. Tom and Sue later fed the dog the small leftovers. It seemed that he took a liking to the kids and enjoyed being with them.

While Sue was cooking one of the freeze-dried meals, Dan went to the stream flowing quietly about fifty feet away and moistened a towel with cold mountain water. He returned to the woman and said, "This is going to hurt."

"Close your eyes now," he said as he gently washed her dusty and dirty face with the stream's icy water. There was caked and dried blood on her face and in her matted, dirt-filled hair. He carefully washed her dusty swollen lips. It took several trips to finally get her face clean. She gasped a few times when Dan touched a particularly sore spot, but otherwise said little.

"I think you'll have some black and blue eyes for a couple of days," Dan said. "Sue, can I borrow your towel to dry her face?"

"Sure, Dad. Just a second and I'll get it for you."

"Here, I'll dry her face for you," Sue said as she gently wiped the woman's face. Sue thought it was a little like washing her Ginger's face.

"We don't even know your name."

The woman smiled at Sue, "I'm Lorraine Fairly, but my friends call me Lor."

"Hi! I'm Sue Peterson, that's my brother, Tom, and my dad."

"Hi, my first name is Dan. I kind of believe that it's good to meet you," Dan smiled.

Lor was regaining feeling in her hands and arms, but she still had difficulty in holding anything. She kept her deep, dark soulful eyes on Dan as he, with almost infinite gentleness, washed her face and hands. Dan locked eyes with her several times with fundamental human desires and needs flowing effortlessly and silently between them. Dan could hardly break the eye to eye, or more precisely, heart to heart contact.

Sue and Dan had to feed her because her hands were still useless. Sue gently teased, "All right, open wide now," as if she was feeding one of her dolls or like she used to feed her baby sister, Ginger. The woman smiled at Sue as she "opened wide." She still could not hold anything in her hands, but she said that they were tingling almost unbearably. She said that she hadn't eaten all day and was very thirsty and hungry.

When Sue fed her a cup of cold water and a little dribbled down her chin onto her shirt, Sue scolded her with a smile, "You have got to learn to drink better than that."

Later, Sue fell asleep in Dan's arms, only occasionally whimpering in her sleep. Dan eventually tucked her in her sleeping bag as the nighttime temperatures fell to the fifties. Tom stretched out by the fire with the dog under one hand. He was soon fast asleep.

Dan and Lor talked long into the night. He unrolled her sleeping bag and carried her to it. Her arms, legs and body were very painful from the beating she had received and she could hardly move.

"Here, I have some aspirin tablets; take two now and two more in the morning," Dan said. "I've got Tylenol and ibuprofen, but this should work faster. That's all I have in the way of pain killers," he apologized.

"Thank you," she whimpered when he tucked the sleeping bag up around her shoulders to keep her warm.

He made some precious coffee and helped her drink it. As he periodically added more wood to the fire, the clearing became quiet and secure as the stars moved slowly overhead, the fragrant towering pine trees stood like sentinels around them as if to protect this small group of humans from the rest of the world. Other than their two quiet voices, the only sound was the snap and crackle of the pine wood in the fire.

"Where are you from, Dan?" Lor smiled through badly bruised lips. "Besides being sent by my guardian angel."

"We're from Southern California, traveling up to Durango to try to find my little daughter, Ginger. Once we find her, we're going to try to make it to my parent's home in Wisconsin."

"How about you, Lor. What are you doing out here in the wilderness?"

She had been visiting friends back in the mountains and was returning to Durango when she was captured. She had been surprised early that morning by two of the men and had been dragged to the camp. Apparently, the leader and two other men had just returned to the camp when Dan had the misfortune to come along. She told Dan how she had fought, but that she had been overpowered by the two men. She said that she had kicked one man in the groin which was the reason for majority of the beating she received.

"Just a minute," Dan said as he walked back to the stream. "I want to get this towel cold again for your face. You need to keep your face cold to decrease the swelling."

As he pressed the cold towel to her face, she asked him, "What happened? What happened to the world, Dan? It has something to do with electricity, but nobody knows anything."

"Well, I do know what happened," Dan said heavily. "Sometimes I wish I didn't know."

He paused for a minute and then said, "Let me give you a little background, and then you'll understand."

Dan told her of his former work in Southern California and of his conversation with his friend, Joe Robinson. He told of the meteor coming to earth containing the life force, and what Joe Robinson had tried to do to fight it.

He concluded by saying, "My friend felt, and I believe him, that as of this moment, that force, that Green Ghost, was unconquerable."

"I thought something like that had happened. A number of people around Durango and out in La

Plata County lost their lives when that stuff attacked before people started realizing what was causing the accidents."

After a moment's silence, she continued, "It didn't hit us too hard, however. We have some nasty winter storms up here and our electrical power goes out frequently. Most everyone has a few gas or propane lanterns and wood stoves in case of an emergency, and so we can easily make do without electricity."

"You said sometime about your daughter, what was her name?"

"My littlest daughter's name is Ginger and she is six years old now." Dan told of his ex-wife, Kathy's psychological problems and her problems with his kids, Kathy's leaving him to join a commune or something up near Durango, and of his and his kids' long journey and the search for their beloved Ginger.

They talked long into the now gentle, now quiet, starlit night, the big cat occasionally strolling through the camp. The cat would stop for a back or belly rub and then wander off. The second time he came into the camp, Dan whistled softly for the cat to come to him. The cat looked for long seconds at Dan, then ambled over. Dan scratched him behind the ears, then down his back. The cat rolled over and Dan rubbed his belly. The purring could be heard yards away. The big cat reminded Dan of a few much smaller regular cats on his parents' farm in Wisconsin, they too would purr when someone rubbed their head or back.

"You're just a big old kitty, aren't you?" Dan murmured to the big cat.

"I am really impressed, Dan," Lor's velvet voice caressed him. "He will accept anyone I tell him to, but very rarely does he voluntarily go to a person."

Periodically, Dan walked down to the stream and soaked the towel with icy mountain stream water so he could place a cold compress on Lor's face. Each time, Lor's eyes searched Dan's face as if to memorize or engrave it in her mind. He rubbed her hands and arms to assist in regaining her blood circulation.

They slept late the next morning, a noisy red headed woodpecker pounding on a tree woke them. Dan, an infrequent dreamer, dreamed of being lost in the depths of soft brown eyes. He awoke to feelings and emotions he hadn't had for a long time. . ..

━━◆◆◆◆◆◆━━

CHAPTER SIX

"Dad, do I have to? I don't want to go back there!"

"Well, Sue, do you want to stay here by yourself?"

"Dan, if it's all right with you, your Sue will be with my baby, he'll protect her," Lor said.

Sue nodded at her father, her big eyes wide with pleasure.

They had decided to return to the men's camp to retrieve their weapons, but before they left their little camp, Lor rubbed the cougar's broad head in her hands and called Sue over to her. Lor focused on the big cat; the cat's yellowish eyes gazed into Lor's face, then it turned and purring, nuzzled up to Sue.

She giggled as she hugged the cougar, "His whiskers tickle me."

"You wear your jacket," Dan warned. Tom and Dan exchanged glances; they knew that she kept her little .22 automatic in her jacket pocket.

Dan looked at the big cat in the tranquil morning light as it rolled onto its back, its soft underbelly being rubbed by Sue. It looked even more intimidating in the sunlight with its powerful chest and sleek body weighing about a hundred and fifty pounds. The animal's broad face, framed by about a dozen long white "whiskers" seemed to hold a perpetual expression of quizzical amusement as if he had looked upon the world and wondered what all the fuss was about.

"In California, we would call him a mountain lion," said Dan.

As Dan, Tom, Lor and her dog walked slowly back to the men's camp, she clutched onto Dan's arm hobbling like an old woman. "I'm sorry Dan, but I can't walk any faster, my back and legs hurt too much," she said, her face pale with perspiration beading on her forehead.

The men's camp was a filthy, disorganized dump. Empty wine and whiskey bottles were strewn about, pieces of rotten partially eaten food lay on broken plates, and piles of equally dirty clothes (a few of which appeared to be blood stained) emitted a foul, decaying odor. Even Lor's dog seemed disinclined to enter the camp, he lay down on the outside seeming to stand guard.

"Look, Tom, Lor, these are booking slips from a jail," Dan gestured with some yellowed, crumbled documents he found in one of the tents. "According to the slips, these men were inmates at some kind of honor farm south of us. I bet they escaped when The Green Ghost attacked."

"It looks like these guys robbed anyone who came along," Tom said.

"Ah, Lor, Tom, I don't think they let anyone go either," Dan said, pointing down a ravine at the back of the camp. "Don't look down there. There are things that you don't want to see." The stench of decaying flesh hung over the ravine with a cloud of flies. He shook his head, "We couldn't get down there without a gas mask."

The loot that the men had captured consisted primarily of money, watches, rings, and other jewelry that might have been valuable before the arrival of the life force. Dan, after his conversation with his friend, Joe Robinson, knew that money was useless. There no longer was a United States government, nor any other government either, for that matter.

"What were these men thinking of?" Dan asked rhetorically. "They couldn't use that stuff for trade, money is essentially useless now, and of what use are rings and jewelry?"

The food that the men had was mostly spoiled or rotten. Tom found their weapons piled with about a dozen other handguns and rifles; the remaining weapons were old and uncleaned with little usable ammunition.

"Dan, Tom, would you help me look through these personal things?" Lor asked. "I want to find any identification or belongings that someone might remember. We'll take those things back to Durango in the event that someone is missing a relative or loved one."

After a search of the filthy camp, they retrieved a small pile of drivers' licenses and wallets, lockets, watches, rings, and small trinkets that someone might recognize.

"I'll give these to Deputy Hank, our Deputy Sheriff for our area. Maybe someone reported these people or things missing," Lor said, her deep eyes somber.

After retrieving their arrows, and locating a shovel in the camp, Dan and Tom buried the men they had shot. The leader had stumbled about twenty feet from the camp before he fell onto a small pine tree, crushing it.

Tom shook his head bitterly, "Even in dying, he simply had to ruin something: a perfectly good little pine tree. What we did for them is a lot more than they deserve."

They walked slowly back to their camp, Lor clutching onto Tom and Dan for support. Her walking consisted of one painful step after another while the bruises on her face, arms and legs were turning black and blue.

Dan touched her forehead, her soft skin felt warm, "I think you have a slight fever, but it's probably due to the bruises. We'll give you some more aspirin when we get back to our camp."

At the camp, Lor retrieved a bar of soap and a couple of towels from her backpack.

"Come on, Sue. How about a bath?" she asked.

Sue looked at her father for permission.

Dan nodded his approval, "It's all right, I think there is a pool about a hundred yards around that bend in the stream. Bring along some soap, your towel, and a change of clothes. You can wash those you're wearing as well as your other clothes that need washing. I think we'll be here for a few days until she's able to travel."

Lor took Sue and they slowly walked around a bend in the stream to take a bath, the big cat following, its long tail twitching from side to side. Dan could hear them laughing and splashing in the cold, crystal clear, mountain stream water. Later, a shiny faced squeaky-clean Sue with Lor, still heavily limping, returned to the camp with washed and clean clothes. Tom and Dan had strung a rope between two trees which served as a clothesline.

"Daddy, she's got some really bad bruises on her legs and side," Sue worried. "There's a bruise that looks like a footprint from a shoe on her back, too."

"Well, there's not much I can do about that. We'll keep cold compresses on them for a while."

Tom and Dan looked at each other and said, "Your turn."

They laughed, and together, walked around the bend for their bath. After putting their change of clothes on the bank by the pond, Tom simply emptied his pockets, took off his shoes and belt, and jumped into the steam, clothes, and all. After shouting at the sudden shock of the cold water, Tom started splashing water on his father, yelling for him to jump in too. Dan, less exuberant, took off his clothes and slowly waded in. The cold water was like steaming ice on sweaty, dirt encrusted bodies, but it was refreshing after the sweaty ride up from New Mexico and the capture by the escaped inmates.

After the bath, Tom and Dan walked back to the camp, their chests bare. For some reason, Dan's clean jeans seemed too large. "I thought these fit me when we left Southern California," he complained to Sue.

Sue was drying Lor's hair and trying to tie it into a ponytail, but she looked at her father's bare chest. "Dad! You've lost weight. Look, Tom."

"Sure enough," Tom grinned. "I never would have believed that beneath that old flabby body, you had those muscles."

"Do you realize, Lor, that he used to be old, fat, flabby and dumpy looking?" Tom asked. "Now, he's no longer fat and flabby."

"Yeah," Sue giggled, "Now, he's just old and dumpy looking."

"Thanks a lot, kids. I'll remember your admiring comments next time you ask for an allowance."

They spent several days at the camp, just resting and trying to help Lor recover. Her hands and arms recovered quickly and by the second day, she was able to use them normally while the bruises on the rest of her body took nearly a week to subside.

Dan discovered that by just watching the big cat, he could tell if there was something going on in the surrounding area. The cougar's small rounded black tipped ears normally were flattened or laying close to his head but when it was alarmed or curious, its ears stood up straight; its large yellow orbited eyes seemed to concentrate their focus like a commanding, omniscient magnifying glass. Sue, and Dan too, for that matter, were fascinated with the big cat. Sue and the cat played together almost as if the big cat was simply an overgrown kitten.

"Doesn't he ever get wild or vicious," Dan asked.

"Oh no. From the very first day that I found him, I made sure that he knew he couldn't scratch or bite anyone I made him smell. I gently touched his nose with a piece of paper if he did something wrong. As it turned out, both my dog and cat just sort of grew up together. This last winter when it was so cold and below zero and snowing, I found them snuggled up in the haystack almost sleeping next to each other."

And strangely, as large, and as powerful as the big cat clearly was, it seemed to be infinitely gentle when it played with Sue.

Tom went hunting with the dog and kept them well fed with a continual supply of pheasant or rabbit. When he wasn't hunting, Tom and "his dog" just explored the area around their camp; they had become almost inseparable but both refused to return to the "other" place.

More than once, Lor thought to herself, that while she had lost her babies to two kids, she might have gained. . .

"I used to be a licensed beautician," Lor told Dan on about the fourth day. "I left the beauty field to work as a legal secretary because I got sick of coddling pampered rich old ladies and getting groped by their old men. I was going to college because I really wanted something better, but when the force or whatever you call it came, I had to have a job, so I went back to cutting hair."

She looked at the Petersons, "I think all of you need a haircut."

Lor had carried her scissors and combs with her. She trimmed Sue's hair and cut her bangs off her face. "Well, now, you look more human and less like a sheepdog," Tom teased. It had been several months since Tom's hair had been cut, and since he usually wore it long anyway, it was a shock when he asked Lor to give him a crew cut. He went in appearance from a shaggy St. Bernard to a sleek Great Dane! He walked around for nearly a week rubbing the top of his head.

Dan laughed, "You should wear a hat now, otherwise you'll get sunburned on the top of your head."

"Sure, Dad. Now it's your turn." In truth, while Dan had tried to shave every other day, his hair hadn't been cut since they left Southern California and it was uncomfortably long and shaggy.

Dan sat down on a log that Lor was using as a barber's chair and smiled at her, "Just a trim please."

She smiled back but both could feel the magnetism of the other. For some strange reason, what was normally a twenty- minute haircut took over an hour. Her hip or abdomen would occasionally brush Dan's shoulder, or she would stand straddling his legs while she cut the hair on the top of his head. Her full breasts, covered by a reddish plaid outdoor shirt, strained toward Dan's lips while she was in front of him. He could imagine dark nipples standing up, reaching, reaching . . . His groin ached from just being near her.

Dan could feel her presence and could smell her mountain stream-fresh desiring woman's body next to him. Once her breasts nearly touched his face and lips as she reached over him to snip just one more hair. . . She would brush the cut hair off his head and shoulders, periodically gently touching his face to ensure no hair lingered there as her fingers did. . .

While she refused to meet Dan's eyes as she finished his haircut, his eyes were liquid pools of need and desire. He just wanted to hold her body to his and, Dam (!), for once in his life, he was sorry that his kids were with him.

After Lor finished the haircut, Dan walked to the icy cold stream to wash his face and head, and more importantly, to cool his aching groin. He hadn't hurt this much since he was a teenager in Wisconsin, necking in the back seat of his car with a healthy farm girl.

Later that afternoon, Lor asked, "Can I see those postcards your little one sent to you?"

She looked at the postcards for a moment and said, "Why, I think I know exactly where this is."

The undivided attention of the Petersons was almost a physical blow.

"This is a small post office right on the outskirts of a tiny town a few miles generally north of Durango."

She continued thoughtfully, "If I remember correctly, it's in very mountainous country, one road in and out."

She asked, "Is this some kind of religious camp that your little one is in?"

"Yes, Yes!"

"There are a couple of them in that area. Somebody saw the Madonna or a cross or a star or something up in that area a couple of years ago and now, half of the nuts in the state congregate in those camps."

"Most of those camps have no electricity or running water, a few just live in hovels dug in the hillside, just waiting to be saved or something."

She added, "La Plata County and the state tried to enforce better living conditions a couple of years ago. As a matter of fact, a couple of the ministers or leaders or whatever came to my boss and asked him to represent them. One of them was even dressed in purple and green robes with nothing else on." She giggled, "He had the skinniest legs! My boss refused to handle their case because they wanted to pay him in prayer or Tuesday morning services or some dumb thing."

She smiled, "I told him absolutely not because I couldn't pay my bills with Tuesday morning services."

"We can stay at my place while we figure out what to do about your Ginger," Lor said. Dan noticed warmly that it was now "We!" and nodded his thanks.

Once they left, it took more than a week for them to make their way into Durango and out to Lor's farm. She had difficulty in walking and riding one of the bikes at first, but eventually the swelling in her body subsided and her muscles loosened. In addition, of course, since Dan and his family didn't have a spare bike, someone was always walking.

Lor's face lost most of its swelling, but the black and blue bruises around her eyes remained sensitive to touch for several weeks.

"You look like our pet raccoon," Tom teased.

"I think that you might have a slight hairline fracture around your left eye or left orbit area, but without x-rays, there is nothing I can do," Dan said.

Her face and eyes captivated Dan. Her full lips and a slightly wide mouth smiled frequently through her long light brown hair. When they shared glances, Dan kept losing himself in her big, deep eyes. Dan felt like a frisky young colt. He hoped that he wasn't showing his interest in Lor, and tried to hide his feelings when the kids were around. Her frequent touch on his arm or hand was like a gentle spark between them.

He had an enormous amount of respect for her. When he tenderly with a very light touch wiped away her tears because her pain grew too much to bear, she never once complained!

When her pain increased, Dan noticed that the animals were always nearby. They would whimper and whine for her and lick her hands as if, somehow, they could cure her pain. At first, when Dan pressed cold compresses to her face, both animals growled deep in their chests.

Dan murmured, "Easy guys, easy, this is supposed to help her."

Dan let them smell his hands and the cold compresses before he again touched Lor's face. The next time, both animals rubbed their bodies against Dan's legs as if to give him encouragement. Dan occasionally felt that he was sorry the men didn't survive longer: he wanted them to suffer as Lor was suffering.

Dan found that she was articulate, sensitive, and fun to be with. She had managed to eke out a survival of sorts when normal citizens and neighbors were abandoning reason or concern for others. Dan communicated ideas, thoughts, and feelings with her that he hadn't shared with another human being for a long time. He was fascinated to learn that her interests in music were like his: all over the spectrum: from Patsy Cline to Mahler's First.

Tom asked, "I know who Patsy Cline was because we have-had," he amended sadly, "a record by her, but who is Mahler."

Lor explained to Tom and Sue who Gustav Mahler was and why he was famous. She concluded, "I think you might have liked some of his music, it is so, so huge. Each time you listen to his music, you get something more out of it. I hope that someday we can hear his music again."

She paused with a slight smile remembering, "His music, particularly his 'First' always reminds me of these snow-capped mountains, an occasional melodic rain shower running through it, the deep canyons with violent rivers running through them, the occasional crescendo of lightening striking these tall fragrant pine trees." Her arms were outstretched encompassing the mountains, "Grand vistas-all!"

"Do you know Bolero by Ravel?" Tom asked.

"Oh no," Dan exclaimed, knowing what was coming.

"Sure, that's a classic piece by Maurice Ravel. Why?"

"We don't need to go into this, kids," Dan stated flatly.

Tom laughed, "Sure we do. Lor, one day, Sue and I were coming home from school and as we were walking down the sidewalk near our house, we could hear this very loud music coming from our home."

"We could hear it all over the neighborhood," Sue giggled.

"Anyway, when we walked in our house, there was Dad standing in front of the stereo with his eyes closed. The stereo was blasting out Bolero and Dad was conducting the music with a large dinner fork by waving his arms and body to the music. The music and heavy drums were rattling the windows, when it stopped with that downward beat, the silence was incredible. Sue and I were standing behind him and he never saw us. We started clapping. I thought he was going to have a heart attack!"

Dan's only reply to the laughter was a sputtered "Aw."

Dan loved his kids with all his heart, but he had been so lonely so long for adult companionship that he almost couldn't stop talking. At night, his dreams were full of long light brown hair surrounding a deep set of eyes over a wide generous mouth reaching out to

touch his. . .

Of course, Dan's attempt to hide his feelings only caused them to be much more evident. It didn't take very long for Tom and Sue to realize what their father and Lor felt for each other, even if Dan and Lor refused to acknowledge such feelings.

During a moment alone while on the road, Tom asked Sue, "Did you hear Dad whistling the other day?"

"Sure did, I thought it sounded like the cry of a wounded buzzard."

She quietly asked, "What do you think of her?"

"Well," Tom thoughtfully replied, "I think I really like her; she never complains about her injuries and she treats us with respect. Do you remember how. . . how . . .," he searched for a word, "how 'bitchy' Kathy always was? She always kept demanding more and more from Dad, more money, more jewelry, more gifts for her, and how badly she treated us after Ginger was born!

"You may not remember, but Dad tried to find another job, just to keep enough money coming in because Kathy was spending everything Dad made. Right after Ginger was born, I had to borrow money from friends just to buy school supplies. Kathy had, just had to contribute to something!" Tom remembered bitterly.

Sue said, "I've never told Dad this, but I was glad when she left. I only wish she hadn't taken Ginger. I love Ginger so much! And you're right, I like Lor a lot too, she's. . . she's so cool."

Tom reflectively continued, "You know, Lor said that we could stay at her home while we look for Ginger. And, if you remember, not once has she asked for anything in return. Not once! Kathy would have asked for payment of money or jewelry or something. You don't remember much about Mom, but Lor is a lot like her: warm, generous, and I think Lor really likes Dad."

Dan, on the other hand, while not aware of his kids' interest, could not recall when he had felt so good. He had lost his excess weight, his body was firm, his legs were solid from peddling his bike the many miles, and his lungs were in great condition. He was with his kids whom he loved, and they were coming closer to a major goal: to find their Ginger.

About a day's journey outside of Durango, Dan was walking alongside Sue who was peddling her bike, and he asked quietly, "Honey, what do you think of Lor?"

She smiled at her father, "She is so nice. She never complains and I know she still hurts. I like her a lot."

She paused for a second and glanced sideways at her dad, "I think you like her a lot, too, don't you, Daddy?" Dan could not stop the smile and the blush flooding his face. Sue started giggling so much that she nearly fell off her bike. They hugged, a warm moment of shared human secrets in the middle of the mountainous wilderness.

Lor led them through the southern part of Durango, past the now deserted and useless airport, and past the abandoned South Durango-Bodo Industrial Park area. She pointed out the start of the narrow-gauge railroad station.

"Oh look, they're working on that old steam engine. Maybe they'll get it working again."

They rode and walked past some of the old bright reddish bicolored historical buildings with Lor explaining a little history of each building.

A considerable number of people were busily engaged in trade by hauling goods to an informal market near the narrow- gauge railroad. Once at the market, interestingly, most people refused to accept United States cash or paper money, and instead, negotiated for goods or services.

"We've got about 20,000 permanent residents in Durango itself and about 27,000 more in La Palta County. Fort Lewis College up on the hill, our local college where I went to school has about 4000 or so students. The tourists don't count, they come and go, but we're always here." Lor smiled with a sense of pride, "We're a pretty hardy bunch here."

Many of the people that they met knew Lor. She was obviously well-liked and respected. Frequently invitations were offered to spend the day and eat. When Lor's friends or acquaintances heard that the Petersons had just come from Southern California, they could hardly leave the Petersons alone, the townspeople were so desperate for information and news.

Lor didn't want to delay much on the highway or spend much time talking to her friends. She borrowed a bike from a friend with the promise to return it in a few days. Later, Dan realized that he hadn't seen the cougar since they arrived near Durango.

"Where's your big cat?"

"I sent him home. He isn't comfortable in a city or with groups of strangers. He will stay with me if I make him, but he's usually a solitary animal and prefers the wide-open spaces."

Dan, unsure of the townspeople's opinion of the religious camps, said quietly to his kids, "I don't think we should discuss our search for Ginger and where she might be until we find out how the locals feel about those camps."

Tom nodded somberly, "I think that's a good idea. Those people in the camps have to get food and supplies somehow and they might have friends down here."

They arrived at Lor's place near sunset. Her home, not too far from Durango, nestled up against a towering mountain and overlooked a small valley with a small tumbling steam running through the valley. Starting from Lor's home, extending southeastward into the valley was a cleared area of about forty acres in size surrounded by trees. It was obvious that in previous years, the forty acres had been farmed and cultivated, now, it is overgrown with alfalfa and sweet clover.

Several generations ago, her ranch style house had started out as a log cabin and over the years, additions had changed it to a sprawling single-story home with plenty of bedrooms. Each bedroom overlooked either the valley or the mountain. The center of her house, the original log cabin, had smoke darkened high wooden beams, to the side of the living room was situated a stone fireplace large enough to roast an ox. A now useless television set and a stereo system sat against one wall. A very pleasant aroma of burnt hickory and pine logs permeated the home. The living room had large, insulated bay windows overlooking the valley and surrounding mountains. Her ample kitchen contained an old, black, but very usable wood stove.

"My father put that old wood stove in when I was a child. We lose electric power out here frequently, and that old stove will burn wood, coal, and bottled, natural gas," Lor explained. "I've got three large tanks of gas which should be enough to last for a long time."

She had a small garden that needed tending, plus an old barn housing a now useless small tractor and an old John Deere combine. She had stalls in the barn for a few horses with some hay and grain left from last year.

"My babies sleep in the barn except when it gets very cold, then they beg to come into the house," Lor said.

"They're so spoiled," she smiled as she gently roughhoused with the dog.

"This is really nice, Lor," Tom said as he looked around the living room.

"Thank you," Lor said, pleased. "Come, let me show you to the bedrooms. I have enough space for an army here."

She lit several kerosene lamps and escorted the kids to "their" individual bedrooms. She smiled, "Tom, you can use this room as long as you want. Sue, this other bedroom is yours for as long as you need it. There's linen in the hall closet and towels in the cabinet in the bathroom. You'll have to use the outhouse outside because we lost our power. Make yourself at home."

"We can unpack our things in the morning, kids. We've come a long way to get here before dark and I am exhausted," Dan said. Tom and Dan brought in firewood and they lit a roaring fire in the fireplace and a cooking fire in the wood stove. Sue took off her shoes and socks and nearly fell asleep before dinner.

Lor pointed out the large cistern and shower in the back of the house. The cistern, up inside the roof of the original log cabin, was kept full of water by an ingenious arrangement of pipes and storage valves storing both rainwater and water from a spring higher up on the mountain. She said that the nice thing about the cistern inside the house was that it didn't freeze in the winter.

Immediately after dinner, Dan took a towel, borrowed a bar of soap from Lor, and had a refreshing and very cold shower.

When he got back into the house, both kids had gone to "their" rooms and were fast asleep. Lor took a quick shower while Dan, carrying a small kerosene lamp, looked in on his kids. It was the first time they had slept in clean sheets for quite some time. He covered Sue with a soft blanket, her hair sprawled out on her pillow like a shining halo. She did not even move as he gently kissed her cheeks. Tom was sound asleep but he had managed to take off his shoes and pants. Dan covered him also, noticing that Tom had the start of a beard. Dan smiled wistfully at his son, knowing that soon, all too soon, he too would be a man.

Dan and Lor sprawled out in front of the somewhat slumbering fireplace, just relaxing, Lor drying her damp hair. They watched a full moon creep up over the mountain tops flooding the valley with light. The room was warm, lit only by the firelight and the moonlight. Long moments passed, each feeling a tension in the air, an awareness of each other, an anticipation . . .

Looking deep into the flickering firelight, a thought came to Dan, *What the hell am I doing? Here, I'm with a woman who I'm falling in love with and I have absolutely nothing to offer her. I'm trying to find my little daughter and if we find her, we're on our way home.*

A feeling deep in Dan said, *I can't lead her on, she's too precious a person to do that to!*

Dan quietly cleared his throat, "Lor, I want to say something. . ." when warm fingers touched his lips.

"Shhh," came the whispered interruption.

Lor took a deep breath, slowly sat up and stretched. She loosened her hair and let it fall naturally over her shoulders. She looked at Dan, their eyes meeting with slumbering pools of need and desire. She rolled over and semi-crouched over Dan, her still slightly damp, but fresh smelling hair falling in his face. She slowly moved her face down and her lips gently touched his face, his eyes, and his cheeks. Slowly, her lips reached out and gently, oh so gently, touched his lips.

Dan moaned deep in his throat; he could spend his entire life lost in her mouth.

Their lips parted, their breath starting to quicken, again, their lips touched, longer this time and harder. Lor's hair fell around them, Dan reached up and gently stroked her face, bringing it down to his searching lips. His lips tasted her lips, now open with a flavor of mint toothpaste, their tongues touching gently, as a butterfly's wings, fluttering now, more and more. A moan like a soft wind escaped from Lor's mouth. Dan gently kissed her face, then her neck, first one side and then the other, then back to her lips, greedy on his. His lips searched down her throat, parting the shirt that covered her upper body.

He slowly unbuttoned her shirt and kissed the part that was revealed. Slowly, as if they had all the time in the world, they undressed each other, his heart pounding heavily in his chest.

When Dan unbuttoned her shirt to release her brassiere covered breasts, a shutter ran through her body. Her breasts were standing like ivory statutes in the moonlight, her hidden nipples causing the statutes to point straight out. He slowly unhooked her stark white brassiere and loosened the bra straps from her shoulders. Before he released her breasts from their bondage, his lips found hers and their hands grasped each other's face to hold while their lips became more demanding.

Dan's lips broke from Lor's and again found their way down to her breasts. He gently and slowly pulled her bra off her full breasts, allowing them to spring free. The moon and the flickering firelight cast glistening rays of soft light, highlighting her proud ivory-colored statues. They were perfect, as if made like a statue of white marble by an admiring sculptor. Dan's lips kissed softly at the bottom of each breast, and then he blew gently on each dark round nipple. Her breath was panting now. With each breath on first her right, then her left dark nipple, she moaned softly, her hands clutching, almost mindlessly, his body.

He cupped each breast and lovingly took a nipple in his mouth. It tasted fresh, like a mountain spring. He gently twisted each nipple with his tongue, each stood higher, as if each was demanding to be touched, to be fondled, to be kissed! Moans were coming from deep within her chest.

Her hands were roaming over his nude chest, fondling his nipples, and just grasping him. She felt his belt buckle, and with a small struggle, released it. She pulled his pants off him and cast them aside. In the meantime, Dan's lips were traveling downward. They paused at her navel, alternatively wetly penetrating, and blowing it dry. He fumbled for the clasp that held her calico skirt on and released it. He pulled it free and it followed the general direction of his trousers.

His lips were still traveling downward. He nuzzled the top of her stark white panties with his tongue and lips, and while growling softly, grasped her panties with his teeth and pulled them off her willing slim hips! She laughed gently as he did this and lifted her hips to assist him.

Her skin was like soft velvet. His lips returned to her mouth to be mashed together. Her proud breasts were crushed against his chest, his curly hair slightly tickling her erect nipples. He broke the kiss and again blew gently on each nipple, taking each one in his mouth.

He released her breasts and his lips started downward, kissing as he went. As his lips touched the dark triangle at the top of her legs, her body went rigid, moaning his name with desire. Lor spread her legs, her breathing simply panting. When Dan kissed and nuzzled the soft inside of her legs, her sweet woman's smell flooded his senses. As he took a long loving swipe with his tongue, separating that which needed to be parted, her body arched and she cried out his name. While her hands clutched his head, his tongue and lips treasured her as she climaxed, crying, "Oh My Darling, My Darling!"

She pulled him up to her face and almost ravished his lips. She abruptly changed positions, and now her lips were traveling downwards. Both of her hands held his throbbing erection as her lips and mouth smoothly and wetly clasped him! Dan thought he was going to explode; it had been so long! There had been very little sex since Ginger had been born, and he had forgotten what it was like to have a woman love him. Lor's mouth and lips moistly stroked him while her hands gently caressed his sack. Dan twisted and groaned; the feeling was almost too much!

Lor suddenly released Dan and crouched over him, straddling him, her breasts floating down onto his face, her long fine hair flooding around his face and lips. She moved her glistening nude body down and Dan could feel her moist entrance demanding to be filled with him. She moved slowly, and he could feel himself enter her! She was very wet and tight; she grasped when he gently entered her and then shuddered as she pushed herself onto him.

She straightened and Dan slowly slid all the way in her! Her vortex was consuming him in a white heat of need and desire, their movements now slow, then rapid, then again slow! Her body was trembling, her face was smilingly angelic, then fiercely passionate. The moonlight and firelight reflected and highlighted her body above him. Her long hair swept over her full breasts, first hiding, then revealing one dark protruding nipple, then the other. Dan reached up to touch her nipples. As he caressed them, and bent his face up to kiss and suck each nipple, her body arched and convulsed as another climax racked her. She started to move up and down on him, crying, "Come, Come, Oh please, My Darling, Come to me!"

Dan grabbed her hips to prevent her from moving, he wanted this to last forever. Lor just simply ignored Dan's hands and continued to move up and down on his erection, harder and harder, faster, and faster, crying his name. Dan's breath was coming in lung filling gasps and then, he exploded into her, filling her, crying her name as he climaxed in mindless, primeval ecstasy.

Later, Lor led Dan to her bedroom for sleep, and again, that night, they awoke to love, to treasure, to care for each other.

Dan vaguely remembered hearing a long wolf-like howling that night, but it was a howl of happiness, of contentment rather than the tortured howls he and Tom heard in the dark forest.

CHAPTER SEVEN

The next morning, bright sunshine flooded the mountains and valley. In the valley, standing like statutes in the waist high dark green alfalfa and yellow-blossomed sweet clover, was a small herd of three female elk, what looked like two or three ungainly baby elk, and a huge male with a large set of antlers.

Sitting by the window overlooking the valley, Sue said, "Dad, look at them. Aren't they beautiful?"

The elk, sensing the activity in the home, faded out of sight into the brush and trees surrounding the fields.

After breakfast, first Tom and then Sue took a shower. Their cries of "Ohhh, that's cold," could be heard echoing through the valley. The big cat paid a visit, strolling through the house as if he owned it. He nuzzled Dan's hand and received a big hug from Sue and Lor. Tom found the dog and soon, they disappeared into the woods and trees, just happily exploring together.

Around noon, a man on horseback rode up to the house. His brown wrangler jeans and long-sleeved plaid shirt were faded, but clean, while a brown leather vest covered his chest. He was clean shaven except for a full mustache sprinkled with gray that drooped over his upper lip. A black leather holster hung on his right side from his black woven belt, the bottom tied to his right leg. It looked like it contained a well-used .357 Colt Trooper with rubberized non-skid hand grips. Partially hidden in a saddle holster protruded a 30-30 Winchester lever action rifle. The man's calm hazel eyes seemed to take in the entire area in a single sweeping glance. Lor was inside and Dan was lounging on the porch with a cup of coffee.

"Howdy," the man said cautiously. "Miss Lorraine around?"

"Yes Sir, just a minute," Dan replied. Somehow, it seemed appropriate to call the man "Sir!"

"Lor, someone here to see you," Dan called.

Wiping her hands on a dish towel, Lor came to the door and exclaimed, "Deputy Hank!"

She ran out of the door to the man who had now dismounted from his horse. They hugged closely for a long moment, Lor kissing his cheek and face. A small flash of dismay crossed Dan's face; a tiny flame of jealousy ignited in his chest.

"What happened to your face," the man asked as his hand gently touched Lor's still slightly swollen black and blue features.

"I'll tell you about that in a second, Hank, but, come here please, I want you to meet Dan Peterson, the man who saved my life!"

Grasping onto his arm, Lor led Hank over to the porch and the two men shook hands. When the men shook hands. Dan felt he was shaking hands with a rock or a vise; this was the hand of a man accustomed to hard labor. Dan saw a medium built man in his middle to late forties with graying hair who appeared to weigh about one hundred and seventy pounds. Hazel eyes peered penetratingly from beneath bushy eyebrows with a self-confident, but cautiously reserved look Dan had seen before. His brown hair with white streaks at the temple was covered by a battered, but clean, cowboy style, tan felt hat.

Dan then saw a shiny gold colored sheriff's star pinned on the man's left chest. The badge had been covered by the man's leather vest.

"Dan, Deputy Hank is the Sheriff around here. I've known him all my life. He and his family own a farm further down the valley and he's been a Deputy Sheriff for . . .oh how many years, Hank?"

"Well, I've been a Deputy for La Plata County here for about twenty-three, twenty-four years, and Miss Lorraine and her parents, may they rest in peace, have been family friends for years," the officer drawled.

"Come on in. How about some coffee?" Lor asked.

"Thank you, I've been up since before daybreak and a cup would be welcome."

Later, eyes constantly scanning over his hands clasping a steaming cup of coffee, Hank asked, "Now, what about your face? And what's this about saving your life?"

"Here's what happened, you remember that I had gone to visit my friends Marcy and her husband?"

"Did they do that?" Hank gestured at her face; his eyes locked on hers.

"Oh no! I know you never cared for them, but they had nothing to do with this."

"Are they still growing that marijuana down there?"

"Hank!"

Lor took a deep breath, "Getting back to what I was telling you, I was walking back with my babies, and I got captured by some ex-convicts." She went on to tell Hank where Dan and his family were from and what they had done to save her. Hank said nothing, his face rigidly emotionless, but he occasionally nodded; his weather-beaten hands, however, tightened around his hot coffee cup. There was a look of respect and something else deep in his eyes when he glanced at Dan. As Lor finished her story, she was standing behind Dan with her hands clasping his shoulders. The magnetism between them filled the air.

Hank nodded as to himself and said, "Well, Mr. Peterson, I ain't much for orders but . . .," with cold steel in his eyes, he continued " . . .You take care of her now, you hear!?"

Dan flushed, a little embarrassed by the story. He nevertheless looked back at Hank with deep emotion, "Deputy, I found something so precious with her, you can rest assured that I intend to do so."

He reached up, grasped her hand, and said, "It's kind of strange, we've traveled what, a thousand hard miles to find our littlest daughter and I find Lorraine."

"Let me call my oldest daughter, she's around here somewhere."

He went to the front door and called "Sue? Come here please and bring that postcard from Ginger."

Dan explained their long journey to Deputy Hank, what they were doing here and their search for their little Ginger. He related his conversation with Joe Robinson about the life force and described his observations of the life force between Durango and Los Angeles, the huge fires in Los Angeles, the general breakdown of law and order, and no ascertainable government in the United States.

The telling of his conversation with Joe Robinson, their journey and the search took about fifteen minutes. Meanwhile, Sue had entered the room and was standing alongside Lor.

"Sue, this is Deputy Hank, he's the Sheriff around here."

"Glad to meet you, little missy. You sure are a pretty and brave little girl."

Sue, usually outspoken, was for some reason, flustered and even a little reserved. She blushed, and interestingly, clutched Lor's hand. Deputy Hank's smile broke through her shyness and she gave a small trembling smile back at him.

"I've got kids your age," he smiled at her.

"Honey, did you bring those postcards?" Dan asked.

She gave him the postcards which he handed to the deputy. "Do you know where this is, where it was postmarked?"

"Well, sure, that's a little post office up north off of Highway 550. It's off at an angle in the mountains not too far from that big hotel and golf course complex that used to be up there."

"Used to?"

After a moment's thought, Deputy Hank continued softly, "I don't know if there are people still living or alive up there. A month ago, there was an enormous forest fire that swept through that whole area. It's been very dry up here and the forests were like matchsticks. And once that force thing came, we couldn't do anything to stop the fires. I heard that almost everything was destroyed through those valleys."

Dan with a sinking, cold feeling in the pit of his stomach asked, "Have you been up there since the fire?"

"Nooo," Deputy Hank drawled. "But I've been meaning to go up there, seeing that I'm about the only law out here in the county. The Durango police, there were only about 32 of them to start with anyway, stay pretty much in Durango. He nodded at Lorraine, "Lor, you remember that folks out here didn't care much for their dark blue uniforms."

Lorraine laughed, "Well, folks out here don't care much for any kind of uniform, much less the Durango dark blues. I remember a while ago that Durango had an officer that gave tickets only to the locals, never the tourists, until he got into a big fight with one of the tourists. The locals, probably half of which he had given tickets too, just stood around watching him get beat up. No one raised a hand to help him!"

"I heard about that," Deputy Hank said, shaking his head. "I heard that the crowd even cheered for the tourist."

"Sure, but when he stopped writing tickets on the locals, the next time he got into a fight with a tourist, they had to admit the tourist to hospital."

"Well, I guess it takes longer for some men to grow up. When you're young, this badge can get pretty heavy."

After a comfortable pause, Deputy Hank sighed, "So much for war stories, I guess you think your daughter might still be up in one of those camps?"

"Yes Sir. The last information I received said that my ex-wife had joined one of those communes up there, but that's about all I know."

"Some of the people in those camps are dangerous and not very cooperative."

"Well, Deputy Hank, we came many very hard miles to find our Ginger, and with all due respect to you, Sir, I've got to try to find her, one way or another."

"Absolutely correct," Tom echoed. He had wondered in during Dan's comments. The dog followed Tom into the kitchen, his long pink tongue dripping small drops of saliva on the floor as Tom's fingers scratched behind his ears.

"Deputy Hank, this is my son, Tom."

The deputy, noting the relationship between the dog and Tom, approvingly shook the boy's hand.

"That's interesting: that dog doesn't take to hardly anyone, he's very picky about who he chooses for his friends. It's good to meet you, Tom."

He nodded over at Dan and Lor, "Your Dad and Lor told me what you did to save her life."

He paused for a second and then with surprisingly deep emotion, grabbed Tom's shoulder and said, "Good job!"

"Well," Tom stammered, "We had to do it; we didn't have any choice."

"Mr. Peterson, let me do some checking. I'll make some inquiries from the townspeople and maybe they'll have some idea of the conditions up in that area. Give me a couple of days and we'll ride up there together."

Dan noted with relief the "We" and agreed with the suggestion. He and the kids had just traveled many long miles and could use the recuperation of a few days' rest.

A few days later, Deputy Hank rode in to Lor's place.

Over a cup of coffee, he said, "I've been talking with the folks around here about those camps up in the mountains. I couldn't find anyone who personally had been up there since the forest fires, but one of the lieutenants on the Durango Police Department, they all are real good guys, said that he had heard rumors that there may be survivors still up in that area. Others told me that they heard that there is total devastation there. Decent folks around here think that those people up in those camps are fanatics and three-quarters crazy. Hardly anyone around here will have anything to do with them. I don't know how you do it out in California, but here, my department was in charge of the Durango/La Plata detention facility in Durango."

"Detention facility?" asked Tom.

"AKA the county jail," laughed Lor.

"Yes, and after that force thing came, we had to kick all our prisoners loose. I heard that one or two of them made their way up into the hills and I would like to look in on them. Most were just dopers and drunks anyway."

After a contemplative sip of Lor's hot coffee, his eyes continuously scanning over the warm cup, Deputy Hank continued, "I suggest that you and I ride up there and sort of scout the area first. I've heard that a few of those camps flatly do not want to be disturbed and might even shoot first and ask questions later."

He added after a moment's thought, "Back when we had radio and computer communications with access to the National Crime and Information Center (NCIC) run by the FBI, more than a few of the other police and sheriffs thought that some of those people were heavily armed and dangerous. We used to receive occasional NCIC or FBI inquiries about one or more of the cults or radical groups that might be up in that area. Every so often, some police department or sheriff's department would ask us to check that region to see if we knew or could find the whereabouts of some dingbat or wanted person."

Dan replied, "I'm familiar with NCIC and the computer network because of working for my city, but did you or your people ever follow up on those inquiries?"

"No, usually not. The reason was that we were always understaffed, and the questions usually were for intelligence purposes only."

He shook his head, "Our philosophy was that if that particular police or sheriff's department wanted to send men up there to find their escapee or whatever, we would certainly cooperate and assist them, but we weren't able to go to war by ourselves. And let me tell you, from some of the information that we did receive, it would be a major fight because a few of those groups were very heavily armed with everything from guns to explosives to large caliber weapons."

Deputy Hank, like a typical hometown sheriff, added with a shrug of his broad shoulders, "Plus, they seldom, if ever, bothered us down here. Just occasional begging or scrounging for food, but usually not much trouble. And there were very few reports of any actual violations of the law. I've had twice as much trouble with the local hillbillies."

A comfortable silence settled over the kitchen. "As far as whatever of my sheriff's department is left, we're essentially letting things go back to where they were a hundred years ago. We got about 1900 square miles in La Plata County to handle, but only a few deputies."

Dan nodded, "Let's face it, it is not a nice world now. People were spoiled, a person's word meant little, crime, litigation, rules, laws, regulations were always increasing."

"I agree," said Deputy Hank. "Every time we turned around, our representatives over in Denver passed something new, not useful, mind you, just new to justify their existence. Our local voters never understood that when they sent these nitwits to Denver or Washington, D.C., their only purpose was to pass new laws. Now, it seems that most laws, rules, or regulations will mean little or nothing. Maybe, if we're really lucky, those nitwits will be stuck wherever they are."

After a moment of thoughtful silence between the two men, Dan continued, "I think that the fundamental values will always apply. There will be less crime, people simply wouldn't put up with criminals, they bury them."

Deputy Hank looked at Dan for a moment and with respect in his eyes, said, "I agree with your comments, darn it, its tough right now, but we don't have television anymore, we're not worried about the national debt or the balance of trade with some foreign country any longer. We don't worry about terrorists' threats; they simply can't get to America. As a matter of fact, I'm starting to see more people in church every Sunday. Maybe some good will come out of this after all."

"Well, Officer, regardless of the conditions, I have to try to find my daughter. I've simply got to know, one way or another."

"Oh, of course. If we figure out where your daughter is, or if she's still. ... well, alive, we could go back up there with whatever force is necessary to rescue her."

Dan whole-heartily agreed with the officer, but asked, "How are the roads up there? Can we take our bikes, or do we walk, or what?"

Hank laughed, "No problem, I have extra horses at my farm and tack for them. Can you ride?"

"It's been a long time, but yes, I can stay on a horse."

"Sure, Deputy Hank, it's when the horse moves that he has the problem," Tom grinned.

"All right Son, you just wait. Deputy, let me show you our weapons and we can decide which ones to take with us."

Tom handed Deputy Hank the power bows. "So those are the famous bows. Good job!" Hank said, his calloused hand gripping Tom's shoulder. Tom explained how the bows worked and how they were set up for firing.

Lor picked up one of the bows and pulled the string, "Hank, I'll never, ever forget seeing those arrows flying out of the darkness." She reached over and hugged Tom, "He's my hero!"

When Dan showed Hank the package of plastic explosives, Hank exclaimed, "Good heavens! Where did you get that stuff? Do you know how to use it?"

Dan then had to relate their fire fight with the gang on the overpass. Hank's only reaction was a slow nod or two as his eyes searched Tom and Dan.

Tom opened the book or manual on how to use the explosives, "This should tell us how to use this stuff."

"Oh sure. Handling those explosives is like doing self-brain surgery with a hatchet by reading a book and looking in a mirror," Hank remarked. "There has got to be somebody around here that knows how to use those explosives, maybe an old Vietnam or Desert Storm or Gulf War vet or someone; I'll find someone."

He added, "In the meantime, I suggest that you keep that stuff in the barn, far away from us."

They decided to leave the next morning. Hank said he would be back with the horses and that they would spend a few days up in the mountains. Both Tom and Lor were unhappy that they weren't going, but all agreed that this was only a scouting trip, and if force were necessary, Dan and Hank would come for help.

The next morning, Hank returned with an extra horse for Dan. He also brought along soft leather saddle bags and a saddle holster for Dan's AR-15. The smell of the soft leather and its oil triggered memories in Tom: they smelled like his old favorite baseball glove.

They loaded the saddle bags with food and supplies for about a week. In addition, raincoats and sleeping bags were tied to the back of the saddles.

Hank tossed a set of Bushnell 10 X 50 adjustable binoculars to Dan and said "Hang these over your saddle horn. We'll need them."

When they were ready to leave, Sue planted a wet kiss on her father's cheek and hugged him fiercely. Tom grasped his arm and said quietly, "You be careful, Dad!"

Lor grabbed Dan and held him for a long moment, her face and eyes moving to not let Dan see the tears, her face pressed against his chest. "You take care, my darling, please," she whispered to him. Dan held her for just a moment longer, loving her had simply become a natural part of his life!

Lor then ran to Hank and hugged him, "You two take care of each other, understand?"

Hank returned the hug, nodding and kissing the top of her head, "We'll be all right, don't you worry."

Hank and Dan rode out, Hank leading the way. They went through the northern part of Durango and crossed the Animas River. Hank thought that by staying on the main roads, at least until they become impassable, they could make the best time. They found Highway 550 and headed north. Hank pointed out to the north and the northwest was the rugged San Juan National Forest with its geologically young snow-covered peaks and steep valleys and canyons.

He said, "There are several four-wheel drive roads up in that area, but the roads are only open a very limited amount of time because of rain and snow. We'll follow this highway for a while. The railroad people asked me to keep an eye on their track and see if it was usable. I guess they'll try to get that old steam engine working again because it doesn't use electricity."

They had traveled through the day with only an occasional rest and it was approaching dusk. They had just passed a few abandoned houses when they came to what looked like the back side of the moon! A forest fire had swept through the area and burnt its way up and into the mountains.

Dan and Hank camped that night at the edge of the burnt area. The horses were a little spooky and Hank hobbled them so they wouldn't wander off. After their meal, Dan and Hank talked long into the night over their small campfire. The air was crisp and cold with a harsh odor of burnt land and trees, the Milky Way shining with a million lights, so bright that a person could almost read by their light.

Next morning dawned cloudy with a heavy promise of rain. The devastation around them was almost unbelievable. The fire had swept from valley to peak to valley, burning everything in its path. Varying degrees of grey and black soot and dirt covered the entire area. An occasional burnt tree still standing like a sentinel punctured the gloomy scene. A heavy smell of burnt wood was everywhere. True to its promise, the weather started to drizzle as they saddled the horses and broke camp.

"Now, we get the rain," muttered Hank.

They followed what was left of the river and road. The falling cold rain, combined with the gray dust and dirt made for a dismal day. In places the heat had been so intense that the road appeared to have a glaze like a piece of pottery on it. The glaze flaked off like a grinding wheel throwing sparks when the horses' iron shod hooves struck it.

They passed what appeared to be an almost flattened and burnt rubble of about a half-dozen buildings.

Hank pointed quietly, "That's the post office from where your little one mailed those postcards. This was a popular tourist stop and some of those commune people would come down here to beg for supplies or food."

Dan felt his heart sink.

Hank gestured, "Over there was a tiny gift store. That is probably where she obtained the postcards. The owners were an old generous retired couple who were always giving things away. Your little girl might have begged for the cards from them."

Hank didn't want to look at Dan's emotion filled eyes when he told Dan of the buildings. Deep in Dan's heart was the consuming question: Would he ever find his precious little daughter?

Hank's hazel eyes glanced over Dan's face and quickly looked away. He said, "Well, my friend, don't worry. We'll try our best to find your little one."

Hank led them up a canyon that appeared to be less burnt than others. There was a single lane dirt road, now heavily covered with ash and half burnt debris.

"I think that there are or were a few of the religious camps up in these side canyons," he remembered.

They rode into a small side canyon that appeared to be a dead-end canyon, the soft plodding of their horses' hoofs quietly echoing off the partially scorched evergreen trees. They found what was left of a few small houses or cabins at the end of the canyon. Dan, with a heavy heart, closely examined the burnt ruins. He found what might have been a family, or something, huddled together in death. It was impossible to tell if these were humans or not, the fire had burnt so thoroughly. Dan searched though the ruins, looking for any evidence that might tell him something! Traces of red hair, anything!

Finally, Hank called Dan away from the ruins stating, "We're looking for your Ginger, a child. If you have kids, you must have toys. And there were no toys in the ruins!"

"Sure. And I didn't see anything that looked like it belonged to a child. Let's go." Dan mounted his horse and they rode out into the main canyon.

Hank halted at one of the side canyons that, amazingly, had apparently escaped the fury of the fire and looked unscathed. A narrow dirt road meandered its way between the trees.

"I remember a similar thing happening out in California during some of our frequent forest fires," Dan said. "Some areas are totally devastated, but the fire had somehow missed whole houses or areas."

"Let me have the binoculars," Hank motioned. He carefully scanned the entire area, muttering that something didn't seem right. Dan could see no movement and the only sound was the falling rain and the soft snicker of their horses.

Hank quietly said, "I think there used to be cabins down that canyon. Let's take a look, but be careful, something isn't right."

Hank nudged his horse forward into the canyon. It was wider than a canyon and narrower than a valley. With the rain falling and the dust and mud, it was impossible to see any tracks on the road. They were forced to follow the road because each side was heavily covered with trees and bushes. As they went deeper into the canyon, it became darker. The high walls shut out whatever light was seeping through the clouds until they were riding in near twilight.

Suddenly, they rounded a curve in the road, approximately two hundred yards ahead of them lay a few small cabins in a clearing. There was no movement or smoke from the cabins. Nor was there any sound other than the soft breathing of their horses. No birds chirping, no bugs or crickets, nothing.

Hank loosened his revolver in its holster and said softly to Dan, "Well, let's see if anyone is home."

"Hello The Cabins, Anyone Home?" Hank yelled.

Dan's horse jumped.

Dan's heart almost stopped; the yell was so unexpected! The yell echoed around the cabins but there was no response.

"Hello the cabins!"

Nothing.

Hank looked at Dan and shrugged, "Well, let's go see what's there. But stay loose."

They slowly rode up to the cabins, but as they got closer, it was clear that they were deserted. There was no glass in the windows, the doors hung ajar and one or two of the cabins appeared to have partially collapsed.

"Dan, would you check out the cabins, I'll keep an eye on things out here."

Dan examined the cabins. Each cabin had a small altar or shrine in it and had been used as living quarters. There was no electricity in the cabins nor were there any electric power lines in the area. Each cabin had a large fireplace at the rear with small partitions in the main living area. He looked for castoff toys or anything that might tell them who had lived there. Nothing. Each cabin, while dusty from nonuse, was vacant.

"Hank, each cabin is vacant and has been for some time. There is not a thing in any of the cabins."

"Well, I think there are more cabins further down this canyon. Let's see if we can find anything."

They returned to the single, now muddy lane and resumed their ride. They came to a six-foot high, six strand barbed wire fence and gate with a red and white sign fastened on it: "Stay out!"

"It sure looks like someone doesn't want any visitors. When someone doesn't want visitors," Hank said softly, "I always question what they're up to."

He smiled at Dan, "Well, I'm the law around here and aren't we in hot pursuit or something?"

"Sure. Seems we forgot our red lights and siren, but you know, they scare the horses."

Hank opened the gate and tied it open. "We may not want to stop to open the gate on our return."

They rode on, the trees and bush forcing them to stay single file on the trail. The dismal rain continued to fall while the cold seeped beneath damp clothes. Dan shivered, even though he was wearing heavy clothes and a raincoat. They plodded on for several miles and rounded a small curve in the trail.

"Halt, Heathens!" a voice commanded from behind them.

"Crap," Hank muttered. "I didn't even see him!"

Dan's heart froze!

The voice was accompanied by the clear and unmistakable ratcheting of two hammers being pulled back on a gun. Both Dan and Hank stopped their horses and raised their hands.

"Easy, man, easy, we're friends," Hank said.

They slowly turned their horses around. Dan's mouth dropped for a second. Holding a long, rusty, double barreled 12-gauge shotgun was a wild eyed, skinny, long haired, heavily bearded man of unknown age. His army camouflage clothing was covered with mud from head to foot with pieces of branches or leaves stuck here and there on his body.

"I gotcha! Hee, Hee. He'll be proud. I'll get some blessings tonight!" He cackled showing missing teeth while one eye slipped to the side.

After a slight hesitation, he waved the shotgun up the road, "Keep on going, but go slow, I'm right behind you! And no talking!"

They came upon a camp consisting of about ten or twelve cabins with smoke emitting from most of the chimneys. There seemed to be several sheds and small corrals on the other side of the cabins. One corral contained several hogs happily rooting in the mud. There were several cattle in the other corrals. Dan saw a large dog chained near one of the cabins, it was on its feet but it only barked once or twice when they entered the camp.

A few pale faces quickly glanced out of several cabin windows and then retreated from sight.

Two men met them. The younger, obviously a follower with somewhat vacant eyes and a slack jaw, wasn't of any interest. Still, he had an approximate 12-inch knife in a leather holster attached to a rope tied around his waist. The rope took the place of a belt and kept his pants from sliding off his skinny hips.

The other, clearly the leader, had a set of white or pearl handled revolvers in black leather holsters with shiny chrome crosses fastened onto and hanging from each holster. He wore a buckskin jacket that had been dyed black but had seen better days; the vest portion of the jacket had white fringes hanging from it. Hanging from most of the fringes were tiny chrome crosses. The jacket had a large chrome cross hanging on the outside of each shoulder; on the left part of the chest was an embroidered, multicolored sunburst. Beneath the sunburst hung several gold and chrome crosses in a row like soldiers' metals.

"Dan, I think I know who that guy is," Hank murmured quietly.

The leader wore jeans that looked like they hadn't been washed in months. The total sinister effect was of some fanatical evil cowboy; he reminded Dan of someone, who? After a second, it hit Dan, this guy looked like photographs he had seen of Charles Manson! He had the same unkempt long hair and pockmarked face, but his wild eyes radiated a cunning, Machiavellian look that emitted danger. There was no other movement in the camp, no one else met Dan and Hank.

Both men stared at Dan and Hank. The leader glanced briefly at "The Thing," following Hank and Dan with the shotgun as if to ask, "What did you do?"

The Thing said, "Your Grace, they were just coming up the trail and they passed right by me. Hee, Hee, they didn't even see me!"

"I captured them. Did I do good? Can I get some blessings tonight?" he cackled.

The leader didn't reply. He just stared at Dan and Hank.

"Howdy. OK if we relax a little?" Hank asked. "We come in peace."

Out of the leader's body rolled a mellow bass senatorial voice that echoed around the cabins: "All Peaceful People Are Welcome Who Worship The Power!"

Despite himself, Dan was impressed with the force and personality of the voice. It had a rich vibrant timber that certainly didn't need a loudspeaker. If one closed his eyes and didn't look at the speaker, a person could easily be hypnotized by the dynamic, charismatic voice.

By now, both Dan and Hank had relaxed their hands, but kept them in plain sight.

"We are just traveling through, looking for a little girl," Hank said.

"By the way, I'm the Sheriff around here." He revealed the badge pinned on his left chest. "Would you mind telling your friend back there to lower that cannon?"

The leader quickly nodded to The Thing who lowered the shotgun and released the hammers. Dan felt like a big target had been removed from between his shoulder blades.

Dan leaned forward over the saddle horn and asked, "We're looking for a woman by the name of Kathy Peterson and a red headed little girl. Have you seen or heard of them?"

Upon hearing Dan's question, the three men on the ground jerked and involuntarily glanced at each other.

"You Imbecile!" the leader screamed, his voice echoing throughout the clearing.

"They Don't Come In Peace!" He yelled at the thing, "They come for us! They come to take away our people!"

The Thing, surprised and scared, started to raise his shotgun again. Dan, fed up with being a target, yanked his H & K 9 mm. chrome semi-automatic from his shoulder holster and commanded, "Freeze!"

As Dan was doing this, Hank snapped his .357 Colt Trooper from his leg holster and glared at the other two, "Don't even think of doing something stupid!"

The man with a rope around his waist, whom Dan had nicknamed "The follower," suddenly threw himself on his knees beside the leader and screamed, "Oh Your Grace, save us from them infidels, these heathens! Oh, Your Grace, Oh Your Grace, Oh Your Grace," he babbled on, saliva dripping down his unshaven chin.

Hank, dismayed with the action of "The Follower", after a few seconds of listening to him, told the leader, "How about shutting your friend up so we can talk like reasonable people?"

The leader said nothing, a hate filled stare blazing flames at Hank.

Meanwhile, Dan's attention was directed at "The Thing." Dan and "The Thing" locked eyes; Dan raised his 9 mm. automatic, yanked back the sliding mechanism of his handgun with his left hand and released it. The metallic sound of metal locking into metal rang throughout the clearing. The barrel of the weapon pointed between "The Thing's" beady eyes. His eyes grew large and round. The black hole in Dan's 9 mm. semi-automatic handgun seemed to increase in size the longer he stared at it.

The weapon was rock steady in Dan's hand.

Dan ordered, "Drop the shotgun!"

The Thing hesitated.

"Now, Moron!"

The Thing, seeing an icy coldness in Dan's eyes, threw the shotgun away from him, dropped to his knees, clasped his hands in front of him, and started repeating over and over, "Oh Your Grace, Your Grace, help us!"

Hank told Dan, "Let's back out of here slowly."

"Yes! These people are crazy!"

Dan and Hank slowly backed their horses out of the clearing, closely watching the three men until they turned the bend in the road. After galloping their horses a few miles back down the trail, they stopped at the original cabins.

"Well, what do you think?" Hank asked.

"Something's fishy back there. Did you see their reaction when I mentioned Kathy and Ginger's names? They either have Ginger, or know where she is."

"I think so too," Hank replied. "One other thing is perfectly clear: they wouldn't give up either without a fight. And, most importantly, they're paranoid, unusually paranoid for some reason, and they're armed and dangerous!"

"What do we do now?"

"Well, I suggest that we need more information about that camp." Hank added reflectively, "It would be nice to know, if in fact, your ex-wife or your Ginger is in the camp. I suggest that we do some scouting up there."

"I agree."

They rode back down the canyon and watered and tethered their horses in a small clearing.

"They'll be all right here for about a day," Hank said. "You got your hiking boots on? Bring that AR-15 and those binoculars, but remember, all we want to do is obtain information."

They walked back up the canyon road through the gate.

Hank looked around and then pointed at the top of the canyon, "I think we might be able to get above the camp if we follow the top of that canyon or ridge."

They pushed their way through trees and bushes; it was arduous climbing and Dan was soon disoriented. He turned the AR-15 upside down to keep the barrel free from water and hung it over his shoulder. The rain continued to fall, thankfully not heavy, but more than a drizzle.

As they came to the top of a ridge, Hank paused for a moment and looked around.

"I think that camp is about a mile or so ahead of us and down toward our left," he pointed.

"Oh," panted Dan. Hank could have said that Denver was a mile that way and Dan would have taken him at his word.

Later, a whiff of wood smoke drifting through the rain caressed their nostrils and Dan knew that they weren't too far from the camp. They moved cautiously, the rain masking any noises they made. The brush and trees had become thicker and progress was difficult. They came to a trail which was merely a winding opening in the brush and trees.

"I don't like following a trail because that means someone else travels on it, but this looks like it hasn't been used for a while," Hank whispered as he knelt to examine the footpath. "I bet that this path leads to the back of the corrals at the rear of the camp."

Once they were in a position that Hank judged to be above the camp, they left the path and pushed their way through the thick underbrush. When they appeared to be close to the edge of the ridge, Dan and Hank got on their hands and knees and crawled up through the cold, wet grass, and bushes to the edge, pushed aside a few branches and peered down at the camp. In the cold drizzle, they could see part of the backs of several cabins and all the corrals and sheds. The sheds looked like they were used for storage. There were four corrals, one occupied by several hogs. One of the other corrals had three young Holstein heifers in it while another corral contained several Holstein cows with a large mean looking bull. The bull was restless and rumbling around the corral as if he knew something wasn't right. Snorting and pawing the wet earth, he had herded his cows into an opposite corner from Dan and Hank.

Hank whispered in Dan's ear, "That bull is going to be trouble if we try to go through his corral. Try to memorize the entire layout. Hand me those glasses, please."

After a few minutes of looking closely at the entire camp, he handed the binoculars to Dan, "Here, see if you can find anything."

At the edge of the camp, Dan could see a few small swings made from a tire, hanging from a tree. A small, but deep and swift stream flowed directly through the center of the encampment. It probably was the source of the water for the camp.

Hank breathed into Dan's ear, "Look for sentries, there must be some someplace."

Dan closely searched what he could see of the surrounding area through the falling mist, but saw no movement, the only sound was the patter of raindrops on the trees. The smoke from the cabins mixed with the pungent odor of fresh manure from the corrals flooded the area. Dan thought he could hear some yelling coming from the largest cabin.

Hank whispered, "Do you see any dogs?"

"Just one. They had that one large dog chained to a tree just north of the cabins, but I haven't heard or seen any others; I wonder why."

"I think we have learned all we can from this little excursion," Hank whispered. "We know that they are armed and it's too dangerous for us to just stroll in and ask for your daughter. I suggest we get out of here while there is still some daylight."

"Ok," Dan nodded. "Let me take one last look." He wanted to memorize the entire layout of the cabins and tried to estimate distances.

The return trip to the horses, while very exhausting, was uneventful. Later, the sky cleared and the drizzling stopped. They rode back to the road and camped early in a grove of trees that had once held a campground. After changing into dry clothes and lighting a small fire, Dan cooked a light meal while Hank cared for the horses.

They talked long into the night over the campfire, writing down notes and attempting to draft a map that accurately portrayed the camp.

"I think I know who that leader is. I want to get back to my station and pull a few old files to check, but some time ago, we had an intelligence survey on radical religious leaders with militant philosophies and I think he was part of that bunch," Hank said, thoughtfully.

"Well, I don't think that they will give up my daughter willingly, do you?"

"No."

"This really isn't your problem, my friend, but I'm going back there to find my daughter. From the reaction to my questions, I really think she's there. I sincerely appreciate your help, but I think that going back there will be dangerous. I, I can't ask you to expose yourself to that."

The silence of the night was broken only by the soft whisper of a breeze in the tall pines and an occasional snap and crackle of the flickering fire, its pungent smoke occasionally caressing their faces.

Hank stared into the glowing campfire and said almost inaudibly, "Well, let me ask you a rhetorical question. If a person had saved someone very precious to you, someone that was a part of you, from a fate worse than death, and if that person needed help, would you help that person?"

Dan, surprised by the question, said slowly, "Well, sure, of course, yes. But what has that got to do with me finding my daughter?"

Hank, after a few more moments staring into the flickering campfire, heaved a deep sigh and said slowly and quietly, "Well, what you and your son, Tom, did for Lorraine could never be repaid. You see, my relationship with her goes back years . . . even before she was born."

"Well, I understood that you knew her parents before they died, didn't you?"

Hank softly mumbled, "You might say that I knew them, but it's more accurate to say that I knew her mother . . . very well . . ."

After a few seconds, Dan jerked up straight.

"Wait a second!"

"A part of you? My, my God!"

He stuttered, "Are, are you trying to tell me you're, you're her father, her real father?"

Hank just nodded.

"Oh, my Lord! Does she know?"

Hank emphatically shook his head, "Absolutely not! Only her mother and I knew. You see, things were different in those days!"

He said, slowly dredging up memories from the sad canyons of his mind, "I had and was nothing, just a wild Polish kid. Lorraine's mother's parents were staunch Germans. They and my parents hated each other almost as badly as the old Hatfields and McCoys hated each other. Lorraine's mother and I accidentally met and from that moment on, we loved each other, but any marriage would have destroyed both of our families. The differences between our families were just too much."

He paused briefly, smiling in memory, "We used to sneak out of our houses late at night and meet!"

Hank paused for another long moment, reliving part of his life, "Lorraine's mother's husband-to-be had courted her for a long time before we met and he was approved of by her parents. And as it turned out, it was a good marriage. Lorraine was an only child because her mother couldn't have any more kids."

Hank continued after a moment, "Now you understand why I'm here, Dan. I'm proud of what she has become, and I've tried to keep an eye on her. I've never told her, and I'm not going to tell her! If she looks upon me as simply 'Deputy Hank,' I'm satisfied. And as you know, I married my wife later; we too have a good marriage. But Lorraine is still a part of me."

"As a matter of fact, I've never told anyone else before," he said, looking deep into Dan's eyes. "I'd rather this information didn't get around."

"Oh, don't worry about that."

"Now," Hank said heavily, "Let's get back to your daughter. We will need more help to get into that camp to find her. I have a few friends that might be willing to lend us a hand or equipment. I suggest that we head back home and plan this much more."

That night, around the flickering campfire, Dan reflected that during the long ride from California to here, he had looked deeply into his heart. He discovered that his only interest in his ex-wife was to know how she was involved with his Ginger. He could remember with deep emotion how his little girl's two tiny arms had encircled his neck and kissed him whispering, "Daddy, I lub you!"

Dan had made up his mind he was going to find and take Ginger, no matter what Kathy felt or wanted. He once toyed with the idea of attempting to convince Kathy to "come back", but she had caused too much unnecessary sorrow and despair in his and his children's lives to even consider such an idea. In addition, he knew, knew, that both Tom and Sue would have nothing to do with her. Most importantly, since he had found Lorraine, he had experienced a love, a caring, a feeling, he thought existed only in poems or books.

The next morning, they started their return to Lor's place, each deep in thought and memories.

CHAPTER EIGHT

As they rode into Lorraine's place late the next afternoon, Sue saw them first.

"Daddy, Daddy. Tom! Lor. Daddy's back!"

Sue ran out to the road where her father had dismounted; after he received a flurry of hugs and kisses from her, he heaved her up on the horse and remounted behind her. Hank just smiled and smiled.

Tom, followed by his dog, squirted out of the barn like a rabbit out of a hole and ran over to them. By this time, they had ridden to the front of Lor's house and dismounted.

Tom ran to his father, "Did you find her?"

"We think so, but we'll have to go back up in those mountains to get her."

The front door of the house banged open. "You're back, Oh My God, you're back!" Lor exclaimed.

She ran across the porch and flung herself into Dan's arms. "See," she tearfully told Sue as she buried her head on Dan's chest, her arms clutching him, "I told you they would be back! Sue was so worried that something might happen to you!"

"Just Sue, huh?" Dan murmured as he bent to touch her lips.

Still sitting on his horse, like a minister smiling and blessing his congregation was Hank. His and Dan's eyes met and

unspoken were heartfelt promises.

She left Dan's arms, ran to Hank's horse, and nearly dragged him off the poor animal. She hugged him and kissed his now whiskery cheek saying, "It's good to see you, thanks for taking care of my man."

Over a quick cup of coffee, his eyes always constantly roaming, Hank said, "I have a few friends that I want to talk to; the two men I have in mind know that area and both are ex-military. One of them I know is an explosives expert and they might help us. Plus, I want to check in our station's files and see if we have anything on that leader."

Hank left soon after, saying he wanted to get home to his family before dark. He suggested that Dan draw a full diagram of the camp what he could remember.

A few days later, Hank rode in with two other men.

"Hi Mike, Hi Smiley," Lor said, surprised. "I didn't know you were the two men Hank had in mind."

"Dan, this is Mike Osborne and Smiley over there is known simply as Smiley."

Dan shook hands with "Smiley." Smiley, the shorter of the two was dark complexioned, his long grey hair tied in a ponytail like an old hippie. He was wiry and thin, but his dark eyes seemed to occasionally drift off into another world. He was called "Smiley" and Dan could see why; he was always smiling.

Mike Osborne was the opposite; he was about 6-1 with little excess weight (Dan noted that almost everyone was thin now since food was difficult to find.). His hair was whitish blond cut in a short crew cut. He seemed to have an inherent great bodily strength as his arms strained the sleeves on his heavy flannel shirt to the breaking point while his broad shoulders tapered to a slim waist. When he moved, however, there was no sound. Dan thought he had heard cats making more noise.

"Good to meet you, Hank says some nice things about you," Mike said, his surprising sensitive hands shook Dan's hand with a bone-crushing grip. Somehow, Dan felt that even with the grip, the man put nowhere near the power he could have into the handshake. Dan quickly retrieved his hand, it felt like it had been mangled.

"Dan, I've known these two for years. Mike and I went to high school together, but I've seen little of him since graduation," Lor said. Smiley (Dan never did find out his true name), much older than Mike, was one of those individuals who seemed dreamingly only half in the present universe!

"This is my son, Tom, and our little girl, Sue, is wondering around here somewhere."

Lor, Tom and all four men crowded around Lor's kitchen table to review Dan's map of the religious camp. He had spent nearly two whole days drawing everything he could remember about the camp on a piece of four foot by four-foot drafting paper.

Lor remembered one night late, they were both asleep in her bed when Dan suddenly awoke and jumped out of bed, scaring her.

He exclaimed, "I forgot something on the map. There were no windows in the back of the cabins, the windows all face into the center of that compound."

After a moment of silence, Mike said, "Well, one thing is abundantly clear: whoever determined the location of this camp either was familiar with the establishment of places for maximum security coverage or was very lucky."

"I agree," Smiley said. "It seems to me that the major weak spot is here, the south side," as he pointed to the top of the ridge where Dan and Hank had scouted the camp. "According to you, the brush is very thick around the northern or opposite end of the camp. I think that anyone trying to trash their way through the brush would be heard a mile away."

"What about sentries?" Mike asked.

"Only the retarded that got the drop on us," Hank said. "We didn't see anyone else, but then, it was raining."

"Did you see any other way into that camp?" Mike asked.

Both Hank and Dan shook their heads.

Smiley quietly reminisced, "This camp reminds me of a camp I was in about twenty clicks at the end of that war. It had a stream flowing through the center of it, too."

Tom asked, "Iraq?

"Yes, a long, long time ago. I was the rookie on our team, my first time in Iraq, and my first assignment. Our Special Forces team floated a tiny boat down the stream with a remote-controlled bomb on it. We set it off when it got to the other end of the village, and let me tell you, it sure diverted everyone's attention away from our end."

Tom, awed by the calm recitation of the tale by Smiley, asked, "You were in the Special Forces? What were you doing there?"

Smiley thoughtfully replied, "You know, it was an almost identical assignment; we had to extract an old man from the village because they had discovered that he worked for us."

"We don't have any remote control now," Dan pointed out.

"Man, that's ok. I hear you have Plastic and I've got yards of primer cord and a bunch of detonators. It seems that somehow, they found their way to my place before I was discharged," Smiley drawled with a feral look in his eyes. "And what I don't have, there are a few of my buddies still around and they'll supply me with whatever I need."

He smiled, "I thought they might come in handy sometime. Why- we could float a little boat with the plastic explosives tied inside of it down that stream. The only questions I have are what kind of Plastic you have and how much cord I need. We'll light that sucker before we sail it off and try to time it to explode wherever you want."

He paused dreamingly and smiled to himself, "Man, that's going to be so cool. If it goes off in those trees, we'll have firewood for acres around!"

"Say, can I see your Plastic? I need to find out what kind it is."

"Sure," Tom said. "Come on, it's in the barn."

Tom led Smiley out to the barn. An owl hooted at them from the upper rafters of the dusty and now unused building. Motes of dust danced in the light beams shining through the wooden sides of the musty smelling barn. A few lonely mice scurried away at their approach.

"Here it is," Tom said as he removed an old piece of protective canvas and handed the bundle of explosives to Smiley.

Smiley's hands fondled the package and unwrapped it as if it was a divine gift.

"Here, Tom, see! This is what they call Semtex. You can tell the difference between this and C-4 because this is yellowish in color while C-4 is grayish in color. We don't see much Semtex in the States because we used other types more that were manufactured here."

Tom looked at the substance, fascinated. "Isn't it dangerous to handle that stuff?"

"Naw. You can mold this into almost any shape you want. Here, watch!"

Smiley dropped the package of explosives onto the concrete floor of the barn.

Tom froze, his heart in his throat!

He swayed, lightheaded, a moan escaping from his chest!

Seconds passed.

Nothing happened.

"See, Tom, you can drop it on the floor, throw it against the wall, jump up and down on it and the stuff wouldn't go off," Smiley grinned.

"I," Tom took a shaky deep breath, trying to calm his pounding heart, "I, I wish you had told me you were going to do that!"

"Well, it's like anything else; you have to treat it right," Smiley replied as he picked up and fondled the package. "And you have to know what you are doing. You see, this stuff was made in Czechoslovakia from equal parts of two other explosives. If I remember correctly, they were called PETN and RDX that are short for some unpronounceable Czechoslovakian names. Terrorists preferred C-4 if they could get it because it was essentially odorless and that made it easier to smuggle. I question where they got this stuff? Semtex has a slight odor that dogs can pick up. Here, smell."

Tom sniffed the package. He could easily detect a mild caustic or acidic odor, almost like glue.

"What's the difference between Semtex and dynamite?" Tom asked.

"Well, if you start at the bottom without considering the hard powders such as gun powder or the soft stuff like ammonium nitrate that was used in the Oklahoma bombing, dynamite is pretty much at the bottom. Then comes trinitrotoluene . . ."

Smiley grinned at Tom. "Know what that is?"

"I can't even pronounce it. What is it?"

"The good old-fashioned T.N.T. It's about twice as powerful as regular dynamite. Then comes our Semtex here which is about half-again as powerful as T.N.T. Then the American made C-4 which has more force or velocity than Semtex. The government did and probably still does a lot of research into more powerful explosives and there's about a half-dozen levels above C-4. C-5 is probably my favorite. A lot of them aren't very stable though."

"We'll leave it out here, although it would be safe in the house," Smiley said as he gently wrapped the package. "The only thing you have to be careful about is that you never carry detonators and this stuff together; if a detonator blows, it will set these explosives off."

Tom led them back into the house. Smiley said to Dan, "Say, you don't want these people hurt, do you?"

"Oh no, all we want is our Ginger back."

Hank interrupted, "You must remember that they are armed. I found what seems to be a warning from NCIC with a description that matches that leader. If he's the same one, his name is William Addler Webber, AKA Adler or Addler."

"What kind of nick name is Adler?" asked Mike.

"Like the snake."

"Oh."

Hank continued, "He got chased out of New Mexico and Arizona. Both states have or had warrants out for him for weapons violations. And we must consider him and his bunch dangerous; besides, as you know, they're half crazy! I believe that they will fight if we try to take one of their people."

"Well," Dan said, "I don't care about Kathy, they can keep her, and good riddance; all I want is our Ginger."

"Absolutely!" Tom agreed.

Dan and Tom's heartfelt comment earned a long deep look from Lorraine.

"By the way," Mike asked. "Do we know what cabin your kid is in?"

Hank and Dan looked at each other, "Ah, no, we don't. All the cabins seemed inhabited, too."

Mike said, "Well, we'll have to find that out before we go in there. I don't want to walk through that whole dam camp, banging on doors."

"I can see it now," he continued in falsetto with a limp wrist, prancing around the cabin, "Pardon me sir and madam, have you seen a little girl I can kidnap? Would you direct me to the correct cabin? Bless you sir, I assure you my parole officer says I'm not much of a child molester anymore. By the way, madam, where *are* your young juicy children?"

Hank drawled, "Well, I suggest that you don't give up your day job."

While the others laughed, Dan had to grin despite himself.

Mike continued, "If what you say is true, those people will be like a stirred-up hornets' nest, and just as nasty."

"You've got a point there. I guess we'll just have to hope for the best, maybe we'll see her by one of the cabins," Dan said.

After much discussion, it was decided that they would leave the next morning.

Lor and Tom looked at each other in surprise, "Do you think what I'm thinking: they believe they're going without us!"

Both turned to Hank and Dan and said together, "Wrong!"

Tom pleaded, "Dad, she's my sister and I want to go, please!"

Lor, following his lead said, "Absolutely correct, plus I think I can find Ginger."

"How?" both Hank and Dan blurted.

"I might, just might be able to get my little kitten to find her. He has an extraordinary sense of smell and he follows my instructions if I can make it clear to him what I want. Do you have anything of Ginger's that might have her scent on it?"

"Sure!" Tom replied, excited. "We brought her doll all the way across the country. It might still have her scent on it."

"All right, all right," Dan said. "Sue, please get Ginger's doll. I guess you both are coming. Hank, could your wife take care of Sue while we're gone?"

"Oh sure, no problem."

Mike had a puzzled look on his face, "What kitten?"

Lor explained that she had a "little kitten" she raised from birth and that it followed her and sometimes obeyed her.

"Haven't you seen him?" she asked Mike. Upon receiving a negative answer, she went to the front door and called and whistled softly, "Here, Baby. Here, Baby."

Smiley grinned at Mike who obviously didn't know about the cat and said, "Just watch! Don't be startled. And don't make any moves!"

Suddenly, a full grown one-hundred-and-fifty-plus-pound male cougar strolled into Lor's house as if he owned the place, walked to Lor, and rubbed himself against her leg. Lor bent down and scratched him behind his black tipped ears. Sue ran up to him and gave the big cat a hug and scratched the soft brown fur on his back. She then tickled the soft white fur under his chin, his eyes closed, the cat's purr filled the house.

The quizzical look on Mike's face was replaced by large round eyes and a dropped jaw. With some effort, he closed his mouth and, forcing his eyes off the big cat, looked around. All the others were grinning at him.

"How do you like her 'kitty'?" Hank asked.

Mike just shook his head, "After tours in the Army in some nasty places, I thought I've seen everything, but this, this is unbelievable!"

The big cat arose from the floor where he had been hugged and scratched by Sue and just flowed over to Dan, his nails clicking softly on the hardwood floor, his long black tipped tail twitching slowly. He haughtily allowed Dan to scratch his tawny colored head.

"What a magnificent animal," Mike breathed.

Lor smiled proudly, "Thank you, but he doesn't know he's an animal. He thinks he's part people; I found him when he was only a day or so old and his eyes were still closed. I don't know what happened to his mother, but I fed him a combination of cow and goat's milk with some cat food thrown in. He was just like a kitten except that he never stopped growing." She took Mike's hands and said, "Come here, I need to introduce you to him."

She rubbed Mike's hands and then rubbed the big cat's face. He purred and allowed Mike to scratch his back. "Once I do that, he knows that you are a friend and he wouldn't attack you."

"Wait a second," exclaimed Mike. "About six months ago, while I was on duty in our E.R., some punk low life dragged himself in. He looked like he had tried to make love to a barbed wire fence, and the fence won. He had huge deep scratches on his buttocks, legs and back, and his front looked like he had crashed through a bramble bush."

He looked at Lor, "You didn't happen to have a prowler or peeping-tom around that time, did you?"

Hank looked at Lor, "I bet that's what happened to that guy." He looked at Mike and grinned, "We had a prowler in the area about that time, and then, he just disappeared. Now, I know what happened to him."

With difficulty, Hank changed the subject, "There's six of us and I only have four horses. Could you men use your own horses? And does one of you have a pack mule? I think we should take enough supplies for at least a couple of days."

Mike said, "Sure, Smiley and I will use our own horses, and I've got an old mare we can use for a pack horse. She's gentle and will just follow the horse in front of her. Oh, one other thing: clothes."

"Clothes?" asked Tom.

"Yes, clothes," replied Mike. "For all of us, do not wear anything that has yellow or red in it. Jeans are ok, but I want us to blend in with the trees, not be visible as if we were hunting deer."

"Good thinking," said Hank as he turned to Dan and Lor, "I'll bring Betty and the kids early tomorrow morning. Your little one can go back to our farm with them."

The arrangements completed, Hank, Smiley and Mike said good-bye and left.

After dinner that night, Dan, and Tom cleaned their weapons and checked their bows. The sleeping bags were rolled and stacked by the door with the weapons, ammo, and freeze-dried food.

"We'll take all of our medical supplies. I hope we don't need them, but . . ." Dan murmured to Tom.

Tom and Sue went to bed early.

That night, Dan and Lor lay silently awake in her bed. Both of their thoughts were on what they would face in the near future. It just seemed natural they would share their feelings, doubts and hopes. Lor's head lay on Dan's shoulder, the silences were easy and unforced. Slowly, the heat arose between them. They tenderly flowed together, their lovemaking slow, soft, and caring except the final moment when they clutched each other.

The next morning dawned bright and clear. Shortly after sunrise, Hank, his family, Mike and Smiley rode in followed by a dun-colored old mare with a few packs stacked on her. Also attached to the pack was a tiny saddle.

Lor came around the side of the house, trailed by her cougar.

She said, "I'm going to have him with us and I need to get the horses used to him."

She rubbed the cougar's face and head with her hands. She then went to first one horse and then another, holding their heads in her hands and rubbing their noses with her cougar scented hands, murmuring with each horse. Each horse started being skittish at first and then quieted under Lor's hands. Mike, Dan, and Tom were impressed: she seemed to have a special way with animals.

Lor told them, "I probably could get the horses to allow the cat to ride on their back, but neither would be very happy."

After Dan talked for a minute with Sue and Betty, Hank's wife, Sue willingly went off to play with Hank's kids.

"Don't worry, she'll be fine with us; we'll head on over to our house after a while. She can sleep with our youngest, they're about the same age," Betty said. "You just go find your little girl and don't worry about Sue."

A few minutes later, all six rode out. The dog followed Tom while the big cat roamed far afield.

When they came to the northern outskirts of Durango, Lor called the cat to her and they brought up the rear of the party.

"I'll keep him with me until we get out of this populated area," she said.

People stopped what they were doing and just stared at the spectacle: five male riders on horses with a large dog followed by a beautiful female on a horse with a large light brown colored cougar by her side. Many knew either Hank or one or more of the groups, and waved and called out greetings.

They retraced the same route Hank and Dan had taken except this time, they did not stop at the burnt area.

Dan pointed at a pile of burnt rubble, "Tom, we think that Ginger mailed those postcards from a store and post office that used to be over there."

Their eyes met, unspoken was the question, "Would they ever find their Ginger?"

Hank led them up the side canyons without stopping. They camped that evening several miles below the original cabins that Dan and Hank had found and inspected. They made a small fire and had a light dinner. The horses were hobbled near some grass and Lor had the big dog stand guard over the camp.

Lor also sent the big cat out to scout to see if there were any people nearby. She explained that if the cat saw or found anyone, he would return and alert her. Meanwhile, the cat would hunt and find food for itself.

Mike looked at Dan, "This is your show. How do you want to handle it?"

"I think we should leave our horses near where we left them before," Dan nodded at Hank. "It seems to me that the best way is to retrace our steps to the back of that camp. We know that they have a sentry guarding the road, and now, they'll probably have more than one."

"Makes sense," Hank agreed. "Plus, they wouldn't expect anyone to crawl through that brush and trees behind the camp; at least, I hope so."

"Lor, your pets must be our point leaders," Mike said.

"Sure."

Smiley had taken charge of their plastic explosives and his primer cord and blasting caps. Each carried a small pack including whatever weapons they brought along. Dan gave Lor his .38 Smith & Wesson revolver strapping it on her waist.

"Tom, we will be walking through some heavy brush; I don't want these arrows or bows snagging on branches," Dan said, "so make sure your arrows are snug in your quiver."

He asked, "Mike, do you want to carry the AR-15?"

"Oh yes!" Mike smiled and said to Tom, "I love these Colt rifles, I just don't like the actions on their revolvers. I prefer the smoother actions on Smith and Wesson or Berettas. This," he gestured with the AR-15 rifle, "is just like the military M-16's except that this isn't fully automatic. Colt put out a couple of combat models, some that are shorter in length and others that have a heavier caliber."

Mike broke open the action and pointed, "This is the older model of the AR-15. You could make this into a fully automatic rifle with a paper clip. The newer models of this weapon are supposed to prohibit you from making it into an automatic weapon, so they say. However, in full auto with this weapon, once you pull the trigger, it will fire your entire clip without stopping. The effect is that you could burn out your barrel. In this type of a problem (Dan noticed that he referred to almost everything as a "problem"), we don't want to fill the air with lead like we would if we were in combat."

His practiced hands fondled the rifle and inspected the parts, "This one is almost new, I would venture to say that there's been only about thirty or forty rounds through it. The Sear needs work and the trigger pull is still rough."

Tom glanced at his dad, impressed, "I think that's right. We only fired it twice."

They rode out the next morning shortly after sunrise and made their way to the lower cabins. It was a dreary morning and Dan thought it looked like it would rain again. He wondered to himself if it always rained up here. They hobbled their horses in a small clearing with plenty of grass.

Hank observed, "We don't want to tie them up, we'll be gone at least a day and they need to move a little."

Hank led the way, with Lor following close behind. She sent her animals out ahead to scout for sentries. Shortly after the last set of cabins and past the barbed wire gate, they left the road and branched off into the thick underbrush, generally following the original route Hank and Dan had taken. It drizzled, the only sound was their breathing, and the light patter of the falling rain on the trees. The big cat roamed ahead of them, but the dog stayed either with Lor or with Tom. There was little conversation between them; they were concentrating on making their way through the brush quietly.

Closer to the top of the ridge, Lor called the cat and dog to her and had both scouting ahead. They finally came out on the tiny trail that Dan and Hank had originally found. The ground and fallen twigs and leaves from the trees were wet and soggy. A cold raindrop wiggled its way down Tom's back, a brisk rubbing of his back only spread the chilly moisture. He shivered as the drop felt like an ice cube dripping down his sweaty back.

After Mike squatted and carefully examined the trail, he whispered to Smiley, "No footprints!"

"Yes, that's right," said Lor. "My babies don't see anyone around here."

"I suggest that we stop for a little rest and a bite to eat," said Mike. "Once we get to that camp, I don't think they are going to invite us for dinner."

After a brief rest, they trudged on.

They approached the area where they could overlook the camp and crouched in a circle to rest. It had been a very strenuous walk up the side of the wooded canyon through the heavy brush, particularly since everything was wet. Lor soothed the big cat while Tom rubbed the back and head of "his" dog. Clearly, neither animal was particularly enthused about being out in the rain.

While they were resting, Smiley brought out a supply of camouflage paint he had "liberated" from his combat days.

"Here," he whispered, "Put this on your face and hands." He had each wipe their faces and hands with the paint until they looked like something out of a war movie.

Tom thought the camouflage paint looked great. Though he was excited, the adventure books he had read said nothing about the taut, tense feeling in his stomach. His chest was tightening; it didn't dawn on him that everyone else was much quieter with lines of tension outlining their faces.

Could they find their beloved Ginger?

After their rest, they decided to see what the camp looked like. Each crawled to the edge of the ridge, one behind a bush, another between some tall weeds, one crawled under an evergreen tree. Dan found a place between two bushes where he peered out. The rain and mist made it difficult to closely examine the camp; however, there was smoke coming from nearly every cabin and occasionally, someone would run through the rain from one cabin to another.

Dan passed the binoculars around, whispering, "Here, everyone takes a look."

They could see there were thirteen cabins in a semicircle with the front of each cabin facing inward to the center of the circle. The stream flowed between the cabins, separating eight on the right or east side and five on the other or west side. Two of the five on the west side were connected by a canvas covered walkway. At the far north end of the encampment, next to the stream was a large pile of cut logs and firewood plus a few small sheds. There were two small foot bridges over the deep and fast flowing stream. The swings that Dan had seen on their first visit were on the far east side near the end of the eight cabins.

As they examined the camp, an acidic odor of fresh manure from the corrals directly below and to the right of them drifted on the moisture laden air. The stream flowed from their lower right, through the corrals (obviously providing water for the animals), and out through the encampment. Next to the corrals were a few more small sheds, probably containing supplies for the animals, Dan thought.

"What are those for?" Tom whispered, pointing to burnt poles standing in the middle of the cabins.

Smiley looked and whispered, "They pour oil on top of those poles and burn them at night. It gets very dark up here at night and those poles give them enough light to see to do things outside."

The big Holstein bull in one of the corrals was restless again. He sniffed the air, pawed the ground, occasionally let out with a soft bellow, and generally forced "his" herd to the far end of the corral.

Lor called the animals to her and held their heads in her hands for long moments. She had Ginger's old doll and had both animals smell it. Both whined and lay on their haunches; occasionally one or the other would snarl softly.

Lor, dismayed, quietly shook her head at Dan. "I can't get them to understand what I want. They don't know the difference between a red headed child and another child. And this scent may be too old."

Hank, Mike, Dan, Tom and Lor retreated from the edge of the ridge and had a quiet conference.

Dan whispered to Tom, "I think that since only you and I know what Kathy looks like, you and I should make our way over to the east side and examine each cabin in turn looking for either Kathy or Ginger. OK?"

Tom nodded, his face tense.

"Lor, would you send your dog over to try to quiet that camp dog?"

Lor nodded, "Sure, that dog hasn't been treated well, anyway."

"Everybody, keep an eye out for a bright red headed little girl! The last time we saw her, she had long hair, and I don't think there are too many children with bright red hair," Dan whispered. "If you can get her, grab her and run! Once we have her, we're gone too!"

Mike suggested, "Hank, Lor, how about you two filtering down to the area near the western part of the corrals to serve as back-up. See those bales of hay down there? We'll use that as a meeting place if necessary."

Dan nodded and explained their plan to Smiley. Smiley agreed and said that he would hide by the stream and try to time how long it took an object to float from him to the pile of logs. He thought that would be a good place to set off a diversion since, if he was lucky and timed it right, the plastic explosives would explode by the pile of logs and throw all sorts of wood and debris throughout the entire encampment, causing even more confusion.

"Man-oh-man, I hope I get to do this!" he smiled dreamingly.

"I'll go with you two," Mike said to Dan and Tom. "I think I can be of more assistance if you run into problems."

Dan was glad to have Mike along; Mike seemed to flow though trees and bushes with hardly a whisper of sound whereas Dan thought he (Dan) moved through the trees and bushes with all the subtlety of an elephant in heat.

"Dan, Tom, you two hit the cabins at dusk; there will still be enough light to see, but if things fall apart, it might be dark enough to hide," Mike suggested. "Once we start, I want to go through this camp as fast as possible. When, not if, someone figures out that we're here, all hell will break loose."

"Makes sense to me," Dan said.

"Lor, would you hang onto our bows? Tom, you and I will keep our guns with us."

"Be careful, please!" Lor whispered as she touched both Tom and Dan's arms.

Dan, Mike, and Tom left soon thereafter. Mike thought it would take them several hours to make their way quietly around the east side of the camp to the northernmost cabin.

Later, near dusk, after an arduous journey that included part walking, part crawling, and wading through a small stream, Dan, Tom and Mike lay at the edge of the forest looking into the campgrounds. While the rain had ceased falling, the sky was still cloudy and everything was still saturated with moisture. Cold dribbles of mist meandered their way under shirts and pants causing instant shivers. They were just south of the swings that were swaying back and forth from a gentle breeze. Near the camp dog, Tom could see his dog hiding in the shadows as if he was just secretly visiting a friend. The camp dog was near them, but strangely, it was squatting on its paws almost asleep.

"Tom, crawl to that first cabin and sneak a look inside; see if anyone is in there," Dan whispered. "Remember, if we get separated, we'll meet at that far corral by those bales of hay."

"Just a second, Tom," Mike whispered. "If someone comes out of one of the cabins, freeze! even if he is not looking directly at you. His eyes will pick up motion from the side. If his back is to you, only then can you move. Understand?"

Tom nodded, his heart thumping in his chest.

"Tom, as soon as you get back here, I'm going to filter on over to the cabins on the other side of that stream, OK?" Mike pointed.

After crawling in the shadows to the north side of the first cabin, Tom paused for a moment. His hands shaking, his heart pounding so loud he thought everyone in the cabin could hear it, he stood and quickly peered into the lived-in cabin.

Nothing.

No one was there!

He then hastily crawled back to where Mike was hiding.

"Mike, that cabin's been lived in, but there's no one there," Tom whispered.

At the same time, Dan crawled to the second cabin, keeping in the now lengthening shadows, and quickly peeked in the side window. At first, he could see nothing, but as his eyes adjusted to the dim light, he could see that the cabin was also empty.

A man walked out of the last of the cabins in the semicircle in front of Dan.

Dan froze.

As soon as the man turned in the opposite direction, Dan sank to the ground at the side of the cabin. The man, wearing a poncho, was loudly chanting some kind of unintelligible prayer. He was carrying a can and a lighted torch. He approached first one of the poles, then the other and poured what looked like used motor oil on each pole. He lit each of the poles with his torch, all the while continuing his chanting. After lighting the poles, he stomped his torch into the ground and threw it into the steam. He then marched back to his cabin.

Dan, his heart, now quieting, crawled back to Tom and Mike and told them of his findings.

Suddenly, at that moment, the clouds broke and the sun shined through a crevice in the far mountain top, illuminating the center of the campground. Now, Dan understood why this campsite had been chosen: In the evening, just before the sun set, it gave an appearance of divine bright blessing at a certain location in the center of the camp.

Just as the center was being illuminated, the man who had been addressed as "Your Grace" led a group of people out of their cabins to the center of the illumination. He was dressed in a bright yellow and red robe with red epaulets with chrome or silver medallions hanging from the epaulets. The sun reflecting off the bright yellow and red robe with the hanging medallions gave the Leader a flashing radiance that was almost blinding!

Very clever, Dan thought. He wondered what happened to the leader's guns. Once in the center of the illuminated area and facing west, "The Leader" and his followers started chanting softly, and then increasingly louder, swaying slowly back and forth.

Dan looked carefully at the group singing and swaying in the center of the camp, "Tom, Kathy's not in that bunch. I'm going to crawl over to those other cabins."

Dan crept to the side of the third cabin, and peaked into a side window. No one appeared to be in the cabin, but it was lived in. He then crept to the fourth cabin and again peered in a side window.

Nothing.

This cabin also appeared to be empty, but someone lived there, too. This cabin looked in much more disarray than the previous cabins.

Dan crawled around the back of the fifth cabin. He could hear voices inside. This cabin had two doors, one in the front facing the center of the campground and one facing the side. Dan crept to the side door and listened. He could hear a few mumbled voices, all females. By this time, Dan was getting frustrated in his search for his little daughter: where was she?

"What the hell!" Dan thought to himself. "Maybe someone inside knows what's going on!"

Dan drew his 9 .mm chrome H & K semi-automatic handgun from its holster, quietly pulled the rawhide latch on the wooden door, very slowly pushed it open, and squeezed inside the cabin.

An odor of unwashed bodies with an almost overpowering smell of incense permeated the heated room. Several lanterns emitting a fair amount of light hung from the wooden rafters of the cabin.

Dan's look swept the interior of the cabin in a single glance. Three women were all sitting in a semi-circle facing the fireplace talking or sewing or something.

Dan pulled back the upper part of his 9 .mm semi-automatic handgun and released the slide; it loaded itself with the sharp clank of hard metal on metal! He had the instant attention of the woman.

"All I want is my daughter! Don't try anything and you won't get hurt. Where's Kathy Peterson or Ginger Peterson?"

Silence.

Dead silence!

What Dan had forgotten was his appearance.

He had gotten filthy and weed and damp grass stained from crawling through the mud, grass. and bushes. He was covered with dirt and leaves. A piece of a branch was hanging from his left shoulder holster, his face and hands were covered with camouflage paint all topped by a battered California Angel baseball cap with weeds sprouting out of it. The three women saw an apparition holding a shiny 9 .mm semi-automatic that somehow just appeared in the shadows that had a perfectly good human voice coming from it.

Silence.

Absolute silence.

Suddenly, screams!

All three of the women screamed for help.

Dan, startled with the unexpected response from the women, jerked and accidentally fired a deafening round into the roof of the cabin. The only response to that was an even louder volume of screams from the women, and a pile of dirt on his head from the hollow nosed bullet going through the roof.

Meanwhile, Smiley hearing the screams and the shot decided that now was a great time to set off his diversion. He had determined that it took between thirty and forty-five seconds for an object to float from him to the pile of logs. He had fastened a plastic garbage can top with a few wooden sticks that would float the kilo of explosives down the stream. After lighting the primer cord to the detonators, he pushed his "boat" down the stream.

He sat back with a dreamy smile on his face, softly singing, "Row, row, row your boat, gently down the steam . . ." and waited to see what would happen.

Dan, getting little or no response to his, he thought, reasonable request, was trying to figure out how to stop the women from screaming. He sidestepped from in front of the side door to the door facing directly onto the clearing, trying to keep a better angle between him and the screaming women.

Suddenly, the front wooden door behind Dan flew open, the sharp edge of the heavy door striking him in the back.

Dan's gun flew from his hand, skidded across the floor, and lodged against the base of one bunk. He was knocked to the floor, dazed by the force of the blow.

Above him towered the leader.

"You!"

The leader threw off his robes and yanked a huge pearl handled hunting knife from the belt around his waist. (Dan, in a remote part of his mind, wondered if everything this person had was pearl handled!) Still dazed, Dan fumbled for his Marine Corp dark metal K-Bar knife and rose to his knees, waving his knife in front of him to fend off the attack of the leader.

The leader, snarling, lashed out with a heavy silver metal-toed cowboy boot, and struck Dan on his left shoulder. The unexpected kick drove Dan to the floor. Despite the sharp blow, he frantically clutched onto his knife.

Dan rolled to his right side and attempted to get to his knees, his left shoulder felt numb. The leader swung his metal-toed boot at Dan's head. The heavy boot just grazed Dan's temple, drawing blood. Dan recovered his balance, grabbed the boot, lifted it, and threw the leader, off balance, back out of the open doorway.

Dan, still dazed, half stooped, half crawled through the door after the leader.

The leader fell on his back, grabbed a handful of dirt, and threw it in Dan's face when he came through the door. Half blinded, Dan fell to his knees, desperately wiping his eyes.

The leader, still snarling, jumped to his feet, and again kicked Dan. The heavy boot just grazed Dan's left arm and struck his left rib cage. The shock of the blow stunned Dan. Almost by reflex, his vision blurry, he took a quick slash with his knife at the leader's leg. The K-Bar's razor edge struck the leader's leg approximately one inch above his cowboy boot and sliced a one-half inch deep and three-inch long laceration across the back of the leg.

Several of the leader's followers, alerted by the screams of the women and seeing their leader falling out of the doorway, crowded around Dan. Their yells were enforced on Dan with their boots and bare feet. A few had clubs and were attempting to hit Dan. While more than a few blows effectively struck Dan, most of the clubbing blows either glanced off him or outright missed him. Dazed and fighting for his life, Dan struggled to his feet, and frantically waving his knife, attempted to fend off the kicks and blows.

The leader cursing, shoved aside two of his men and tackled Dan from the back, rolling them both over and over in the dust, dirt, mud, and grime of the yard. The leader came out on top swearing, his knees straddling Dan's chest.

Suddenly, Smiley's dreams came true!

His "boat" had floated down the stream and lodged against the pile of logs at the edge of the steam. It detonated with a duel, thunderous violent red and yellow explosion, hurling logs, debris, dust, water, and firewood into the dark air.

A shed near the logs contained the camp's explosives; these explosives sympathetically detonated causing the two-part explosion. The concussion knocked the leader off Dan, the followers flung to the ground from the blast.

The logs, a few trees and four nearby cabins collapsed. One cabin burst into explosive flames, its screaming inhabitants fleeing the fallen cabin like gophers out of a hole. Incredible confusion reigned in the campground. Debris, logs, and tiny pieces of kindling were falling from the sky.

Huge clouds of dust and dirt stirred up by the explosion swirled around the cabins.

The explosion collapsed the gates holding the animals. The Holstein bull, crazed out of his tiny mind by the fire and explosion, attacked anything in sight. Pigs were squealing and running frantically through the camp!

Dan, still dazed, had somehow suffered a knife cut on his chest while being beaten and badly clubbed by the leader's followers. Flattened on his back, he was struggling to rise, but his body refused to obey him.

The leader got to his hands and knees, and dragging one leg behind him, crawled through the mud and dirt to Dan. Screaming profanities, he knelt over Dan.

Raged, the leader clutched his pearl handled knife above his head and started a vicious downward swing into Dan's chest!

Dan could see the pearl handled knife stabbing down toward his chest, but his numbed arms refused to block the attack.

A spear of helpless fear thrust through Dan; a moan escaped from his clenched lips.

Suddenly, a one-hundred-and-fifty-pound snarling cougar with his jaws wide open appeared out of the dust, fire, and confusion, and launched himself against the leader's arm. The downward swinging arm was engulfed by the fang filled mouth of the cougar, slicing it, and breaking it cleanly. Dan vaguely remembered a distinct popping sound as if a brittle branch was being broken. The force of the cougar's attack dragged the leader off Dan and flung him several yards away.

The cougar stopped in his tracks, straddling Dan, and with a terrible screaming snarl erupting from his powerful chest, directly faced the leader's men who had surrounded Dan.

They took one look at these horrible razor-sharp teeth filled apparition, dropped their clubs and knives, and fled, dragging their leader with them.

The cougar roared a challenge at the fleeing men, but it was unanswered.

Dan, on the ground, his left shoulder and arm useless, numbed, in shock and half-conscious from the savage kicks and fight looked up at the cougar. His left chest knifed shivers of pain through him each time he drew a breath, the center part of his chest felt wrongly wet, and the left side of his head pounded with each beat of his heart. The big cat carefully stepped over Dan, sniffed Dan's head, took a distasteful swipe with his tongue, looked around and stood over Dan.

Dan looked with blurred vision westward toward the general direction of the fires.

A tall figure with a battered felt hat and a star flashing on his left chest was striding toward him through the all-encompassing fire, dust, dusk, and smoke. The fire and setting sun were behind the tall man, creating an outline that towered above Dan. The tall man was carrying a tiny package.

As the tall figure strode closer, Dan saw that the tiny package had long red hair and was clutching the man around the neck.

"Oh my God!"

"Is it her?"

"Is it her?"

"IS IT HER??"

"Could it be . . ."

A tiny body launched itself at Dan, crying, "Daddy? Daddy!"

"I think this small person belongs to you," a pleased Hank drawled.

Dan clutched the tiny, starved body of his Ginger to him! He could not get up, but his Ginger was hugging him and planting wet kisses and tears over his face. Some of the tears were Dan's.

He attempted to rise, but the pain was too great. He said with a husky voice and brimming eyes to Hank, "God, I didn't even know if she was still alive! If there is anything you ever need, anything!"

"Well, we're kind of even, Son," smiled a pleased Hank.

Hank looked around, "I suggest we get out of here; we've caused about enough damage for one night."

He bent and grasped Dan under his armpits and lifted him from the ground, "You don't look very good, but you're going to have to walk, my friend."

Each breath Dan took sent radiating pain shooting down his chest and ribs. Ginger was hanging onto Dan and refusing to let go of him. Hank draped Dan's right arm over his shoulder and half carried, half walked him toward the corral and meeting place, the big cat leading them.

When they appeared out of the dust and confusion at the corral, they were met by Lor.

She looked at Dan, blanched and exclaimed, "Oh my God!"

She grabbed Dan's free arm and made him sit on a nearby bale of hay. She smiled at Ginger who just stared back, clutching onto her father.

As Dan collapsed on the bale of hay, he gasped, "Where's Tom?"

Lor said, "I don't know, but we'll find him!"

She called the big cat to her and took its face in her hands. The big cat briefly licked her hand and waited, focusing on Lor. Suddenly, the cat's squeaky voice growled softly and bounded away.

Mike materialized out of the dust and confusion followed by Smiley, "It's good to see you, I've been talking to some of the locals about your Kathy." Upon seeing Lor's glare, Mike hastily amended his comments to, "Well, I didn't mean "your" whatever the hell she was."

Dan, seeing the grim look in Mike's face, didn't ask how he was communicating with the locals, except that he was glad he wasn't "one of the locals!"

Mike continued, "It took a little persuasion, but they told me what happened. Apparently, about two, maybe three weeks ago, she suffered some kind of appendicitis attack and the entire camp, she included, refused to get competent medical help. They all sat around her praying or chanting or something. She got worse and they still didn't seek a doctor. She became unconscious and," Mike hesitated and looked at Ginger, "she passed away about eight or nine days ago."

Hank said thoughtfully, "I bet that's why they were so paranoid of us when we rode in that first day. They thought we had come to arrest them or seek revenge or something. Now things make sense."

Out of the dust materialized the cougar, followed by Tom and the dog. He, too, was covered with dust, mud, and dirt. He had been knocked flat by the concussion from the explosion and then nearly been trampled by the terrified herd of cattle; he had been crouching near one of the cabins, attempting to make sense of the confusion.

Ginger saw Tom, jumped from Dan's lap and launched herself at him, yelling, "Tommy, Tommy!" As little sister hugged dusty, muddy, and dirty big brother, even burley Mike had a wet furrow running down his grime covered smiling face!

Hank cleared his throat a couple of times and said, "Come on people, we got what we came for. Let's get out of here before they get organized."

Lor exclaimed, "Hank, Dan can't make it back the way we came, look, he can hardly walk!"

Mike observed, "Well, we aren't worried about ambushes anymore, we can take the road like normal people. The only thing I'm worried about is that big bull, but I think your cat and dog here will keep him occupied."

Lor grabbed their bows, "Come on, let's get out of here!"

Hank and Mike assisted Dan to his feet. Dan mumbled a request to Smiley to retrieve his 9 .mm automatic from the fifth cabin where he had been attacked by the leader.

Ginger had attached herself to Tom to his great pleasure.

They slowly walked through the camp nearly dragging Dan since his legs didn't seem to work well; the dust, dirt and confusion was starting to subside. The fires were burning themselves out and the dust was settling. They could hear the leader screaming and berating his followers from behind a far cabin, his bass voice echoing around the camp. Hank led the way with Tom bringing up the rear. Mike, with Lor's mother-hen-like assistance, was helping Dan walk. The big cat stayed with Lor, but the dog roamed behind with Tom.

They crossed over the steam, their steps drumming on the wooden bridge. At the edge of the camp Smiley joined them, having retrieved Dan's weapon from the cabin.

"Boy, those people don't like you, Dan."

"The feeling is mutual," Tom growled. "Look at what they did to my sister and my Dad."

At the beginning of the road, a large black and white object in the dim shadows moved.

They froze!

The dog bounded ahead of them, barking loudly. The large black and white object gave off a startled "Mooo" and ran crashing through the bushes.

"Aw," Tom grinned, "It was only one of the cows." He bent down to rub the dog's head. "You didn't have to scare her half to death, but good boy," he praised the dog.

A three-quarters full moon gave them a little light to see as they trudged down the road. Their progress was slowed by Dan's inability to walk any distance without resting. The blows he had suffered had taken their toll. He was feeling a little less dazed, but all that did was to make his head hurt more; he thought something was wrong with his chest because besides the pounding pain, it felt damp.

They came to a small grassy clearing surrounded by tall pine trees just off the road and stopped.

"We're not going any further," Lor adamantly decided. "He needs to rest and we can't carry him much further."

"Think we'll be safe here?" Mike asked, looking around. "We're not very far from that camp."

"Sure, my babies are the best sentries there are," Lor smiled grimly. "No one will come near us without them knowing about it."

After they made a small campfire, Lor looked at Dan, he had just been sitting where they placed him, his hunched body shivering in pain. She screamed, "Oh My God!" when she took a closer look at him: his chest, shirt and undershirt were covered with blood!

Mike ran over to Dan.

"Calm down, Lorraine! Calm down! Let me look at him."

"Hank, Tom, would you bring the horses up here? I left my medicine bag and supplies in my pack by the horses. Smiley, would you make us a bigger fire, I need to see what I'm doing."

"Dan, Mike was a paramedic in the Army and he works as an Emergency Room nurse over in our main hospital," Lor said. "Will he be all right, Mike?"

"Lorraine, relax! I've fixed up much worse at the hospital: we have those hillbillies coming in every Friday night after they get drunk and beat the hell out of each other."

"Dan, for right now, just keep bending over with your arms across your chest; that'll stop any major bleeding until I can see what happened to you."

As soon as Lor had made Dan as comfortable as possible, she turned her attention to Ginger who had stayed behind with Dan, clutching onto him. Lor had a little trail-mix food and water from her canteen that she gently fed Ginger. Then, she pulled from her jacket a small candy bar she had been saving just for her. Ginger's big eyes lit up and a trembling smile creased a grimy face.

Tom and Hank soon arrived with the horses and their packs. Lor immediately started boiling water to sterilize Mike's instruments. Most of his instruments, however, had been wrapped in a sterile package. She hovered over Mike as he gently removed Dan's shirt.

"Here, Lorraine, I'm going to cut his undershirt off; it's in tatters anyway," Mike said.

"That's fine. I can sew his shirt back together, but those T-shirts are too flimsy to sew; at best they can be used for a rag."

Mike ran his hands and fingers over Dan's ribs and back; though Dan moaned deeply a few times, Mike said, "I don't think you have any broken ribs or bones, but you have some very nasty bruises. For all I can determine, you might even have a slight concussion from being kicked in the head."

He grinned at Dan, "Why didn't you pick on somebody your own size?"

Dan, Lor and Tom didn't even smile.

Once the undershirt was cut off, Mike dropped a few drops of bleach into the boiled water, "Heat and bleach will kill anything."

After washing and disinfecting his hands with a little alcohol, he slipped on a pair of sterile gloves and gently washed Dan's chest. A jagged knife wound started just on top of Dan's left nipple and went across his chest to just under his right nipple. The deepest laceration was just to the inside of each nipple in the meat or fat part of his breasts.

As Mike cleaned the oozing knife wound with a precious little dab of hydrogen peroxide, he said, "Guy, I've got to take some stitches; most of this I can use butterflies on, but the deepest parts need to be stitched. The best part of your knife wound is that you bled quite a bit; bleeding cleans wounds, too."

He went on, "I have just a very little pain killing medication that I could inject in your chest, but I want to save it for emergencies. I don't know when we'll ever have any more."

He looked Dan in the eye, "Think you can do it without dope?"

Dan, with beads of sweat pouring down his grey face, just nodded.

"Tom, Lor, come here and hold his hands and shoulders, I don't want him jerking or moving while I'm sewing. This isn't like my E.R and the light isn't the best out here."

Lor and Tom obediently grasped Dan hands and shoulders. Smiley attempted to entertain Ginger while Hank served as Mike's nurse. Mike's large, very strong hands with the calmness of long practice, tied a small amount of surgical string to a very fine curved suturing needle; he then disinfected it as well as he was able to considering that they were in the middle of a mountainous forest!

He looked at Lor and Tom and nodded. After Hank poured a little alcohol over his hands, he pressed the jagged edges of the knife wound together. When he made the first penetration of Dan's skin with the needle, Dan jerked and moaned in his throat.

Lor grasped Dan's hand and shoulder as hard as she could, tears streaming down her face. Mike made eight stitches on the inside of each breast to close the knife wound; the remainder of the jagged laceration, he closed with butterfly bandages. After carefully placing a large sterile dressing on the wound, he then unsealed a large bandage holding the dressing in place and tightly taped Dan's chest.

Once he was finished and while he was washing Dan's blood off his hands, Mike said, "Well, when your grandkids ask you what you did in the war, you can open your shirt and tell them that you had your boobs operated on!"

Despite themselves, both Tom and Lor laughed.

Dan wasn't amused!

"Here, I'm giving you 800 milligrams of Ibuprofen which should help a little with your pain and bruises," Mike said.

They ate and rested that night. The cougar and dog were introduced to Ginger. The dog licked her hand and went back to lie by Tom. The big cat's chest, however, purred when the back of his ears was rubbed by Ginger. She was enchanted by the big cat and it seemed that the feeling was mutual. He even allowed her to touch his long white whiskers.

Hank told Dan how he found Ginger, "Right after that leader led his followers out of their cabin and started praying, I checked the cabins on the other side of the stream. They kept the kids in the second cabin. I just walked in and asked for Ginger. She was the only red-haired girl there who raised her hand!"

He smiled gently at Ginger, "I asked her what her last name was and she said Peterson. I told her that her daddy and brother had come for her, but I don't think she really believed me. But, as soon as I heard that shot, I knew things were falling apart. I grabbed her and got out of there."

Ginger started by sleeping with Tom, but sometime during the night, Dan was awakened by a tiny body crawling into his sleeping bag with him. Dan, with tears in his eyes, remembered how she used to crawl into his bed at night and snuggle up to him. He hadn't always slept well because she radiated heat like a furnace and liked to push her strangely cold feet into his armpits. Now, he didn't care, she was with him.

During the night, Dan, dozing through his pain, awoke to hear the dog growling softly beside Tom. Both the big cat and the dog crouched and slowly moved up the road, both growling deep in their chests. Suddenly, both growled fiercely and charged up the road! Dan heard a large animal crashing through the underbrush away from them. He couldn't tell if it was one of the camp's cattle or what; whatever it was would not come back this way again.

The next morning dawned bright and sunny. Mike and Lor examined Dan's body. Massive bruises raised great welts of black, yellow, and blue on his body and face. He could hardly move, but he, and Tom, too could hardly stop smiling-they had their Ginger!

Through his pain, Dan mumbled to Tom, his eyes brimming, "We got her, Son! We got her."

In the daylight, though, clutching her doll that Lor had given her, she looked thin and frail. Obviously, the people in the camp hadn't taken decent care of her. Lor gave her a light sponge bath, Later, she said angrily, "That poor little girl hasn't had a bath in weeks or months. What was wrong with those people?"

It took nearly an hour for Lor to brush Ginger's matted and filthy hair. Her hair was so dirty, it looked brown in the bright sunlight, rather than bright red. Lor furiously told Dan that Ginger's hair hadn't been brushed or even washed for several weeks. While Lor was brushing Ginger's hair, Tom walked over, squatted down by her, and smiled warmly, "Well, Sis, Sue's waiting for you when we get to Lor's place. Everything will be all right now." He gently reached out and caressed her cheek. Her big bright blue eyes glowed warmly; a small smile broke though.

Both Hank and Lor assured Dan that a couple of weeks of good food and lots of loving and Ginger would be all right.

They loaded the horses and Ginger fit nicely on Hank's tiny saddle. Hank, Mike, and Tom had to help Dan onto his horse. Once in the saddle, he sat there with perspiration dripping from his forehead, shivering. Any movement sent flashes of pain pounding through his body. He hoped he could stay on the horse. Clutching the saddle horn with both hands, he tried to cushion his severely bruised body, but they had no choice, they had to move. They could not stay here.

They slowly moved out, the horses picking their easy way, the dog and big cat scouting behind and ahead. Lor smiled at Ginger, "Don't worry, Honey, they'll protect us."

They walked the horses out of the canyon. Dan was having trouble staying on his horse because every movement of the horse seemed to aggravate his bruises. They stopped to rest several times before they even got to the remains of the main highway. Each time, Hank and Mike helped Dan off his horse. Lor would place wet compresses on his head or on the bruises on his body. She apologized, "I don't have anything cold to put on your face or body, but when we get home, you will feel better."

Dan's chest and ribs seemed to hurt the most, but the steady, gentle rocking motion of the horse numbed his ribs.

He told Lor, "It only hurts when I breathe or laugh."

While traveling down the road, Ginger rode between Lor and Dan. She told them she and her "Ma Ma" had been at the camp for nearly the whole time they had been gone from Southern California. She said that the winter was the hardest because they had little food or clothing. The leader required them to go out and beg for money from the tourists down by the hotel and in the small town near them. (That was where Ginger mailed the postcards to Tom and Sue.) If they didn't come back with money or food or clothes or something, they received no "blessings" that night. As best as Dan could ascertain, "Blessings" were any favor, including food (!) granted by the leader to his followers.

The longer Dan listened to Ginger's story and the terrible conditions she lived under, the angrier he became. At one point, delirious from the pain, he painfully pulled up his horse and mumbled, "I'm going back there and teach that . . .that thing a lesson! He can't treat kids like that!"

"No, Dan!" Lor said worriedly, "It's over, we got what we came for!"

"Hank?" she called, "Come here please."

"She is absolutely correct, Son!" Hank said when Lor explained what Dan wanted to do. "Those people who are there have an option to walk out of that camp every day. That's their life, let them live it under those conditions. Plus," he added with a smile, "we got the most important person, your little one!"

Through a red-rimmed fog of pain, Dan reluctantly had to agree; in addition, he was in no condition to even change his clothes, much less, as much as he wanted to, break the remaining bones in the leader's body.

They camped that night in a small camping area north of the outskirts of Durango. Tom had used his bow and arrows and shot five rabbits that day. The first two rabbits he gave to the big cat and the remaining three were used in a delicious rabbit stew. Ginger's eyes were big when she was told she could eat all she wanted. Her thin, nearly emaciated body made it obvious that she hadn't had a decent meal in weeks. With pleasure both Tom and Dan told her that never again would she have to perform "Blessings" before she could eat.

Dan had tears of joy in his heart when he saw Ginger sitting between Lor and Tom, all three eating their dinner together, talking quietly and smiling at each other. Dan couldn't eat much because the left side of his face was heavily swollen, (Apparently, during the fight, someone had kicked him on the side of his face), but his smile radiated through the pain.

"I think you might have a T.M.J. problem with your jaw," Mike said. "Does it click when you move it?"

"Yes, it does," Dan nodded, painfully.

"What is T.M.J.?" Tom asked.

"T.M.J. is medical shorthand for a temporo-mandibular joint dysfunction which is a condition that is essentially a dislocated jaw," Mike said. "There is nothing I can do about it without x-rays to determine the severity of the condition; he will live, but it'll be a little difficult to eat for a while."

He looked in Lor's direction and smiled. "Maybe you can get her to feed you for a few days."

That night, before Ginger crawled into her sleeping bag, she gave "her Tommy" a good night hug, then

Dan got a long hug. Ginger then went to Lor and gave her a long hug. Lor looked at Dan over Ginger's flaming red hair with tears brimming in her eyes.

She murmured to the little girl, "You sleep easy tonight, Sweetheart, you're safe and you're with us." She reluctantly let go of Ginger and tucked her in her sleeping bag.

That night, Lor and Dan lay next to each other under the bright stars, surrounded by the smell of pine trees with an occasional whiff of campfire smoke. Their hands touched and caressed. They talked long into the night; sometime later that night, Ginger crawled again into Dan's sleeping bag. While her occasional movements and kicks against his sore body caused sweat to break out on Dan's head from the pain, and more than once, a soft groan escaped from his clenched lips, Dan dozed with a smile on his face: He had his little girl!

The next morning after a light breakfast, they broke camp. Dan, still suffering from the beating, needed to be lifted onto the back of his horse. Once there, it felt worse, the back-and-forth movement caused his heavily bruised body to announce in no uncertain terms it didn't appreciate such treatment.

They made their way back though the northern part of Durango. Lor sent the big cat home; Hank and Mike both thought there was no danger any more from the camp followers, and in addition, the big cat was uncomfortable around people he didn't know.

"Let's go to my place," Hank suggested. "Your Sue is there and my wife will have plenty of food and extra clothes for your little one."

As they slowly rode up to a typical, but large ranch style house, Tom's dog ran ahead barking. The front door flew open and a stout woman with an apron over her blue jeans hastened out.

"You're home, thank heavens you're home!" Betty, Hank's wife exclaimed.

She ran to Hank's horse and nearly dragged him off the animal. They embraced for long moments.

"It's ok, Mother, its ok, everything turned out fine." Hank murmured to her. Hank's eyes met Dan's over her head. Unspoken volumes of thought went into that single exchange.

"Come, come meet the little one," Hank said.

At this moment, Sue, with a couple of other kids in tow, came around the corner of the house. She saw the group standing by the horses in the yard and let out a scream "Daddy, Tommy."

She ran to Dan and flung herself into his arms; Dan nearly passed out, he fell to his knees, the pain was so severe!

Lor quickly reached out and took Sue out of Dan's arms and said, "We have someone for you!"

Then, for the first time in over two years, Sue laid eyes on her little sister. They ran to each other and after hugging, touched arms, danced together, rubbed hands while each talking a mile a minute. Big eyes in little cherub faces surrounded by long fine hair radiated pleasure and happiness.

After a large meal, Mike, and Smiley left. Before they departed, Dan painfully hobbled to them and said with deep feeling, "Mike, Smiley, there is no way I can ever repay you for helping us the last couple of days. The words 'Thank You' are inadequate; if there is ever anything I can do, just call." He shook each man's hand with a heartfelt "Thank You!"

Smiley, a little embarrassed, replied "Aw, it was nothing, I'm glad to have helped. It's kind of nice to see some happiness now. And man-oh-man," he grinned, "That sure was a great explosion. I guess I've still got the touch."

Mike shrugged off Dan's thanks, "Oh, I'm happy for you, and for Lorraine, too. I'll come back in a day or two to check your stitches. You just rest now."

That evening, Dan and his family returned to Lor's place. He needed time to rest and recover.

CHAPTER NINE

S everal days passed.
Daniel Peterson's temperature soared, his face ached from being kicked in the fight and every muscle in his body hurt. He slowly healed, the black, blue, and yellow bruises he had received in the savage beating from the followers in the commune eventually disappeared. A massive bruise about three inches to the left of his spine and just under his left shoulder blade covered the spot where a steel toed boot had found its mark.

"Keep putting cold compresses on his bruises for the first two-three days, and after that, put on warm compresses to aid the healing. Some aspirin or Tylenol will help with his pain," Mike told a very worried Lorraine and Tom. "Keep an eye on his temperature, he was beaten quite badly, but I think he'll be all right in about a week or so. He'll just be stiff for some time. Lorraine, feed him soup or some other light substance for about a week; if he doesn't have to chew something hard, his T.M.J. or jaw where he was kicked should heal."

Mike rode out to Lorraine's farm a few times to examine Dan. He removed the stitches from Dan's chest commenting, "Well, two years of medical school sure helped here."

Upon noticing Dan's expression of surprise, Mike explained, "I exhausted my personal funds to attend medical school as far as I did, and I couldn't borrow enough money to finish. I saw no options, but to join the Army. I received one of those guaranteed assignments to a medical unit and hoped to save enough money to finish school."

"I was sent to Africa and a few of the other conflicts our government was involved in. There was always a shortage of competent and sober medical help and we did everything from triage to actual emergency surgery."

"Besides," he grinned at Dan, "If you don't like my services, just pick up your telephone and call for another doctor."

"I had just enough money saved to return to medical school and was planning on returning in the fall when 'all this' happened," Mike continued. He had a slightly haunted and frustrated look on his face realizing there probably would not be any more medical schools.

As the days passed, Ginger gained weight. Her emaciated body started to fill out; in addition, her previously perky personality forcibly repressed for nearly two years blossomed with the love and care showered upon her by the entire household. Many smiles were on Dan's face as he saw Sue and Ginger skipping through the front yard or around the house, singing some childhood song. Ginger's long bright red hair was a splash of vivid color in the dark green trees and house as the two girls played with the big cat and Tom's dog.

"Tom, Lorraine, I'm worried if some of that religious group might try to rescue Ginger," Dan mumbled their first night back at her home, his body shaking with fever.

"You don't need to be concerned about whether somebody would try to kidnap the girls," Lorraine smiled gently. "Both of them, and Tom too, have become part of my home. And you've seen that the big cat and dog follow them almost everywhere."

Lorraine smiled tenderly at Dan, "I think, my Darling, that _my_ babies will take good care of _your_ babies. This is home to my babies and they are very territorial about who comes near here."

She paused for a moment, "I remember about six months ago, we had Peeping Tom wondering around here. Late one night I heard my kitten snarl, the dog starting barking, and then I heard someone screaming. I looked around, but I could not find anything. The next day one of my neighbors told me that a young man had been admitted to the hospital with huge bite marks on him, but he refused to say where he got them." She grinned, "But, now Mike and I know where he got them and I never had any more problems with prowlers."

About the fourth night back at Lorraine's place, Lorraine was sitting in front of the fireplace, mending a hole in the knee of Sue's worn jeans by the light of one of their lanterns. The night was warm and quiet; a gentle pine flavored breeze flowed through the open windows. Tom, Sue, and Ginger were preparing for bed, each had brushed their teeth and the girls had changed into hand-me-down nightgowns generously contributed by Hank's family.

Tom called both girls over to the corner and spoke quietly to them. They smiled and nodded.

Both girls skipped over to Dan. He was lying on the couch next to Lorraine, still in pain.

"Good night, Daddy," they chorused as they gently kissed him.

"Good night, little tykes," Dan smiled as he painfully struggled to sit up. "You guys sleep well tonight, ok."

Then, Sue and Ginger looked at each other, and together they walked over to Lorraine with shy smiles on their faces.

Sue said, "Excuse me," and took the jeans and darning needle from Lorraine.

Lorraine stared at the girls; her eyes big in the flickering fireplace light.

They then both reached out, their small arms hugged her as tiny lips gently touched her cheeks. Lorraine's big dark eyes brimmed with tears as she hugged the two little girls back.

"Aw! You girls sleep easy tonight, my babies will take loving care of you," she murmured to their smiling faces. "Come on, I'll tuck you both in."

Before Hank, Smiley and Mike had left after the rescue of Ginger, Lorraine told them, "How about we have a party here in about two weeks, the Friday after this coming Friday? By then, Dan should be feeling better and we really have something to celebrate."

"Sure," the men chorused. "We'll spread the word, it's about time we had some fun."

Two weeks later, around noon, the first of Lorraine's friends arrived at the house. Most rode horses or bicycles, four had horse and buggy combinations and several had horses pulling wagons on which they had piled the whole family. People just streamed in throughout the remainder of the day.

Each person was introduced to Dan and his family. Repeatedly, Lorraine told the story of how Dan and Tom saved her, and how they rescued Ginger. After about the second time, they took her aside and asked, "Hon, we did what we had to, but please, let's just drop it, OK?"

"No! I can't stop telling them what you two did and I wouldn't stop!"

There were other boys Tom's age and soon, they wandered off together. Deputy Hank arrived with his family including a new grandchild. Sue and Ginger quickly became fast friends with a about six or seven girls their age and soon, they were busily discussing whatever girls of the age of about six or nine discuss.

Many were the questions asked Dan about conditions in Los Angeles. Some guests had relatives there, and more than once, after Dan calmly and factually told what he had seen in Los Angeles area, a few people shuffled off by themselves, weeping because they knew, then, there was little hope for some of their loved ones.

Dan tried, as much as he could, to be accurate about what he saw and the devastation through which they had traveled. Often, he related his conversation with Joe Robinson, thinking these people needed to know what caused the breakdown of society. He knew these survivors had learned to avoid electricity, now they understood exactly why they had to stay away from it.

Deputy Hank approached him later and said, "Son, some of these people can't tell you now, but they appreciate what you have done and what you're telling them."

He continued quietly and solemnly, "It was hard for some of these older folks, not knowing about conditions and their kids and things in Los Angeles and along the way. Now, they have a better idea how things are. I think it's not-knowing that's so hard."

"Well, I'm sorry to have to tell them about the difficult conditions between here and Los Angeles, but I refuse to lie to them, they need to know what happened. Let's face it, it is not a nice world right now, we're going back to basics in many ways," Dan continued reflectively, "maybe someone, somewhere will find a way to fight that Green Ghost and we can start our society over."

Deputy Hank looked at Dan for a moment with respect in his eyes, "I agree with your comments. Darn it, it is tough right now, but I see people reverting to the fundamentals because those worked. Maybe some good will come out of this after all."

Each family had brought with them a large supply of food. One family had butchered a heifer three days ago and brought most of it along for barbecuing or roasting. The wonderful fragrance of baked bread, cookies and pies permeated Lorraine's kitchen. Each time Dan strolled through the house, besides receiving a happy hug or a kiss from Lorraine, he got to sample just about everything. By the time the folks ate, there was enough food for twice that many people.

Dan, Tom, Sue, and Ginger were quickly stuffed. Many families asked them to "Just taste this. . .!" "You'll like this. . .!" "You must try this; the recipe has been in our family for years. . .!" Fresh ground coffee, fresh milk, and even a few homemade brews were available.

Dan quickly realized that most people intended to spend the night and the next morning before they went home. Most had brought with them their sleeping bags, and bright yellow, red, and green tents dotted Lorraine's alfalfa field. A makeshift fence held the horses.

"Lorraine, what about your big cat? We have all those horses around here. Will he bother them?"

"Oh no. He is in the mountains looking for food and he will not return for at least a day or so. With all these people around here, he will not come until I call him."

In the general scheme of things, it was doubtful if anyone other than the small children would sleep. This was the first real chance for most to truly visit with their neighbors and friends since the change in their world, and they intended to make the most of it.

Dan ambled out into the front yard and saw two men setting up a small portable dance floor. The boards or planks were hardwood tongue and grooved and they fit together tightly so people could dance on the floor.

"Where did you get that from," he asked a blue-jeaned farmer.

With a sideways glance, the response was, "Well, someone borrowed it from one of those big hotels over in Durango. I don't think they had much use for it now."

They then lit lanterns and hung them from posts at the corners of the floor.

Three fiddles and two violins were taken out of their containers and tuned. There was even a wheezy old accordion, two horns from the local high school, two silver plated harmonicas, an ancient banjo and three guitars and a small set of drums.

An old farmer grumbled to Dan, "That old banjo sounds out of tune."

Not gaining much in the way of points, Dan looked at him and asked, "It has a tune?"

A viola and an alto saxophone completed the makeshift orchestra. An air of expectancy hung over the dance floor.

The women had changed from the universally worn work clothes or jeans into dresses or medium length gowns, the men had changed into white shirts with ties. Hair was slicked down with water; precious and very limited makeup was carefully applied to rosy checked faces. Tiny amounts of perfume and cologne flavored the still night air. This was the first real enjoyment they could look forward to since the life force had attacked their town, and their pulses quickened, their eyes were brighter, their laughter and joy higher.

Teenage boys' glances met teenage girls' glances with age-old thoughts of, "Will she dance with me?" or "I hope I don't make a fool out of myself when I ask her to dance with me!" or reversely, "I hope he asks me to dance!" Shy smiles met shy glances.

A hush settled over the valley at sundown. Lorraine had changed to a bright red, blue and green calico skirt with a short-sleeved, white-laced blouse. Dan could hardly keep his eyes off her, she was so radiant. Four men, carrying an old wooden chair, came to Lorraine, placed her in the chair and physically lifted her above their heads. They laughingly carried her to the center of the dance floor, twirled her in circles and gently put her down.

Cries of "Speech, Speech!" rang through the crowd.

Lorraine smilingly raised her hands and said, "Thank you all for coming, there's plenty of food left. Enjoy yourself!"

One of the men, a gnarled old farmer and obviously an informal leader of the community, hobbled slowly on his cane to the center of the floor and spoke to Lorraine and to the crowd, "Let's give a hand to Lorraine for having us tonight!"

After the cheers rang out, the old farmer went on, "It is sort of traditional around here that the hostess has the first dance of the night. Please pick your man and your song."

Lorraine, flattered by the attention, spoke, her voice caressing the gathering, "Thank you all so much. I think most of you have heard what Dan Peterson and his family did for me, and how they found their little girl."

She looked over the crowd and met Dan's eyes. Even at that distance, their eyes locked and looked within each other's heart.

Lorraine said shyly, "Dan Peterson, would you dance this first dance with me?"

As Dan nodded "Yes!", he started to walk onto the dance floor. Hands reached out to shake his hands and touch his arms, and several women even kissed his check.

"What's going on?" he asked in confusion.

The crowd started clapping and cheering. Dan saw Tom, Sue and Ginger standing on the side of the dance floor, their smiles nearly breaking their faces.

"What are they cheering for?" He asked Lorraine, bewildered. "What's going on?"

Lorraine, her dark eyes shining from laughter and pride said, "Don't you know? You saved my life! You rescued your little girl against overwhelming odds. You brought hope and news to their lives, you gave them vital information for their future; they really appreciate what you have done. And they admire you and your family for traveling under such harsh conditions. I too, so much, so very much, appreciate what you have done."

Lorraine went on in a whisper, a blush coloring her cheeks, "Especially last night!"

By now, the crowd was yelling for Dan, "Speech, speech!"

Dan, now thoroughly embarrassed, said, "Well, thank you, but give thanks to my kids, Tom and Sue. They were there too." More cheers rang out for the two very flustered kids while their bright-red-haired little sister hugged them.

"And give more thanks to my son, Tom; he had a big part in saving us and finding our Ginger."

More than one shapely teen aged beauty in tight jeans and skimpy well filled halter tops looked at Tom with something much better than friendship in her eyes. Unknown to Dan, Mike had slipped two small foil wrapped packages to Tom saying, "I think you know what these are for."

Tom, blushing slightly, "Thanks!"

Three cynical old farmers grinned at each other agreeing, "In the morning, that boy very likely will call himself a man!"

Lorraine and Dan walked over the leader of the music group (lacking a better definition, they most certainly were not an orchestra) and whispered a song title. The leader went into a quick conference with the musicians and then called, "Crystal, would you come up here to sing with us?"

"Dan, Crystal has been a friend of mine for years. She has a great and, some say, a powerful voice. And more importantly, she is good people."

Soon, a rendition of Patsy Cline's "Crazy" drifted through the valley.

Tears flowed from more than one matronly figure's eyes when they watched the love flow between Dan and Lorraine on the dance floor. Dan had not danced in years and his body was still sore, but somehow his body and Lorraine's body melted into a smooth flowing motion of gentle touching.

Dan whispered in her ear, "If we keep dancing like this, you and I will have to sneak off into the woods for a little bit!"

A smiling giggle against his chest was her only reply, except that she danced even closer.

Soon, other couples joined Dan and Lorraine, and for that night at least, there was peace and happiness in the valley!

❖❖❖❖❖

As the days passed, Dan, however, was starting to worry. He still needed to make their way to Wisconsin, but he was unsure about Lorraine. He knew he loved her, fully and deeply, and her gentle caresses each time they passed or came near each other strengthened and intensified his feelings for her.

"Is it fair to her ask her to leave all she has here to come with us to Wisconsin?" Dan mumbled to himself. *"Her home is here and her friends are here. She's well known here and could even earn a living of sorts as a beautician or barber."*

Dan became increasingly withdrawn as he worried about the problem. He knew he and his family had to make it to Wisconsin. There was nothing for them here in Colorado except Lorraine. And Dan needed to plan for the future of his family, not only for work, food, and shelter, but his children needed to obtain whatever education was possible. He knew that he had a family back home, and they could work together as a commune of sorts, each providing support to the rest of the family. He simply had to attempt to get his children to Wisconsin, but he desperately wanted to take Lorraine with them.

One evening after dinner, Dan was sitting on the front porch of Lorraine's place. The sun was setting behind the dark mountains to the west, a tranquil hush spread over the valley, the colors of the light green alfalfa field and darker evergreen trees seemed sharper. A small herd of deer had appeared at the far end of Lorraine's land, quietly grazing on the fresh alfalfa. It had showered that day and the pungent aroma of fresh wet earth and pine needles laced with the sweet fragrance of honeysuckle flowed through the valley.

Lorraine came out carrying two cups of aromatic Columbian hot coffee and sat next to Dan. She handed a cup to Dan who nodded his thanks as he cupped his hands around the steaming container.

After a moment or two of silence, quietly sipping her coffee, she said, "All right, Dan, what's the matter? You have been noticeably quiet the last couple of days. Is something wrong?"

She paused for a moment, worried, "Have I done something wrong?"

"No," Dan replied slowly, shaking his head. "No, you haven't done anything wrong."

After a moment he asked, "How do I want to say this?"

Lorraine looked at him, her big dark eyes wide with apprehension, the coffee cup in her hand trembling.

Dan said slowly, "We came here to find our little Ginger; we were unbelievably lucky, we found her and you! With my kids, you have become, you are the most important person in the world to me." Dan's eyes, deep with feeling, searched hers.

Dan stopped and then almost desperately, he blurted, "But our journey isn't over yet."

"I, I don't understand. What's the problem?"

"We have to try to get to Wisconsin."

"I still don't understand."

"I want you to come with me, with us, to my home!"

"I, I still don't understand."

After a second or two, Lorraine exclaimed, "Oh! Oh, now I see. You're worried that I would not want to go to your home with you. Is that it? Is that right?"

"Yes," Dan nodded, his heart thumping deep in his chest.

Lorraine responded with a peal of laughter, spilling her coffee on the wooden porch. Dan stared at her surprised; laughter was the last thing he expected. Lorraine finally stopped laughing with tears running down her cheeks.

"Is that what is bothering you? Oh, my darling, don't you understand? As long as you have me, wherever you go, I will follow! You are part of me, Dan! Tom, Sue and now Ginger are starting to accept me as a part of their life."

She paused, then asked worriedly, "You do want me with you?"

A huge burden had just been removed from his shoulders by what Lor said! His still painful body sagged with relief. His arms grasped and held her to his chest. A gentle pine scented breeze caressed the two lovers as tender lips touched, not with a promise of lust, but with a promise of peace and happiness together.

A day or two later, Mike Osborne rode in to share lunch and talk with Dan and Lorraine.

After the girls ate, they disappeared to play, but Tom sat with the adults at the table. They talked of the camp and their experiences in it.

Lorraine told how she had overheard Smiley singing, "Row, row, row your boat," right before he blew up the woodpile.

After the laughter and smiles subsided, there was a quiet lull in the conversation. It was obvious that Mike had something on his mind, but Dan decided to let him broach the subject in his way.

"Lorraine, Dan," he began slowly, "I don't know if you knew that I have family down in southern Illinois. My Dad is still there and I have a couple of brothers and sisters scattered around that area. I talked to my Dad months ago, before all this happened, and he and a couple of my brothers were doing ok on their farm."

He went on, "I understand that you are planning to travel to, where: Minnesota?"

"No, Wisconsin, but it's the same area."

"Well, I met this woman and we've sort of been together for a while. She is divorced (Dan thought it interesting because the "divorce" comment was unnecessary). She and her two kids were spending the winter and going to school in Durango and they were stranded here when the life force, that Green Ghost problem attacked us. She's from a tiny town over in Indiana and wants to try to return home."

He stopped for a moment "I guess what I'm asking is for permission for us to come with you. It seems to me that the more people we have with us, the safer it would be traveling."

Lorraine and Dan looked at each other and both looked at Tom. They nodded together.

"Of course, Mike, you and your friends would be welcome," Dan said. "After what you did to help us find our Ginger, you didn't even have to ask. I do not know the conditions between us and Wisconsin or Illinois, but they'll probably be quite harsh. Coming here from Orange County, California, we found it fairly easy going in some places, and downright dangerous in other places."

"How old are your friend's kids?" Lorraine asked.

"I think her boy is about Tom's age, and her daughter is about twelve or so."

"Why don't you bring them out to meet us? How about tomorrow? He is interested in leaving soon," Lorraine suggested with a nod at Dan.

"Sure," Mike said. "When Dan?"

"I don't know yet, my friend. But soon, I don't want to travel in late fall or winter, and it will take us probably several months to get home. Ginger is recovering well and I'm feeling a whole lot better," Dan said. He smiled at Lorraine, "I've got a great nurse."

Lorraine smiled and then blushed deeply. Mike laughed, watching the emotion flow between the two.

"Let's get together tomorrow and discuss the trip," Dan continued thoughtfully, "I know most everyone around here uses horses, but I don't think they can keep up with our bikes. In addition, we can travel much faster with bikes than horses or mules or whatever."

"Well, I've got some horses and they are of more use than bikes when we get there," Mike argued.

"Sure, but can your friend's children ride horses?" Lorraine asked.

"Ah, good point. Her boy would be all right, but her daughter would: number one, refuse to ride, and number two, if we could convince her to ride the horse, she would irritate it with her constant whining and complaining. I have to tell you that she may be a little problem."

He paused "Thank you both. I'll bring them out tomorrow to meet you."

Over the next several days, Mike brought his "friend" and her two children out to Lorraine's place. Mike's "friend" was Mary Ann Kreiger from a small town near Valparaiso, Indiana. Her son, Geoff, a slim, quiet, brown-haired boy, was about a year younger than Tom. Her daughter, Jennifer, however, was an overweight, largish, complaining and whining twelve-year old.

Geoff Kreiger and Tom Peterson became friendly almost immediately. Jennifer Kreiger was another story! When introduced to Sue and Ginger, Jennifer made a mistake.

She said, "Well, let's go outside and play hide and seek, you'll be it and I'll hide."

Sue listened to Jennifer for a moment and then, she and Ginger just simply walked away, ignoring Jennifer thereafter.

Jennifer's mouth dropped open. Nobody had ever done that to her. Dan smiled to himself.

The last several months had changed Sue and made her much more self-reliant; if someone was going to boss her around, that person had to earn her respect.

They discussed the upcoming trip in detail. After much conversation and some argument, Mike finally resolved himself to use bikes rather than horses when he discovered that Mary Ann and the kids could ride bikes, but that Mary Ann and Jennifer had never ridden horses. Later, both Mike and Lorraine, and eventually Hank became involved in bartering or trading for whatever bikes were obtainable in Durango.

"What route are you planning to take to get to Wisconsin?" Mike asked.

"Well, it will be difficult riding over those two major passes crossing the Continental Divide to the eastern slope of the Rocky Mountains," Dan pointed to the southern part of Colorado on their map, "but it's summer now and the weather will be in our favor."

"Makes sense," Mike agreed. "I think it will be much faster going straight east than to travel south through the northern part of New Mexico. It will be hot down there, and we will have to come back north anyway."

Most importantly, when Dan and Lorraine examined the map, the route south would have taken them near the place where Lorraine had been beaten and nearly raped by the escaped convicts. She wrapped her arms around herself, shivering, "I have very mixed emotions about that place: one was the beating I received and how scared I was; the other was that I found you and Tom and Sue. But, Dan, please, please, I cannot go near there again!"

Dan and Tom exchanged glances, "Well, I guess that settles that."

Hank commented one day, "In Durango with almost twenty thousand people, you would assume that there would be an abundance of bikes; the problem is that since internal combustion vehicles are unavailable, those who have bikes want to keep them." Mike fortunately had several horses and a few cows to trade and eventually, Mike, Mary Ann, Geoff, and Jennifer had bikes.

While all the negotiations and trading were going on, Hank had acquired a sleek new Univega Mountain bike for Lorraine. It had twenty-one different speeds and was a vivid bright green in color.

"Lorraine, can I borrow your sunglasses, that bike is so bright, it hurts my eyes," Tom said.

Hank apologized that he could only find a man's bike, but he said to Lorraine, "Well, you shouldn't wear dresses on the trip, anyway."

That night, Dan, Tom, and Lorraine, sprawling in front of the fireplace, talked quietly after the two girls had fallen asleep. Lorraine was concerned, "Dan, my cat and...," she smiled at Tom, "Your dog can't keep up with the bikes on level roads or downhill."

"Dad, both of those animals would be very valuable as sentries at night and maybe even as an early warning system to tell us if there are people ahead of us."

"I agree, Dan. In addition, they are my babies and I wouldn't leave them here by themselves," Lorraine argued. "They're so spoiled, they'd starve."

"All right, all right," Dan said. "I don't think I could take away your animals from the kids even if I tried. Your big cat and the girls are almost inseparable, and Tom, your dog follows you everywhere."

He mused to himself, "The problem is that we'll have to strengthen the trailers to carry the animals. The animals will have to ride at least part of the time. Lorraine, can you pull a one-hundred-and-fifty-pound cat on a trailer?"

"I think so."

"Well, Dad, if we lighten her load, she should be able to pull a trailer that heavy because she has all of those gears on her bike."

"That goes for you too, Tom. You will have to pull a trailer with a place for your dog to ride. I think we will need trailers for all the adults, Mike, Mary Ann, you, Tom, and Lorraine, and me. We ought to have a small trailer for Jennifer too. I know she'll complain, but that's tough. She's big enough to help."

With Dan's advice and assisted by Tom and Geoff, Hank and one of the neighbors built two trailers for the boys to pull behind their bikes. Tom's trailer was made by Lor's neighbors sturdier than Geoff's because they planned that Tom's dog would ride on his trailer. They also built three larger trailers for Mike, Lorraine, and Mary Ann to pull. Both Mike's and Lorraine's trailers were constructed with dual wheels to manage the weight of the big cat.

Hank commented, "Lorraine, you'll need those twenty-one extra speeds to tow your big cat. Do you think you can do it?"

"I hope so, Hank. I really must. I cannot leave him here, he would starve or worse, get killed by someone who didn't know him."

"By the way, Hank, do you think you could find handlebar extensions for the bikes?" Dan asked. "When we were coming from Southern California, our arms and chest muscles were almost always fatigued. You see, because we were leaning forward with our heavy backpacks on our back, our arms were always supporting that extra weight."

"Consider it done," was the reply.

While Sue had her bike, Ginger was simply too young to keep up on a bike. Dan and Tom built a small seat out of an awful colored green plastic clothes basket and attached it to Dan's bike. The sides of the clothes basket hung down over the rear wheel to protect Ginger's legs from the spokes. Mike also found two bright yellow plastic child's carriers that fit on the back of a bike; Mike attached the carriers over the rear wheels of Tom's and Lorraine's bikes. That way, Ginger could ride with either Tom, Lorraine, or her father.

"When are we leaving, Dad?" asked Tom.

Hank, Mike, Lorraine, and a few neighbors who happened to be helping Hank, looked at Dan. Dan took a deep breath and then with more confidence than he felt, "Three days, in the early morning!"

Hank looked around the group, "All right, the bikes and trailers are ready, all you will need is food and personal things. I would suggest that all of you have your stuff here the day after tomorrow for final packing. I'll bring out all the freeze-dried food I can find."

The next day, Lorraine went to say goodbye to her friends and neighbors. After a stop at the cemetery to say goodbye to her parents, a much saddened, red-eyed and subdued Lorraine returned that night. Upon her return, Dan just held her in his arms, knowing there was little he could say or do to ease the pain. Ginger's tiny, tanned arms hugged Lorraine too, just trying to show her that in her little way, she understood.

The next morning, Hank arrived on his horse pulling a pack horse. He had nearly three hundred pounds of freeze-dried food. "I'm sorry but this is all I could find. People don't want to give this stuff up." After helping Dan and Tom distribute the food between the three bikes, he left, promising to return the next morning before they left.

That afternoon, Lorraine grabbed two towels and a blanket, and told Dan, "Come on, I want to show you something."

She took Dan and walked with him about a mile into the woods. She led him to a small, grass-filled clearing surrounded and hidden by tall evergreen trees next to a hot spring flowing into a larger stream.

She told Dan bashfully, "When I was a young girl, my favorite story was Camelot. I fantasized that a knight in shining armor on a white stallion would come to rescue me and take me to a secret place where we would live happily ever after."

She giggled softly, her white teeth flashing in the sunlight, "This is my secret place and while your stallion has two wheels, you most definitely are my knight in shining armor."

She smiled with a soft blush, "I used to come here as a young girl and sometimes skinny-dip, thinking about my knight."

She spread the blanket and towels in the clearing near the trees, and sat down, motioning for Dan to sit. Looking deep into Dan's eyes, one shoe and then the other was removed. She slowly pulled off her socks, stood and started to unbutton her plaid shirt.

Dan's breath started to catch in his chest. Lorraine slowly unbuttoned her shirt and pulled it out of her jeans. Dan saw the flash of a white undergarment. She slowly unbuckled her belt and dropped it on the blanket, her eyes locked on Dan's. Tight jeans were unzipped. She then slowly removed her shirt, revealing her white brasserie covered breasts.

Dan's breath came rapidly, his heart starting to pound. The shirt was dropped on the blanket. Her jeans were then slowly removed over her perfectly rounded buttocks, revealing a white pair of panties covering her tanned body. The jeans were slowly placed on top of her other clothes.

"Come, my knight, it's not nice to let a maiden skinny dip alone!"

She then giggled, ran to the pool and dived in.

Dan frantically tore off his clothes, heaving his shirt in one direction and his pants in another. He left his jockey shorts on and dived in after Lorraine. The water was bath-warm with a slight sulfur smell on his freshly scarred chest. Lorraine surfaced a short distance away, giggling, and splashed water on him.

Dan splashed back and swam over to her. Their arms went around each other and their lips met with a violent need.

Dan found that the pool was about shoulder deep, and if Lorraine wrapped her legs around his knees, her body just fit with his.

They moved experimentally together, just one partially clothed body slowly rubbing against the other. Dan thought that if they didn't do something soon, he would explode.

She laughed, pushed him underwater and swam a few strokes away. He surfaced sputtering from a mouthful of sulfur tasting water. He dove under the water to her, grabbed her legs and playfully dumped her upside down. She surfaced and clasped him, laughing and their two bodies melded together. Again, her legs went around him, holding him tight as their lips met.

Her bra was unhooked and floated to the top, accompanied by a filmy pair of panties. Lorraine floated on her back, retaining her hold on Dan's legs. Her breasts floated to the surface, the dark brown nipples centering each breast like a dark mountaintop surrounded by snow. She arched her back and extended her arms, causing her breasts to rise higher in the water. Dan's hands went out and as the rough palms of his hands gently caressed the protruding nipples, her body went rigid and her teeth chattered. She drew herself up into Dan's arms, her breasts meeting the hair on his chest. She released her legs, reached down, and pulled off his shorts. Her hands stroked his erection; he felt huge, almost like her white stallion. He thought he would die, it felt so good.

She giggled, then released him, swam to the shore, and ran up on the bank. Dan's heart caught in his throat! She stood there like a Greek goddess in the light shadows of the forest, dripping, one leg slightly bent, her proud breasts heaving, her thin waist flowing to her wide hips centered by a small moist patch of curly dark hair. She giggled again and turned to run to the blanket. Dan half killed himself getting out of the pool as he watched her rounded shiny white buttocks bounce as she ran to the blanket.

She lay on the blanket holding out her arms as Dan ran from the pool to her, his immense erection bouncing against his body. He knelt by her side and gently touched her face.

"No!"

Lorraine, however, would have none of that.

"Come here," she demanded, hoarsely.

She grabbed him and pulled his face down to hers, their lips and bodies met with a fierce craving and rolled together on the blanket. Their hearts were pounding and their breath was coming in pants.

She pulled him on top of her and guided him into her. Her face twisted in fierce savage pleasure, her breath panting, her arms, and hands clutching him.

She moaned in her throat as Dan thrust deeply into her, her body rising against him, almost throwing him off her. Her back and body arched violently into a bow until only her shoulders and feet were touching the blanket. Again and again, Dan thrust into her, her hands clawing his back, her throat calling his name in mindless ecstasy. They climaxed together, their sweating and panting bodies joyfully giving and receiving an essence, a pleasure, a oneness that fulfilled their innermost souls.

Finally, their bodies lay together, collapsed in and on each other. Their breathing eventually slowed; their hearts quieted. Dan moved slightly and gently sought Lorraine's lips, telling her of his love for her.

Tears of love and joy filled the corners of Lorraine's eyes as she said, "I've dreamed of my 'knight in shining armor,' and you're so fantastically better than the dream."

She giggled softly and moved her hips with Dan still in her, "But now I've got his stallion too."

Dan's arms grew a little weary and he moved his body to rest on the side of Lorraine. As he did so, he glanced over at the light shadows by the trees.

He flinched.

Lorraine, following his gaze, laughed.

Resting on his haunches, his head cocked to one side, just looking at them and seemed to almost purr was the big cat. His large luminous eyes in his amused tilted head seemed to question what he was seeing.

Dan relaxed and said, "I can just see what's going through his mind: 'Why don't the humans do it the right way, the way we cats do it?'"

Lorraine laughed, "Well, if he ever finds a mate and becomes as happy and lucky as I am, maybe we will have taught him something."

After a cooling off swim and the retrieval of their underclothes, they toweled each other dry and slowly dressed. It was becoming dusk and they needed to return to the house to feed the kids and finish packing. Lorraine called the cat, and together, all three walked back to the house. The big cat walked first on Lorraine's side and then on Dan's side, their legs rubbing his soft fur, his long, black-tipped tail twitching from side to side.

That night was devoted to the final packing and preparation for the trip. Extra clothes, some canned goods, the freeze-dried food supplied by Hank, sleeping bags for all, and of course, a few irreplaceable items such as photographs, a precious book or two and so on were carefully sorted, packed, and repacked.

Lorraine found a tiny backpack for Ginger, and her doll was carefully inserted into it.

Hank had given Dan a small sleeping bag for Ginger, saying, "My kids have outgrown this, your little one can make good use of it. "A smile creased his face when Ginger skipped over to him and gave him a hug with her tiny arms.

Once out of Durango, weapons were to be carried on the person, not the trailer. Dan had tightened and greased their bikes and trailers, and that last night at Lorraine's place, they loaded their backpacks and trailers. Dan's, Lorraine's and Tom's bikes and trailers with the backpacks nearly filled the living room. While packing their original trailer, which Hank had thoughtfully modified to carry more weight, Tom and Dan's eyes met over a pile of things.

"Remember the first time we packed this trailer?"

"Sure do, Dad. It feels like a long time ago. Been some changes, huh?" Tom smiled, looking at Ginger sitting on Lorraine's lap. Sue sat next to Lorraine with her head on Lorraine's shoulder. Lorraine was reading a child's book out loud to the two girls in the light from the fireplace.

"I never could have dreamed of what we went through and all this."

"You are responsible for this too, Son," Dan said in a soft voice. "We never would have made it without you, your rescue of us and Lorraine, and your help in finding our Ginger; I'm very proud of you."

"Us too!" Lorraine and Sue exclaimed, smiling at Tom.

For once, he was tongue-tied, but his smile spoke volumes.

Early next morning, Mike and his group rode into the yard. Jennifer followed about half a football field behind, complaining and whining about how early it was, how heavy her load and trailer were, how fast everyone else rode and just about everything in general. Dan took one look at Mike and could see he was angry. Mike took a deep breath, walked over to Jennifer's mother, and had a quiet word with her. She nodded quickly and touched his arm.

Mike stalked over to Jennifer and lifted her off her bike. He almost physically carried her around the house out of sight of the others. There was a sharp murmuring for a moment, then a slap was heard followed by a wail followed by sharper slap.

After a moment, a subdued Jennifer walked back, rubbing her buttocks. Dan noticed with secret approval she no longer complained and whined. Mike followed and appeared with a look of grim satisfaction on his face. Mary Ann looked like she was going to go to her daughter, but Mike's shake of his head stopped her. Dan knew that each had to pull their own weight if they were going to make the trip safely and hoped that Jennifer's spoiled attitude had been at least partially corrected by Mike.

When their eyes met, Dan nodded approval at Mike.

Shortly thereafter Hank rode up. He examined each trailer and bike, adjusted a few things, and while he didn't appear satisfied, there wasn't much more he could do.

He motioned Dan to the side and spoke quietly, his hazel eyes deep, "You take care of her, you understand?" Dan firmly nodded his head and both men shook hands, their free hands clasping the other's arm.

"Well, Hank, I don't know when we'll see each other again, but I owe you more than I could ever repay," Dan said, nodding toward Ginger. "I think, too, that I'm sort of your secret son-in-law, don't worry about your daughter, I'll take care of her."

Hank nodded and walked over to his horse and retrieved a small package. He approached Lorraine standing on the porch and gave her the five-inch by twelve-inch object wrapped in an old grocery store brown paper bag.

"I didn't have any gift paper," he apologized. "This is the only paper I could find, but you should try it on before you leave."

Lorraine, surprised by the gift, opened the heavy package.

She gasped.

In it was a new, beautiful, chrome, six-inch, .357 Colt revolver with black rubberized nonskid grips. The sun glinted off the ribbed barrel. With the weapon was a left-handed cross-draw, front clam-shell Bianchi brown leather high rise holster attached to a black plastic belt with Velcro fasteners. Affixed to the front of the belt were two round containers holding speedy loaders for the .357 magnum weapon. Enclosed with the gift was a precious box of fifty .357 high velocity hollow point copper-jacketed bullets.

"I know you didn't have a weapon. Here, try it on," Hank said quietly as he helped Lorraine adjust the belt. He adjusted the holster so the weapon rode on and above her waist just under her left armpit, but low enough for her right hand to draw the weapon easily and quickly if necessary.

"You wear this after you leave here," he ordered, looking deep into her eyes. "You've fired my Colt enough times, so you know how to use this weapon."

She nodded, eyes brimming, "Thank you! Thank you so very much!"

Finally, the bikes were ready, the backpacks mounted on backs, and the trailers were packed and hooked to the bikes. Tom experimentally had his dog climb on his trailer. The problem was that now, the dog refused to come down. The big cat just lounged on the porch. Lorraine said that it would follow them for a while, and then she would have it sit on one of the trailers.

Lorraine took one last look around the inside of her home and with tears streaming down her face, firmly closed the door saying quietly, "Good-by house; thanks for everything!"

She approached Hank, took a sealed envelope out of her shirt pocket, and gave it to him.

"Read this after I'm gone," she instructed him.

She looked at him for a moment and with more tears flooding her eyes, they clutched each other, trembling for long moments. Tears from Hank's weather-beaten face dampened her head on his chest. Finally, they broke apart, again strongly clutched each other, and then, broke apart for good.

"You take care of yourself, you hear!" Hank's husky voice rumbled out of his almost uncontrolled sob-filled chest.

They mounted their bikes.

Mike led the way out of Lorraine's yard, their trailers tossing up tiny clouds of dust from the wheels. Lorraine and Dan brought up the rear, she waved goodbye to Hank until he was out of sight.

Hank, after watching the group leave, stood for a moment, and then slowly walked to the porch and tied his horse. He sat on Lorraine's rocker, looked at the letter for a long moment and carefully finally opened the letter.

"My Dearest Hank. (He could hear her voice!)

Or should I call you My Dearest Father! (Hank's eyes blurred and he was unable to read for a few minutes!) You see, MY DEAREST FATHER, I've known that you were my real father since shortly before Mom died. When she knew that she didn't have long to live, she told me of you and her. She made me promise to never, never tell you. But now, since I'm going with Dan, the man I love (!), and I don't know when, if ever, I'll see you again, I must tell you.

I was fortunate because I had <u>two</u> fathers, both of whom I loved, respected, and admired. Both loved me as well as they could.

I don't know what's going to happen. Maybe this "force" thing will somehow be fought and beaten, and someday we will be able to see each other again. Maybe you'll have more grandchildren. And if we have a boy, I have his name picked out already!

In the stone hearth on the right of the fireplace is a loose stone. Behind that stone are legal Deeds placing this property in your name. Also, with the Deeds are a few old love letters I discovered after Mom died. (I am keeping the remainder!) They were written to my Mother by my Father . . . My real Father! I treasure those letters now as I have treasured your guidance and help over the years.

Take care, MY FATHER, May the Good Lord Bless You and Keep You.

Your loving Daughter,

Lorraine"

It was nearly noon when the now old man with his slumped shoulders shuffled his way to his horse, mounted it and slowly rode back to his home, clutching his letter.

CHAPTER TEN

Mike led the way out of Lor's place, slowly pulling his heavy trailer onto the dirt road. The trailer's rubber tires threw up small clouds of dust as it bounced through the soft dust on the road. After some distance, they turned onto an asphalt street that eventually led to Highway 550. Once on the highway, traveling became easier. After a few miles, they left Highway 550 and turned onto Highway 160 heading eastbound.

They stopped shortly thereafter to rest and for Lor to get her cat. She called him and playfully, he came bounding up to the group, sniffing each person and receiving an almost obligatory back rub and head scratch. Lor coaxed the big cat to jump up on her trailer where it stretched out like a soft brown purring live carpet.

Tom, rubbing the big cat's head, smiled, "He looks like a big warm carpet; this carpet, however, has teeth!"

Ginger had been riding with Dan, but now, dragging her pillow with her, she changed to the back of Tom's bike. Lor had attached a small pillow to the back of Tom's bike that made it more comfortable for Ginger's little bottom. Since Ginger was riding with Tom, Dan took Tom's dog and had it jump up onto his trailer. There he sat on his rear haunches, his tongue hanging, examining the world like a king of all he surveyed.

They started again, slowly at first, but eventually paddled steadily over the paved highway, the purring of the heavy bicycle tires whispering in their ears. Fallen road signs and overgrown portions of the road were detoured around, and in places, trees had crashed on the roadway, blocking the road.

Mike and Dan rode together for a while and talked.

"I would like to try to make it to Pagosa Springs today."

"I don't think we'll make it that far. The roads haven't been maintained and we're not traveling very fast," Mike said. "You people have been riding for nearly a thousand miles; we've been riding for fifteen or twenty miles."

He continued, "Plus this group, right now, is a little like getting a dinosaur moving: You have to grasp the front end's attention first by clubbing it between the eyes and get it moving, then you run around to the back of the dinosaur and kick it in the butt; by that time, however, the front end has forgotten what it was supposed to do and you have to run around to the front end, and well, you get the picture."

Tom and Geoff had ridden up and overheard the last part of the conversation between Dan and Mike. They looked at each other.

Geoff shook his head sadly at Tom, "Can you believe that? We have this old brontosaurus calling us young tyrannosaurs rexes' dinosaurs?" The boys grinned at each other and rode ahead of the group.

Just then, Lor hurried to them, "Dan, Mike, something's wrong and I can't figure out what it is. Look at the animals."

The big cat's ears were flattened and the soft fur on its back was slightly raised. The hair on the back of Tom's dog's head was also raised. Both animals appeared tense and uncomfortable. The dog quietly growled, but he didn't seem to growl at any single object or thing. Both animals continually sniffed the air, as if they were searching, without success, for an elusive scent of some animal.

The group stopped at the side of the road. Both animals jumped down from their perches and almost aimlessly, walked around, snarling over their shoulders, first in one direction and then another.

"What's wrong with them?" Tom asked.

"I don't know," a worried Lor said.

Tom called his dog to him. The animal went to Tom, but he was shivering as he whimpered into Tom's hand.

"Dad! Something's wrong, he's trying to tell us something."

"Easy, boy, easy now. What's the matter, boy?" Tom whispered to his dog. The dog just whimpered more, occasionally snarling at nothing they could see.

Dan examined the area around them, but he could see nothing unusual. They had stopped at the crest of a small incline in the road. Off to their right was the tree covered mountain and on their left was a small ravine. There weren't any trees or heavy bushes or heavy brush nearby that might hide something.

What was wrong?

He looked up and down the road, but there was nothing there, either. The road was slightly damp from a rainstorm that morning but, now the sky was relatively clear. They had almost instinctively come together, except for Jennifer. She had sat down on the side of the road about fifty feet away, her shirt open at the neck and her sleeves rolled up, just playing with her watch.

Dan's scrutiny continued around them, then he froze!

Watch!

Jennifer's watch?

Dan said as calmly as he could with his heart pounding, "Jennifer! Does that watch have a battery?"

"Sure. I put a new battery in just before we left the house, but it's not running very good, now."

"Jennifer, Honey," Mike interrupted, "Take the watch off of your arm. Now, Honey!"

He commanded, "Now!"

Her eyes grew wide and fearful, she unsnapped the watch from her arm and held it out to him.

"Here," she said in a small voice as she offered it to Mike.

"Drop it on the road, Jenny."

"Now, come here, quickly!"

Jennifer, peering over her shoulder at the innocent-looking watch, ran first to Mike and then to her mother.

"Are you hurt, Honey?" her mother asked.

Jennifer shook her head, her eyes wide and apprehensive, not understanding what was wrong.

Both animals' attention was riveted on the watch. Low snarls were rumbling out of their chests; they circled it staying about fifteen feet away from the watch.

"Let me have your bike for a minute," Dan said to Jennifer as he easily unhooked her trailer.

He dropped his backpack on the ground and mounted her bike. He rode up the road about twenty yards and turned back, accelerating as fast as he could. Riding past the watch, he swiftly kicked it with his right foot.

He felt slimy warmth, a tingling and burning sensation starting in his foot and extending up into his ankle. The watch flew tumbling into the ravine next to the road.

As the watch sailed into the air, both animals snarled violently, the hair on the back of their necks standing straight up, their claws protruding from their paws, saliva dripping from their gaping jaws. A very faint greenish almost transparent substance appeared and flowed through the air toward the ravine.

After a second or two, the substance disappeared into the ravine searching for the watch. Both animals calmed, the big cat licking its fur while Tom's dog scratched a wayward flea.

"That, that, was The Force or The Green Ghost or whatever you want to call it," Dan said, limping off Jennifer's bike.

"Jennifer, or anyone else for that matter, do you have any electrical items, watches, games, anything on you?"

Quiet fearful shakes of the head met his question.

"Hon, would you give me some water, please?" Dan said to Lor as he limped to her side, "I think I got a little burned by that energy."

They slipped off Dan's right shoe and sock, and rolled up his pants leg, but Mike couldn't see any physical damage. It seemed to Mike that the body's natural reflex on the bottom of Dan's foot was a little slow when he stroked it with a metal rod, but there wasn't much he could do about it out in the middle of nowhere.

After soaking Dan's right foot and ankle in a little cold water, and a good massage by Lor, the foot seemed to feel better, although it felt like it had severe pins and needles in it for about an hour.

"It feels like my foot suddenly went to sleep and now, I'm getting circulation back into it," Dan groused.

"I bet that there is a very slight neurological or electrical charge to that stuff," Mike said.

"Well, I don't know about the electrical charge, but from what Joe Robinson told me, that stuff will burn through anything to get to electricity."

"Now we know that includes your foot and anything else," a worried Tom said to his dad.

Mike turned to Jennifer, "Jenny, you were about fifteen seconds away from getting terribly burned by that energy! Do you understand; you were awfully lucky that battery probably was nearly discharged when you put it in your watch."

"She just rolled her sleeves up a little while ago. I'll bet that her clothing stopped the faint electricity from escaping until just now," Geoff said. Tears rained down Jennifer's cheeks as she buried her face in her mother's shoulder, "I'm, I'm sorry."

Mike gently patted her back, "It's all right now, sweetheart, but listen after this, ok?"

After a brief rest, they continued on their way. Mike was right: the rest stops grew more frequent and longer. Dan had forgotten that they were at an elevation of over 7000 feet and that the air was thinner than their accustomed to Los Angeles' elevation of near sea level. They eventually passed the now apparently deserted town of Bayfield and, early in the afternoon, camped about halfway between Bayfield and a tiny town with the name of Chimney Rock. They stopped at a small, overgrown park next to the highway with decrepit, but still usable restrooms.

"It beats going in the bushes," Tom commented. "We always looked for these kinds of parks on our journey here."

Dan agreed, "One thing we learned was that we stop in the middle of the afternoon or at least a couple of hours before sunset. That gave us the time to set up camp, cook our meals, and get ready for the next day. It's hard to do that stuff when you can't see at night."

Tom went out for a short period and returned with a few rabbits for dinner. He smiled, "This is easy hunting now. My dog just smells the rabbit and as soon as they run, they're mine."

The cat left and hunted on his own. Lor told the girls he would feed himself, but that they should try to feed the dog.

During the traveling from Southern California to Durango, the Petersons had developed a system of each performing a particular task when they stopped at night. Each would unpack and unroll his or her own sleeping bag after placing a piece of plastic on the ground. If it looked like rain and if they were not near an overpass or an abandoned building, Tom would find long pieces of wood to use as a frame and they would place the frame so the open end was a few feet above the ground and the closed end was sloped to the ground. It was an elongated triangle which when covered with a piece of plastic kept off the rain. The sleeping bags would stay dry underneath the plastic.

Once shelter was arranged, Sue would try to find small pieces of wood for a fire. Dan would light the fire and either he or Tom would cook whatever meal they had. Tom was acknowledged as the hunter of the group because he was a much better shot with the bows than his father.

When the group pulled into the park, it took the Peterson's about ten minutes to set everything up and a small fire burning. Sue, with Ginger in tow, was busily gathering firewood. Mike, Lor, Mary Ann, Geoff and Jennifer watched with interest as the Petersons quickly and efficiently set up camp. It slowly dawned on the Petersons they were the objects of scrutiny by the remaining members of their party. Dan quickly realized that the others were simply wandering around, attempting to look organized, but not having a clue what needed to be done and how to do it.

"All right, everyone, unpack only your sleeping bags. Put your plastic on the ground first and then lay your bags on top. Try to find a soft or at least smooth place, you'll sleep better without rocks in your back. Each person's responsible for his or her own bag; we're up high here. It will get cold tonight," Dan directed. "Also, each person is responsible for his or her own dishes and utensils: they must be cleaned after every meal or you'll get sick."

Mike said, "Right! Geoff, you, and I'll get more firewood for tonight; there was a dead tree back by the road. Grab that ax if you would, please."

"I'm tired, can't you set up my sleeping bag?" Jennifer whined to her mother.

"No!" came spontaneous commands from Mike and Dan.

Mike continued patiently, "Jennifer, each of us must pull their own weight and we all must help each other."

Jennifer's lower lip protruded, "Well, I'm tired and I can't do it."

"Ok, suit yourself."

Mike walked over to Mary Ann who had been busy unrolling her sleeping bag and whispered, "Don't you help her. She's a big girl and she must start to grow up sometime."

Mary Ann nodded sadly, "She's been spoiled all her life; whenever she sees her father, my ex-husband, she becomes unmanageable because he gives her everything she wants. He never made her do anything, no chores around the house, little schoolwork, and no discipline!"

They looked at Jennifer simply sitting on her bedroll, her lower lip bulging from her dour face. Mike just shook his head and walked away.

Meanwhile, Ginger and Sue were busy chattering away while Sue was showing Ginger how to take care of her sleeping bag. Ginger was doing about as well as a six-year-old little girl could while keeping her long red hair out of her face, clutching her doll in one arm, and dragging her sleeping bag with the other.

Dan noticed that while Jennifer ate dinner, she still hadn't unpacked her sleeping bag.

Mike said quietly to Dan, "Wait until later, it will get colder and she'll unpack her sleeping bag."

"Well, after a night sleeping on a rock or hard ground, she'll learn to look for soft spots too," Dan observed. "We learned that very early on."

A small thunderstorm across the valley with lightening dancing on the lower mountain tops was closely watched with concern. They could occasionally just see a malevolent phosphorescence green oozing out of the thunder clouds when the lightning flashed. Small fires broke out in the forest below the thunderclouds, but fortunately, the fires were quickly extinguished by the rain.

Lor told Tom wistfully, "I wish we could play Mahler's First now. This view so reminds me of that music."

Dan watched the direction of the clouds with some apprehension but they seemed to flow away from them. The thunderclouds slowly dissipated into the distance. The night overhead became clear, the stars twinkling like little lights, the broad brush that was the Milky Way lent a calming effect over the camp.

The only sound was a muted sound of crickets and the firewood crackling in the fire. That night, they huddled together, not only because it was cold, and it was, but out of the knowledge they were probably the only humans within miles.

Before they went to sleep, Lor called the big cat and Tom's dog to her. She held each head in her hands and looked into their eyes. Both animals' tails twitched briefly, and then each bounded to the outside of the camp.

She smiled at the little girls, "Don't worry, nothing will come near us now."

Later that night, only Dan and Lor were awake. They wrapped their sleeping bags around them and sat, quietly contemplating the fire.

Shoulders hunched over and looking into the fire, she said softly, "Dan, I have to tell you something."

"What, Hon?"

"If you remember, I gave a letter to Hank before we left."

She paused heavily for a moment, "I don't know if we'll ever see him again, but I had to tell him a secret that I've known for a long time."

Dreading what was coming, Dan asked, "What's that?"

"Before my mother passed away, she told me that she and Hank were lovers at one time. . ., " she stopped for a second and took a deep trembling breath, ". . . and that Hank was my real father!"

Dan smiled wistfully, "Do you want to know something, my darling?"

"What?"

"Hank knew!"

"W-What?" Her hands flew to her face.

"Do you remember when Hank and I went looking for Ginger the first time?"

She nodded, her eyes leaking.

"Well, he told me about your mother's and his relationship. He had known that you were his daughter from the very beginning, but both your mother and he kept it a secret because too many people would have been hurt to reveal it."

"Oh, Dan," Lor exclaimed as tears streamed down her face. He reached out and held her, her face on his shoulder, her body heaving from the sobs and tears. "I w-w-wish I would have known!"

"Well, it worked out anyway. He loved you as a daughter. If you remember, he was always around if you needed something. And under the circumstances, he was as good a man and a father as anyone could want."

"And if you think about it, the reason he helped Tom and me find our Ginger was that we, or at least mostly Tom, rescued you from those convicts," he said to her bowed head. "I guess the highest thing I can say was that he's a good officer, a good man and the best father that he could be."

The next morning dawned bright and cold. The smell of fresh Columbian coffee permeated the small camp. Lor had risen early and made fresh coffee. She brought a cup to Dan's sleeping bag, put the cup down and gently kissed his lips. His eyes fluttered open and he yawned, an early morning stretch racking his body. She handed him the coffee and smiled. He sat up, stretched again and gratefully accepted the coffee, wrapping his cold hands around the warm steaming cup. His smile and eyes whispered thanks as he sipped the aromatic liquid.

He reached up and touched her face and lips. "What a way to wake up," he whispered to her.

He looked at her red-rimmed eyes, "You don't have to cry anymore, Hon, both of you knew, but neither of you knew, if that makes any sense."

"Well, after the shock of finding out that he knew from the very beginning, it explains a great number of things: why he was always there, why he was around as often as he was."

"He was very proud of you, and he loved you, loves you very much!"

Slowly the group awoke. Sore and stiff muscles protested their unaccustomed use from the day before. Only Dan, Tom and Sue walked easily until the others had their muscles loosened by stretching and bending.

Both the big cat and Tom's dog bounded back into the camp and paid everyone a visit receiving the obligatory back and head rub.

Jennifer refused to come out of her sleeping bag even for breakfast. Dan remembered that she had eventually unrolled her sleeping bag when the fire was dying down and the cold was cruelly seeping into regular clothes. The big cat padded up to her bag, carefully pawed open the top, stuck his head into the opening and licked her face. The cat's tongue was like sandpaper except that it was warm, slobbery and wet.

She screamed, "Go away!" and rolled over in her sleeping bag.

The big cat was pushed out of the opening; he, however, gently pushed his head back into the opening and again, licked her face, his tail wagging furiously. He thought she was playing. By this time, everyone watched the drama between the big cat and Jennifer.

Mike advised, "Honey, I suggest that you get out of your bed; he wouldn't leave you alone until you do."

After a few more screams and muttered comments about the big cat's disreputable ancestors, Jennifer finally rolled out of her sleeping bag. She knelt on top of the sleeping bag and pushed the big cat away while wiping her face, "Go away, you, you overgrown dishrag," she grumbled!

The big cat finally grew tired of trying to play with Jennifer and strolled over to Sue and Ginger. Sue had been attempting to teach Ginger how to roll up her sleeping bag. Her problem was that Ginger wasn't coordinated enough or strong enough to roll her sleeping bag tightly and Tom finally helped her. Both girls stopped packing and gently roughhoused with the big cat; he just lay on the ground, and if cats could smile, Dan swore that the big cat was smiling.

Suddenly, the big cat froze, his keen nose sniffing the air and his eyes staring up the road. Tom's dog also sensed something, the fur on the back of his neck rising, a low growl coming from his chest.

Lor said quietly, sharply, "Dan, Mike, something's around here!"

Dan grabbed his AR-15, Tom clasped the recurve bow, and Mike drew his 9 .mm semi-automatic handgun. Lor motioned for the girls to get behind her. She went to the animals and rubbed their backs, holding them saying softly, "Easy, easy, what do you see?"

Both animals' eyes were riveted on the road. Suddenly, approximately one hundred yards up the road, a bush swayed gently back and forth, and then, violently, as if a giant hand was shaking it. Both animal's hackles rose, and both were growling softly in their chests.

Then, a large black mother bear calmly walked out onto the road, followed by two tiny frolicking cubs.

Lor's big cat, while concentrating on the bears, slowly relaxed. Tom's dog, however, was another story.

"Help me hold the dog, Tom," Lor said as she struggled with the dog as he attempted to pursue the huge carnivores, "If he chases that bear, we'll be lucky to find a piece of his tail left."

Fortunately, the mother bear, after glancing later at the humans, ignored them and simply walked up the road. The last thing they saw of the mother bear was her huge swaying black rear end with a short stubby tail walking calmly down the middle of the road followed by her two playful cubs.

Mike said casually, "Yes, she does have that bumper sticker on her rear end."

"What are you talking about?"

"Sure," Mike commented. "Can't you see the bumper sticker on her rear end that says, 'As a matter of fact, I do own the whole dam road!'"

After the laughter subsided, Dan said, "All right, let's get this show on the road."

But that was easier said than done: leg muscles were sore from the unaccustomed paddling, and Mary Ann's family was still unorganized. The Peterson's were quickly loaded and ready to leave. It was clear, however, that the others needed assistance in rolling their sleeping bags, getting their backpacks and trailers loaded, and in simply getting started. The Petersons had learned early in their journey to unpack only those items they needed at that moment; Mary Ann's family, on the other hand, had unpacked almost everything they brought with them!

Dan looked at Mike and quietly shook his head, "We learned very quickly to not unpack everything, but they needed to learn that lesson by themselves."

Finally, everyone was ready, even a subdued Jennifer. Dan led the way onto the highway with Mike bringing up the rear. Sore leg muscles complained, but after a few minutes of easy peddling, they loosened. The first part of the day's ride was generally down a slight grade past the town of Chimney Rock. Tom's dog rode on his trailer and Lor's big cat rode on Dan's trailer. Ginger rode on the back of Lor's bike. Every so often, to Lor's great joy, Ginger would reach forward and hug her.

Shortly after the town of Chimney Rock, the grade turned sharply uphill.

"Lor, Tom, we need to get your cat and dog off of the trailers; we can't paddle uphill with their extra weight," Dan suggested.

"Sure."

Neither animal, however, wanted to leave his lazy perch. Both had to be nearly physically lifted off the trailers, but eventually, they just padded along with their humans.

Several miles or so further, as they approached an overpass, they saw that the road was blocked by a manmade makeshift barrier. Whoever had designed the barrier had chosen wisely. The road had been cut into the side of a steep mountain with the northern side of the road falling into a deep ravine while the southern side of the road was blocked by the side of the evergreen tree covered mountain.

Both animals snarled at the barrier.

Lor said, "Dan, Mike, there is someone ahead of us behind that barrier."

"Send the animals up and around them until we figure out what we have," Dan said.

They stopped about two hundred yards away from the barricaded overpass. Dan gave his AR-15 to Tom, unhooked his trailer, and, alone, peddled slowly up to the fence posts with barbed wire barrier.

A voice rang out, "That's close enough, stranger!"

Dan spread his hands palms up out in front of him, "We're just passing through, friend."

He continued with, "We don't mean any harm to anyone . . ." attempting to convey that if someone started something, he would finish it.

A moment's silence followed.

Dan, attempting to appear that he wasn't doing so, visually examined the barricade. Whoever had built it utilized old fence posts braced together at the top by barbed wire with the bottoms of the posts spread about three or four feet apart. Dead leaves and tree branches were scattered throughout the barricade in an attempt to render it opaque; it had obviously been there for some time. To the right or south side of the barricade appeared to be a small gate.

A man's voice called out from the side of the barricade, "Why don't you bring your bunch up here; we can see how many of you there are and we'll only charge toll for the adults."

"Well, what kind of toll are you talking about? We don't have any money."

A surprised younger voice came back, "Just some salt, and maybe some food, of course. Money ain't worth nothing, no more."

"Well, we are just passing through, my friend, and we have a long way to travel. I sure hate for my kids to go hungry because I must pay you food to get through a public road," Dan stated flatly.

"It looks to me that's your problem," grunted the adult voice.

Dan tried one more time, "I'm not adverse to sharing a little with you if you need food, but just to pay you toll for passage is, is unfair!" He finished frustratingly.

The voice laughed harshly, "You are looking at 'fair,' now, get back to your friends and get some food and supplies or turn around, makes no difference to us."

With that, the unmistakenable sound of a receiver of a pump shotgun being levered and cocked echoed from behind the barricade. Dan's stomach tightened and his hands froze; he slowly spread his hands on the handlebars of his bike and very carefully turned around and slowly rode back to his group.

"What, what's going on?" The boys asked. Mike just looked at Dan with a question in his face.

He related what had happened and added, "They picked a good spot; there is no other way through this area, and to go around them would take days or even weeks."

Mike looked at Lor, "Can your cat tell us how many people are up there?"

Lor shook her head, "Oh no, he's not that smart. He can just tell me where they are."

Mike looked up at the overpass, and up the side of the mountain. He put his finger in his mouth to moisten it and held it up in the air. The finger grew cooler on the uphill side.

He advised the boys who had questions in their eyes, "They made one mistake: the breeze is blowing toward us. Lor's animals will be able to hear or smell them before they see us."

Mike continued, "I've got an idea; let's go back about half a mile out of their sight."

After they retreated, Mike told Geoff and Tom to gather up some firewood for a large fire. He asked Mary Ann if she had brought a few special things with her. Upon receiving a nod, he outlined his plan.

Soon thereafter, Geoff and Tom piled a large amount of wood on the road about two hundred yards from the barricade in plain sight of anyone hiding by the overpass. Mike, Lor and Dan left with the cat and Tom's dog after giving instructions to Mary Ann, Geoff, Tom, and the girls.

After Mary Ann touched Mike's arm and said, "You be careful," she and the kids grinned at each other.

Mike, Lor and Dan climbed up the side of the mountain through the bushes and trees with Lor's animals until Mike thought they were probably above the overpass. They had to stop and rest several times. They were climbing up the side of the evergreen tree covered mountain at about a 45-degree angle and they were above 7000 feet.

Dan thought that if he wasn't out of breath so much, he would have enjoyed more watching Lor's tight jeans moving ahead of him. Right after one of their rest stops, while Lor was climbing above Dan, Dan reached up and gently pinched a rounded buttock. Lor, grinning, waved a slap at his hand.

They traversed the side of the mountain in an easterly direction through the pungent evergreen trees. The ground was carpeted with fallen evergreen needles with a few small pinecones and their footsteps were silent. With their gasps for air, a lowly squirrel chattering briefly at them was the only sound breaking the silence.

As they came closer to where the overpass might be, Lor knelt with her animals and held their faces; both wagged their tails and licked her face. A gentle breeze moved the tops of the trees in their direction.

A short distance later, the cat's ears flattened back on his broad head and his long tail twitched. Both the animals' attention was focused ahead and down from them. Dan and Mike tightened their shoulder harnesses containing their weapons to eliminate any chance of noise. Lor just pushed her .357 Colt Python revolver deeper in her holster. They then moved quietly through the trees, alert for any noise.

On a soft breeze came a whiff of stale campfire smoke. They crept, single file, through the trees until just ahead of them they could see a small camp with a dirty white nylon two-person tent in front of a hole containing a smoldering fire.

Mike looked at Lor to see if the animals saw anyone in the camp, but she shook her head, pointing downward. The animals' attention was directed below them. Mike, never-the-less, waived to Dan and Lor to remain hidden while he checked the tent and camp.

He found a neat and clean interior of the tent, and the camp itself was well maintained! There was no one there and Mike didn't touch anything. He was concerned about the occupants of the camp, not what they had.

The camp was on the side of a nearly overgrown weed covered, single lane dirt road leading from below and curving around the side of the mountain. It apparently had been bulldozed as a fire break in the distant past. Mike signaled for Lor to have her animals lead them descending the road. She called them to her, rubbed each of their heads and looked them in the eyes for a moment, their tails wagging gently.

Both animals left her and padded down the road, one on each side. They were almost invisible in and against the brown grass and bushes on the sides of the road with a background of dark green evergreen trees.

They had traveled down the road about two hundred yards when both animals' ears flattened back and they froze to the ground. Then they heard a booming sound echoing off the far canyon walls as if someone was banging on a large bass drum. To their left and below them, they could see a stream of smoke drifting nearly straight up in the air, and when the smoke reached about five hundred feet above them, the upper air currents moved it away from them. They could hear male and female voices and calls echoing from across the valley, and screams and laughter of little girls.

Mike grinned at Dan: right on time!

Lor motioned for her animals to move on, continuing down the weed infested dirt road. They came to a bend and both animals flattened to the ground again. This time Dan motioned to Lor and Mike to stay where they were; he slowly and quietly crawled ahead of the animals through the weeds and overgrown grass to peer around the bend.

They had come around behind and above the overpass. The road continued over the overpass, but the side of the hill from where Dan was hiding to the back of the overpass and to the road was clear. He could see directly behind and under the overpass.

There were two men crouched together behind the barricade, one with a pair of binoculars focused down the road. Dan could see no one else.

Dan crawled back to where Mike and Lor were waiting.

He whispered, "There are two men, both over to the right of the barricade."

"Lor, do the animals see anyone else around?"

She shook her head.

Meanwhile, they could hear the yelling and screaming of voices dancing around the fire down the road. Occasionally, a boom rang out as someone pounded on a hollow log!

Dan, in a hushed, tight voice, said, "Well, let's take them! Lor, you send your animals, one on each side to back us up. Keep them out of the firing zone."

She nodded and whispered to her animals, they crept away on their haunches, the dog following the road and the big cat oozing through the tall grass down the side of the mountain.

Dan crawled back to the bend with Lor and Mike behind him. He peeked over again and saw that the two men's attention was still directed down the road; they seemed to be arguing over the use of the binoculars.

Dan could now see there was a large fire in the middle of the road and that there were half-nude figures dancing around it! Mary Ann had a light brown bikini swimsuit that made her look almost totally naked. Periodically, one of the girls, half-dressed, would run around the fire, yelling, and screaming, waving their arms; then one of the boys would come out from behind the bushes and run around the fire, yelling, and screaming. He noted that the boys would change shirts and hats each time they ran around the fire.

Dan motioned to Mike and Lor to spread out. He then stood up and carefully walked to the side of the road overlooking the back of the overpass and barricade. His heart was beating rapidly, but his attention was focused on the two men.

He slipped the AR-15 off his back, quietly pulled back the double-T locking mechanism of the weapon and set the safety lever.

He then released the safety and the lock, the upper sliding mechanism containing a copper jacketed .223 cartridge slid into the receiver with a loud, sharp metallic clank!

The two men started to turn.

Dan commanded harshly: "Freeze!"

"Put Your Hands On Top Of Your Heads!"

Upon seeing a hesitation from the men, he barked in a voice coming from deep within his chest, "Do It, Now!"

They slowly complied, the one man holding the binoculars dropped them.

"Now, back away from the fence!"

"Slowly!" upon receiving compliance from the men.

"Now, lay down on your stomach!"

When the men lay down, Dan ordered, "Spread your arms and hands away from your body, palms up! Now!"

"Mike," Dan whispered, "Would you go down, search them and tie them up? We'll cover you from here."

Mike nodded and slid down the side of the mountain to approach them from their back. Meanwhile, Lor had directed her cat to shadow the two men lying on the pavement of the highway. The 150-pound cat arrogantly rose out of the bushes as if He owned the whole road, ambled over to the two men, and smelled their heads. The big cat then squatted in front of the two men and watched them with his large intelligent shining amber eyes. A drooling, yellowish fang protruded through the cat's wide tawny face! If he could speak, he would have said, "Please do something stupid, like trying to run away!"

One man moaned to himself, "Oh Lord! What the hell is this?"

Dan barked, "Don't even think of moving!"

By this time, Mike had reached the men. He quickly searched them and found nothing. He removed their belts and tied their hands behind them. He then waved to Dan and Lor for them to descend to the road.

Dan asked Lor, "Any more around here?"

She shook her head, "No, our babies would have found them by now."

Mike walked over to the binoculars that the men had dropped and looked through them down to the fire. His face then broke in a wide grin with a bit of longing.

"She's pretty enough to cause a mummy to become excited," he commented to Dan. "No wonder these guys never saw us coming."

After patting her cat and dog, Lor pulled apart the gate through the barricade and walked out on to the road. She waved at the remainder of the group. She called, "Come on up."

They ran up to her, both Ginger and Sue hugging her asking, "Are you all right? Is Dad ok?" Tom briefly hugged her as he ran by to inspect what was behind the barricade.

Mary Ann quickly changed clothes and she came soon after. She darted through the fence and ran to Mike's side. She asked worriedly, touching, and rubbing his arms and shoulders with her hands, "Are you all right? Are you ok?!"

He smiled down at her and took her in his arms, "I'm just fine."

She lay her head on his broad chest with tears in her eyes, "Oh, thank heavens!" she whispered as her arms held him in a vicelike grasp, "I was so scared for you!"

After a moment of hugging Mary Ann, Mike looked at Dan, "Good commands! Where did you learn to do that?"

"When we were living in California, I went on ride-alongs with a couple of Los Angeles County Deputy Sheriffs, really good guys, and I saw them do that. It was called a felony stop."

"Well, whatever it was called, good job!"

Mike and Dan went to where the two men were still lying. They assisted the two men to a sitting position. The younger of the two men, a boy little older than Tom, had urinated in his pants. He later told them that while being ordered to "Freeze" was bad enough, when he was laying on the highway and saw the big cat come padding over to him, he thought he was going to die. He had never seen such an animal up close and he now knew what a helpless rabbit felt like when being hunted.

The two men were father and son. They had been there for two months. They had a hunting cabin about five miles up the dirt road and were managing to eke out an existence of sorts.

The father, Roger Duchien, added, "We haven't hurt anyone. Nor have we 'held-up' anyone; you can check our belongings if you want. All we asked for was whatever supplies we didn't have. And we never, never, took everything someone had. My son and I don't need much and we never asked for much, just a little."

Mike asked, "Well, why do you think you are entitled to anything?"

Duchien replied flatly, "I think we earned it! About ten miles up the highway behind us, you'll come to another overpass with a few cabins near it. It looks much like this overpass. Those people used to rob and rape and kill. We," nodding to his son, "wiped them out after they held up our group!"

Roger Duchien's eyes were cold and hard, but they remained steady on Dan's when he continued, "We were the only survivors left after they got done with us. We escaped and went back. They'll never bother anyone again. I think we earned the right to charge a little toll!"

Jennifer, overhearing the statements by Duchien, asked in an almost superior manner, "Well! Why didn't you call 911 or the police? That's what they are for."

Duchien looked at her for a minute and then said coldly, "Where the hell have you been, sweetheart? There is no more '911' or police or rangers, or anything."

Jennifer's face paled as she looked at him; her head shook sideways, attempting to deny what Duchien had said, but his steady eyes held hers, making her believe that what he said was true. Her face suddenly grew older and tiny tears escaped down her face.

"Finally!" Dan thought.

Although his hands were bound behind him, Duchien said slowly and thoughtfully to Dan and Mike, "My reasoning was and is that since the world as we knew it no longer exists, and the monetary or economic system as we knew it no longer exists, we have reverted to a feudal or barter system. If so, since we have provided a service: that of safe passage for the next few miles at least and we should receive something in exchange."

Dan and Mike raised their eyebrows and cocked their heads at each other, but the logic made sense.

Duchien continued, "We don't even have any more shells for the shotgun; that's it leaning over on the fence. If you people would have ridden straight through the fence, we couldn't have and wouldn't have stopped you." Duchien's eyes and face, while concerned for his plight, remained steady on Dan's face.

"Nice bluff," Dan acknowledged.

"It worked before," Duchien shrugged with a small smile.

Mike drew Dan aside and asked, "What are we going to do with them?"

Dan thought for a moment and then replied, "Well, I sent the boys up to the tent to examine it for weapons. They just came back."

"Tom, Geoff, what did you find?"

The boys walked over to Dan and Mike. Tom reported, "We found an old 30-06, bolt action deer rifle and some shells for the rifle, some food, sleeping bags, and so on. We didn't find any shells for the shotgun. Nothing else important," he shrugged.

"Did you find any evidence of anyone else's property, backpacks, supplies, anything else?" Mike asked.

Tom shook his head, "No, I don't think so. I remember all the supplies and stuff we found when we rescued Lor, and all those things we found on that first overpass in Southern California, but there was nothing like that in or around that tent."

"Do you think the father is telling the truth?" Dan asked Mike.

Mike hesitated for a second, "I think so. We haven't found anything to show otherwise."

Dan and Mike walked over to where the two men were seated. Lor and Mary Ann had been talking to them after sending the kids for the bikes.

"I don't think they meant us any harm," Lor said to Dan. "Their major problem now is lack of salt. They can exist on the animals running around up here, but they need salt to cure the meat."

Dan said to Roger Duchien as he untied him and his son, "Well, as I first said, we're just passing through. What do you know about the road or conditions ahead of us if we stay on this highway?"

"As far as I know, the road between us and Pagosa Springs is open. There are some people left in that town and they are pretty friendly. From Pagosa Springs eastward, there will be snow on the mountain tops, but the road, such as it is, should be open. Someone came through here on horseback, oh, about a couple of weeks ago, from Alamosa, and he said that there were washouts in a couple of places, but that it was passable. He told us that there had been a forest fire on the other side of Wolf Creek Pass, but that it had burned itself out."

He looked at his son, "How long do you think it would take them to get from Pagosa Springs to over the mountains?"

Duchien's son (Dan never found out the boy's name) thoughtfully replied, "Well, it's very scenic through there, but with those curves and those switchbacks, and since you're up over ten thousand feet, I'd say at least three to four days. I think it's about forty-five miles."

Duchien asked Dan if he knew what had happened to the world. Dan squatted along-side of Duchien and his son and in about five minutes, told them what he knew about the meteor and the life force.

Duchien was quiet for a moment or two and then muttered, "I kind of thought something like that happened; when everything started, we saw a car driving up this road and in the middle of a storm, it was attacked by a green glowing thing. That stuff only attacked the engine compartment, but they drove over that cliff behind you. We didn't even bother looking down at the bottom; it's about a thousand feet or so down there."

He continued, "We could see green something eating or corroding the 220,000-voltage wires down in the valley and it didn't take a rocket scientist to figure out that that stuff was dangerous!"

Lor looked at Dan, "I think I know where there is a saltlick that they could use. When we climbed up from the road, there was a tiny spring with white mineral deposits all around it."

She turned to Duchien, "If you go back down the road just around the bend and climb up about two hundred yards, you'll find a spring. I think that was salt because both of my animals stopped and licked it."

They left a short time later. Dan wanted to travel a few miles, and while he believed Duchien, he didn't want to tempt fate.

About ten miles later, as Duchien promised, they came upon another overpass. They found a few burnt out cabins. More importantly, bullet holes and gouges on the sides of the overpass indicated that a fierce gunfight had taken place. Spent cartridges littered the sides of the overpass and the road. Off to the side, they saw what appeared to be the remains of a few mounds with crosses on them.

"It looks like Duchien was telling the truth when he said they wiped out this bunch," Dan said. "Come on, let's get going."

They camped that night near a side dirt road with a broken sign pointing south to Pagosa Junction. Tom and Geoff thought they would need horses or goats to get over the road as it appeared to be washed out.

After arriving in what was left of the small town of Pagosa Springs, they spent several days resting and taking occasional baths in the still oozing 160-degree springs. Lor knew a few people there and they spent some time with them. Again and again, Dan had to tell what he knew of the meteor and the life force. People everywhere were desperate for information; there seemed to be a fatalistic acceptance, however, of the life force coupled with a frontier-like determination to overcome the immediate obstacle of life without electricity. A surprising number of parents thought, "The kids didn't need the darn TV set anyway!"

CHAPTER ELEVEN

The days and miles passed.

After looking at their carefully preserved map, Dan wanted to turn north on the old Interstate 25 to travel through Colorado Springs and maybe even Denver.

"I would like you kids to see the Air Force Academy, particularly the chapel because it's really different."

One night, however, they camped with about twenty-five adults and kids fleeing southward from the Denver area.

As they huddled around a giant campfire, Robert "Bob" Ashley, a lean nerdy looking man who wasn't as old as he appeared, said, "I work, worked as a civilian for the U.S. Army in a confidential "think-tank" base just to the southeast of Denver. Our base had a small nuclear reactor for electrical power that ran fine until it was savagely attacked by that green force."

He said bitterly, "We received word about the force thing from a satellite feed from Langley, Virginia, that was a CIA liaison right in the middle of the attack. Here we are trying to fight this thing with water, fire retardants, earth, and anything else we could throw at it without even knowing what in the hell it was."

He went on sadly, "I'll never forget the wording some moron had broadcast: 'You should be advised that there may be a hazardous substance that might possibly have an effect on your power supply!' I called him every name I could think of."

Ashley said the Fort Carlson Military Reservation south of Colorado Springs had been violently attacked by the force. A few adults in the group thought that some of the Air Force bases or Army bases in the Denver-Colorado Springs area had nuclear weapons. While apparently none of the nuclear weapons had detonated, there were several that "cooked" causing low level nuclear reactions that radiated the surrounding area. An ammunition storage area east of Denver near the new airport had exploded. Apparently, the storage area contained many of the Air Force's smart bombs and missiles; the blast laid waste to an area of about nine square miles.

"Joe Robinson told me that they were going to try to arrange a meeting of scientists at the University of Chicago next summer." Dan said. "Did you hear anything about that?"

"Sure, and it was more than just a meeting of scientists. If I understood what I heard correctly, there was going to be a large rendezvous of the surviving military, government workers and scientists at the University of Chicago. Chicago was picked because it was the general center of the United States and June was picked because winter would have been finished by then."

Dan thought that the terrible emphasis was on "surviving," but he was forced to agree that society as he knew it had been effectively destroyed by the force.

"You may not know that the whole area north of us is a war zone, Dan," Robert Ashley advised, quietly. "A couple of the more organized gangs had raided what was left of the various military bases and National Guard armories and stole weapons and anything else they could get their hands on. There was some brutal fighting between the various gangs; what they would do is set fire to their enemy's home turf and burn them out. And as you know, there aren't any fire departments anymore."

"Thank heavens for our usual rains we get up here," a heavy woman agreed, her bleached blond hair showing extensive dark roots. "If we hadn't received a few good storms, there would be nothing left up there."

Ashley wistfully smiled, "Someone told me that Mile High Stadium, home of our World Champion Denver Broncos and the former home of our Denver Rockys was a neutral zone for the warring gangs. Apparently, the gangs meet there to exchange prisoners and things."

"I wanted to take my family up to the Air Force Academy because heaven knows when we'll be here again, if ever," Dan said.

"Well, don't go there," Ashley responded. "It's too dangerous now."

"Well, if we can't do it, we can't do it," Dan said, reluctantly. "Maybe someday"

They continued generally eastward until they crossed the muddy Arkansas River. The old Santa Fe Trail was followed for a short distance with an occasional stop to examine a few abandoned museums. Dan tried to keep the kids' education going as well as he could by seeing an important part of American Old West history. On the far eastern part of Colorado, they eventually turned northward and pushed generally northeast toward the old Interstate 80. "I want to take Interstate 80 across Nebraska and Iowa. It will be much easier traveling on that highway than these small side roads," Dan pointed on their map.

Both Dan and Mike thought that while none of the roads had been maintained for the past several months, the major interstate highways would have the best chance of being open.

Dan said to Tom and Geoff, "Thank goodness for President Eisenhower."

"Why?" Geoff asked.

"Well, I'm glad you didn't ask who? When he was President, he signed bills authorizing the heavy-duty nationwide highway system. The purpose according to Congress was that the major highways allowed the military to much more easily move and transport stuff from one place to another. Remember, our enemy at that time was Russia and the military was afraid of an invasion. It took billions of dollars, but it sure made travel much easier from border to border and coast to coast."

"That's right," Mike said. "If I recall correctly, a good portion of the gasoline taxes went into highways. At least now, we don't have to worry about taxes."

One night, about a day's ride south of Interstate 76, they had sought shelter and camped under a small overpass. It had drizzled that afternoon and they stopped early. They usually would not travel in the rain if they could avoid it. If they saw adverse weather ahead of them, they looked for a shelter.

Normally, towns were avoided and since they had heavy sleeping bags, sleeping in the open had become a matter of routine to them. In addition, towns meant people and people meant delays and sometimes, danger. Dan wasn't interested in delays; he simply wanted to get to Wisconsin.

While they were still in Durango at Lor's house, Tom had quietly asked his father, "Dad, do you think that Grandpa and Grandma are all right?"

"I simply don't know, Son, I sure hope so. Your aunt still lives not too far from them and while I'm worried, there isn't a thing I can do about them here." Thoughts of his parents were frequently on his mind, and whenever a delay seemed inevitable, he grew restless and attempted to expedite matters.

That night, at about midnight the weather cleared and the stars appeared through the breaking clouds. There was no moon to illuminate the all-encompassing deep darkness. The fire was low, its embers flickering in the soft breeze. The only sound was that of a lonely cricket, chirping for a mate with an occasional bullfrog or two lending alto background music. A very mild breeze carried with it the refreshing smell of wet earth and green grass with an occasional whiff of smoke from the campfire.

Suddenly, both the big cat sleeping between the girls, and Tom's dog, which had been sleeping by Tom, sat up and growled softly. Both Dan and Mike, forced to become light sleepers, awoke and crawled out of their sleeping bags.

"What's the matter, guys?" Dan quietly asked the animals as he rubbed their heads.

"What's out there?"

Both animals nuzzled him briefly, but their attention was directed northward. Neither animal appeared to be alarmed, just alert.

Dan threw some extra wood on their fire.

Mike shook his head, "Good move, genius, now we can see even less. My night vision is completely gone."

"Sorry."

Suddenly, they heard the faint sounds of a deep bass grunting emanating from the solid darkness. The grunting sounded like a combination of a huge pig grunting and a small bovine bull snorting. By this time, the boys had awakened and were intently listening to the strange sounds coming out of the darkness.

"What on earth is that?" Geoff whispered.

The grunting seemed to come from several different sources. It slowly passed to the west of the overpass, but was spread out over a wide area.

Tom rubbed the back of his dog and whispered, "What's out there, boy?"

His dog, however, just licked his hand and continued looking out into the deep darkness.

Mike murmured, "I haven't the foggiest idea what's out there, but whatever it is, it is huge; I don't think, though, that it's a danger to us, your dog and the big cat are interested, but not alarmed."

Slowly, the grunting spread around them; whatever "it" was, there were a number of "its."

The night slowly turned into dawn. The group had gone back to sleep, Dan sleeping lightly and rising only to keep the fire lit. Slowly, the stars disappeared with the brightening in the east. Long fingers of bright reds and yellows reached up into the sky as the sun clawed its way into another warm day. The darkness slowly dissipated leaving mounds of darkness, moving darkness, scattered around the camp.

Geoff and Tom again awake peered out into the disappearing darkness with keen eyes.

"Well, I'll be," Tom exclaimed.

"What are they, Son?"

Tom, without answering his father said, "Let's wake the girls; I bet they haven't seen those before."

Dan, a little irritated, squinted out into the breaking dawn at the moving lumps of darkness. His eyes were not as sharp as his son's and he needed a little more sunlight to ascertain what the objects were.

Oh!

"Come on girls, look at what we have around us," Dan said in a hushed voice.

The girls, yawning, crawled out of their sleeping bags and looked around. Their eyes rounded with surprise and delight.

"Buffalo!" exclaimed the boys.

"Wrong, guys," replied Dan. "These are bison, which are distinctly American plains animals. Buffalo are usually on the African or Asian continents."

Scattered less than fifty yards away was a herd of approximately fifty to sixty bison. There were about a half-dozen tiny crimson haired calves cavorting around their mothers while a gigantic bull majestically supervised his herd. Their hair was dark, long and course. Their shoulders were huge with the bodies tapering to slim, almost hairless hips. The tails swung rapidly to chase the flies infesting them. On top of one large female rode a stark white bird, picking flies and lice off the head of its ride. Small polished black horns grew from the massive heads.

Off to the side was a small group of what appeared to be young bulls; obviously, the large bull had driven them away from "his" harem. The bison just meandered along, heads down munching on the buffalo and blue grama grasses. A particular favorite was the occasional patch of wild rye grass where three or four bison would gather around, grunting and munching away-like a bunch of old ladies around a bridge table.

Every so often, one or the other of the babies would stick its head under its mother for "lunch." Besides "lunch," the calves would usually receive a bath from its mother's tongue.

Tom asked Ginger, "How would you like to receive a bath from a washcloth that felt like the side of a tree?"

"Absolutely not," Ginger said as she snuggled closer to Lor and Dan.

The humans simply sat and watched the bison. Ginger and Sue were enchanted, "Daddy, can we go out and play with them?"

"No, I don't think so, sweetie, they are wild animals and if you got too close to them, you might get hurt."

Tom's dog and the big cat just sat on their haunches, not barking or snarling, but simply keeping an eye on the king of the plains.

"Where did they come from, Dad?" Tom asked.

"Well, they either came from Yellowstone National Park or from a large bison ranch in southwest South Dakota, Northern Wyoming area. With no one to control them, they'll go anyplace they want to now."

"We passed just north of a large area known as Comanche Grass Lands about a week or so ago, and I bet that's where they're headed," Mike said.

"I think so too," Dan replied, "At one time, this plains area was their land. Obviously, instinct handed down through generations drew them back to those lands."

Dan thought that the head bull had to weigh over two thousand pounds and was nearly seven feet tall at his shoulders. It was clear that he knew the presence of the humans and he stationed himself generally between the humans and his herd. It was equally understood that he considered this "his" land and that the humans were there only with his permission.

From the north side of the overpass, which had been hidden from the humans, came a solitary male bison. He was smaller and obviously somewhat younger than the chief bull.

"Look!" Both Sue and Ginger gasped and pointed.

"Look Daddy, it's a white buffalo!"

"Well, it is not a buffalo, but everybody called them buffalo and the title continues to this day," lectured Dan.

Not only was he entirely white, but his white fur also glistened with a soft pearl luminescence from the previous night's rain. He was so close to the humans, they could see his pink-rimmed eyes with his off-white polished horns protruding from his stark white massive head. They could smell his heavy musty earth odor since he was only about twenty yards upwind. He walked slowly with effortless nobility to his presence making the grunting sounds they had heard that night.

Dan said softly, "I have heard about white buffaloes, but I don't know of anyone who has ever seen one."

After a moment or two, he said to his kids, "The ancient Indians held the white buffalo as almost a God, or a sign of favor from the earth gods. They revered it, and seldom, if ever, killed it. The Sioux Indians told the legend, handed down from generation to generation, to their young braves of the white buffalo. They believed that if one is true in his heart and spirit, and if he believes in the white buffalo, in time of desperate need, the white buffalo will appear and save him."

They spent the morning watching the animals. After breakfast, they packed and were ready to travel but no one was in a rush to leave the wonderful animals.

Tom said, "See that one over there?" he pointed, "It too has a bumper sticker on its rear end."

Jennifer had to ask, "Which one? I don't see anything on a rear end."

"Oh sure, it's the one that has a bumper sticker on it that says, 'As a matter of fact, I do own the whole dam prairie!'"

After the laughter subsided, they reluctantly mounted their bikes and headed northward.

The animals had followed and walked on the road, leaving large piles of fresh, smelly, droppings.

Dan said to the kids, "You know, in the old days, when the settlers originally crossed these plains in their covered wagons, they used these buffalo droppings or buffalo chips as they are called, for firewood. The buffalo were basic to the Indians, and they used every part of the buffalo. You are starting to see now that since we are out of the mountains and through the foothills, there aren't many trees for firewood. And dried buffalo chips burn too."

Sue and Jennifer, almost together, turned up their noses thinking about eating something cooked over buffalo manure.

Lor, Mary Ann and Dan grinned at each other: "How spoiled our kids are, I bet if they got hungry enough, they wouldn't know the difference."

Dan, seeing the boys eyeing the still steaming piles of buffalo droppings warned, "The first one who rides through a pile gets to do dishes tonight!"

"Aw," both boys said together, grinning at each other.

And as things sometimes happen, while Dan was riding with Lor and talking with her, he felt a soft bump and heard a squishing sound. The aromatic odor of fresh buffalo droppings immediately assaulted their noses.

Both boys laughed so hard, they stopped their bikes before they fell. They had tears in their eyes and their sides hurt.

"Say, everyone, let's get all of our dishes together tonight, they need to be washed!"

Geoff chortled.

Dan just shook his head. The remainder of the day, the boys would ride past Dan holding their noses and asking each other, "What is that strange odor around here? Can you smell something? It sure smells bad!"

The days and the miles passed. Interstate 76 came and was followed to its intersection with Interstate 80. They were forced to detour around the intersection of both highways as the overhead signs had blown down, effectively blocking the highways. The sprawling prairie town of North Platte came and went. Sitting useless and now covered with dust on the outskirts of the town were large lots full of bright yellow and green John Deere combines, tractors and farm equipment. New and used car lots remained abandoned and useless, once highly polished and shiny cars and trucks were now covered with dust and grime.

Just on the east side of North Platte, Nebraska, they had to make a significant detour off the highway. The highway on both sides was completely blocked with wrecked and burned automobiles, small and large trucks and several gasoline tankers (or more precisely, what appeared to be left of gasoline tankers.).

Mike speculated, "I wonder if they got caught in a fog that came off the Platte River. Someone told me that in the spring, they have some very heavy fog around here."

"Well, that force is or was around here; look: our babies refuse to go near that huge wreck," Lor replied. Both the big cat and Tom's dog eyed the jumbled pile of vehicles with distrust, their hackles slightly raised.

The long four-hundred-and-fifty-mile ride from North Platte to Omaha started over the almost flat, gently rolling lands stretching out on all sides of the road. Off to the side, they would occasionally see a burned hulk of a farm tractor or large combine that had been attacked by the force. The sprawling lands of what had been wheat or rye grain fields were now being gradually overtaken by the original grasses. Little bluestem, cordgrass and wild rye grasses started their spotted return intermingled with the original buffalo grass.

During one rest stop, Tom took their binoculars and climbed up on an overpass. Later he came down quietly committing, "Boy, you can see for miles and miles from here, it's so flat."

Off in the distances, herds of shy pronghorn antelope hid in the rolling valleys while each day near the river, whitetail and mule deer made their skittish appearance.

"We've seen a lot of wild animals; are there always that many out here? And how about bears?" Mary Ann asked.

"I've never heard of bears out here, but since there are no cars or trucks or tractors now, there's little for the deer to be afraid of," Dan said.

The boys found great fun in riding against the wind. Since the bike tires made little noise, and if they were riding against the wind so that animals would not hear them or smell them, they would sneak up on an unsuspecting badger or groundhog and scare them half to death. This stopped when Tom got chased by a highly irate badger. "Careful guys, that badger will hurt you or chew on your tires or feet," warned Dan.

It seemed however, that the wild animals were losing their fear of humans, particularly when the humans were on the bikes; perhaps the animals equated the humans on bikes to humans in cars.

Food was never a problem: Tom and Geoff proved to be very good hunters and seldom was the night they didn't have fresh meat or a couple of pheasants or something.

The days remained bright, hot and rainless. The ground was baked hard by the almost merciless sun. A whole day would pass before they even saw a cloud in the dazzling sky. As they crossed over the Platte River, they rested for several days at a campground at the river's edge.

While white sandhill cranes and high-flying eagles watched, Dan roughhoused with Sue and Ginger, dunking them in the river between frantic giggling and splashing. Lor, sitting sedately on the riverbank, just smiled and smiled when the two girls ran to her to get dry. Washed clean clothing was hung to dry in the hot sun on a makeshift clothesline hung between two trees.

Several times during the long trip, Lor had deep conversations with Tom, Sue and Ginger regarding what they should call her.

"You can call me anything that you are comfortable with, from Lor, Lorraine, Mom, Mother, or whatever. You must remember, however, that you had another mother that you must not forget."

The kids fully realized and more importantly, fully approved of the relationship between their father and Lor. Tom and Sue had never seen their father so happy and relaxed until he met Lor.

The second morning at the campground, Lor, Tom, and Sue were down by the river's edge when Tom whispered to Sue, "You know, I think Dad's birthday is sometime around now."

"Mom?" Sue turned to Lor, "Can we bake a cake or something for Dad? How about a surprise party for him?" she said excitedly.

Lor smiled widely, both in her heart when Sue called her "Mom!" and on her face for the idea of a surprise birthday party.

She hugged both kids, "Great idea, guys! How do we get your father out of camp for an hour or two while I bake a cake for him?"

After a moment's thought, Tom exclaimed, "I know, I'll get Mike and Geoff to ask Dad to go fishing. There's a quiet pond about half a mile up the river that might have some fish in it, and remember, Geoff brought along his fishing tackle and a couple of lightweight rods."

"Good idea. And if you catch something, we'll have fish for dinner tonight."

After a few more minutes of planning, they returned to the camp. Tom quietly drew Mike and Geoff aside and told them of their plan. They enthusiastically agreed. A little later, Mike casually walked over to where Dan was working on one of the trailers and asked, "Say, how about taking a break and let's go fishing with the boys. Maybe we'll catch something for dinner tonight."

"Sure."

It had been years since he had been fishing and he thought they could use the extra food. In addition, since he had been pushing the group to travel as fast and as far as possible each day, he could use a little relaxation, too.

Around noon, the males of the group wondered off in search of a fishing hole. Lor, Mary Ann and the girls immediately set to work baking and soon, the campsite was flooded with the tantalizing smell of baking sourdough bread.

Several hours later, the men came back, proudly carrying a four large trout, each weighing several pounds.

"I don't think that hole has been fished for years; the fish didn't seem to know enough to stay away from our fishing lines," Geoff said proudly.

Tom excitedly showed the girls a perfect flint arrowhead he had found. "Indians used to travel through here and they probably hunted around here. Just imagine that this arrowhead might have been shot at a buffalo or a rabbit or something." He couldn't understand the girls' lack of enthusiasm.

After Geoff and Mike cleaned the fish, they barbecued on one of the remaining barbecue stands that had charcoal left in it. After a huge meal of trout, biscuits, and potatoes that Lor had traded for in North Platte, Dan felt like he was stuffed. He was just sprawled out near his sleeping bag about half asleep. After a few minutes, Mike and Lor's eyes met and they exchanged slight nods.

"Dan, can you give me a hand with this trailer? I want to check the bearings and make sure they have enough grease," Mike nonchalantly asked.

"Sure," Dan yawned. He was full and somewhat contemplating taking a nap. It never occurred to him to ask why this trailer had to be examined this minute, but since Mike asked, he would help. They walked over to the trailers; Mike had Dan lift the wheel on a trailer, positioning himself so that Dan's back was to the camp.

Meanwhile, Lor retrieved Dan's birthday cake. The girls, almost besides themselves with excitement, cautiously placed their few precious small candles on the cake and carefully lit them.

Very quietly they walked over behind Dan.

Mike, facing the girls, said, "Dan, put the trailer down and turn around."

Dan, eyes blinking, turned . . .

"Surprise!"

The age-old song of "Happy Birthday," mostly off key, rang throughout the campsite. Dan's mouth, initially wide open, finally closed with tears glistening in his eyes. Sue and Ginger just jumped up and down with happiness hugging their father.

After getting Dan to eat a generous portion of the sourdough birthday cake, Lor said, "Dan, we don't have anything to give you, but if, no, when we get to Wisconsin, we have all agreed to make up for this lack of gifts."

Dan shook his head, "Well, Lor, you are wrong!"

Lor, startled, stared back at Dan.

He continued, "What all of you have given me here tonight, and what you have given me over the past couple of months is the greatest gift of all: that of happiness and care! Thank you all so much, so very much!"

Dan and Lor shared glances, their looks deep into each other's souls promised happiness, pleasure, respect and joy together, not only for tonight, but for all time!

That night, the only sound was a whisper of a soft, gentle wind cooling the star sprinkled sky with a background rhapsody of lonely crickets chirping for mates. Off in the distance could be heard the occasional hoot of an owl, either looking for his mate or for food. Dan and Lor wondered off down the riverbank to be alone for a while. Later, they came back, their bodies relaxed, their arms around each other, smiling into each other's eyes.

By the time Dan and Lor returned, everyone in the camp was asleep except for Mike. He was awake, periodically adding wood to the fire. He was watching a lightning storm far to the southeast. Every so often, intense bolts of lightning would violently cascade down from the storm clouds and strike the ground; forty or fifty seconds later, a faint rumbling would cross the camp.

He remarked, "I hope that storm blows away before we get to it; it seems to be sizeable."

"Well, let's see what our map shows," Dan said.

In the flickering firelight, Dan's carefully preserved map showed, however, that Interstate 80 was turning southeast, generally following the Platte River.

"I don't think we have much of a choice, we have to stay on the highway and, right now at least, it leads directly to the storm," Mike complained.

The next morning, they could see what appeared to be a heavy black cloudbank on the southeastern horizon. They packed, mounted their bikes and returned to the highway, pushing eastward, always eastward, to get to Wisconsin.

Around noon, after traveling a considerable distance due to the flat roadway with few detours, they stopped to rest at the side of the highway near a road leading down to the Platte River.

Lor was becoming alarmed.

"Dan, Mike, there's something wrong. Look at my babies; they're agitated over something."

Dan saw that while both animals were normally lethargic during the ride, now they were alert; their attention seemed focused toward the south and southeast.

"Tom, toss me those binoculars. Mike, this overpass is the highest thing around here, let's climb up there."

Dan took his binoculars and he and Mike climbed up onto a small overpass. The wind had risen and was blowing in their faces from the south and southeast. When Dan looked through the binoculars, he quietly gasped to himself.

"Oh no!"

"What's wrong, Dan?" Mike asked. All he could see was a huge black cloud on the southern and eastern horizons.

"Here, look."

Mike looked through the binoculars to the southeast.

He then looked to the south.

The same, if not worse!

In desperation, he looked back toward the southwest and west; more of the same!

"Dan, what are we going to do? We can't escape from that," Mike exclaimed.

Fire!

Prairie fire from the southeast, the south and the southwest!

Dan, with that wind blowing in our face, we can't outrun that fire!" Mike added with heavy worry, "There's no way that anyone can put that fire out, we can only hope for rain!"

"What do we do?"

"Well, Lor's animals gave us a little time," Dan thought furiously.

He looked around for a place of escape or safety, and then focused his attention southward. His stomach and chest were tightening; the outer fringes of terror were attempting to clamber their way into his mind.

"There!" he pointed. "That road leads to the river. I think we must try for it. Maybe we can make a stand there or try to protect ourselves in or by the river. What do you think?"

"I think so too! We don't have any other choice."

They ran down the small hill and back to their group.

"Listen up," Dan said loudly and breathlessly. "That huge cloud to the south of us is a prairie fire!"

"Oh my God!" Mary Ann exclaimed. "What are we going to do?"

"Everybody pack up and let's get down to the river," Dan directed. "We may be able to protect ourselves there."

With that said, the entire group fled south on a lonely asphalt two lane road, a faint moaning of foreboding wind attempting to claw its way into their minds. They skidded to a halt at an abandoned and partially destroyed cement bridge that tapered out into the middle of the river. Darting across the road ahead and behind them were wild animals fleeing the fire. Fleet antelope, coyotes, rabbits and even a small black bear ran terrified from the fire.

Ahead of them, across the river, they could now see the billowing clouds of dark smoke spread across the entire south and southeastern sky. The wind was blowing directly in their face and they could faintly smell the pungent odor of burning grass. Flames thrust their way high into the sky!

All around the road and the bridge were trees and brush. Dan and Mike knew that the fire would jump the river and continue through or over them. At this point, the river was approximately thirty or forty yards in width and sluggishly muddy.

Dan turned quickly to Mike, "How about a backfire of some kind? If we can start those trees and bushes on fire across the river," he pointed to the opposite side of the river, "the fire might go around us!"

They could now hear the fire: a hollow, terrifying roaring, inflamed by the wind. Dan had read somewhere that in these fires, sometimes the center becomes hot, consuming the available oxygen.

"Good idea," Mike nodded.

"Tom, Geoff, tie a rope to yourselves, take some matches and try to get across the river. It looks slow around here. Start fires about one to two hundred yards up and down the river over there and as soon as they are going well, come back here! OK?"

Both Tom and Geoff nodded fearfully. Lor and Mary Ann quickly yanked two ropes off the trailers, tied them together and then tied one to each boy.

"Empty your pockets. Keep your shoes on, but tie your laces tightly," Dan told the boys.

After he gave both boys heavy-duty water-proofed kitchen matches that had been previously dipped in wax, he said, "You both be careful!" Mary Ann and Lor both hugged the boys with fear in their wide eyes.

"Lor, Mary Ann, girls, bring the bikes and trailers down under the bridge while Mike and I help the boys across the river," Dan directed.

Both boys waded into the river with Dan and Mike holding the ropes. Meanwhile, Lor and Mary Ann and the girls dragged the bikes and trailers under the bridge. The bank was soft and muddy, but it held the bikes. They took pots and cups off the trailers to use to pour water over themselves or the bikes and trailers if things got worse.

"Girls, help me with the babies: they want to escape," Lor asked Jennifer and Sue. Both girls petted the animals, making soft sounds in an effort to calm the frightened animals.

The boys, about ten feet apart were slowly making their way across the river. While the depth was only up to their shoulders, the sluggish, muddy water clutched at them, attempting to drag them under its filthy surface. Frightened animals were swimming down or up the river; they saw opossum, skunks, raccoons, and on the opposite shore, coyotes running frantically up and down the bank of the river. A common goal was paramount: to escape the fire!

Upon reaching the other side, Tom and Geoff tied the ropes to a tree and separated.

"You go to the left and I'll go this way," Tom pointed. "Run down about a hundred yards and start your fires there and work your way back."

The smell of burning grass was getting heavier! Tom and Geoff ran on water-soaked shoes about a hundred yards up or down the riverbank. There they sought dry grass or brush. Quickly, fires were lit and they worked their way back to where they had landed. They left behind them a trail of fires reaching into the parched brush and trees surrounding the riverbank.

Meanwhile, Dan and Mike had grabbed their axes and were clearing the brush away from under the bridge area. The bushes and tiny trees, once green from the rains and spring flooding of the river, were now brittle and tinder-dry because of the lack of rain. Dan and Mike cleared a space of approximately thirty yards in diameter around the underside of the bridge before the boys had returned to their starting point.

Dan waved the boys back across the river. Looking fearfully behind them, the boys tied the ropes to their waists. While Dan and Mike pulled them across the river, they attempted to remain upright. As soon as the boys were safely across the river, Dan hugged each soaking wet boy, "Good job, guys!"

Behind the boys on the opposite side of the river, the backfire set by the boys reached the top of the riverbank with vicious yellow tentacles of fire reaching for the tinder dry prairie grass leading to the main fire.

Dan had another idea, "Mike, what do you think about starting another backfire around here? The focus of the fire might change if there is nothing left to burn on each side of the road and this bridge?"

"Good thinking; let's start small on each side. Tom, Geoff, you guys help Lor with the animals." By this time, the animals had become almost frantic with the approach of the fire and the girls were having difficulty in controlling them.

The wind was blowing directly toward them. The thundering roaring of the fire was like a hundred trains!

Dan and Mike raced to each side of the bridge and started small fires in the parched grass. The grass quickly caught and spread up the embankment and spread to the trees and bushes on their side of the river.

The fire across the river reached the backfires started by Tom and Geoff and exploded into a fusion of flame, smoke and debris hundreds of feet into the air. The mass was, however, at least two or three hundred yards away from the river! Burning twigs and embers, smoke and just plain heat surrounded the group huddled under the bridge.

The temperature rose, until Dan thought it was at least 110 degrees or possibly 120 degrees or more. They poured water over themselves and the animals, always talking gently with them, attempting to calm them. The fire raged its furious rampage around and over them. The heavy blinding smoke, containing white-hot sparks and burning debris flooded over them, searching for anything to ignite.

They, however, had chosen well!

The two-lane wide, heavy concrete bridge, extending about halfway into the river, provided just enough cover and safety to keep the searching tentacles of flames off them.

"It's going around us!" Tom shouted.

"Yes! Those backfires did it," Geoff agreed.

"You are right, boys; good job! Well done!" Dan exclaimed.

While the temperature remained high, it didn't seem to get any hotter. Most importantly, the smoke appeared to be diminishing, the terrible roaring of the center of the fire had gone around them and was trailing off to the northwest. Deprived of ignitable materials by the small backfires near the bridge, the fire raged on, but away from them.

Another immediate problem, however, had manifested itself during the center of the fire.

Snakes!

Rattlesnakes, tiny garden snakes, and large green snakes were crawling over almost anything that wasn't burning! Mike and Dan were forced to use their axes and a shovel to kill the terrified crawlers. The poor snakes weren't aggressive, they simply were desperately attempting to escape the terrible heat and burning that was destroying their homes. Mike and Dan knew, never-the-less that they had to either kill the snakes or try to throw them back into the river or burning brush. The easiest and safest was to simply hack away at them until there was little left.

Pockets of fire remained; larger solitary trees continued to thrust flames and smoke into the sky while parched smaller trees and brush, more easily ignited, were more quickly depleted of burnable material.

The hours passed slowly.

Hours filled with blinding, foul smoke-filled air.

The river, sluggish and muddy at this time of year, gradually filled with debris, burnt animals, partially burned trees and bushes. The water rose inch by inch until it reached the shoes of the group.

They slowly retreated as far as they could under the bridge, but all too soon, there wasn't any more room left for them to escape.

Dan whispered to Mike, "If the river gets any higher, we'll have to either brave the water or the fire!"

"Yeah, well, we don't want to leave this shelter unless we absolutely have to."

Neither man, nor anyone else in the group, wanted to leave their haven. By then, however, the fire had diminished in intensity and the harsh wind blowing from the southeast had calmed considerably.

After an additional hour, with the water clutching at their feet, Dan said, "Well, I think we can get out of here now."

They surfaced from under the bridge, black soot covered bodies and faces peering around them like miners escaping from a deep, dark coal mine. They emerged to view a landscape as desolate as the photographs of the moon beamed back to the earth. Gray or black everywhere; an occasional large tree still smoldered or sometimes, the ground itself was still spewing smoke. Ashes and black soot covered everything. The soil, in many places too, too hot to walk on or even touch. Stones, rocks and boulders and the top of the concrete bridge radiated heat like a winter radiator. The only sounds were those of objects crackling as they cooled and the snap-crackle of a few fires around them.

A now soft wind from the southeast blew the odor of burnt grass toward them. Tom thought it smelled like burning marijuana, but he thought it prudent to not mention to his dad he knew what burning marijuana smelled like or how he knew.

Lor said, "Dan, that asphalt road is still too hot to ride on yet. I think we should just camp here overnight, and by morning, things should have cooled down enough for us to travel."

"Sure. Anyone object?"

Everyone mutely shook their heads, still sobered by the ruined devastation around them. All except Ginger, and even Ginger in her small way, realized that they had been extremely lucky.

"You know, if it hadn't been for Lor's cat or my dog, we would have been caught up on the highway," Tom said. "Good work you guys," Tom said as he rubbed the grimy heads of both animals.

While both animals were filthy from the dark soot and blackened ground, and from occasionally having water poured on them to keep them cool, neither they, nor the adults lavishing love on them, cared.

Camp was quickly established. Tom remarked, "Dad, one of the best things you ever traded for was that old shotgun for these five-gallon water bottles."

"You know," he went on reflectively, "We had just filled those bottles this morning. We can go for another couple of days on the water we have. Hopefully, they'll last until we get out of this burnt area."

"Good point, Son, but we should be frugal with the water. I don't know how far we have to travel to get out of this mess."

They scraped off about two inches of burnt topsoil in a small bowl-shaped area on the side of the bridge. This way, Lor felt, that after placing their plastic sheets on the charred ground, their sleeping bags would not get any dirtier from the soot and ashes.

They fed Tom's dog, but Lor sent the cat out to forage for its own food. She felt there were enough burnt animals in the area to feed a whole army of cougars. She had learned that the big cat, if it had a full meal, would not eat for a couple of days after eating, and usually, simply lay around, half asleep, digesting his food.

That night the cloudless sky glowed with the radiance of the Milky Way while around them for miles in each direction, large trees smoldered with bright yellow and red embers like Roman candles scattered in the darkness. The sparkling yellows and reds slowly diminished throughout the night until near dawn, there were only a few such fires left.

The morning dawned bright and, again, cloudless. During the night, the big cat had crept back into the camp and with his bulging stomach nearly dragging the ground, had rested between Sue and Ginger's sleeping bags.

Lor noticed that more and more, the big cat stayed with or near the two little girls. While the two girls played with the big cat whenever possible, it seemed to her that the big cat had assumed the role of protector of "his" children. Fortunately, Dan hadn't needed to physically discipline his children (and Lor would never, ever spank either Ginger or Sue! but she mildly speculated what would happen if Dan had to spank either of the two girls. There was little doubt which side the big cat would take.

Camp was broken with a light breakfast and a little water. They started back up the road they had traveled less than twenty-four hours before, but what a terrible difference! Black and gray ashes and cinders covered the ground as far as they could see. In many places, the heat of the fire had melted the asphalt with a resulting stream of molten tar coursing to the side of the road like lava flowing from a volcano. In those places, since the tar remained very hot, the bikes and the trailers had to be carefully lifted over the tar. A bonus, however, of the fire was that it incinerated the seedlings, grass and small trees on the side of the road and the ditches.

They pushed their bikes with the animals walking gingerly alongside them. Lor had to almost push the big cat off the "his" trailer, since all he wanted to do was sleep. What originally took them about an hour to ride in panic, now took them several hours. In several places, burnt trees or brush had to be cast aside to make a path for the bikes. Soon they were again covered with soot and ashes; everywhere they stepped, small clouds of fine, gray ashes swirled around them. The odor of burnt grass, trees, bushes, and sometimes, dead animals, overwhelmed their senses. Lor made bandanna like facemasks for the girls to filter out the dust and stench.

They slowly returned to the Interstate 80 highway.

"Mike, I think that since most of the highway is concrete and unburnable, we should be able to make better time," suggested Dan.

"Yes, plus the right-of-way of the highway is wider and usually free of trees and brush," agreed Mike.

They were correct, except that a fine layer of ash lay over the roadway. All the mileage signs such as "North Platte x miles" or "Omaha x miles" were destroyed. Interestingly, a single sign stating "Deer Crossing Next 5 Miles" remained upright and unburnt.

Dan led off eastward on the highway. The others followed single file with Mike bringing up the rear. The fine ash covering ruts and small furrows in the roadway made it treacherous because the bike tires could get caught in the rut or furrow and dislodge the rider. Small clouds of ash thrown up by the bike's trailers' wheels hung suspended in the still air.

"You know, we saw conditions like this in Los Angeles with our fires during the summer. Strange things would happen, in most areas, it laid total waste to everything, completely flattening whatever was in its way. Other fields or houses were untouched," Dan commented to Mike.

Here, the largest unburnt areas were about several acres in size. Once frightened animals still peered out nervously from beneath small bushes and trees while overhead, surviving crows, eagles, a few cranes and bunches of tiny birds wheeled and circled.

They rode for about five or ten miles and stopped to rest. Small buildings on the side of the road were crumbling rubble with an occasional solitary chimney standing like a sentinel. A desolate silence hung over the entire area.

"How far do you think this burn area extends, Dad?" Tom asked.

"I don't know, Son; I hope not too much further. This is very hard paddling through this ash and debris. And it's filthy."

Tom and Geoff smiled at their soot-covered faces, "Well, we can't get much dirtier than we are!"

After a five or ten-minute break and a drink of precious water, they mounted up and rode on. To the southeast they could see another gigantic, black-rimmed cloud formation building into the bright sky. A few miles passed.

Suddenly, as they crested a small hill, they could see before them and as far as the eye could see:

Green!

Green grass!

Live, unburnt green flowing grass!

Soot and ash covered gray faces yelled with joy. Tom's dog started barking with happiness; even the big cat let out with a cry that sounded like a baby screeching!

They had conquered mankind's oldest enemy, and mankind's cherished friend: fire!

CHAPTER TWELVE

They rode for about a mile into the unburnt areas. The huge malevolently black, slowly swirling thunderhead clouds to the south and southeast of them blotted out the sun. Occasional bolts of savage lightning struck the ground or an unfortunate tree standing under the storm clouds. Periodic harsh rumbling came to them as if the gods were bowling in the clouds.

"I don't like the looks of that storm; think we should stop under that overpass up ahead of us?" Mike asked quietly to Dan.

"Sure. It's hard riding through those ashes and we all need to rest."

The overpass was raised above the highway for a four-lane asphalt Nebraska side road. They were protected from the storm while having a front row seat watching the lightening.

"We should push the bikes, trailers and metal backpacks on the other side of this overpass. I'm a little worried about the lightning striking anything metal near us," Dan advised.

"Good thinking," Mike nodded.

After watching the storm for a few minutes, Dan turned to Tom, "Just like having tickets on the first base side of the ball game." They both looked somberly at each other, knowing that they probably would never see another beloved Angel baseball game.

Soft warm rain started to sprinkle. Lor, seeing the rain, retrieved a few towels, soap and clean clothes said, "Come on, girls, bath time. We all smell and look like the inside of a barbecue pit. You guys stay here, we're going to take baths."

She and Mary Ann took the girls over to the north side of the overpass out of sight of the men. They had become filthy and charcoal-gray soot covered from hiding under the bridge and the long ride through the burnt area. The girls' once bright, fine hair now was streaked with gray like old bag women. The sprinkles quickly turned into a heavy warm shower softly blown by the summer wind.

"Jennifer, take your clothes off and wash them first, then your body."

"Motherrr, what if someone sees us?"

"Look out there and tell me if you see someone, anyone, something that can see us."

Both looked out from the side of the overpass and all they could see was waving fields of unharvested green with the shadows of the thunderhead clouds outlined by occasional rays of bright sunshine.

Sue didn't care, she thought it was almost like the showers she used to take back home. She held her face up to the rain while soot and ash covered faces and bodies dripped tiny rivers of black grimy rain.

"Clothes first and then your bodies," Lor said to Sue and Ginger.

"Here is a little shampoo for your hair, but use very little, we don't have any more when this is gone."

Mary Ann whispered to Lor, "Now I can see why some people are nudists; this rain and warm wind is sensuous!"

"You are right," Lor nodded quietly, glancing up and down Mary Ann's nude body, "Now I see why Mike is so interested in you. I saw you two sneaking off the other night after everyone was asleep."

Mary Ann beamed and blushed bright red, covering her face and smile with her towel. She giggled with Lor, each knowing that the age-old wonderful longing of a man and a woman for each other was still prevalent, no matter how terrible the conditions in the rest of the world!

"You know, I really care for him, Lor. He is so kind and sensitive, and the kids really like him, too," Mary Ann said softly. "He's a man, a gentle man!"

Before the men had taken their "showers," they attached a rope from one side of the underpass to the other and hung clothes to dry. A fire was started, and while eating, they watched a spectacular lightening display. The sharp zipping sound that lightning made when traveling through air seemed almost on top of them. It was followed by thunder that shook the ground; they felt like they were in the center of a huge bass drum. Once the lightning strike was less than a quarter mile away and they saw and felt the white-yellow explosion when the lightning struck the ground. The sharp thunder blasted in their ears and caused a ringing for minutes afterwards. The center of the storm appeared to be about a mile or two south of them, traveling from southeast to northwest.

"Some time ago, a group of scientists took slow motion photographs of lightning," Dan said to the kids. "They discovered that there were in fact, frequently, two or more bolts or flashes when we see one flash, some of which even traveled from the ground up or back to the clouds."

"I remember studying lightning in school. That noise or boom we hear is the air being forced apart and then violently coming back together," Tom nodded.

The energy was present: the hair on the back of the heads of both animals bristled. The kids attempted to calm them by talking softly and rubbing their heads and backs. An evil greenish phosphoric substance seemed to drape itself around the lightning like sheer cloth curtains blowing in the breeze. Oscillating waves of violent rain were punctured by places of sun-scorched calm.

The kids sat in a front row, surrounding, and quieting the animals. Lor snuggled up to Dan while Mary Ann, after looking at Lor and Dan for a moment, shrugged her shoulders and quietly sat down next to Mike and put her head on his shoulder. His huge muscular arm gently encircled her waist while they smiled tenderly at each other.

Geoff looked over his shoulder at Mike and Mary Ann, grinned and nudged Jennifer. She looked at Geoff who nodded in the direction of their mother and Mike. Jennifer's eyes opened wide, blinking rapidly; Mary Ann met her daughter's stare and nodded. Dan whispered to Lor, "I hope that Jennifer and Mike get along with each other. I think that she needs someone like him for a father."

Lor, her head on Dan's shoulder, nodded quietly.

That night, and the nights passed as did the miles.

Lincoln, Nebraska, and the Lincoln Municipal airport off to the side came and went, a few giant 727's and DC-10's sitting abandoned on the end of the runways. The once proud brightly colored tails that cleaved the sky with power and pride were now soiled and covered with pigeon droppings. The massive undercarriages, some with flattened tires, were covered with windblown debris. Toward the far end of one of the runways could be seen the charred remains of what could have been a three engine 727. The burnt vestige of the plane's huge tail containing the third engine was tilted at a forty-five-degree angle. The plane had evidently been attacked by the energy while in its takeoff roll. Scattered around it were a half dozen fire trucks; their bright red or white bodies looked like a giant cleaver had hacked away at their engines.

Dan looked at Mike, "I hope that explosion was quick; I don't think those fire trucks did much good."

Mike shook his head, "Not when they're trying to defend themselves."

They continued to generally follow the old Interstate 80 highway except when short detours were necessary. There was no maintenance on the highway, but if an overpass had collapsed or part of the road had been washed out or blocked by wrecked vehicles, previous travelers had hewn out rough passages through those areas.

After Lincoln, Nebraska, they turned northward to pass through Omaha, Nebraska with the intention of following Interstate 80 eastward. About a day's ride before Omaha, they saw huge herds of cattle grazing peacefully in the fields to the side of the road.

"Where did all the cows come from, Daddy?" Ginger asked.

"I don't know, Sweetheart. Maybe someone up ahead of us will know."

Everything from stocky white-faced beef cattle, black and white Holsteins and tan and white Guernsey cows, and even a few rangy Texas longhorns roamed throughout the countryside and over the highway. One or two huge humpbacked Brahma bulls were scattered in the herds as well as a few solitary shaggy bison. A considerable number of very young calves bounced from mother cow to mother cow looking for a warm utter to feed on. It was clear that even if the energy had destroyed intelligent civilization as humans had known it, nature was continuing to take its course.

In small hollows near springs could be heard pigs grunting and squealing. There was no question that they were near a pig habitat if the wind was blowing the right way. When they passed near one specific location, Lor complained to Dan, "That odor is so bad, it would bring tears to the eyes of a buzzard!"

"Sure, but when we are enjoying ham and eggs or bacon and eggs, I think we'll forget this stink," Tom smiled.

During one of their rests stops where they met a few other travelers, Dan was told that when the energy struck, the slaughterhouses around Omaha had been forced to close. Apparently, some kind citizens had released the condemned hogs and cattle before they starved in the stockyards. Once out on the open prairie, the animals had to fend for themselves.

They had just crossed over the Platte River when Dan reminded the kids, "This is the same Platte River that we took shelter in during that fire. Remember?"

Tom, trying to remember his geography lessons from high school, asked, "Doesn't this river run into the Missouri River somewhere ahead of us."

"No, I don't think so," Mike said. "That confluence is quite far north of us."

They talked to some residents who told them to absolutely avoid the southern part of Omaha and the Council Bluffs, Iowa area.

"Stay away from there; there are several different gangs each controlling a particular area and they will require a toll of some kind from anyone traveling through their so-called empire," a few disgusted travelers grumbled.

"Do you know this area?" a resident of the west side of Omaha asked.

Upon receiving a negative shake of Dan's head, he continued, "Well, right now, there is a vicious battle going on between a group generally headquartered near the Rosenblatt Stadium on the west side of the

Missouri River versus a gang headquartered near the Friendship Park area on the east side of the river. Stay away from either area!"

Apparently, neither gang was very friendly.

A young girl and her mother on horseback told them, "I would suggest that the Interstate 680 bypass around the north of Omaha should be safe during the day. It's about a fifteen-mile ride which was generally open and clear the last time we went through there. After that, you can pick up Interstate 29 North until Interstate 680 branches off to the east to eventually connect back on to 80."

It was mid-afternoon and they were just riding slowly along looking for a place to stop when they approached a man on horseback.

"Howdy," the man called. "Where are you folks from?"

"Well, we're essentially from Colorado and California."

"No kidding! You've come a long way. How are things behind you like in North Platte or Denver?"

They talked for a moment or two, then, "Say, I've got an idea. Why don't you spend the night at my place. It's only about a mile or so up the road; I know my wife and a few of the neighbors would sure like to talk with you folks."

Dan looked at Mike and Lor, and upon receiving nods, he said, "Sure, we were about ready to stop for the night anyway."

Don and Sandra "Sandy" Pendergras put them up in a large vacant bunkhouse on their 600-acre farm. That night, they dined on inch thick steaks, or as Don said, "Omaha beef!" Lor had mentioned to Sandy that throughout their trip, because of weight restrictions, they each had a very limited supply of metal plates and utensils. Lor was therefore pleased and flattered when Sandy set a table with a real tablecloth, fine china, and real silverware.

"This is so nice, Sandy," Lor complimented. "Thank you, thank you very much!"

"Well, it isn't every day we get visitors from Colorado and California."

Silver candleholders holding large candles emitting considerable flickering light gave a formal appearance to the dinner. The large windows on the eastern and western sides of the Pendergras home were open, allowing a fragrant breeze to flow through; an occasional odor of cow manure did not detract from the pungent smell of wet grass and blossoming flowers. Even the children, normally rambunctious during a meal, were subdued and polite.

Over dinner, Dan described the conditions from Los Angeles to Omaha to their hosts and a few of the surrounding neighbors. When he told them of his conversation with his friend Joe Robinson, and his subsequent talk with Bob Ashley, their hosts' faces became drawn as they nodded understanding.

"I'm not really surprised," Don Pendergras said. "We didn't know what that stuff was or where it came from, but we learned to stay away from it. We lost one of our hired hands when he was driving one of the big John Deere tractors and the ignition system of the tractor was attacked and destroyed."

"A few of our neighbors have either been hurt or killed too by that force when they tried to use their tractors or combines," Sandy agreed.

"You know," Don Pendergras said heavily, "we have hundreds of thousands of dollars' worth of equipment, tractors, combines, planters and plows lying around here useless. But there isn't anything we can figure out to do about it! We have a couple of horses that we used to cultivate a few acres and I guess we'll get by until that stuff is eliminated."

As Sandy Pendergras related before a roaring fire situated in a large brick fireplace in the corner of the family home, "Well, we are all farmers around here and pretty self-sufficient. We all help each other, and while things will be tough, we'll do all right. We really don't have any choice."

Don Pendergras and his family, typical warm, friendly Nebraskans, were hungry for information. It seemed that nearly everyone Dan talked to had friends or relatives in one of the cities that they had passed. Many were the questions like, "Did you happen to meet so and so?" and they would name a loved one or relative or friend.

After a moment's peaceful silence, Dan commented thoughtfully, "We've traveled a lot of miles so far, and we have a few to go, but from what we have seen, it seems to me that our country, and probably the world, has reverted to an agrarian existence."

When a few heads nodded, he went on, "I think we should probably start studying how our forefathers existed in the early centuries of our country. After all, they did it without electricity."

A few more heads nodded somber agreement.

Sandy echoed the feelings of her neighbors when she said, "We appreciate what you're telling us. We didn't know what had happened, and now, we can try to plan a little for the future knowing that we can't expect much help from anyone else."

"You're welcome," Dan said. "We haven't seen any sign of any organized federal government in our journey. A few of the small towns have developed an informal organization and they use that as a basis for keeping peace and feeding people. And I have no idea of conditions in the rest of the world. As a matter of fact, Joe Robinson told me that the President of the United States tried to activate the National Guard, but that he was unable to even broadcast the decree. So, don't count on any organized or governmental assistance any time soon."

They left at sunrise the next morning after an enormous breakfast of fried bacon and fresh chicken eggs with country gravy and homemade biscuits. Much to Dan's surprise, a precious pot of fresh Columbian coffee had been made by Sandy Pendergras.

When Dan attempted to thank her, she refused saying, "No, Dan, it is us who should thank you. We know now what to look forward to. I know I speak for all of us when I say, "Good Luck" to you and your family." She smiled, "And your little redheaded girl is an absolute doll! If you come by these parts again, be sure to stop in, OK?"

After fond goodbyes, and as the sun was climbing over the flat eastern horizon, they made their way back on to Interstate 80.

They took the recommendation of their hosts and followed Bypass 680 up and around Omaha without incident. They paused to rest over the bridge crossing the mighty Missouri River as they rode into Iowa. At this point, north of Omaha, although the river was low and sluggish, they could see an occasional small rowboat or canoe on it. Far to the south billowing clouds of black smoke ascended into the still air. Mike couldn't see anything though the binoculars, but thought the smoke was probably from the south Omaha area.

They followed Interstate 680 through the wide curving connector to Interstate 29 North. About twenty miles further, they turned onto Interstate 680 Eastbound. They had to make a short detour around the connection of Interstate 680 and Interstate 80 since the high overpasses had fallen and blocked the road. Fortunately, others had been through the road ahead of them and rough roads had been hewn out of the brush and debris.

The miles, days and towns passed. The great central, flat, waving grasslands of western Iowa seemed to extend almost forever into the distance. In some areas, original prairie grass fought to reestablish itself against uncultivated and unharvested fields of corn and grain. Des Moines came and was ridden through without stopping; as much as possible, large towns or cities were avoided.

The weather was warm and frequently humid. Lor and Mary Ann usually rode in shorts and halter-tops while the men rode without shirts. Their laborious paddling had slimmed and conditioned their bodies; Dan loved to ride behind Lor, watching her body move in conjunction with her paddling of the bike. The first time Lor and Mary Ann put on their shorts and halter-tops, it took them all about ten minutes to see why they were leading and Mike and Dan were following. The sneaky grins on Mike and Dan's faces were proof.

About two days east of Des Moines, the land became a little rolling or hilly. The wind was behind them, coming gently and generally out of the west or northwest. They had just approached the crest of a small hill when, suddenly, the cat sat up and snarled.

A rider on a horse galloped up behind them from around a small grove of trees. At the same time, five more men mounted on horseback rode out from the trees on the opposite side of the road. The cat snarled, jumped off the trailer, and vanished into the brush on the side of the road.

The leader, a large, bearded man on a gray horse, drew a dark black Ozi 9. mm automatic handgun and ordered, "Hold it right there, folks!"

When the group had skidded to a stop, he directed, "Get off the bikes!"

Dan quickly looked around behind him. The rider who had ridden up behind them had a shotgun and was waving it in their direction.

"Keep your hands in plain sight," he said.

"We're just passing through, friend," Mike said, his eyes locked on the leader. "We've come a long way and we don't have anything worth taking!"

"Then you don't mind if we check you out, do you," the leader said coldly.

"Josh," he asked the rider behind the group, "See anybody else coming?"

"Naw, just them."

"Ok, see what they got in them trailers."

"Josh" got off his horse and walked over to Lor, leering at her breasts. By this time, Sue had jumped off her bike and had run to Lor's side, clutching her.

"You leave her alone!" Sue yelled.

Josh sneered, "Beat it kid," grabbed Sue, and flung her to the side of the road. She rolled over and over on the ground,, more angry than hurt.

Dan, flames of red fury encircling his vision, crouched, his right hand jerked to his left shoulder holster when the clear sound of a pump shotgun being loaded and cocked rang in the still air.

He froze!

"That's the way! Don't do anything stupid and you wouldn't get hurt," the rider with the pump shotgun jeered.

Josh, smiling with blackened, cavity-ridden teeth and breath that would have nauseated a cockroach, reached out and ran his fingers up and down Lor's halter top, outlining her breasts.

She struck his head with her right clinched fist, but he caught it in his filthy left hand. He laughed as his right hand continued to outline her breasts.

Dan, still in a crouch, his eyes darting everywhere, was desperately looking for a way out.

"Leave her alone!" Sue lying on the ground off to the side yelled again.

Josh and the rest of the riders ignored her.

Mistake!

With tears blinding her eyes, and sobs racking her tiny body, Sue reached into her jacket on her bike, unzipped an inside pocket and pulled out her little Smith & Wesson pearl handled, chrome .22 caliber automatic. She had been carrying it since they left Orange County, California.

She flipped the safety off on the left side of the weapon like her father had taught her, pulled back the slide mechanism and quietly released it.

She pointed the weapon in the general direction of the leader, and with tears blinding her eyes, she fired as fast as she could pull the trigger.

The first .22 caliber Long Rifle lead hollow nosed bullet, traveling approximately 900 feet a second, went in the general direction of Minnesota. The second hollow nosed bullet struck the leader in the center of his left ear. It penetrated the ear canal, through the spongy bone surrounding the eardrum and entered the brain cavity, mushrooming constantly. By the time the lead hollow nosed bullet crashed into the leader's brain cavity, the bullet had expanded to twice its size. No longer having to worry about earwax, he was dead before he hit the ground.

The third Long Rifle bullet grazed the top of the leader's head; the remaining bullets thudded into his falling body.

As soon as Sue started firing, the big cat, which had been circling behind the horsemen, attacked!

With a savage snarl coming from its broad chest, it leaped upon one of the horses. It's one and one-half inch razor sharp claws slashed the hide on the poor horse's back to ribbons. The horse screamed, reared, and threw its rider off its back. This rider, unfortunately, was too close to one of the other horses and he landed on top of this second animal's head.

The second horse, startled by the gunshots, the scream of its fellow horse, and having a 150-pound human dumped on its head, panicked!

He reared, throwing the first rider off his head and trampled him under his front feet.

The man's last conscious sight of this world was looking up to see the shiny bottom of an iron horseshoe clad front foot come crashing down onto his face!

Meanwhile, the big cat had jumped from its original victim to the back of this second, terribly frightened horse and was slashing the second rider on the head and shoulders. The big cat's razor-sharp front claws, normally used for pulling down and killing wild deer, met little resistance from the human's neck and shoulders. A one and one-half inch long front claw sliced and pierced the right jugular vein, punctured the larynx, carved through the neck muscles, and glanced off the man's neck vertebrate like a hot knife through butter! A full operating room might have saved him if it had been available at that instant, but he would never have been normal again.

Josh was just standing there astonished at the confusion going on with the horses, the big cat, and the gunshots.

Spotting Josh's hesitation, Dan clutched his H & K 9. mm chrome plated automatic, snapped it out of its holster and, swinging backhand, swung the weapon with all his force.

He hit Josh full in the face with the top of the barrel of the three-pound gun. From the shock in his right arm, Dan could feel the right-front of Josh's face collapse. The front sights tore through the center of Josh's nose, ripped open his cheekbone and lacerated his left eyeball. The "I" shaped front sights shredded and partially welded an approximate one-quarter inch deep by one-half inch wide by four-inch-long strip of skin from Josh's face onto the top of Dan's 9. mm barrel!

Josh folded like an accordion.

Meanwhile, Mike, seeing the distraction, yanked his Taurus PT-92 9 .mm automatic from its holster and, firing double action, fired three quick shots at the remaining two horsemen. The shots were so fast, it seemed like one continuous blast!

One copper jacketed bullet, weighing slightly less than one ounce, traveling at a muzzle velocity of around 1150 feet per second, hit one of the riders in the left front thigh, glanced off the femur and continued burrowing its way up into the hip where it lodged in the pelvic bone. The second shot ricocheted harmlessly off the saddle horn; the third shot bounced off the rider's handgun and penetrated his left shoulder! The rider screamed, yanked his horse around and galloped off, bleeding profusely.

The last rider's shocked eyes locked with Dan's cold, cold stare!

Dan slowly raised the chrome plated H & K 9. mm automatic with Josh's blood and skin hanging from the barrel.

The barrel stopped, pointed between the rider's eyes. The black hole in the automatic looked about the size of a cannon with Josh's skin and blood hanging and dripping from the front sight. The last rider slowly raised his hands with a terrible sinking feeling in his stomach.

Dan's mouth smiled, the smile never reaching his cold gray eyes.

His finger slowly tightened on the trigger; the weapon rock-steady in his hands. The rider, seeing this, moaned and voided his bladder in his saddle.

"Don't, Dan! Don't!" Mike whispered. "It's over!"

"I know, but I want to make sure he knows," Dan coldly acknowledged.

"Keep your hands up and get off the horse!"

"Face down on the ground!"

"Tom, Geoff, watch him!" Dan ordered.

He ran over to his daughter Sue and gently took the still smoking. 22 small automatic handgun from her trembling hand. Lor, however, had reached her first, and kneeling, was holding her shivering small body in her arms.

"Good job, Honey, well done," Lor whispered in Sue's ear as she stroked her hair. "Good girl! I am so proud of you. They were very bad men, and you did what was right."

A small smile was creeping out of her by the time Dan reached her. After he repeated essentially what Lor had told her, the smile grew larger. A big heartfelt hug from her father and her shaking had stopped.

Even Tom called over to her, "Thanks, Sis, they had us, and you turned the tables on them."

Lor ran her hands up and down Sue's body, "Do you hurt anywhere?"

Sue shook her head, looking at her arm, "My elbow and knee hurt a little, but I'm allright."

"Aren't you glad you practiced shooting up our closet back home?" her father grinned at her.

She started to brush off her clothes and Dan thought that she might be more upset over getting her clothes dirty then worried about the shooting.

Ginger had jumped off Tom's bike and ran over to Sue. The two little girls hugged each other. Both grinned at each other, one proud of her big sister, and the other, happy that she had done what was right.

Jennifer dashed over to Sue and hugged her, "That was the bravest thing I've ever seen! I was so scared. I never knew you even had a gun," she admired.

Dan ordered Josh, semi-conscious, whimpering, and oozing blood, and fluid from his face, to get on his horse and leave.

The leader's body, the man's body who was trampled by the horse, and the one who was "fanged" by the cat, were dragged to the side of the road and simply dumped there.

Tom and Geoff sat the remaining man up with his hands tied tightly behind him watched closely watched by Tom's dog and Lor's big cat. The big cat simply sat on his haunches, licking his claws, and occasionally glaring at the man. If one could read the big cat's mind, one might hear "Please run, please move, please do something stupid!"

Dan stalked over the remaining suspect, and wiped "Josh's" blood off the barrel of his gun with the shirt.

Dan, his eyes as icy cold as an executioner eyeing his next "client" demanded, "You have one minute to live unless you tell me the truth! Do you understand?"

His face a white sheet, the man quickly stuttered, "Y-Y-Y-Yes Sir."

"Are there any more of you?"

"N-N-No Sir."

"You're sure?"

The man, shaking, shook his head. When questioned, the man answered that he and the other robbers were from a small town about a mile or so to the south of the highway. They had elected themselves the town dictators and ran the town their way. They could see a bend in the highway and by the time anyone traveling would get to this point, the poor victims would be stopped. The robbers would keep an eye on the highway and "toll" was charged, usually in the form of supplies.

After much questioning, Dan said to Mike, "I don't think he knows much of value. He says he hasn't traveled much eastward, and his conversations with travelers were not about how enjoyable their journey had been."

"Any thoughts as to what we should do with him?" Mike asked.

"Release him, he's no threat to us anymore."

Tom and Geoff rounded up the two remaining horses and after being searched, the man was placed in his saddle and his hands were tied securely to the saddle horn. Tom tied the other horse to the back of the saddle and Tom's dog, barking fiercely, chased both horses out of the area. The handguns, shotguns, rifles, and ammunition were confiscated by Mike and Dan.

"We can trade the weapons in our next town." Dan commented to Mike.

Mike nodded through a small smile, "I don't think that there will be any retaliation from the townspeople. We took good care of their nemesis."

"True. However, I suggest that it would be prudent if we leave right now. Five or ten miles will make me feel more comfortable."

They immediately left the battle scene. Sue seemed to be unaffected, and the fact that she had just killed a man did not seem to bother her much. Lor, and the rest of the group, reinforced that she had done something necessarily good and correct, she had saved their lives.

That evening, Lor gave Sue a bath with a little of their precious water. Later, Lor told Dan that while Sue had four small bruises on her hips and shoulders, she was in fine shape. Except for the fact that her family treated her as a heroine, Sue put the entire episode behind her. Dan was concerned, but there was little he could do about it. She realized that what she did was necessary, and that was the end of that!

Later that evening in front of a smoldering campfire under the bright stars, after the girls had gone to sleep, Tom said quietly, "You know, Dad, you've really changed since we left home."

"Really, how?"

"Well, you used to be so laid back, so quiet; I can't imagine you doing what you did today months ago when we still lived in California. I hated it when Kathy used to treat you so badly. Now, you seem so much more in charge, in many ways so much stronger. What you did today was incredible!"

"Well, son, look at what we have: we have Lor, we have you, we have Sue, and" he smiled, "we have our Ginger."

He reflected for a moment, "The key word, Son is 'we.' Lor," he smiled deep into her eyes, "You are the best thing that ever happened to us; you, Tom, I am extremely proud of because you have matured into a sensitive young man, and, importantly, we have our girls."

"I agree," Lor said as she hugged a smiling young man, "Where were you when I was sixteen?"

One or two nights later, on the outskirts of Davenport, Iowa, they gathered around the campfire and examined the creased and folded map that Dan had safely carried across the country. It was getting close to the time for them to separate, for each family to go their individual ways. Their ultimate destinations were pointed out. Dan's home was about ninety miles north of Milwaukee near Lake Michigan. Mike's home was in Southern Illinois and Mary Ann's destination was in Indiana. By unspoken agreement, no decisions were made by the that evening.

In the morning, they decided to spend another day or so where they were. They had camped at a campground off the main highway that had sheltered toilets and barbecue pits. Nearby was a stream that in the spring and early summer, would be a full river. That afternoon, each party walked alone for quiet personal conversations.

Lor and Dan walked off in one direction, hand in hand. Lor could tell that Dan was getting excited about getting near his home. "I hope they are all right. I have a sister that lives not too far from them, but I simply do not know," he said to her, his eyes off in the distance.

"The big question now is what about Mike and Mary Ann?" Are they going to stay with us or go their own way or what?" Dan murmured to Lor.

"I don't know either, but whatever they do will be with each other."

Dan was certain of one thing: he was happier than he had ever been in his life. The terrible loneliness that he had suffered when married to Kathy, and after she left, and the bleak, forlorn lack of adult companionship and communication with a loved one that had haunted Dan was now completely reversed. He had suffered the typical malaise of a single parent who was doing all he (or she!) could raise children as a single parent. He, as well as others, more frequently "she," had difficulty in explaining to young minds why they couldn't go on nice vacations or have great cars or have what the boy or girl down the block had.

Dan had been genuinely concerned with Sue. In many ways, she had suffered the most by not having a decent mother to guide and care for her. Dan believed a little girl, or in this case, two little girls, needed a mother, period. Tom, Dan was not quite as worried about because he was made of sterner stuff and he was older when their mother died.

As the relationship between Sue and Lor grew, it was obvious to Dan that Lor was becoming the mother that Sue never really had. The love showered upon both Sue and Ginger by Lor was returned in spades. Lor would just beam when a tiny pair of arms hugged her and an equally tiny pair of lips would place a gentle kiss on her cheek. Interestingly, the relationship between Lor and Tom was not that of a mother and son, but more of an aunt and nephew who would share thoughts and feelings with a comfortable trust of confidentiality.

Very simply, Dan loved Lor fully with a profound respect that approached awe. When their paths crossed, she would just quietly reach out and touch him on the face or arm, or occasionally, just impetuously hug him. Every so often at night, after the children were asleep, they would sneak off by themselves, their love blossoming and overflowing in the warm wind under the benevolent smiling stars.

For the rest of his life, Dan would remember the feel, the sensation, the ecstasy-joy of his Lor's naked body over him in the warm gentle breeze driven night.

That afternoon, Mike and Mary Ann walked off together and spent time alone. Dan thought they might have walked up steam for privacy. Even the kids were somber; they knew that major decisions needed to be made today.

Before Mike and Mary Ann returned, a small family rode up on horseback, pulling a laden mule behind them. They were armed, as everyone Dan and his group met, but they kept their hands away from the weapons. It was obvious that they were not looking for trouble, only normal travelers as was Dan's group.

The new travelers' name was Cline. They were escaping from the North side of Chicago, heading for Des Moines, Iowa, to stay with relatives. Joseph Cline and his wife, Abigail, were about forty or so. Their son, Toby, was around twenty and their teenage daughter, Carrie, was about sixteen or seventeen. She was beautiful! Even as thin as people were now, with her tight jeans and plaid shirt, she was a striking teenage beauty with bright blue-green eyes and long dark blonde hair. Tom and Geoff were in love at first sight. And that was Love with a capital L!

(Later, Mike confidentially grinned at Dan, "Where was she when I was sixteen?")

The Clines made camp next to Dan's group and shortly thereafter, the families visited.

"We were living in Evanston, a small suburb north of Chicago when that stuff struck," Joseph Cline explained. "I am, I was, a police officer for the City of Chicago and I had attempted to walk to work, but conditions prohibited me from even making it much past our immediate neighborhood. Riots broke out almost immediately, people just went crazy like your riots in Los Angeles. People were stealing anything they could get their hands on, and what they couldn't steal, they burnt."

"Yes, I'll never forget those first couple of days, no electricity, and later, no gas or water," Abigail agreed. "Fortunately, our neighbors and us all looked out for each other for a while, but then, that changed too. Pretty soon, it was every family for themselves."

After a moment of silence, Joseph Cline continued, "The west side of Chicago from about a mile or so on each side of Cicero Avenue had suffered a firestorm of some kind. We were told that a tornado had touched down a mile or so south of O'Hare International Airport and swept northward. I heard that it stopped about in the middle of O'Hare after destroying a bunch of grounded airplanes."

Abigail Cline agreed, "With no fire engines or water or electrical power, we were powerless to stop the fire. Fortunately, after a day or two, a heavy rainstorm saved the remainder of the city and eventually extinguished the fire. The life and property toll throughout that whole area is enormous, however."

"There's no more law and order in that entire area. I heard that the National Guard and three or four remaining police stations just barricaded themselves in their buildings," Joseph Cline said, somberly.

Mary Ann leaned forward worriedly, "Have you heard anything about the area extending over into Indiana? That's where I'm from."

"Well," Abigail said, "I had heard that the entire area around the south-eastern part of Lake Michigan extending into Indiana was a war zone."

"That's what I heard, too," Joseph agreed. "We had some of the Black gangs which had originated in Los Angeles over the drug trade down in that area. My last briefing at the police station said that both Crips and Bloods, and various subfactions, including our local Lords were fighting with each other and everyone else. Worse, there were numerous Mexican street gangs and Polish gangs that were quickly forming for self-protection, even the Mafia had again reared its head in an attempt for control of not only their own neighborhood, but of the rest of my city."

"I wouldn't go anywhere near that part of the country if I were you," Joseph warned. "At least not now, maybe in six months or so and then only if you are heavily armed, but not now."

Mike and Mary Ann, upon hearing the Clines' story, somberly looked into each other's eyes. Mike nodded his head off to the side; they both rose and walked a short distance away to talk quietly together. Their hands clasped; it was evident that a major decision had been made!

"Geoff, Jennifer, would you come over here for a minute?" Mike called.

Geoff and Jennifer looked at each other, distress lining their faces. They met with their mother and Mike and all slowly walked away. Mike talked for a moment and then Mary Ann talked for several minutes.

After a moment or two, Geoff grinned and hugged his mother. He then reached over and vigorously shook Mike's hand. Jennifer, a little reticent, hugged her mother and then hugged Mike.

Dan was anxiously watching the entire scene. He said to Lor, "They're telling the kids what everyone already knew, that each had found in the other a person that they simply wanted to be with and live with, or in normal times, would probably marry."

She smiled, "I wondered when they would finally break it to the kids. You know, of course, that both kids were fully aware of the romance from the first night that they even held hands."

"I thought that Mike and Geoff got along well together, but I don't think Jennifer was too enthusiastic about Mike," said Dan.

"Well, she needed and needs a firm father figure, someone to look up to. And I don't think she really respected her real father. Haven't you noticed that she has grown up quite a bit since we started our journey? Remember how she used to complain and whine all the time?"

"Yes, I remember that he had to spank her before we even left your home. I guess he got her attention."

"Well, now, she doesn't complain at all. Mike nicely made her work and made her take care of herself, but he gives her encouragement. And he is so gentle with her, but firm too. Don't you remember about two nights ago, when he complimented her on her cooking, she positively beamed and almost danced. Oh, do not worry, my darling, Jennifer and Mike will be all right together," murmured Lor.

Mike, Mary Ann, Geoff, and Jennifer walked slowly back to Lor and Dan.

"Mike, you ask," Mary Ann said, her eyes reflecting worry.

"Dan, Lor, we've come a long way together and it doesn't look like we can get to her home," Mike started slowly. "It seems to me that we all make a pretty good team for self-protection and I think we should stay together." He paused and then said slowly, "Would you mind if we traveled with you to your home? Do you think that there might be someplace for us to stay, at least for a couple of months or until next summer?"

Mary Ann added, "As you know, the reason my kids and I left Durango was that there was nothing there for us. I had no money or any way of earning a living or supporting my kids. While we had little in Indiana, it was home. I don't have many relatives, but it was someplace to go to."

"Now, however," she smiled up at Mike, "I have him! And wherever he goes, we go."

It suddenly seemed that not only were Mike, Mary Ann, Geoff, and Jennifer concerned about Dan's answer, but his kids and his Lor were also anxious about his response. Dan's eyes met Tom's and they exchanged knowing looks. Dan next looked at Lor and she smiled and nodded at him. Dan found it interesting that both Sue and Ginger were holding onto Lor. It was obvious that whatever Lor wanted, Sue and Ginger would agree with.

"Yes! Of course!"

There was a sudden lessening of the tension like the abrupt deflation of a balloon. Geoff and Tom grinned at each other and slapped high fives. Mary Ann hugged Lor and then hugged Dan with tears in her eyes. Mike's hand crushed Dan's right hand in a bone crushing grip while his left-hand clasped Dan's shoulder, "Thanks, thanks so very much, my friend!"

Dan shook his head in the direction of Ginger, "No thanks are necessary, Mike. I owe you! We owe you more than I can ever repay!"

"Mike, Mary Ann, I think my folks have an extra house up there; I don't know if anyone is living there now, but it will hold two families easy. And if that's not available, well, we'll find something."

Dan and Mike decided to move out the next morning. While both Geoff and Tom both wanted to stay until the Cline's departed, Joseph Cline said that they, also, were leaving the next morning. That night, the Clines and the Petersons shared dinner. Tom and Geoff had gone hunting and the tantalizing aroma of barbecue rabbit and pheasant filled the air. Abigail had found an abandoned garden with a row of new potatoes and carrots that she shared. Wild ripe strawberries found by the girls was dessert.

The boys and Carrie Cline got little sleep that night. After dinner, they wandered off together in the moonlight, all three shy and bashful, totally unaware that they were making memories. Memories that would last them a lifetime: memories of a love found and a love lost! Gone from Tom's mind, for the present at least, were the warm (or more precisely hot!) memories of the girl in Colorado and what they did (several times) in Lor's barn. Both he and Geoff were living for this one moment in time.

Since Dan's home was north of Milwaukee and near Lake Michigan, they decided to follow Interstate 80 to Interstate 88. According to the map, a short distance after the town of Rock Falls, Illinois, Interstate 88 turned into the Illinois East West Toll-Way.

"We came through that way and the road was open and clear," Joseph advised. "I suggest that you turn north on Interstate 39 and follow it into Wisconsin."

Dan and Mike told Joseph what had happened to them east of Des Moines and gave him the location. Joseph nodded and said that worse, much worse had happened in Chicago. He said that their horses were their early warning system, but he didn't say how they obtained their horses.

The next morning, after having the Clines introduced to the big cat, sad goodbyes were said. Carrie Cline gave each of the boys a warm hug and a soft kiss on the lips. As the Clines rode out of the camp, the last the boys saw of Carrie with her slim body and long blonde hair was her waving goodbye from her horse.

Dan smiled and murmured to Mike, "Looks like the boys can float to Wisconsin."

The time and the miles passed. Rock Falls came and went while abandoned tollbooths and toll barriers were simply avoided.

The boys saluted and Dan grinned as they crossed the Wisconsin-Illinois border. The large wooden sign "Welcome to Wisconsin," while bullet riddled, was certainly welcome. They passed Interstate 43 just outside of Beloit.

After carefully looking at their map, Dan said, "I don't think we should follow Interstate 43 down here. It goes through Milwaukee and then turns north and we'll pick it up later, but I want to avoid that city now."

"How about Madison?" Tom asked.

"Later. I want to come back down here to the University of Wisconsin to see if anyone is doing any research on that force, but let's get home first. I think we should skip it now."

They attempted to stay away from any large city as much as possible. While the country had revered an agricultural culture, the conditions inside the cities were hazardous. They had also, as much as possible, traveled on major highways. While there had been no maintenance of any roads or highways, they had found that the smaller state, county, or town roads were more frequently blocked, washed out or otherwise impassable.

After following Interstate 90 past Janesville with its huge, but now abandoned General Motors' plant with about half of the windows shot out, they branched off on a small highway running northward. Off to the side of the road, they saw the typical rolling farmland of southern Wisconsin, spotted with hilltops and lake banks covered with evergreen, popular and maple trees.

They could see that many of the farms were being actively farmed, but only on a small scale. Huge, expensive aluminum or steel silos were useless since there was no way for the farmer to fill them. Horses, mules and even the few oxen were worth their weight in gold! Antique plows, planters, and cultivators were dragged out of storage where they had lain, collecting dust for years.

They had stopped and spent the night at a campground northeast of Madison, Wisconsin.

The next morning, they had left early while the dew was still on the grass.

Dan kept walking around and asking, "All right, is everyone ready? Let's go! Come on," until Mike grabbed him and sat him down on his sleeping bag.

"Dan, it will take us three days or more to get to your home; relax, we'll get there."

Dan mumbled, "Sure, you're right, I'm just a little anxious, I guess."

A chorus of "Ha!" came from the group.

Lor smiled at him, "You got us this far, Hon; we'll get there. Don't worry."

As they rode off, the rolling hills with their attendant streams and lakes of Southern Wisconsin made riding difficult, particularly when the animals had to be removed from the trailers when climbing a hill. The big cat and Tom's dog were usually recalcitrant about jumping off the trailers. They obviously much preferred riding to walking.

"They're spoiled," Lor smiled.

They passed farmers on wagons being pulled by teams of horses, mules, and teams of oxen, however, they seldom stopped to talk and just waved as they paddled by.

In the early afternoon, they were following a narrow two-lane asphalt road that led through a dense forest of mostly popular, sugar maple and evergreen trees. The forest extended for about two miles ahead of them, dropping down to traverse and follow a river and then climbing the opposite hillside. There was a mild breeze blowing through the forest, pushing the group on the bikes ahead of it.

They followed the road that reached the river, crossed it, and then turned right or towards the east and went out of sight through the heavy forest. They had just crossed over a narrow old concrete bridge and were entering a sharp curve turning toward the east when ahead of them, they heard three quick gunshots.

Dan, who was leading and pulling the trailer with Tom's dog on it, skidded to a stop. The group nearly ran into him as they slid to a halt. By the time Dan stopped, he was in the turn and could see ahead of him.

A man wearing army combat fatigues was standing over two figures on the ground. He was holding what appeared to be a sawed-off Colt AR-15. As Dan skidded to a stop, the man swung his rifle in Dan's direction, obviously surprised. As the bikes stopped, both animals leaped from the trailers and vanished into the thick underbrush surrounding the road.

"Hands up!" the man shouted, backing away slightly from the two figures lying on the road.

"Easy, guy, easy, we're just passing though," Dan said as he stood straddling his bike.

"Get off of the bikes!" the man yelled, waving the sawed- off rifle in Dan's direction.

"Now!" as he fired a shot over their heads.

The group jumped off their bikes, keeping their hands in the air.

"Easy, fellow, we're just passing through here," Mike said.

One of the figures on the road whimpered. Dan couldn't tell if the figure had been shot or not. The man skittered sideways over to the figure, kicked it in the head, yelled, "Shut up!"

The figure jerked once and then was still.

Dan got a good look at the man. He was very thin to the point of being almost emaciated, his long unkempt hair hadn't been cut in months, his combat fatigues hadn't seen soap in an equivalent number of months. His eyes radiated a frenzied cunning above a long gray and black streaked beard and mustache. An old sweat stained baseball cap with a faded "G" on it was perched on top of his head.

"Keep your hands up where I can see them! Everybody: down on the ground," the man ordered.

When Dan and Mike hesitated, the man jerked the AR-15 to his right shoulder, pointed the gun at Ginger and said, "When I say down, I mean now!"

"All right, all right," Dan exclaimed. "Just take it easy, we'll cooperate."

Dan tuned to the group, "Everybody, lay down."

Dan knelt, trying desperately to figure out a way for him to reach one of his guns.

As soon as the group was lying on their stomachs, the man walked over to one of the figures laying just in front of him. He nudged it with his moccasin covered foot; the figure jerked slightly and moaned. The man lowered the front of his AR-15 to the figure's head and pulled the trigger.

A loud click echoed off the surrounding trees.

Mary Ann grasped, "Oh my God!"

Dan's heart sank.

He had to do something now.

Right now!

But what?

The man swore, tapped the magazine release lever, and ejected the empty magazine. Almost all in one motion, he reloaded the rifle with a filled magazine. He pulled back the T-slide mechanism on the top of the AR-15 and released it, thereby loading the weapon with a metallic clank that echoed throughout the small clearing.

He again pointed the rifle at the head of the figure on the ground in front of him, and smiling slightly, started to pull the trigger.

Though a sinking feeling in his heart, Dan knew there was nothing he could do to save the figure; he couldn't pull his shoulder weapon fast enough.

Suddenly, a twang echoed off to the side and to their back.

Tom knew that sound!

He had heard it before!

They heard a swish as a 490-gram single edge broadhead thirty-two inch, dark red and black graphite arrow flew past them.

It impacted on the man with a dull thud!

The arrow, driven from a 90-pound release weight compound recurve hunting bow, traveling just under 500 feet per second, struck the man just below his left ear. The arrow penetrated completely though the man's neck, the razor-sharp single edge broadhead severing the spinal cord. He was dead before he hit the ground! As he fell, a final reflex pulled the trigger of his AR-15, the shot went wild into the upper branches of a huge maple tree, scaring a flock of crows.

Dan climbed to his knees, yanked his chrome plated 9-mm. H & K automatic from his shoulder holster, cocked it, and frantically looked around. He could see nothing but trees and underbrush.

"Stay here," he ordered softly.

He ran to the man crumbled on the road with an arrow sticking out of his neck, his legs jerking spastically. Dan pulled the AR-15 from his lifeless hands and quickly moved away from the body. He flicked on the safety and looked around. All he could still see was trees and heavy brush.

A voice rang out from near the concrete bridge behind them, "Please put the gun down, stranger. I'm on your side."

Dan nodded, released the hammer on his 9-mm. handgun and snapped it into its holster, slowly lifted the AR-15 over his head in plain view, removed the magazine from the weapon and ejected the live round from the chamber; the bullet clanging as it hit the pavement. He then gently placed the rifle down on the ground.

"All right," the voice called. "Would somebody call off these animals? I know they are stalking me and I don't want to shoot them."

"They are my babies!" Lor cried. "They wouldn't hurt you if you don't hurt us."

That's right," Dan called. "How about showing yourself, they wouldn't harm you."

A bush shook slightly just to the side of the bridge and a man stepped out. He too was dressed in army combat fatigues, and his face and hands were covered with black and green camouflage paint. He had on a very battered and beaten tan colored "Smoky the Bear" hat, but what drew their attention was what was fastened on his left chest.

A highly polished gold star.

The man was a deputy sheriff.

"Howdy," he said as he walked closer. He carried his camouflaged recurve power bow in his left hand. On his back was slung a 30-30 Winchester lever action hunting rifle. At his waist hung a dark leather quiver containing brightly feathered arrows. From a distance, he looked almost like a moving green and brown bush with legs. His seven-pointed star, however, flashed in the sunlight.

"Let me take a look at these people. I'm pretty much the law around here and this outlaw has been robbing and murdering people for months."

By this time, the two figures that had been on the road sat up, one of them bleeding from the mouth and nose where he had been kicked. The other figure appeared to be a girl, judging from her long hair.

"Oh, they're just kids," Lor exclaimed. "Look Dan, they're not much older than our kids."

"Thank you, sir!" the boy mumbled through his bloody mouth and nose, his body shaking. "He was going to kill us!"

"Deputy Bakowski, oh my Lord, am I glad to see you," the girl sobbed, her arms clutching the boy. "Where did you come from?"

"Well, hello Chris," Deputy Bakowski said his deep voice ringing through the clearing. "I've been trying to capture this guy for months now. He has robbed and murdered over a half dozen people through these woods around here. We thought that he lived in one of those caves about two miles up the river, but we could never catch him. Are you two all right?"

"Bobby here is pretty beat up, but outside of that, I think we're all right, I, I was so scared," the girl wept, her slim body shaking. "We, we, were just walking up to my mom's house when he jumped out of the bushes over there and held us up."

"Here, let me take a look at him," Mike said.

"Geoff, bring that first aid kit that's on top of my trailer over here, would you please?"

Dan walked over to the Deputy and said, "I'm Dan Peterson and we're just passing through trying to get home up near Manitowoc-Two Rivers. This is my family, Lor, Tom, Sue, and Ginger. That's Mike Osborne over there treating the boy with his family, Mary Ann, Geoff, and Jennifer."

As Dan and the Deputy shook hands, Dan said, "We owe you, officer! We owe you a lot. That, whatever he is, got the drop on us and I was afraid to try to make a move for my gun because of our kids."

The rest of the group gathered around the Deputy, trying to relax and thank him. Both Ginger and Sue were almost hiding behind Lor as they shook hands; the little girls were suddenly very shy as the officer smiled at them.

He shrugged off the thanks saying, "I'm just trying to do my job; I took an oath to protect the people in my county. While there isn't much of a government right now, and certainly no court system, this star means a lot to me, and to a lot of good people."

Deputy Bakowski examined the slain robber, yanked his arrow out of the robber's neck and carefully wiped it in the former robber's clothes. He searched the robber's pants, and placed the contents of the robber's pockets in a plastic bag. "I'll see if anyone can identify what he had in his pockets."

"By the way, what kind of animals are those? I could see them coming through the brush, but I couldn't see much about them."

"They're my babies," Lor said. "Here, I'll call them."

As the animals bounded out of the brush, both Sue and Ginger ran to the big cougar and hugged it while Tom's dog trotted over to Tom for his head-rub.

"Well, I'll be! Those are some babies!"

Lor called the big cat over to Deputy Bakowski; she rubbed the Deputy's hands with hers and then rubbed the big cat's face with her hands. The big cat, a purr rumbling out of his powerful chest casually walked over to the deputy and submitted a back rub by the deputy.

"Rub him right behind his ears and on his shoulders; he likes that," Sue said, her arm draped over the big cat as she patted its broad shoulders.

The Deputy smiled as he tentatively stroked the big cat, "We don't see many like him down here; most of the big cats are west and north of us. Boy, he sure is tame."

After looking at Mike bandaging the boy's face, he said, "Say folks, my home is just up the road about a mile or so. I have an empty house just next door and you're welcome to spend the night there."

Dan nodded, "Thank you. It will be nice to have a roof over our heads."

The deputy looked in the direction of the slain robber and said, "Leave him there; I'll send somebody to pick up the body in the morning and get him buried. He doesn't have any family that would claim him, anyway."

"Bobbie will be all right. I've bandaged his face and showed him and his friend what to do about his face," reported Mike.

That night they were the guests of the deputy and his family.

Deputy Joseph Bakowski, his wife Chris, their two little dark eyed girls, and Dan's group filled the Bakowski's candle-lit dining room. Lor's "babies" stayed outside after being introduced to the Bakowski girls. Neither girl wanted to leave the big cat; it just lay on the grass and purred as the two little girls crawled over him almost like he was a large stuffed toy.

The Bakowskis could hardly believe that Dan and his family had traveled from Southern California through Colorado to get to here. After Dan finished telling their story, including that Deputy Hank in Colorado was Lor's father, there was an awed silence.

After a moment or two, Deputy Joseph Bakowski, nodding his head, said, "Well, I'm glad to see that there are a few of us officers still carrying the badge or star. We certainly don't do this job because of the money or the benefits; I think that I can speak for most decent officers or deputies when I say that we are performing a duty, almost an obligation for our society, for our country, that was handed down through generations of men who wore this star."

Chris Bakowski nodded and said, "His grandfather and his father were police officers. He doesn't talk about it much, but it is something he feels deeply."

Joseph Bakowski paused for a moment and then quietly stated as a fact, "I feel that now, more than ever, what our star represents separates us from total anarchy!"

Jennifer had to ask, "Deputy Bakowski, why didn't you shoot that robber with your gun?"

Chris Bakowski burst out laughing, "Well, he'll never admit it, but he can't hit the broad side of a barn with a gun. He would do better throwing his gun at a suspect. With that bow, however, he was the State Champion in archery in the Wisconsin and Midwest Regional Police Olympics. He received four gold medals in their last competition." She pointed, "Look, they're hanging on the wall over there."

She smiled at her husband, the look of pride and respect on her face served to reiterate the point., "He almost didn't make it through the police academy in Milwaukee because he nearly didn't qualify with his handgun."

The next morning, they packed and bid a fond goodbye to Deputy Bakowski and his family.

"Thank you again for what you did," Dan said.

"Oh, forget about that. Good luck to you people. If you get back down in this area, be sure to stop by," Joseph Bakowski said, his star flashing brightly on his chest. "And bring your cat, too."

The next day, they arrived at Interstate 43 going north through Port Washington toward Sheboygan and beyond. Off to the left side, behind huge trees, they could see the world-famous sprawling Kohler plant.

"They used to make toilet facilities there. They were known worldwide for their quality. I think we had some of their products in our first house," Dan said.

At sunset, they arrived just outside of Manitowoc, which was originally famous for its gigantic Manitowoc cranes and a now quite rusty World War II submarine that had been built there during World War II. They camped near a red brick constructed Holiday Inn Motel. It appeared to be ransacked with only a few windows left; a nearby motel and a restaurant were vacant.

"Dan, how far are we from your place?" Lor asked.

"Not far! We'll be at my folks' place in the morning."

"O.K., kids, bath time tonight," she ordered. "I want us to look nice for them."

Later that night, after dinner and after everyone had somewhat of a bath with their limited water, they gathered around the campfire. Dan was a little surprised that there were so few mosquitoes, usually, during this time of the year, the area had been bombarded by them.

Suddenly, Sue gasped and pointed up in the sky, "Look!"

There! The northern sky was floodlit with moving beams of soft pastel lights. They seemed to change colors from a soft pink to a moving white to a slightly sharper blue and soft greens. At times, the lights were almost bright enough to read by! It was eerie because there was no sound coming from the lights.

"What are they, Daddy?" Ginger asked worriedly.

"That is the Northern Lights, Honey. When I lived up here, we'd see them almost every summer."

"They are so pretty! How far away are they?"

"Tom, you did a very good term paper on the Northern Lights. Why don't you tell her about them?"

"Well, ok," Tom said a little reluctantly. He spoke to the whole group: "The technical name for them is the Aurora Borealis. The ancient Indians and settlers up here in Wisconsin thought they were reflections off the northern ice cap around the North Pole. Scientists today think that they are caused by solar particles coming from the sun hitting the earth's atmosphere after being speeded up by earth's magnetic field. And to answer your question, they are about sixty to several hundred miles up in the air."

"Well, I'm impressed. The boy who I have such respect for also has some knowledge," Lor smiled, "Like father, like son."

"Well, we learned about it in class. And I thought it was interesting."

"Yes, I saw his research project; he got an A on it; the teacher was impressed with his research and he did a good job," Dan said to Lor.

Then, as suddenly and as quietly as the northern lights came, they faded away.

"Ohhh," a disappointed Ginger said. "Will they come back?"

"Sometimes they will come every night for weeks, and at other times, they wouldn't come all summer. I guess it depends on the sun."

That night, Dan scarcely slept, he was so excited; and his excitement was contagious.

Very early in the morning, with Lor and his family asleep by his side, Dan was still wide-awake, staring into the small flickering fire. Both animals nuzzled up to him.

"We're almost home, guys," Dan whispered. "I bet you feel it too."

Both animals just lay by Dan as he gently rubbed their heads and backs, both perhaps aware that their long ride was nearly over.

So close, so close now. . ..

CHAPTER THIRTEEN

"Come on everyone, let's get ready!" Dan demanded after a sleepless night.

"Here, I'll help you," he said as he rolled up a just vacated sleeping bag. "I'm worried about Grandpa and Grandma, and I want to get there."

"I know, Dad," Tom replied, his hand touching his father's shoulder, "but take it easy, we'll be there in a little while."

Lor, however, insisted on taking the time to dress the girls and herself in whatever good clothes they had brought with them. She also used a little of her scarce makeup. She was worried about her reception by Dan's parents and she wanted to look as well as she could.

Finally, the cougar and Tom's dog jumped on the trailers and they left. North, past the outskirts of Manitowoc, they took a wide county asphalt road named #10, east bound through a "round-about" ,which later turned northbound into a smaller asphalt winding two lane road named "Q".

The road was followed over several small bridges.

"Look, Ginger. Aren't they pretty?" Tom pointed at red winged blackbirds chirping noisily from weeds and bushes with cattails in a swamp.

The cougar looked at the red winged blackbirds: lunch!

Once, Dan had been leading and paddling faster and faster when a shout came from the group, "Slow down! We can't go that fast."

"Aw, I'm sorry," Dan said. "I was in a little hurry."

"Ha!"

Finally.

At the crest of a small hill and around a small bend in the road, there (!) off to the right about three quarters of a mile from the main road sat a small group of buildings. A once white barn, built in 1911, with a rusty tin roof, an old, dilapidated cement-block silo with a tree growing out of it, a granary, nearly as old as the barn, and small shed surrounded a two-story house, part of which dated to 1890. A stream of smoke was coming out of one of the two brick chimneys on the top of the house.

"There! And it looks like someone is home," Dan exclaimed.

On the West side of the house was an old apple orchard with a few trees older than Dan. Surrounding this were fields where grain, corn, soybeans, and alfalfa once grew, but now mostly covered with weeds. Former line fences, now overgrown with chokecherry trees and a few evergreen trees starting to push their way toward the sun.

"Home!" Dan whispered through tears blurring his vision.

He felt a nearly overwhelming tightness in his chest so he could hardly breathe. He couldn't swallow, his throat felt so full, his eyes brimming. . ..

"I almost can't believe it. I was never sure if we could ever make it!"

"We did it, people. We did it!" Dan's face was suddenly wet.

"You got us here, Dad. Nobody else could have done it," beamed Tom as he hugged his dad.

"Ginger, that's Grandpa and Grandma's place," Tom said. "You've seen their photographs, remember?"

At that moment, Lor realized something with deep sadness and a sudden joy, "Sweetie, you've never seen your Grandpa and Grandma?"

When Ginger shook her head, Lor's eyes filled with tears. She briefly hugged Ginger, then went to Dan to clutch his arm. She was speechless, her heart welling up into her throat with conflicting deep emotions: happiness they had overcome enormous odds to get here and that Ginger would finally see her grandparents, but worry about whether Dan's parents would accept her or if they were even alive.

They stopped for just a moment at the beginning of the single lane dirt road with wide weed and sweet-clover hay overgrown ditches leading to the buildings. A narrow path wove its way through the weeds carefully skirting a large mound of dirt created by an enthusiastic badger chasing a hapless gopher.

Lor's cougar and Tom's dog sat up alertly as if they knew that their journey was nearly over. Tom's dog barked briefly, cheerfully; he knew.

Lor said, "Just a second, Dan, please," as she freshened her makeup, brushed Ginger and Sue's hair and made sure the kids looked as neat as possible. She even fussed a little over Dan's shirt.

A voice filled with heavy emotion rumbled from deep within Mike's chest, "Dan, my friend, please lead the way. I imagine there are some people over there that might want to see you."

Dan mounted up and led his group down the dirt road. Riding the bikes through the overgrown weeds and sweet clover was laborious, however, Dan never noticed the exertion. As they neared the buildings, Tom's dog started barking. Somehow, he knew that he was home. And if one could read the big cat's face, a smile would be found there.

As they turned the corner to ride past the ten-foot-high lilac bushes planted by Dan's mother, into the front yard of the buildings, the front door of the tin-roofed, faded old white house opened. A tall, grey haired old man with a weather-beaten face wearing worn and patched Oshkosh overalls stepped out, looked, staggered back, and clutched the side of the door.

He opened his mouth, but nothing came out; then, after several attempts, "Mother! Mother!"

A voice came from inside of the house, "What, Poppy?"

A chocked sob came out, "Come here, Mother! Hurry!"

He slowly hobbled to where the group and the bikes had stopped. Tears were streaming down the old man's face. He grasped Dan and just looked at him as if he was seeing a ghost. His whole body was shaking. He was trying to say something, but words just couldn't come out. His gnarled, roughened hands reached for Tom and the kids to touch them, his face disbelieving and sobbing.

The front door swung opened and a short, slightly plump, matronly woman came out wearing a flour covered apron. She stopped, stared, and screamed with her hands to her face. She too clutched onto the side of the house as she nearly fainted for just a second and then rushed to Dan and the kids.

She clasped them to her bosom, crying, "Oh my God, we thought you were dead! You're here. Oh my God, you're here!"

Tears streamed down her face as she grasped the kids, holding them away from her for just a second to look at them, unbelieving, and then clutching them to her.

Dan's father just held onto Dan, his whole body shaking, his chin quivering with tears running down his cheeks, "How did you do this, Son? How did you do this?"

A revered grandmother hugged her beloved grandchildren, although smothered or half crushed is perhaps a better definition. Throughout the joyful confusion, Mike, and Mary Ann, with their arms around each other, just stood and smiled, happiness reflected in their glistening eyes.

After a few moments, Dan led his mother to Lor. "Mom, this is my Lor."

Mom didn't need to say a single word; she just reached out and grabbed Lor and hugged her, her short flour scented body just shaking with sobs and happiness. There was absolutely no doubt in Lor's mind of her reception and acceptance by Dan's mother.

After a few more moments, when things calmed somewhat, Dan introduced Mike, Mary Ann, Jennifer, and Geoff to his parents. Welcomes were heart warmingly extended.

The big cat was introduced, and when the story was told of how he had helped save their lives, the elder Petersons both rubbed the tawny cat's head. The rumbling could be heard throughout the entire front yard.

The first night home, the old father, wearing faded and patched but clean Oshkosh overalls, slowly climbed the rickety stairs to the second floor of his old farmhouse to look in on his grandchildren and family. His shabby bedroom slippers made almost no sound as he carefully placed each foot on the well-worn stairs.

"Well, now I have a good reason to fix these stairs," he thought as he carefully carried his oil burning lantern with its glass chimney. He quietly hobbled over to a small bed. He looked down at a tiny figure with long bright red hair spread like a shining red halo on the stark white pillow; a granddaughter he had never seen before this day.

His chin quavered; tears fell from the weather-roughened features to softly land on her tiny face. She awakened and looked up at her grandfather, a grandfather she hadn't known before today. A smile broke through her tanned face as she reached up to hug her grandfather.

"It's ok, Grandpa; we're here now," she whispered in his ear as her slim sun-browned arms embraced his weather-beaten neck.

He was amazed at the flashes of understanding and maturity exhibited by his littlest granddaughter.

"You sleep well now, Honey," he whispered back as he tucked her in the bed. "You're home, sweetheart, you're home!"

After a brief examination of the rest of his family, he quietly and cautiously crept down the broken wooden stairs. He hobbled over to his wife and said, "They are all fine, Mother. I, I can still hardly believe it." He shook his head in quiet wonderment.

"I can't believe it either, Poppy," she said, her knitting needles flashing in the lamplight. "It's been, what, over seven years, eight years since we've seen our boy."

"Yes, I think that's right."

"Well, after he married that Kathy, she refused to have anything to do with us. He, Tom and Sue used to come home about every year or so before he and Kathy were married."

The old father didn't even question his wife's utilization of the term "that Kathy." She had called Dan's wife such since she discovered that "that Kathy" had refused to come home to visit them. The problem had been compounded when "that Kathy" would hardly carry on a telephone conversation with her mother-in-law. Dan's mother could not understand the mentality of such a person, even the United States and Russia talked for goodness sakes.

"Let's get some sleep, Poppy," she smiled at her husband of many years. "We have a long day, no, we have a wonderful day ahead of us tomorrow."

Two days later, a lonely figure walked through the fields of ripened grain or what was once a field of grown grain. The sun had just risen above the cloudless eastern horizon; the dew on the grass and grain was quickly being burnt off by the morning sun.

A heavy two-gallon sealed thermos jug was strapped on a calico shirted back. Long brown hair was tied in a ponytail while tight jeans covered shapely hips. She approached the road leading to the farmhouse and started down it. As she neared the overgrown side road to the farmhouse, Tom's dog barked and trotted up the road to meet her. His drooping tail was wagging back and forth, his bark friendly. She bent over and scratched his head behind his ears when he licked her outstretched hand.

"How are you doing, boy?" she asked the dog. His only reply was a more vigorous wagging of his tail.

"Where did you come from?" she asked. She could see that the dog, while somewhat thin, appeared to be in good health, its heavy coat of fur was well brushed and free of the usual farm dirt.

She continued down the road, past the ancient lilacs and walked up to the house. About a dozen white chickens pecked in the barnyard and a few geese noisily hissed in the old orchard. On the side of the house, she saw a small pile of freshly sawn hardwood boards sitting on two sawhorses. She didn't see, however, the eight bikes and several trailers parked in the shed by the run-down barn. The dog followed her to the wide cement and brick step by the front porch and lay down on an old piece of carpet. He acted as if this was where he belonged.

She banged on the front door with her fist and called, "Anybody home?"

She then opened the screen door to the porch, strode into the kitchen and saw the old couple sitting around the now-extended wooden kitchen table finishing a cup of coffee, "Hi Dad, Hi Mom! Here's some milk for you."

It was Sarah, Dan's sister.

"When did you get the dog? He sure seems friendly," she asked.

"Hi, Sarah. Thanks for the milk, we'll put it down in the basement to keep it cool. Help yourself to some coffee," her mother said. The smell of freshly perked coffee being heated by an old wood stove permeated the well-used and sunlit kitchen.

"Oh, the dog is one of our recent additions," her father replied with a grin.

"Really? You didn't have that dog last week when I came over here. Where did you get him?"

"And how come the coffee?" she asked as she retrieved a well-used cup with a big green G on it from the kitchen cupboard and reached for the pot of precious coffee.

"Where did you get this stuff? Coffee is worth its weight in gold," she asked again.

Her back was to the living room door.

"Well, we've had a few changes since you were here last time." Her father's grin grew even wider.

"What's going on here? What happened?" Sarah asked, looking back and forth from her mom to her dad. Both looked as if their smiles would break their faces.

Dan silently walked into the kitchen from the living room behind Sarah.

"Hi Sis," he said quietly.

Her face turned white; the cup dropped out of her hand to fall to the floor, unnoticed. Her hands went to her face, she shook her head numbly and slowly turned to face Dan.

Her eyes bulged, her face slack. She swayed back and forth as if she was going to collapse. Her father reached out to grasp her arms and support her, her knees weak.

She tried to swallow through suddenly dry lips, slowly shaking her head.

Her face blurred through suddenly wet eyes, she whispered, "Dan? Dan? Oh my God! Is it really you? We, we," she stammered "We thought you were d-d-dead!"

Sarah just stared at him for a second longer, then flung herself into Dan's arms, her body shaking, with tears and happiness. She pulled back from him for just a second to look at him, to touch his now older, heavily suntanned face with unbelieving hands. She then clutched him again, his rock-like frame holding her quaking body. Quivering, her knees weak, she mumbled, "Let, let me sit down, p-please."

"I, I can't believe it," she whispered through her sobbing, "I knew how hard things were for you out there in California, and after this thing attacked us, there was no word from anyone."

She said to her parents after collapsing into a kitchen chair, still clutching onto Dan, the moisture from her tears staining her calico shirt, "When did he get here?"

"Two days ago," her father exclaimed.

"Two mornings ago, he rode in and you wouldn't believe everything," Dan's mother said as she hugged her son for about the hundredth time in two days.

"Everyone else still asleep?" she asked.

"Yes. We're not used to sleeping in clean sheets and soft beds."

"We?" Sarah asked, still shaking, and trying to dry her tears.

"Yes! We! I brought all of my kids: Tom, Sue and Ginger."

"And" Dan continued with a soft smile on his face, "I brought someone special with me."

While the coffee cup was retrieved and the spilt coffee cleaned off the floor, Dan told Sarah and his parents in some detail what happened to his life.

He told of his ex-wife Kathy's actions in taking all their savings and running off to Colorado with Ginger to live in the commune (which they knew from his letters), the coming of the life force and his conversation with his friend, Joe Robinson, their escape from southern California and their search for Ginger. He told of the meeting with Lor and of her assistance in finding Ginger. He brushed over the fight at the commune except to advise them that Kathy had died of an apparent appendicitis attack when she and the commune refused to obtain medical help. He told of Sheriff Hank finding Ginger for them and the long ride home to Wisconsin.

The telling of the story took almost a half hour. A few moments of somber silence fell over the family.

"My God, Son, I didn't realize all of that," his father muttered, shaking his head.

He said to his daughter, "We haven't talked too much since he came home. Things have been a little hectic around here since they rode up. Every time I look at him or see the grandkids, I…I…," he stopped and fished out a large red handkerchief out of his pocket and noisily blew his nose, his chin quivering.

At that moment, Lor came down the rickety stairs into the kitchen, concerned, her hair freshly brushed, looking as neat as possible. In her heart, she was worried about her reception with Dan's family. While she loved him deeply and fully, she wanted to be accepted by them.

"Good morning, Lorraine, "Dan's mother said as they hugged each other, also for about the hundredth time in two days.

"Lorraine Fairly, this is Sarah, our oldest daughter. She has a small farm about two miles from here."

"So, you are the woman who has made an honest man out of my brother?" Sarah asked. Both women shook hands and hugged each other. An almost identical thought crossed their minds, "*I think this is someone I could like.*"

"I heard Dan telling you about what happened. Did he tell you how he met me?" Lor asked Sarah.

"No, or at least, not much," Sarah said, shaking her head.

After obtaining a cup of coffee, Lor sat on the other side of Dan and grasped his hand.

"He wouldn't tell you much, but I will," she started. "I owe my whole life to him and Tom."

She related how she had been captured by ex-convicts on the road to Durango. She told them that just before she would be gang-raped by the ex-convicts, Dan, and Tom, with their power bows and graphite arrows had slain two of the men and had scared off the other three men. She told how she had been badly beaten and how Dan, Tom and Sue had nursed her back to health.

Dan, a little embarrassed, mumbled, "Well, we were lucky. And much credit goes to Tom: he was smart enough to recognize the situation and rescue us with the power bows."

Dan's father looked at Dan with pride and considerable respect, "You have done very well, Son. It's so good to see you and I'm so proud of you."

"So am I," Lor exclaimed. "Without him leading and guiding us, we never would have made it here."

Dan's father continued heavily, "We didn't have any knowledge of what caused the force thing; we know that a number of neighbors around here lost their lives when they tried to run their farm machinery or cars. Sarah's husband lost his life because of that green thing. The animals knew, though, they ran from that force. It's interesting, the big animals like cows and horses do not seem to sense the force, but wild animals, dogs and cats seem to know when it's around."

He continued after a moment of silence, "I still can't believe that you're here."

"Is the rest of the family up?" Dan asked Lor to change the subject.

"They were stirring when I came down. They should be down in a few minutes."

A few minutes later, the rest of Dan's family carefully came down the old rickety stairs. Introductions or reintroduction were made to their Aunt Sarah: "My how you've grown, Tom," and "I remember you, Sue, when you were just a little girl; now you are a young lady," and "Ginger, this is your Aunt Sarah," and so on.

Later, due to the commotion in the kitchen, Mike, Mary Ann, Geoff, and Jennifer awakened and drifted into the kitchen. More introductions were made. Soon, the smell of eggs, smoked bacon and toast filled the kitchen and spaces were made either at the table or kitchen counter for everyone to eat. Standing off to the side and overlooking the entire group was Dan's father and mother, their arms around each other, their smiles nearly breaking their cheeks, a happy tear or two wove its way down a seamed and weather-beaten face.

After breakfast, the kids wondered off to explore the farm or farm buildings while the adults sat over a final cup of breakfast coffee.

"Mr. Peterson, Mrs. Peterson," Mike begin, "We sincerely appreciate your hospitality, but we can't impose any more on you. Is there any place around here we can stay, a vacant house we can rent or something?"

"Well. . ." Dan's father said with a thoughtful look in his eye, "Sarah, that Clement's place is vacant, isn't it?"

"Yes, I believe so. I went past it about a week ago and no one was living there."

Sarah looked at Dan, "Dan, do you remember that old Klotsky place over on the other road, overlooking the river?"

Upon receiving a shake of Dan's head, Sarah said, "Sure, you remember that place, we used to steal apples from their orchard when we were kids; I heard that you and a few of your friends used to tip over his mailbox at Halloween."

Sarah smiled at Dan, "I also heard that he caught you and some girl skinny dipping in his pond one night."

There was much laughter at the expression on Dan's face, now he remembered what house Sarah was talking about. He mumbled, clearly flustered, "Well, I was young then... and it was a good thing he didn't see his daughter hiding in the bushes with my best friend."

Lor hugged Dan, "So my man is not an angel after all," she kidded as she kissed his reddened cheeks.

Sarah continued, "They sold it to old man Clement about six or seven years ago, and it has been vacant for, oh, about a half year or so now. I think the state took it over or something. In any event, it is available for whomever wants it."

"Sounds good. Can we look at it today?" Mike asked after a glance and nod with Mary Ann.

"Sure, I'll walk over with you," Sarah said. "Dan, will you and your family be staying here?"

Dan's father interrupted, "He," and with a nod at Lorraine, "and his family will be staying here. We have enough room and this has always been your home. That is, unless you don't want to stay here?" he looked at Dan.

"Of course, Dad, we would like to stay here; it took a long ride home for us to get here," Dan said as he warmly hugged his father.

"Sarah, do you have any extra cows on your place?" Dan asked.

"Sure, I've got one that just had a calf. You'll need milk for your kids and what the calf doesn't drink, they can have," Sarah replied. "We can walk over there and you can bring them back here."

"Dad, is your barn in any condition to keep that cow and her calf?" Sarah asked.

"Sure; I've still got a barn full of grain and hay that was never used this summer. And now, I've got a good reason to fix that old barn up," he smiled at Dan.

"Once we get settled in up here, do you have any plans for the future?" Mike asked Dan.

There was a sudden silence in the kitchen. "Well," Dan began. "We're finally safe here. I've had time to think during our long ride, and there must be some way to fight that Green Ghost. The United States, or what's left of it, got lucky that this force came in the spring. It gave people time to somehow adjust."

The silence grew deeper. "I want to visit the libraries around here, and maybe even travel to Green Bay or Madison at the University of Wisconsin to try to research anything that might help. There must be something that will help us conquer that life form. And I'm hoping that there are others who have the same goal."

Dan looked at Lor's expression. "Oh, don't worry, I'll never leave you, but this is something I feel I must do. I need to search for scientists and anyone else who might have some idea how to beat the Green Ghost."

Little did Dan know that others with the same idea were searching for him!

THE END

TO BE CONTINUED:

THE
SEARCH